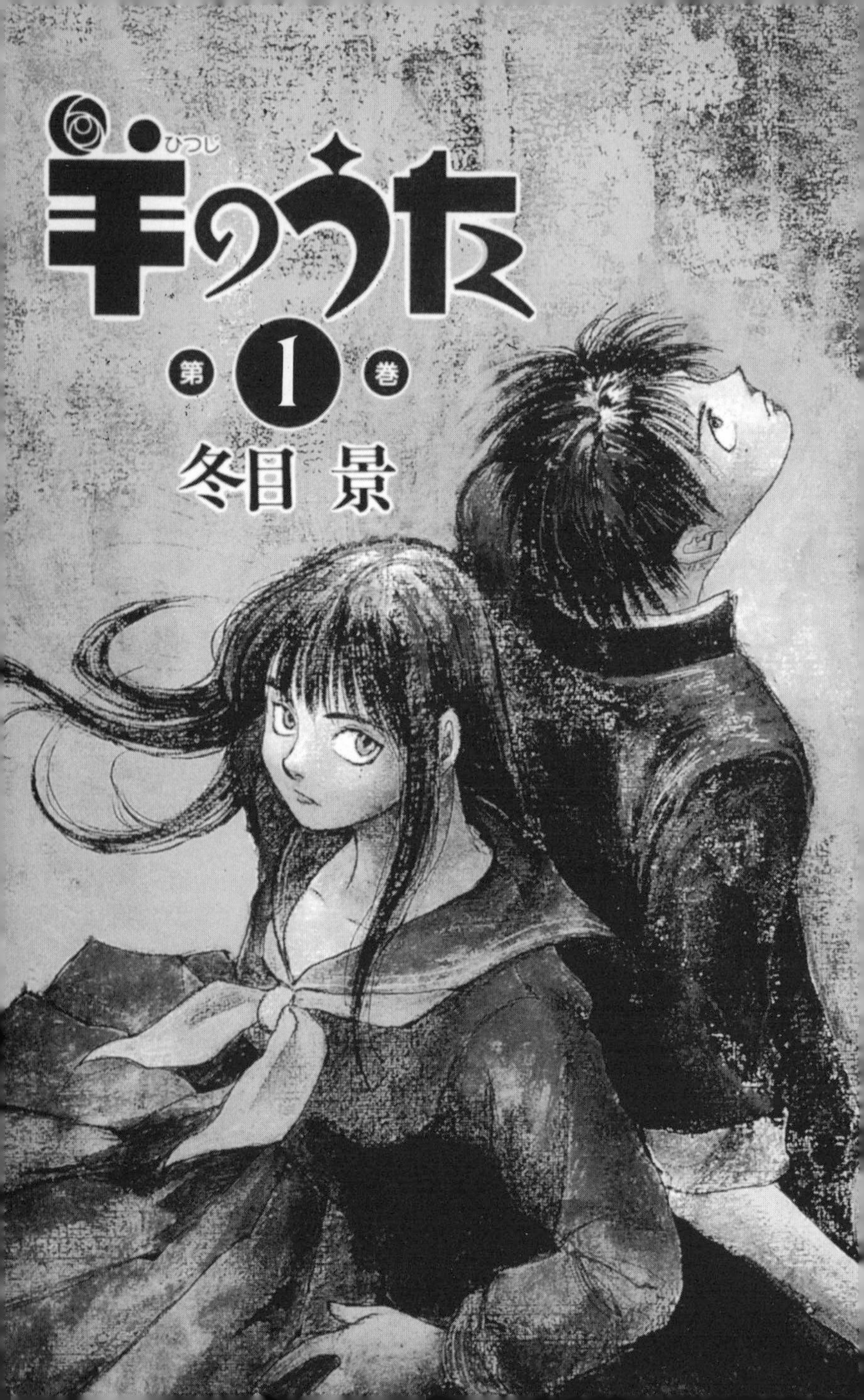
羊のうた
ひつじ
第1巻
冬目景

Translator - Ryan Flake
English Adaptation - Jay Antani
Copy Editor - Nicole Monastirsky
Retouch and Lettering - Keiko Okabe and Jose Macasocol, Jr.
Cover Layout - Gary Shum
Graphic Designer - Jose Macasocol, Jr.

Editor - Paul Morrissey
Digital Imaging Manager - Chris Buford
Pre-Press Manager - Antonio DePietro
Production Managers - Jennifer Miller and Mutsumi Miyazaki
Art Director - Matt Alford
Managing Editor - Jill Freshney
VP of Production - Ron Klamert
President & C.O.O. - John Parker
Publisher & C.E.O. - Stuart Levy

E-mail: info@TOKYOPOP.com

Come visit us online at www.TOKYOPOP.com

A  TOKYOPOP® Manga

TOKYOPOP Inc.
5900 Wilshire Blvd. Suite 2000
Los Angeles, CA 90036

Lament of the Lamb Vol. 1

© 2002 KEI TOUME. All Rights Reserved. First published in Japan in 2002
by GENTOSHA COMICS INC. TOKYO. English translation rights arranged with
GENTOSHA COMICS INC. TOKYO through TOHAN CORPORATION, TOKYO.

English text copyright ©2004 TOKYOPOP Inc.

ISBN: 1-59182-814-7

First TOKYOPOP printing: May 2004

10 9 8 7 6 5 4 3 2 1

Printed in the USA

LAMENT of the LAMB ™

VOL. 1

BY KEI TOUME

TOKYOPOP ®

LOS ANGELES • TOKYO • LONDON

LAMENT of the LAMB.

羊のうた

第 ① 巻

CONTENTS

CHAPTER

MINGLED AMONG THE SHEEP
THERE IS A WOLF--

AND BY HIS OWN LONELY
FANGS HE IS RENT.

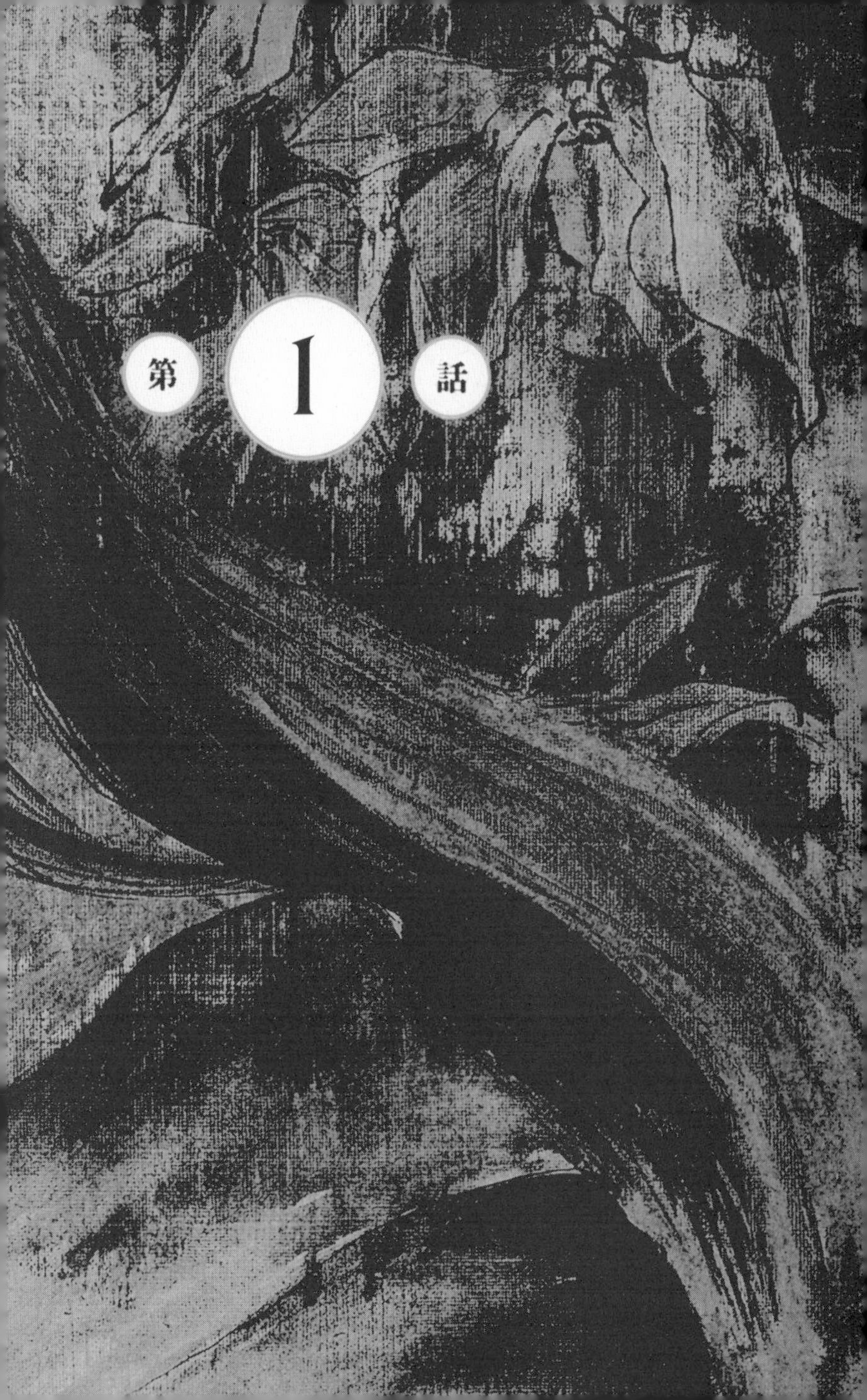
第1話

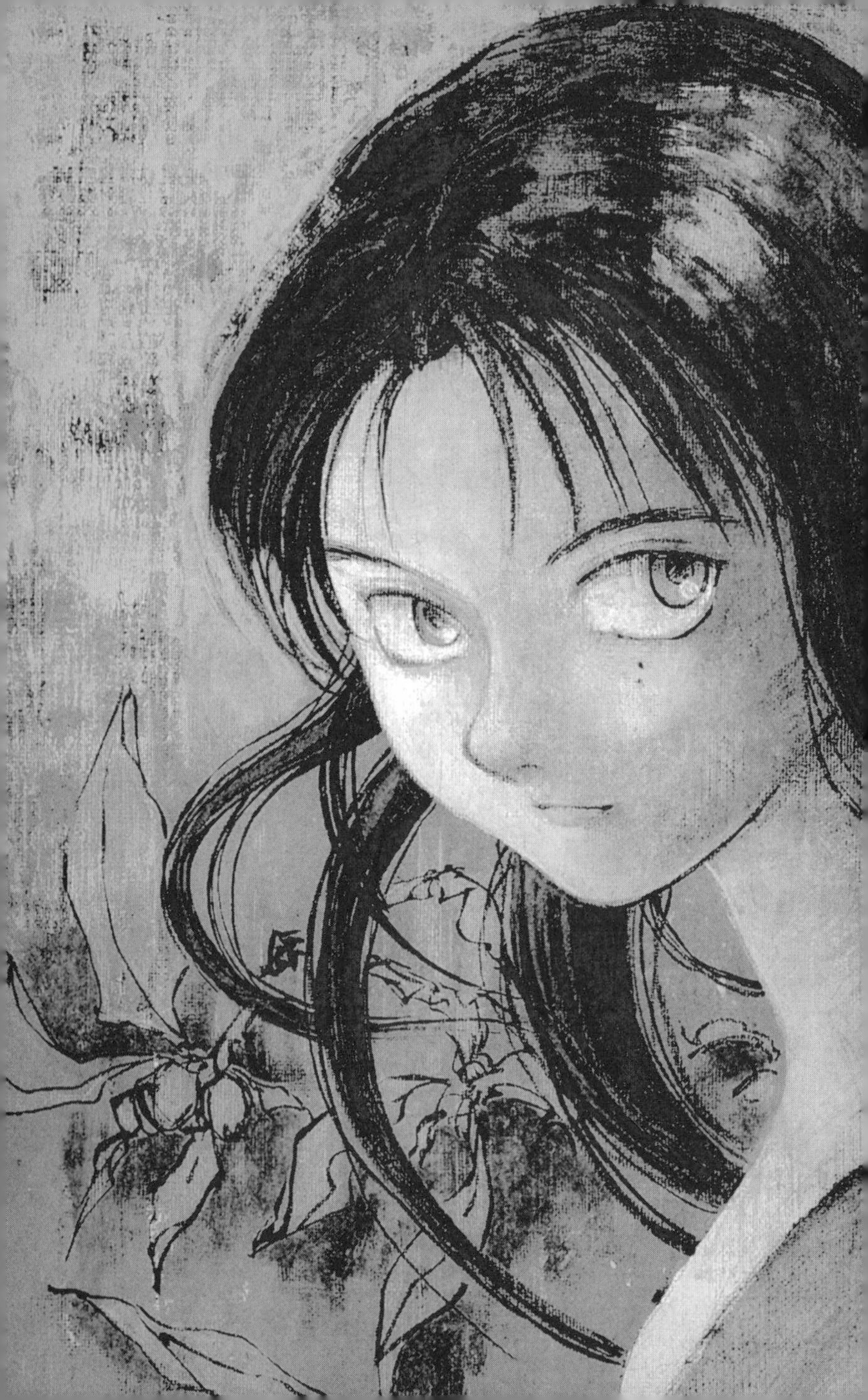

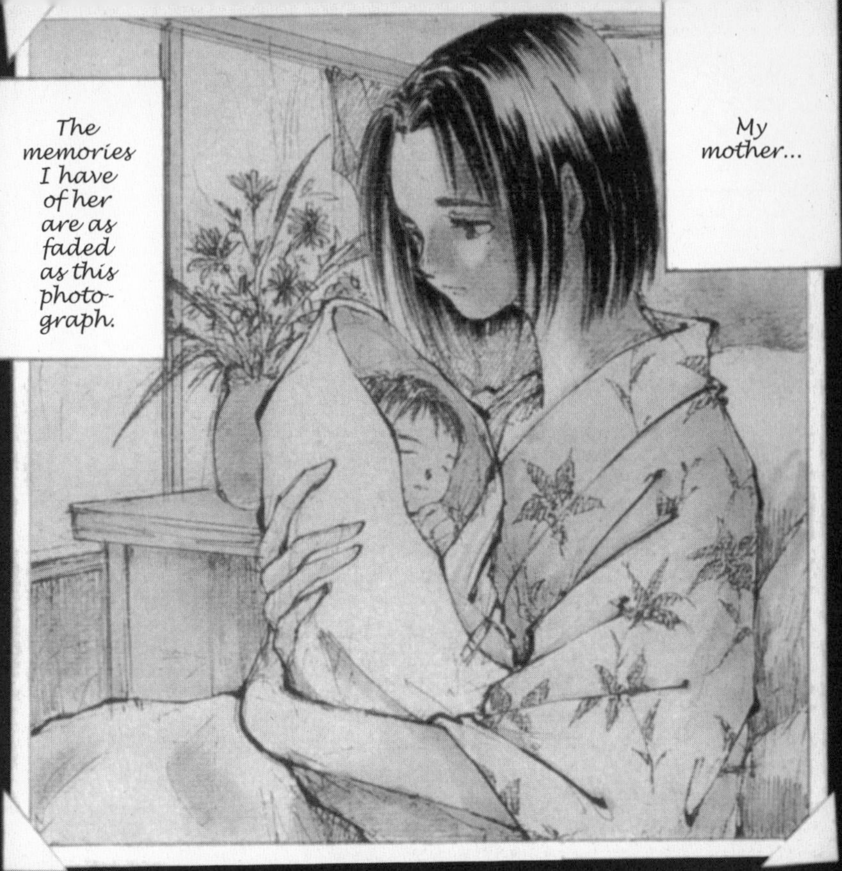
My mother...
The memories I have of her are as faded as this photo-graph.
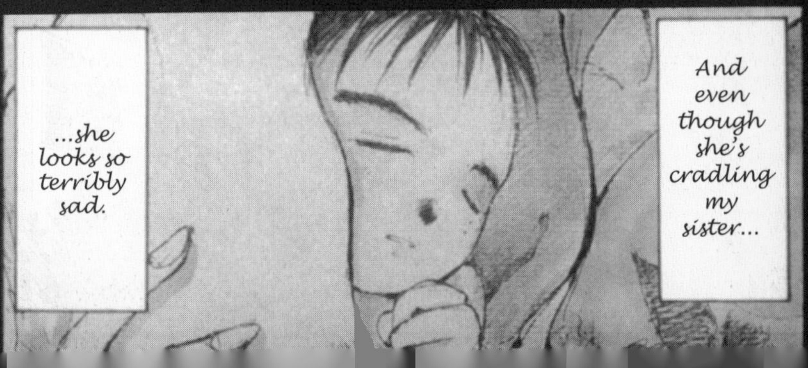
And even though she's cradling my sister...
...she looks so terribly sad.

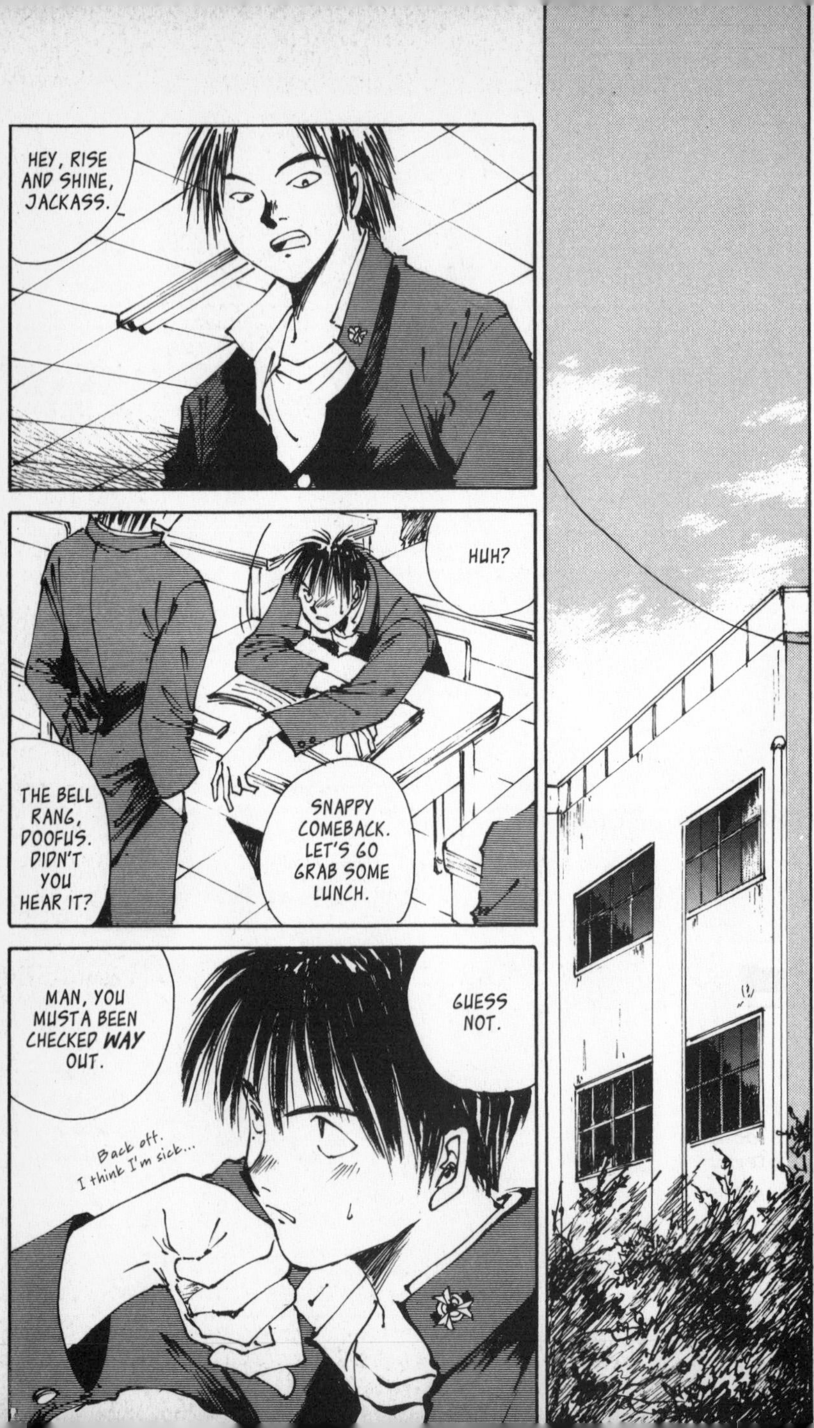
!?
HEY, RISE AND SHINE, JACKASS.
HUH?
THE BELL RANG, DOOFUS. DIDN'T YOU HEAR IT?
SNAPPY COMEBACK. LET'S GO GRAB SOME LUNCH.
GUESS NOT.
MAN, YOU MUSTA BEEN CHECKED WAY OUT.
Back off. I think I'm sick...

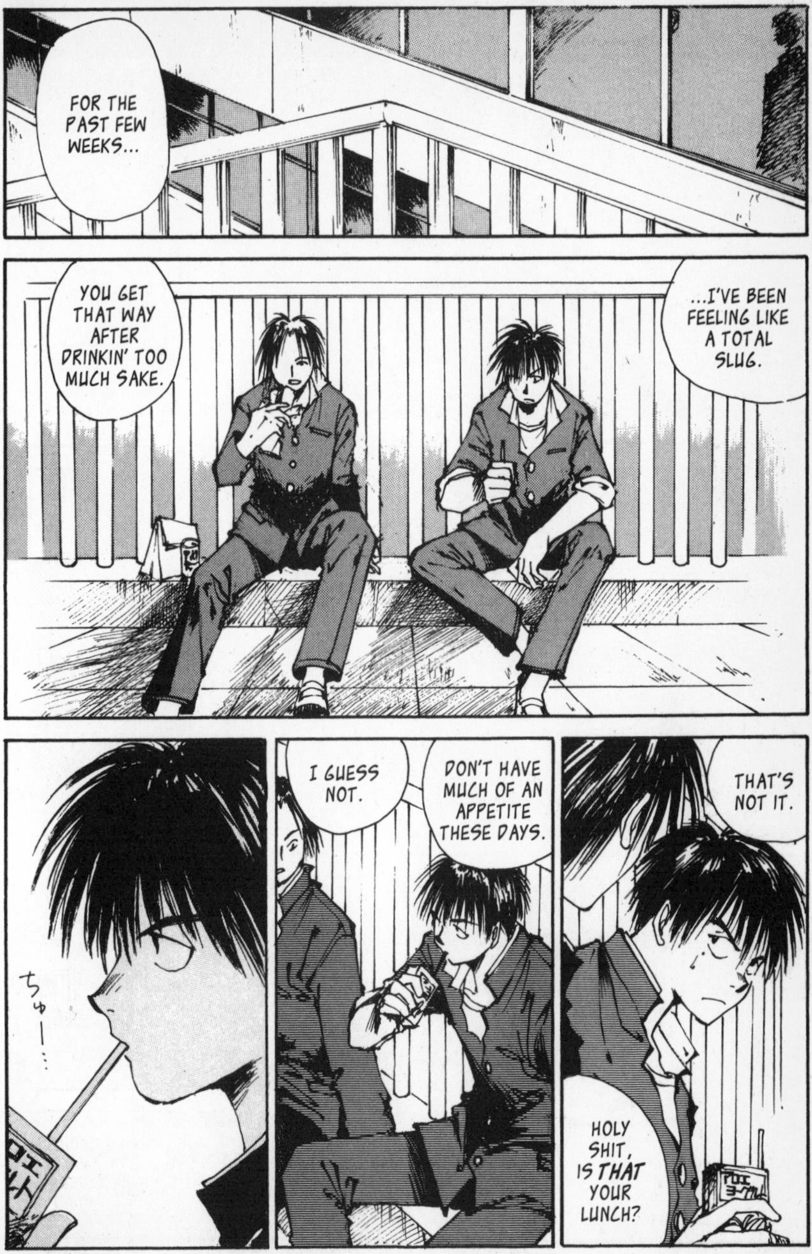
FOR THE PAST FEW WEEKS...
...I'VE BEEN FEELING LIKE A TOTAL SLUG.
YOU GET THAT WAY AFTER DRINKIN' TOO MUCH SAKE.
THAT'S NOT IT.
HOLY SHIT, IS *THAT* YOUR LUNCH?
DON'T HAVE MUCH OF AN APPETITE THESE DAYS.
I GUESS NOT.
ちゅー…

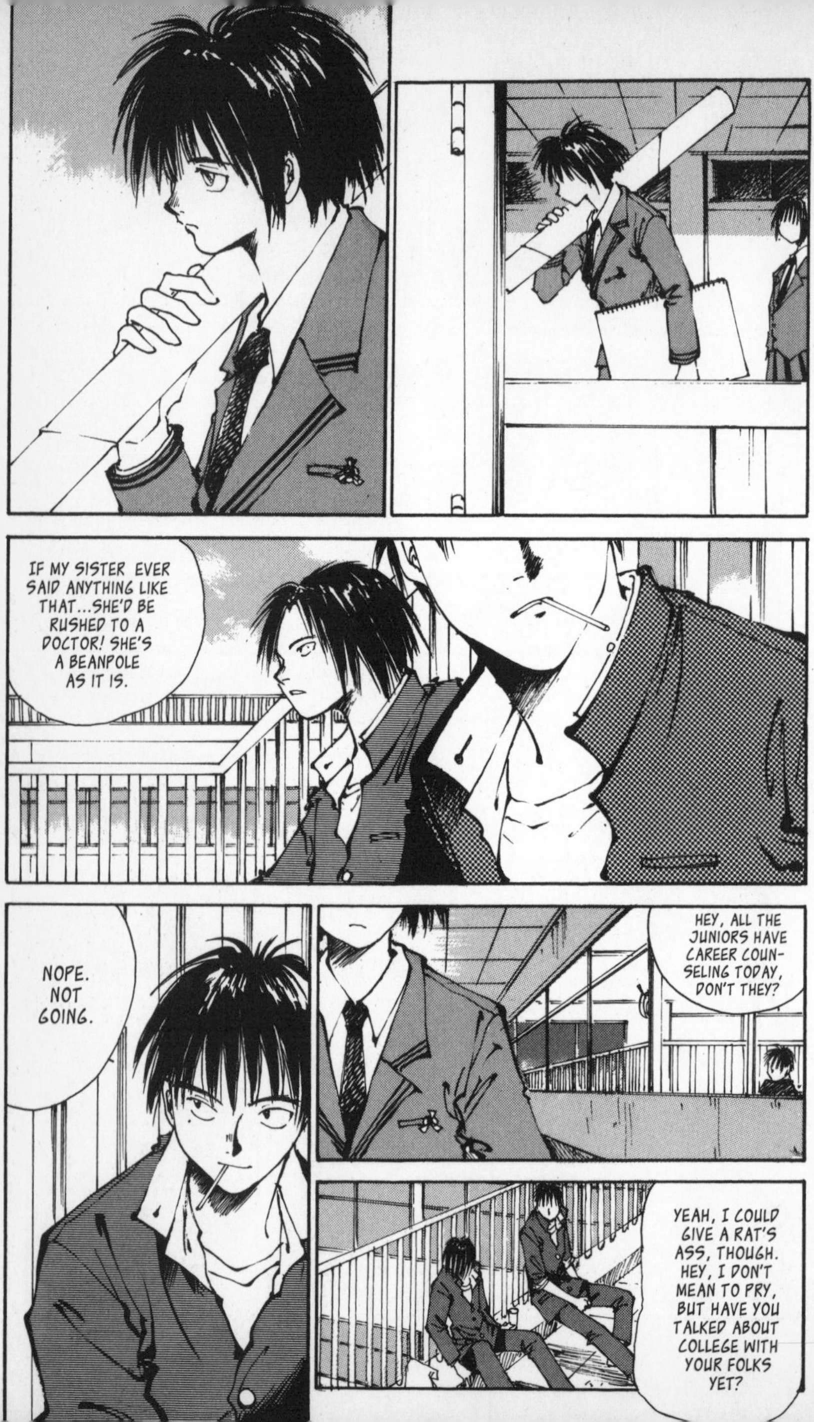
IF MY SISTER EVER SAID ANYTHING LIKE THAT...SHE'D BE RUSHED TO A DOCTOR! SHE'S A BEANPOLE AS IT IS.
HEY, ALL THE JUNIORS HAVE CAREER COUN-SELING TODAY, DON'T THEY?
NOPE. NOT GOING.
YEAH, I COULD GIVE A RAT'S ASS, THOUGH. HEY, I DON'T MEAN TO PRY, BUT HAVE YOU TALKED ABOUT COLLEGE WITH YOUR FOLKS YET?

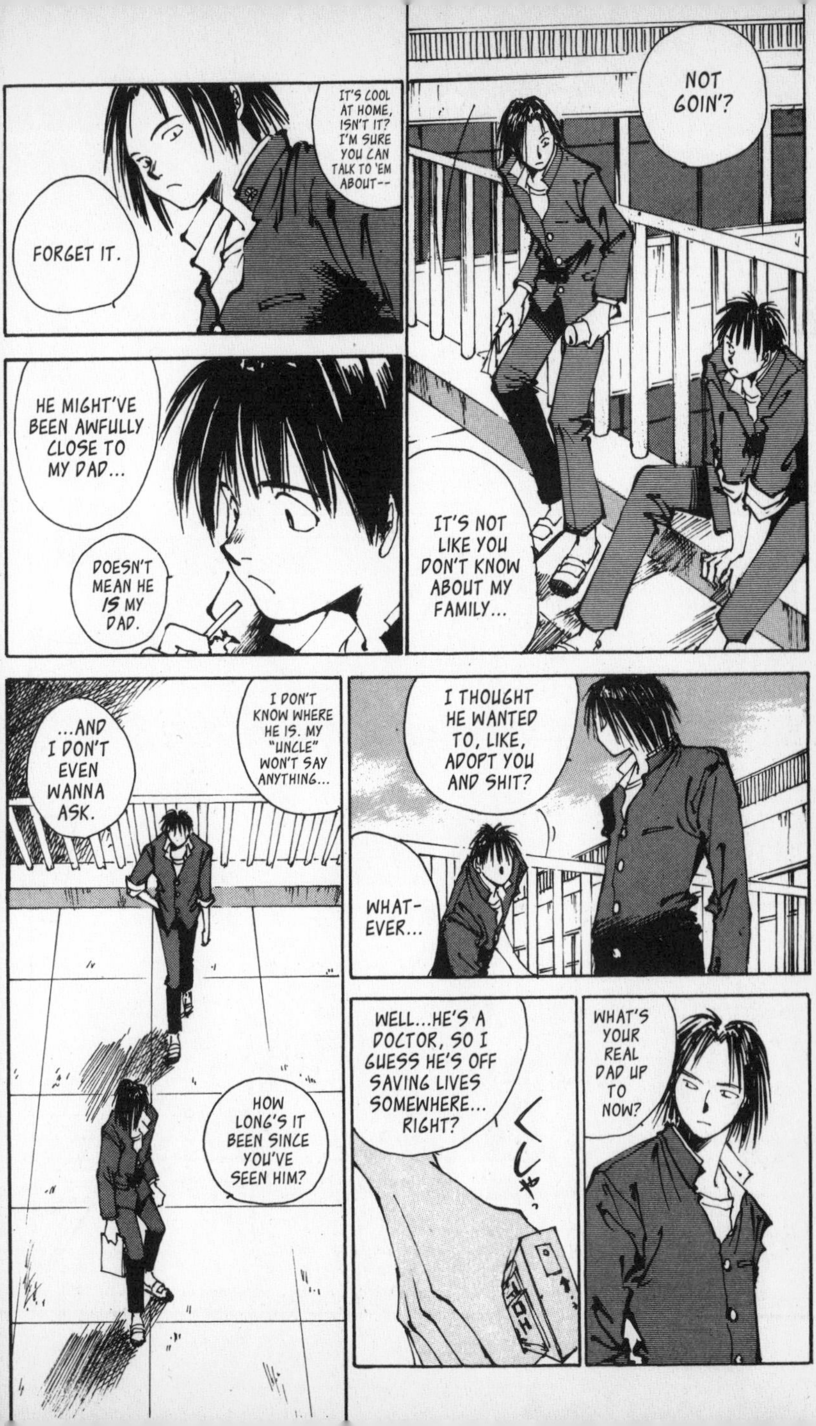
NOT GOIN'?
IT'S NOT LIKE YOU DON'T KNOW ABOUT MY FAMILY...
IT'S COOL AT HOME, ISN'T IT? I'M SURE YOU CAN TALK TO 'EM ABOUT--
FORGET IT.
HE MIGHT'VE BEEN AWFULLY CLOSE TO MY DAD...
DOESN'T MEAN HE *IS* MY DAD.
I THOUGHT HE WANTED TO, LIKE, ADOPT YOU AND SHIT?
WHAT-EVER...
WHAT'S YOUR REAL DAD UP TO NOW?
WELL...HE'S A DOCTOR, SO I GUESS HE'S OFF SAVING LIVES SOMEWHERE... RIGHT?
くしゃっ
HOW LONG'S IT BEEN SINCE YOU'VE SEEN HIM?
I DON'T KNOW WHERE HE IS. MY "UNCLE" WON'T SAY ANYTHING...
...AND I DON'T EVEN WANNA ASK.

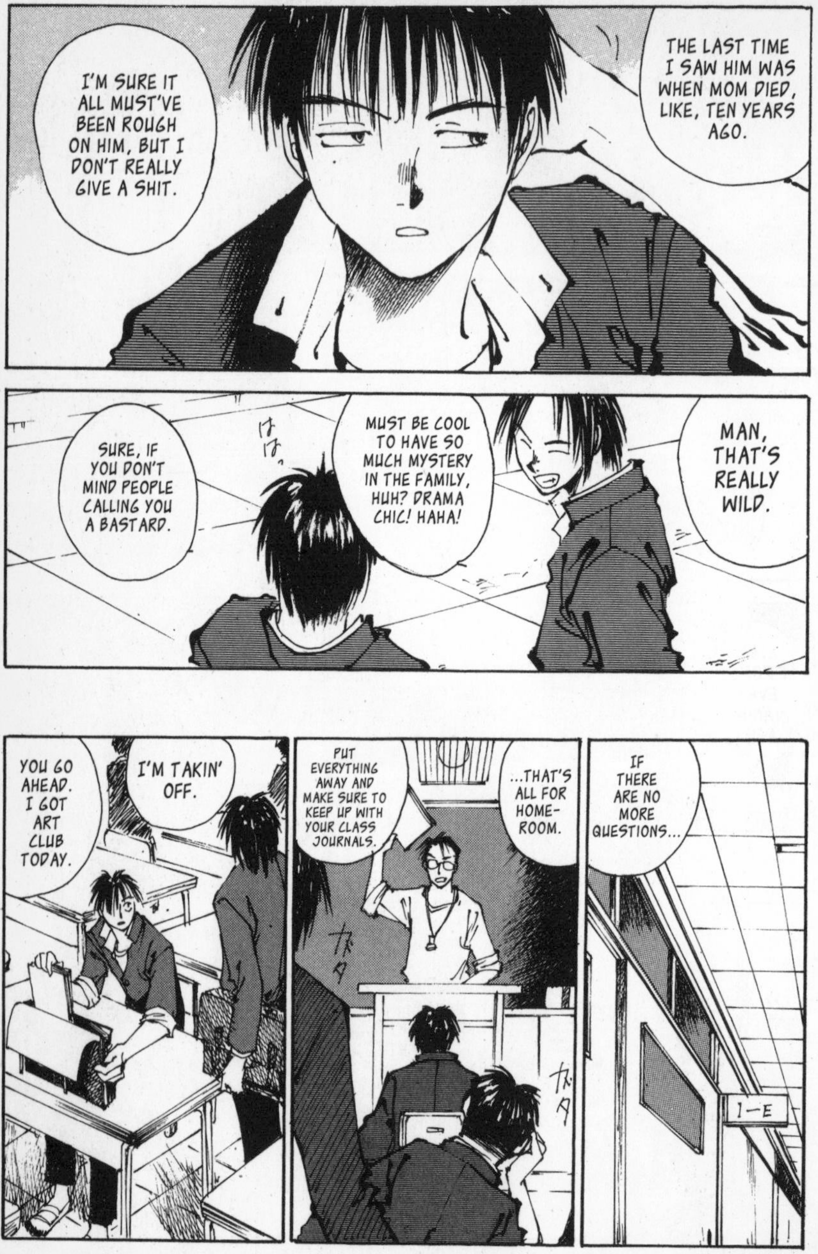
THE LAST TIME I SAW HIM WAS WHEN MOM DIED, LIKE, TEN YEARS AGO.
I'M SURE IT ALL MUST'VE BEEN ROUGH ON HIM, BUT I DON'T REALLY GIVE A SHIT.
MAN, THAT'S REALLY WILD.
MUST BE COOL TO HAVE SO MUCH MYSTERY IN THE FAMILY, HUH? DRAMA CHIC! HAHA!
はは
SURE, IF YOU DON'T MIND PEOPLE CALLING YOU A BASTARD.
1-E
IF THERE ARE NO MORE QUESTIONS...
...THAT'S ALL FOR HOME-ROOM.
PUT EVERYTHING AWAY AND MAKE SURE TO KEEP UP WITH YOUR CLASS JOURNALS.
ガタ
ガタ
I'M TAKIN' OFF.
YOU GO AHEAD. I GOT ART CLUB TODAY.

LATER ON, MACHO MAN! HAVE FUN WITH THE OTHER GIRLS. HAHAHA!

SCREW YOU.

......

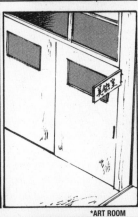

*ART ROOM

WHAT THE--?

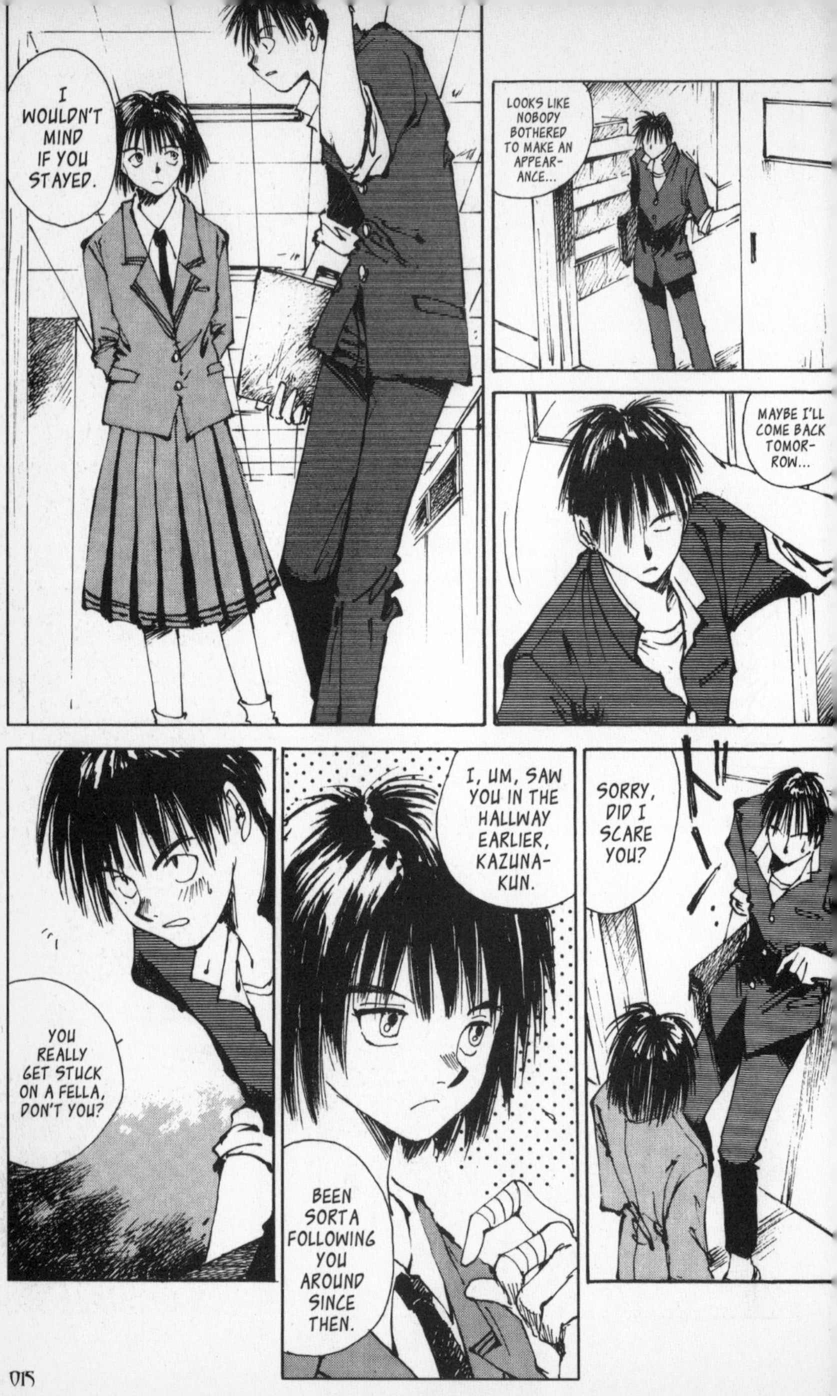
LOOKS LIKE NOBODY BOTHERED TO MAKE AN APPEAR-ANCE...
MAYBE I'LL COME BACK TOMOR-ROW...
I WOULDN'T MIND IF YOU STAYED.
SORRY, DID I SCARE YOU?
I, UM, SAW YOU IN THE HALLWAY EARLIER, KAZUNA-KUN.
BEEN SORTA FOLLOWING YOU AROUND SINCE THEN.
YOU REALLY GET STUCK ON A FELLA, DON'T YOU?

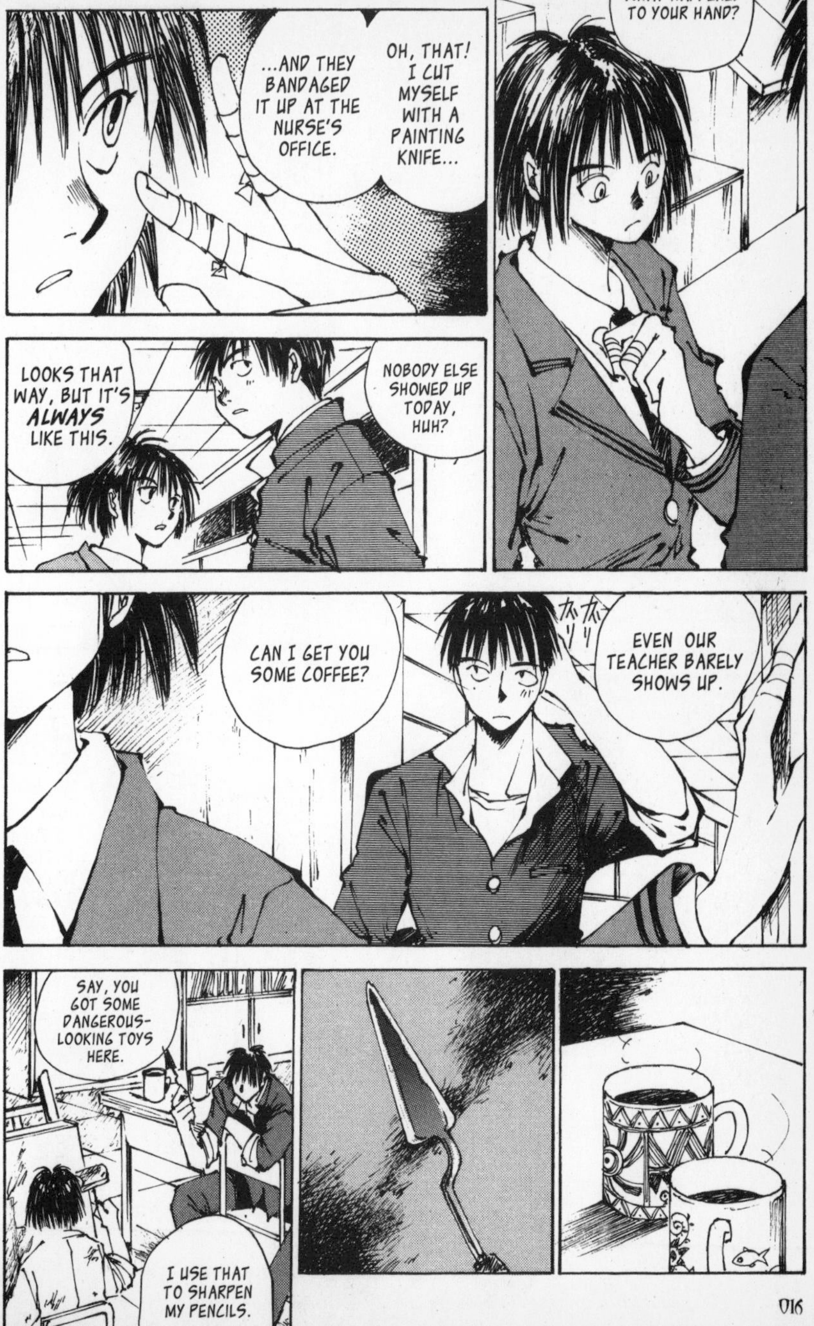
WHAT HAPPENED TO YOUR HAND?
OH, THAT! I CUT MYSELF WITH A PAINTING KNIFE...
...AND THEY BANDAGED IT UP AT THE NURSE'S OFFICE.
NOBODY ELSE SHOWED UP TODAY, HUH?
LOOKS THAT WAY, BUT IT'S ALWAYS LIKE THIS.
EVEN OUR TEACHER BARELY SHOWS UP.
CAN I GET YOU SOME COFFEE?
SAY, YOU GOT SOME DANGEROUS-LOOKING TOYS HERE.
I USE THAT TO SHARPEN MY PENCILS.

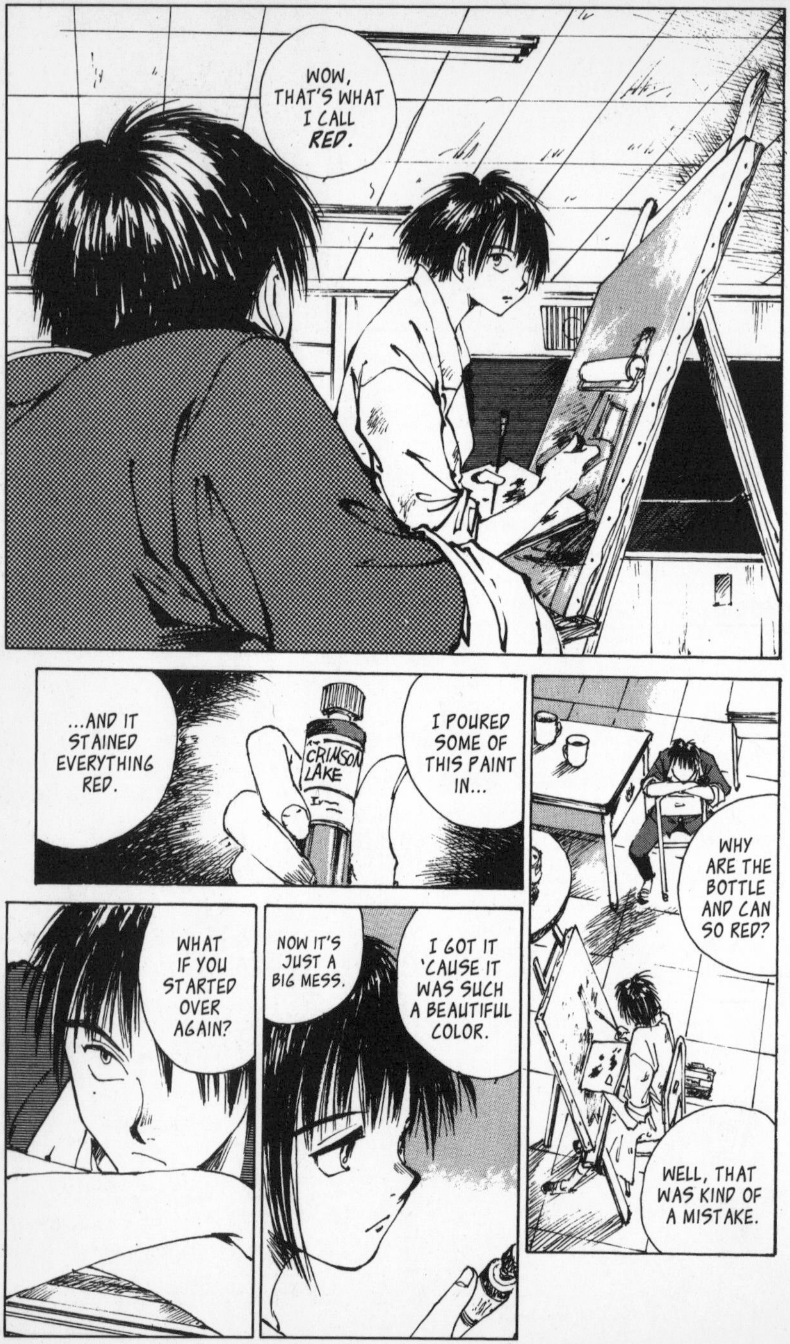
WOW, THAT'S WHAT I CALL RED.
WHY ARE THE BOTTLE AND CAN SO RED?
WELL, THAT WAS KIND OF A MISTAKE.
I POURED SOME OF THIS PAINT IN...
CRIMSON LAKE
...AND IT STAINED EVERYTHING RED.
I GOT IT 'CAUSE IT WAS SUCH A BEAUTIFUL COLOR.
NOW IT'S JUST A BIG MESS.
WHAT IF YOU STARTED OVER AGAIN?

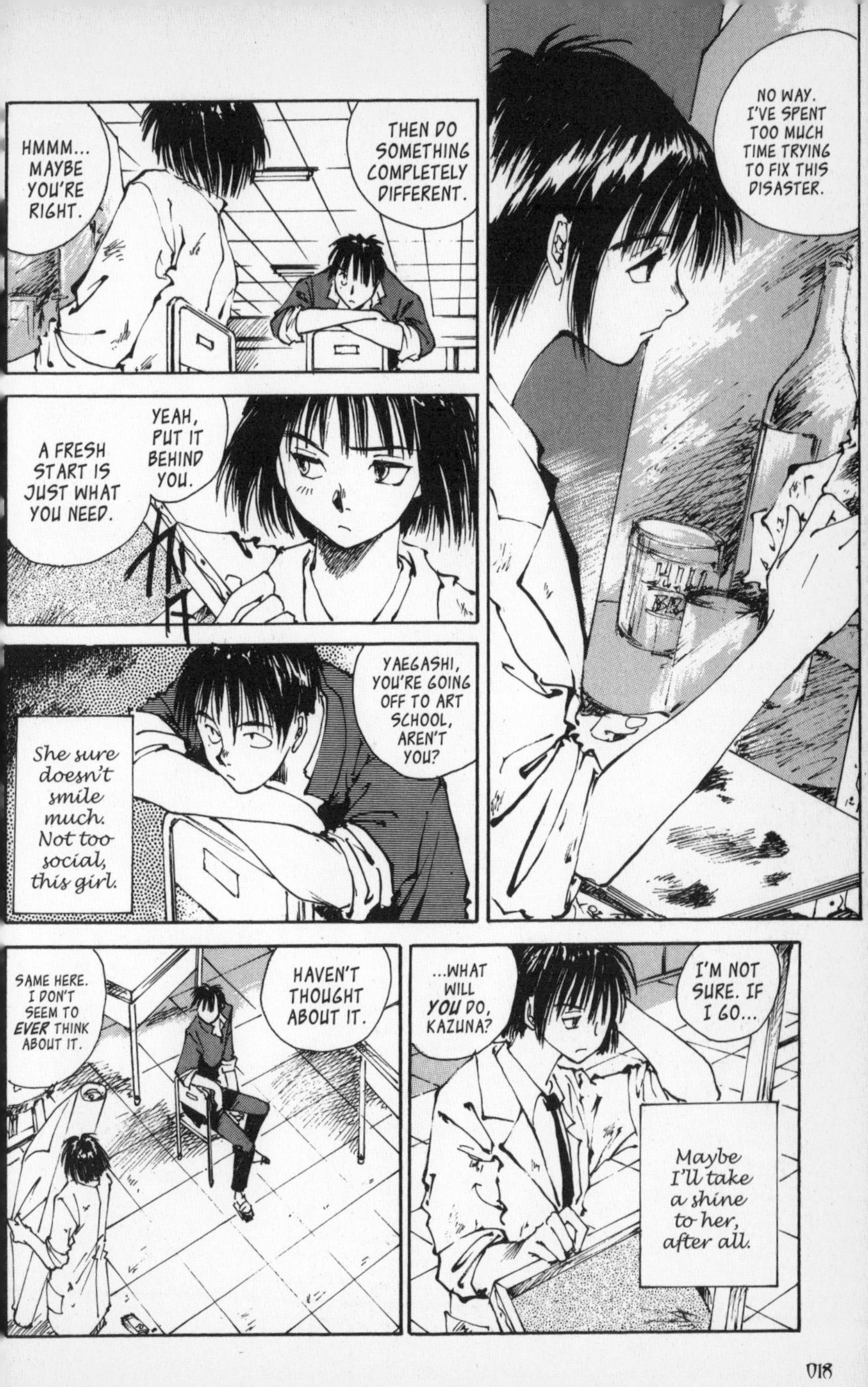
NO WAY. I'VE SPENT TOO MUCH TIME TRYING TO FIX THIS DISASTER.
THEN DO SOMETHING COMPLETELY DIFFERENT.
HMMM... MAYBE YOU'RE RIGHT.
YEAH, PUT IT BEHIND YOU.
A FRESH START IS JUST WHAT YOU NEED.
YAEGASHI, YOU'RE GOING OFF TO ART SCHOOL, AREN'T YOU?
She sure doesn't smile much. Not too social, this girl.
I'M NOT SURE. IF I GO...
...WHAT WILL ***YOU*** DO, KAZUNA?
Maybe I'll take a shine to her, after all.
HAVEN'T THOUGHT ABOUT IT.
SAME HERE. I DON'T SEEM TO ***EVER*** THINK ABOUT IT.

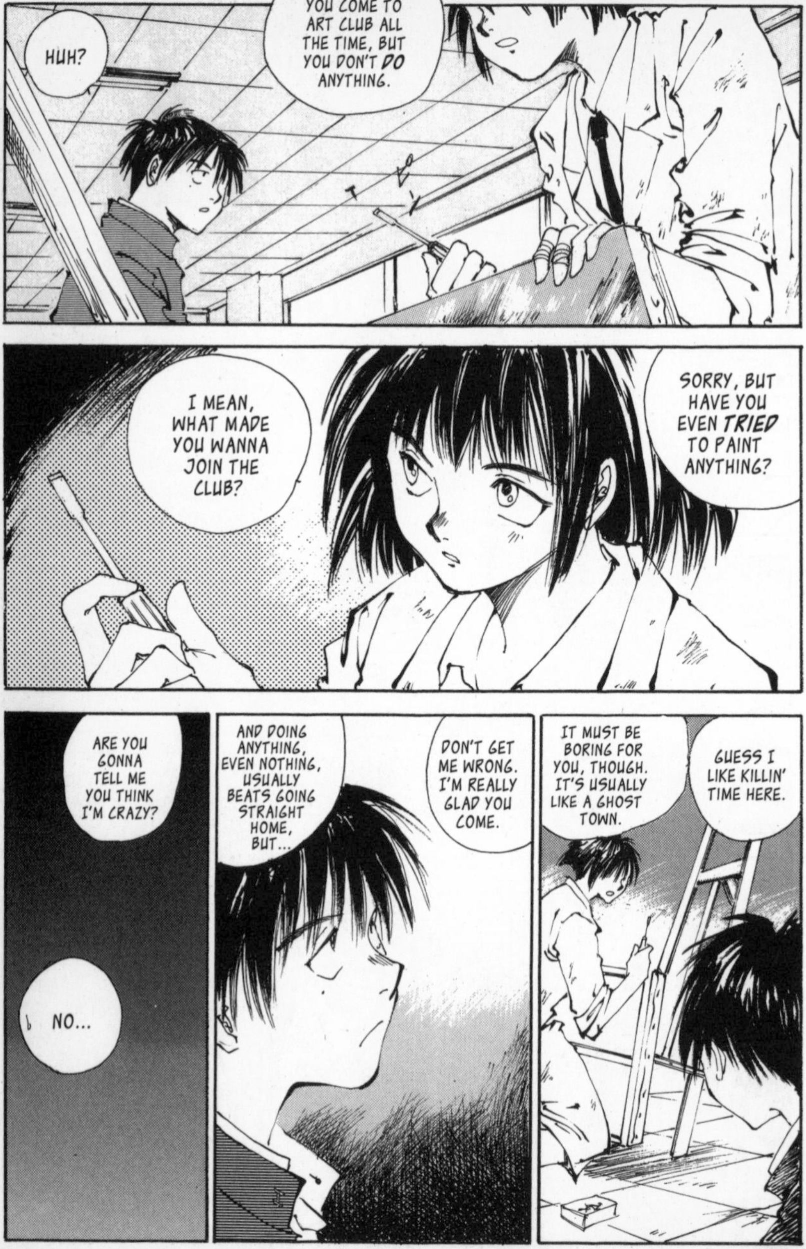
KAZUNA-KUN, YOU COME TO ART CLUB ALL THE TIME, BUT YOU DON'T *DO* ANYTHING.
HUH?
SORRY, BUT HAVE YOU EVEN *TRIED* TO PAINT ANYTHING?
I MEAN, WHAT MADE YOU WANNA JOIN THE CLUB?
GUESS I LIKE KILLIN' TIME HERE.
IT MUST BE BORING FOR YOU, THOUGH. IT'S USUALLY LIKE A GHOST TOWN.
DON'T GET ME WRONG. I'M REALLY GLAD YOU COME.
AND DOING ANYTHING, EVEN NOTHING, USUALLY BEATS GOING STRAIGHT HOME, BUT...
ARE YOU GONNA TELL ME YOU THINK I'M CRAZY?
NO...

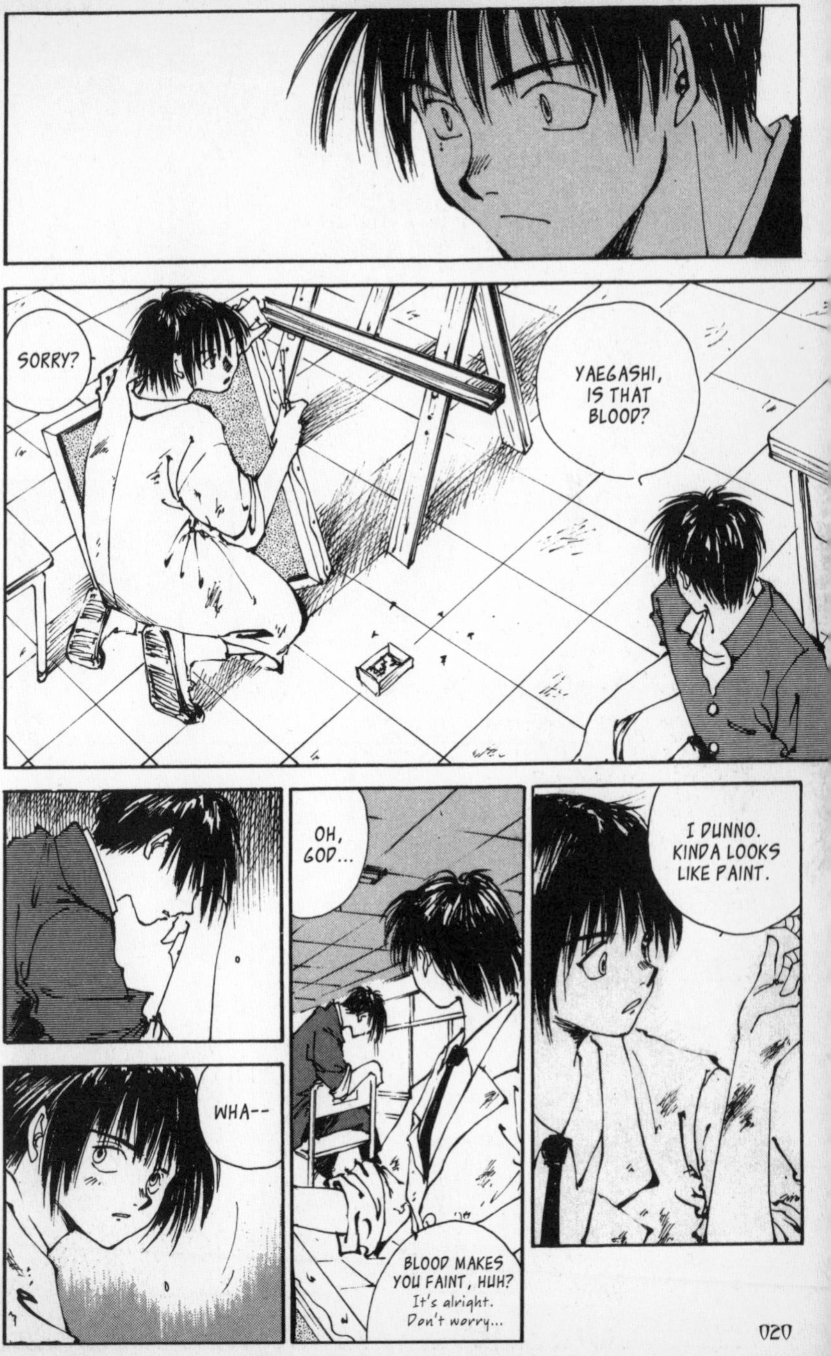
YAEGASHI, IS THAT BLOOD?
SORRY?
I DUNNO. KINDA LOOKS LIKE PAINT.
OH, GOD...
BLOOD MAKES YOU FAINT, HUH? It's alright. Don't worry...
WHA--

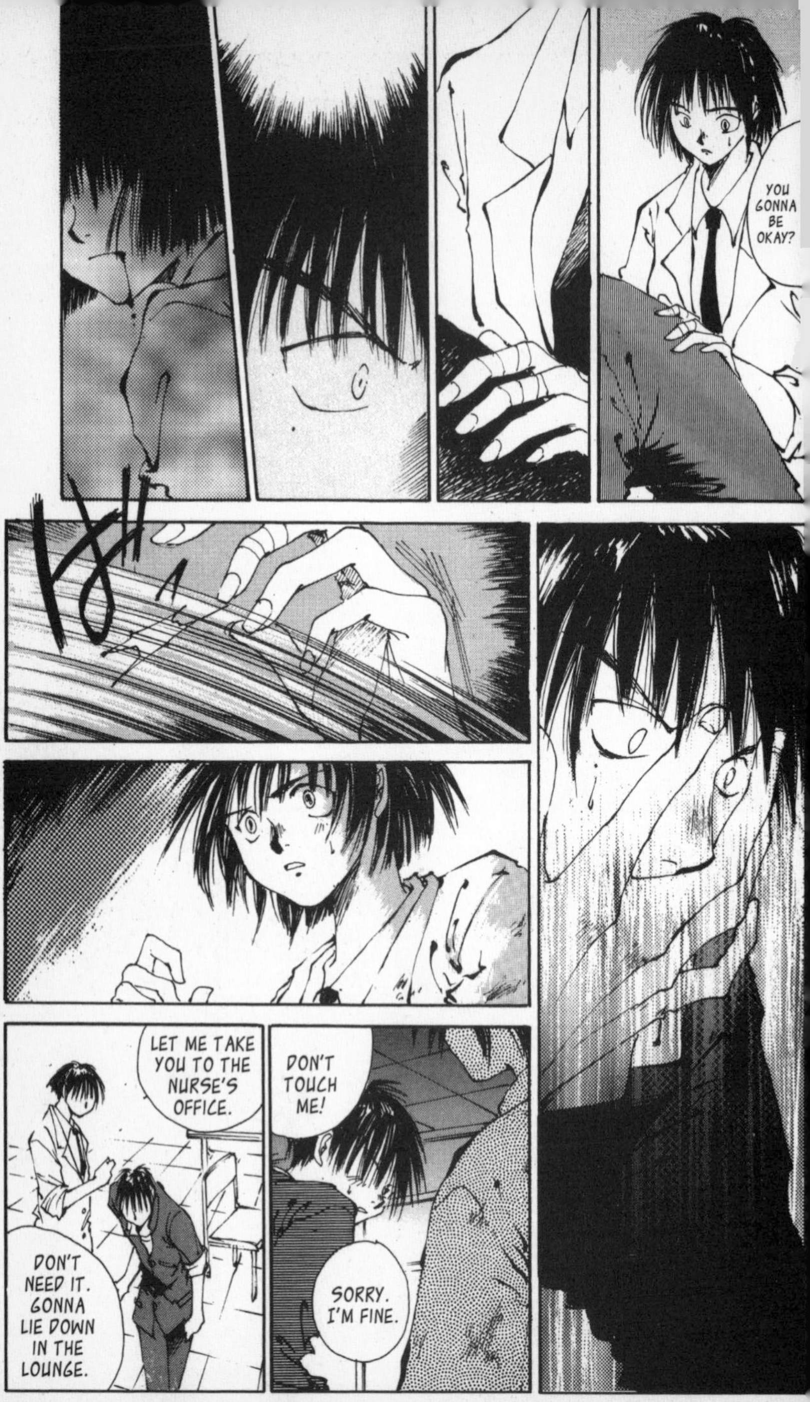
YOU GONNA BE OKAY?
DON'T TOUCH ME!
SORRY. I'M FINE.
LET ME TAKE YOU TO THE NURSE'S OFFICE.
DON'T NEED IT. GONNA LIE DOWN IN THE LOUNGE.

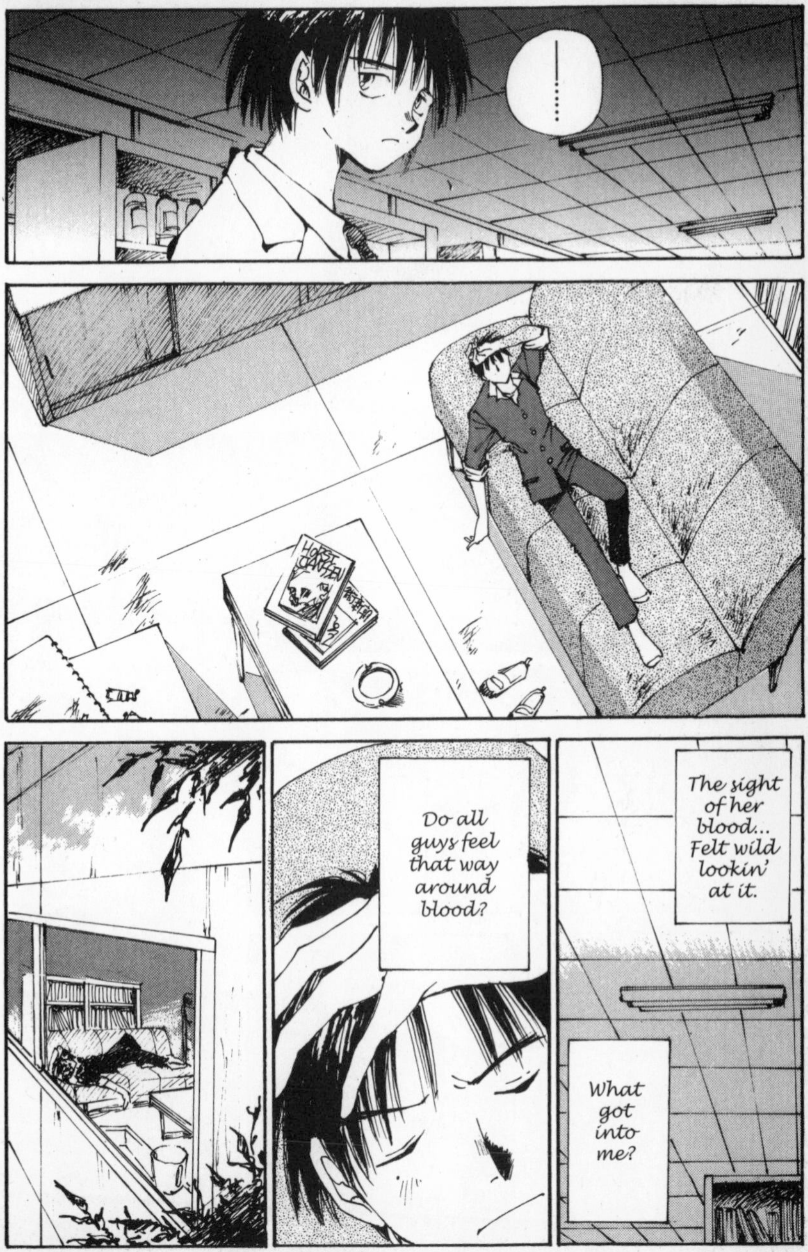
……
The sight of her blood... Felt wild lookin' at it.
What got into me?
Do all guys feel that way around blood?

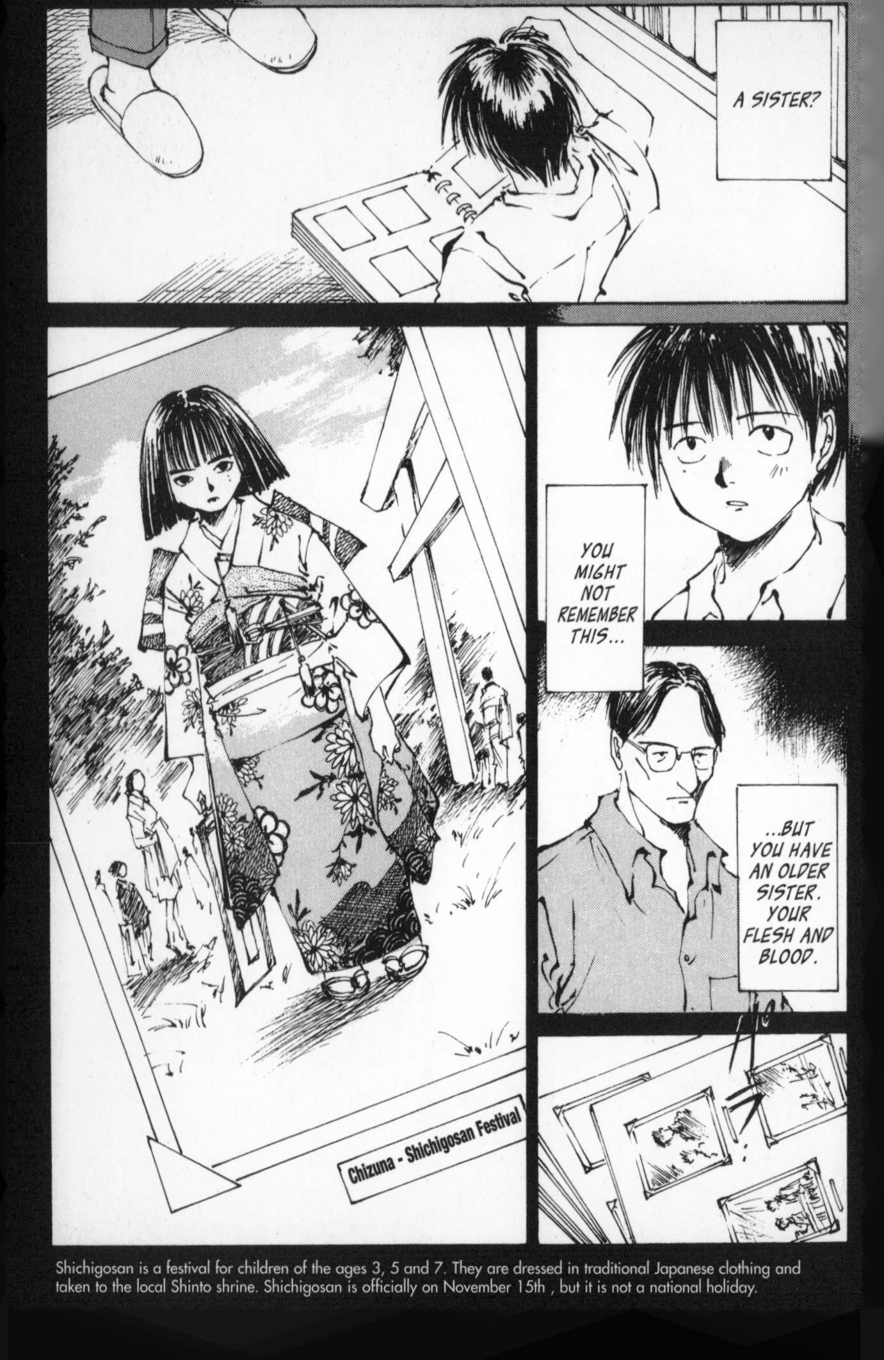
A SISTER?
YOU MIGHT NOT REMEMBER THIS...
...BUT YOU HAVE AN OLDER SISTER. YOUR FLESH AND BLOOD.
Chizuna - Shichigosan Festival

Shichigosan is a festival for children of the ages 3, 5 and 7. They are dressed in traditional Japanese clothing and taken to the local Shinto shrine. Shichigosan is officially on November 15th , but it is not a national holiday.

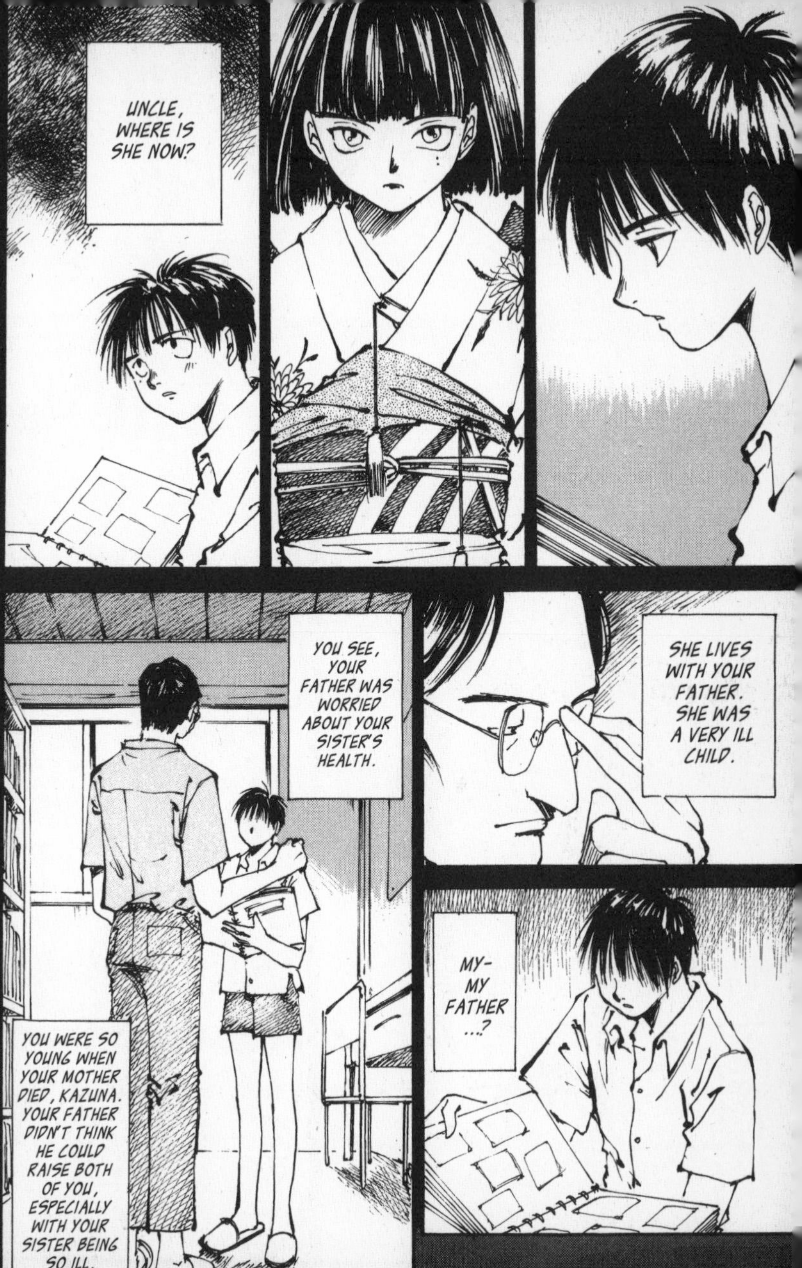
UNCLE, WHERE IS SHE NOW?
SHE LIVES WITH YOUR FATHER. SHE WAS A VERY ILL CHILD.
MY- MY FATHER ...?
YOU SEE, YOUR FATHER WAS WORRIED ABOUT YOUR SISTER'S HEALTH.
YOU WERE SO YOUNG WHEN YOUR MOTHER DIED, KAZUNA. YOUR FATHER DIDN'T THINK HE COULD RAISE BOTH OF YOU, ESPECIALLY WITH YOUR SISTER BEING SO ILL.

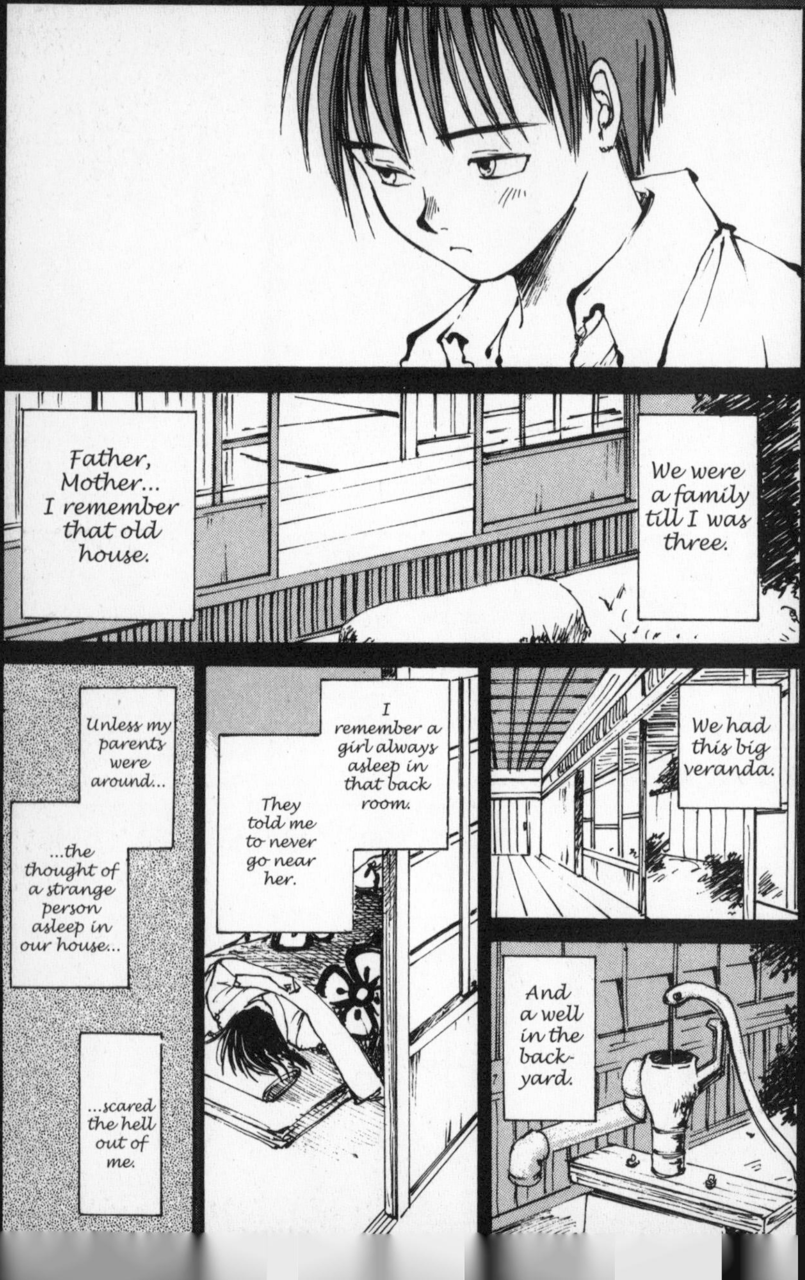
We were a family till I was three.
Father, Mother... I remember that old house.
We had this big veranda.
And a well in the back-yard.
I remember a girl always asleep in that back room.
They told me to never go near her.
Unless my parents were around...
...the thought of a strange person asleep in our house...
...scared the hell out of me.

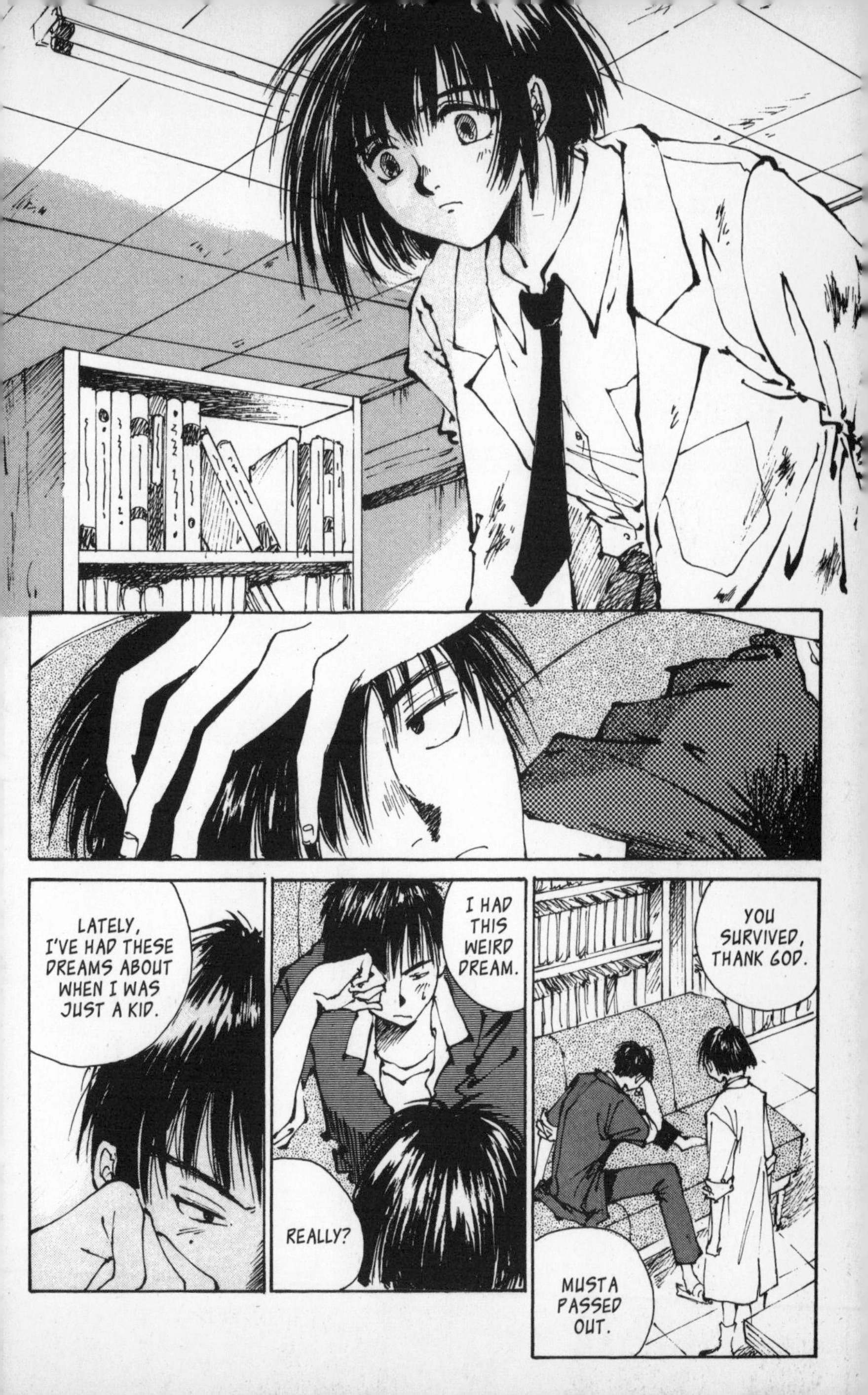
YOU SURVIVED, THANK GOD.
MUSTA PASSED OUT.
I HAD THIS WEIRD DREAM.
REALLY?
LATELY, I'VE HAD THESE DREAMS ABOUT WHEN I WAS JUST A KID.

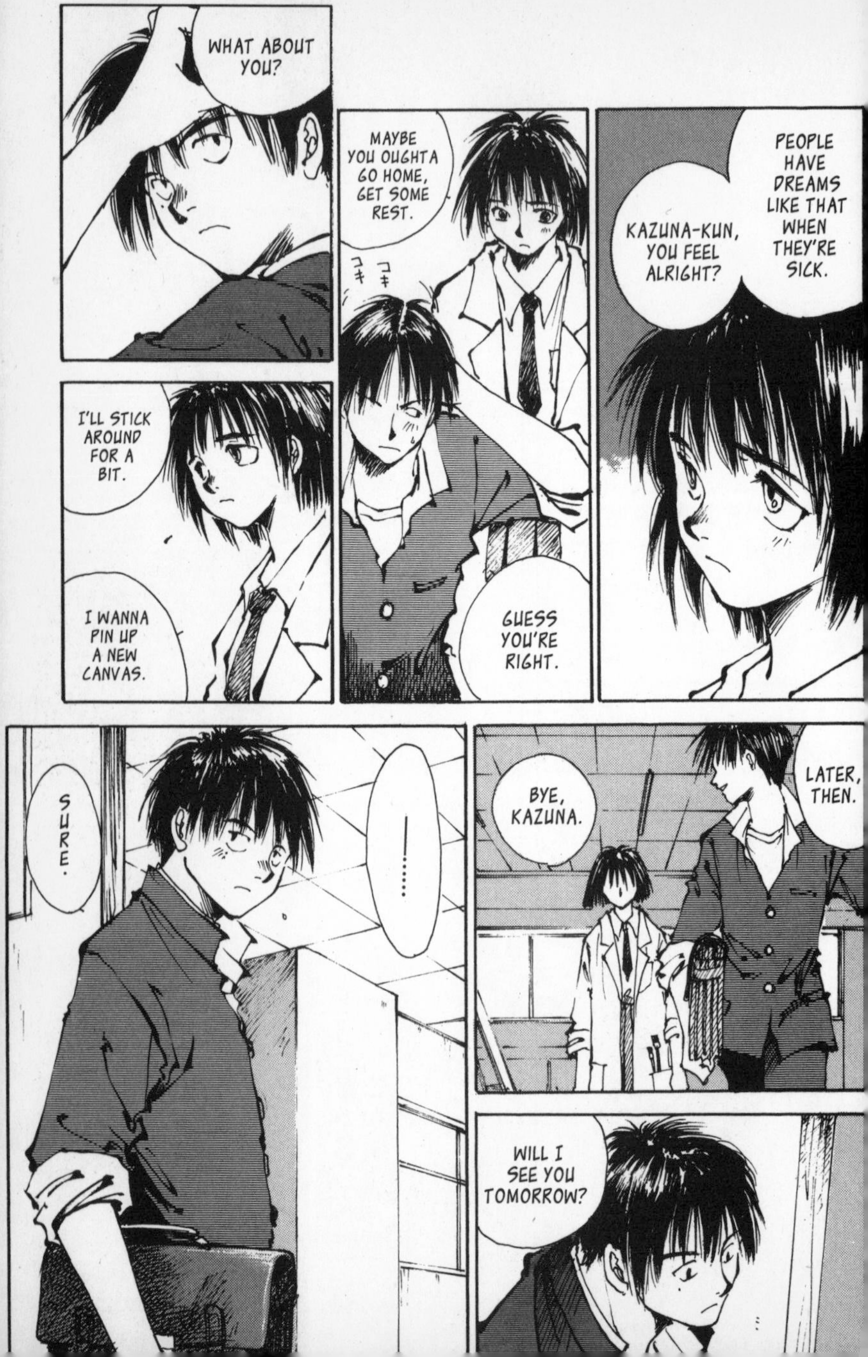
PEOPLE HAVE DREAMS LIKE THAT WHEN THEY'RE SICK.
KAZUNA-KUN, YOU FEEL ALRIGHT?
MAYBE YOU OUGHTA GO HOME, GET SOME REST.
コキ コキ
GUESS YOU'RE RIGHT.
WHAT ABOUT YOU?
I'LL STICK AROUND FOR A BIT.
I WANNA PIN UP A NEW CANVAS.
LATER, THEN.
BYE, KAZUNA.
WILL I SEE YOU TOMORROW?
!......
SURE.

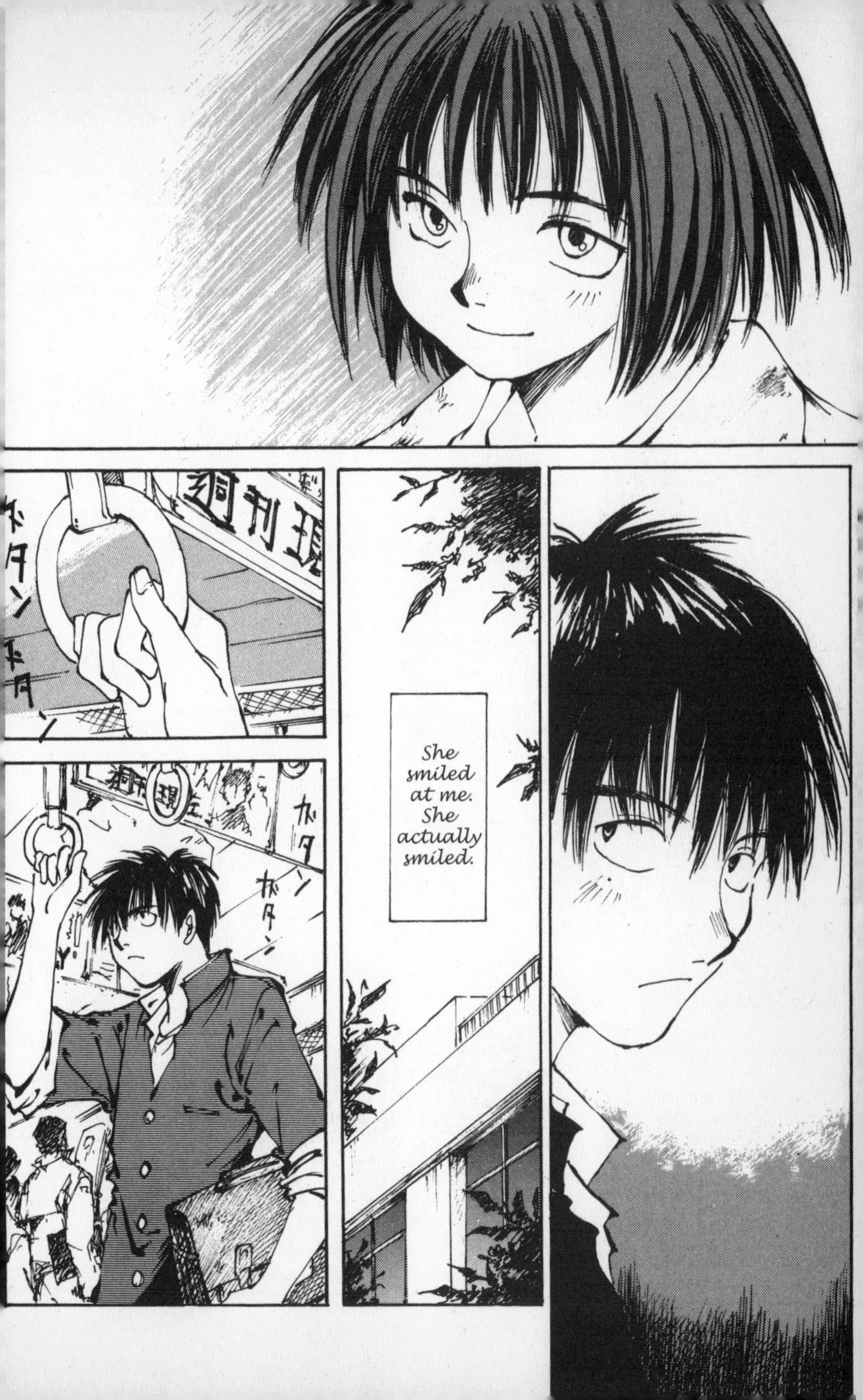
She smiled at me. She actually smiled.
ガタン
ガタン

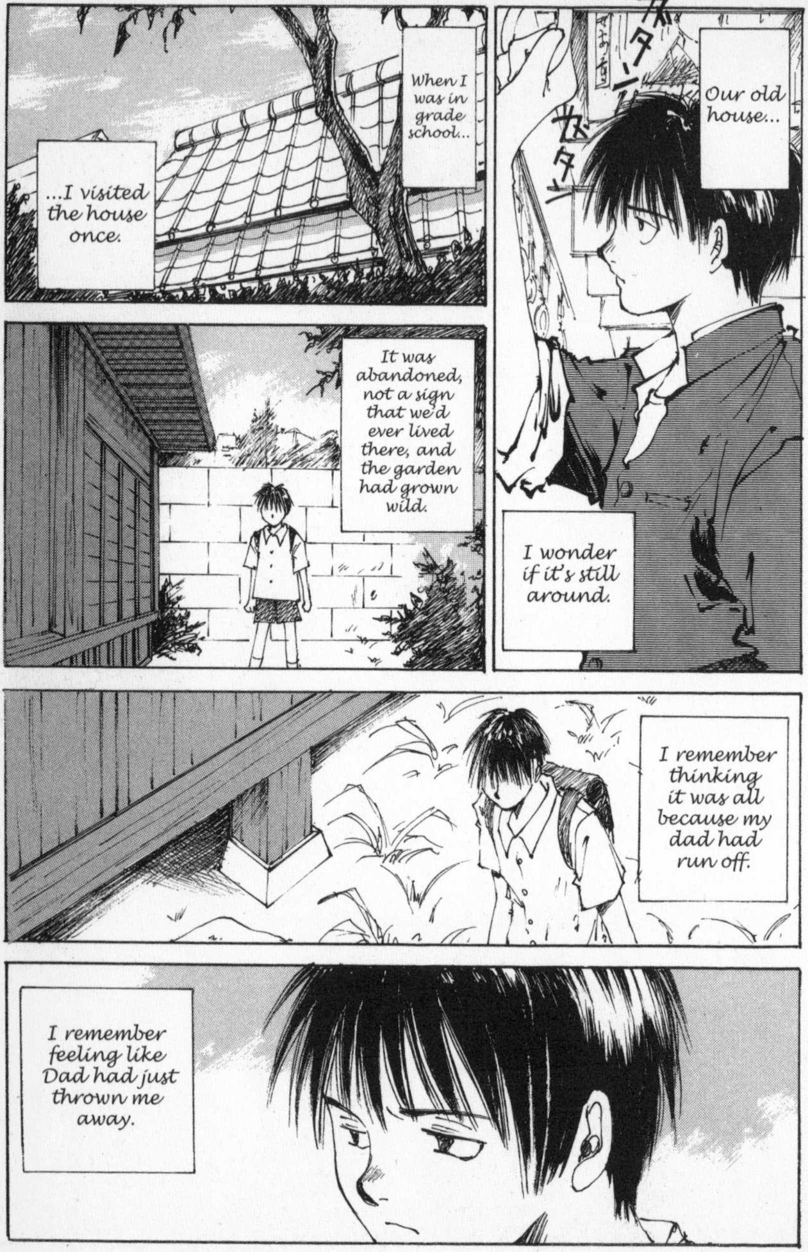
Our old house...
I wonder if it's still around.
When I was in grade school...
...I visited the house once.
It was abandoned, not a sign that we'd ever lived there, and the garden had grown wild.
I remember thinking it was all because my dad had run off.
I remember feeling like Dad had just thrown me away.

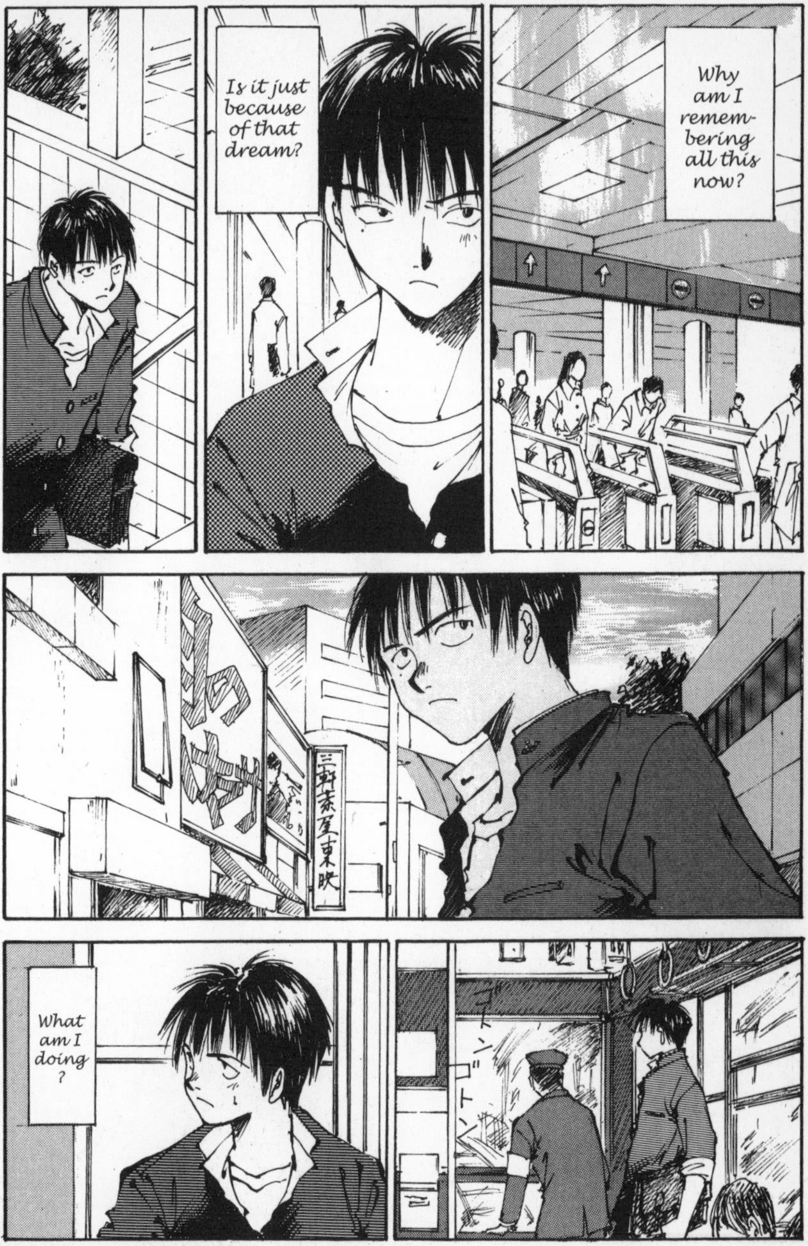
Why am I remem-bering all this now?
Is it just because of that dream?
三軒茶屋東映
ゴトン
ゴトン
What am I doing ?

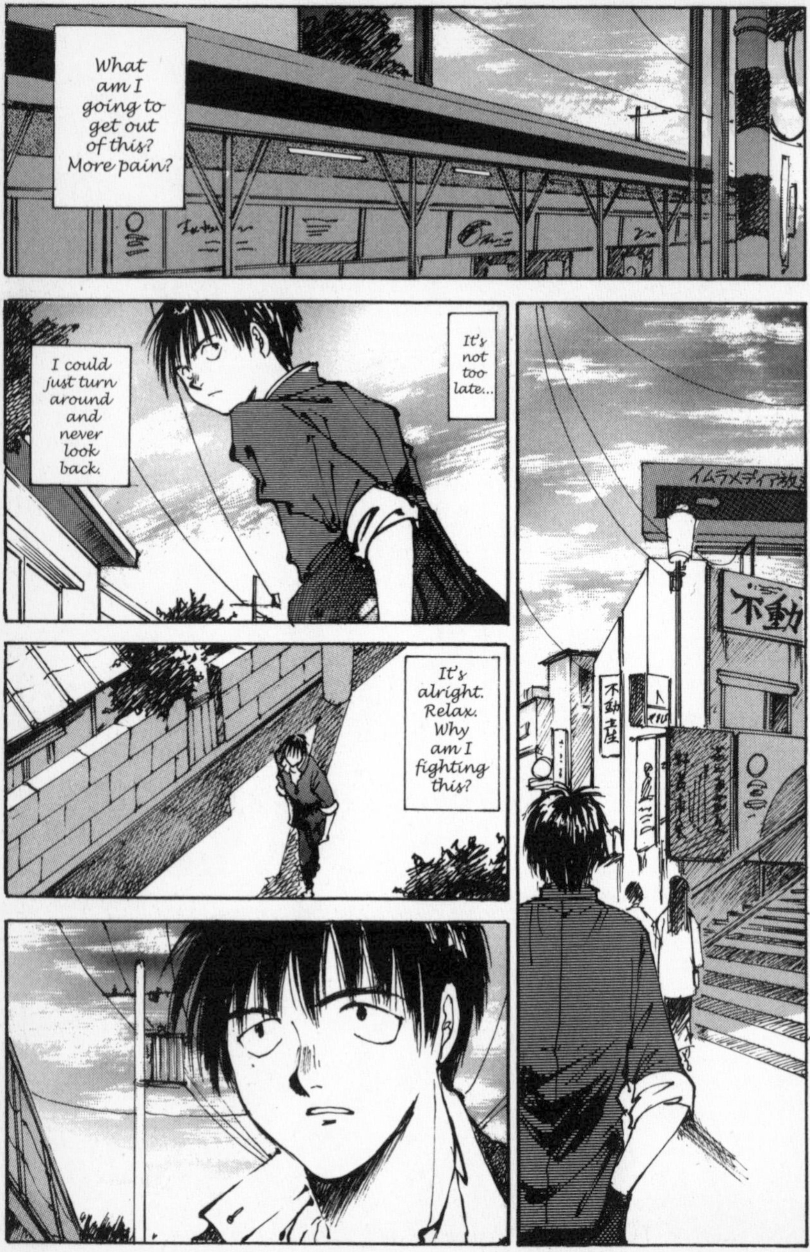
What am I going to get out of this? More pain?
It's not too late...
I could just turn around and never look back.
It's alright. Relax. Why am I fighting this?

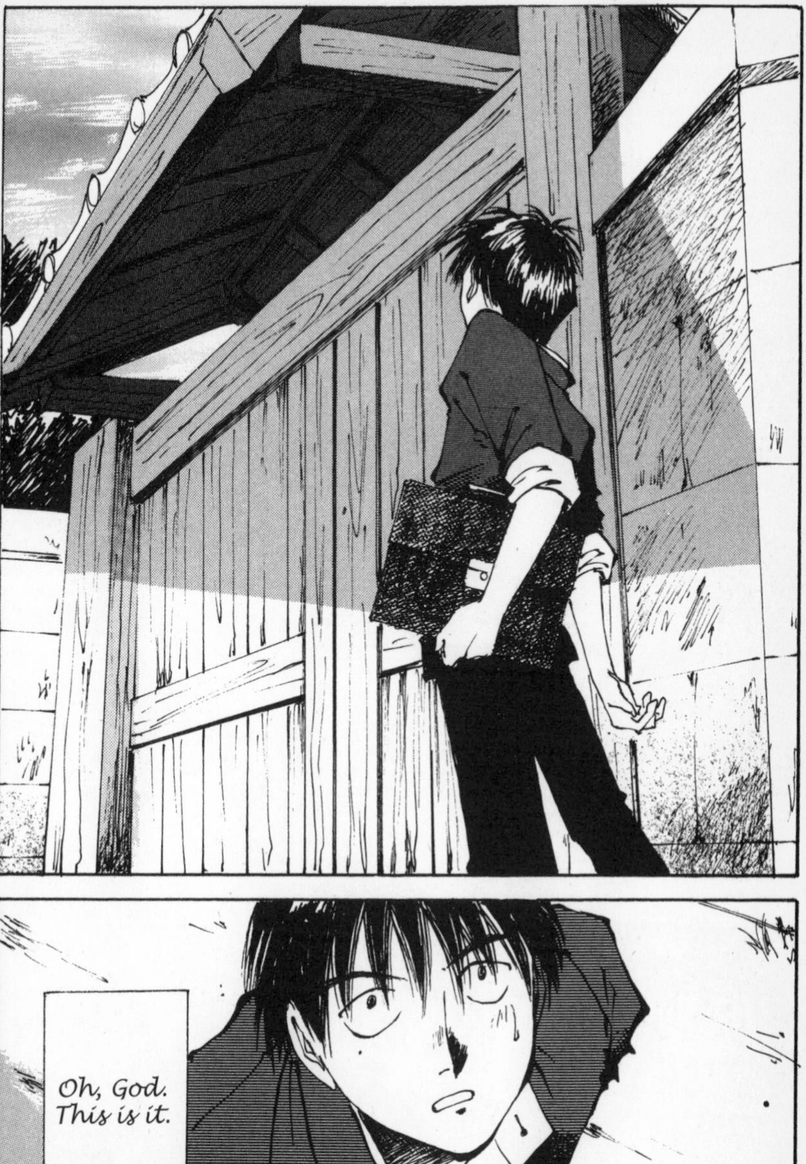
Oh, God. This is it.

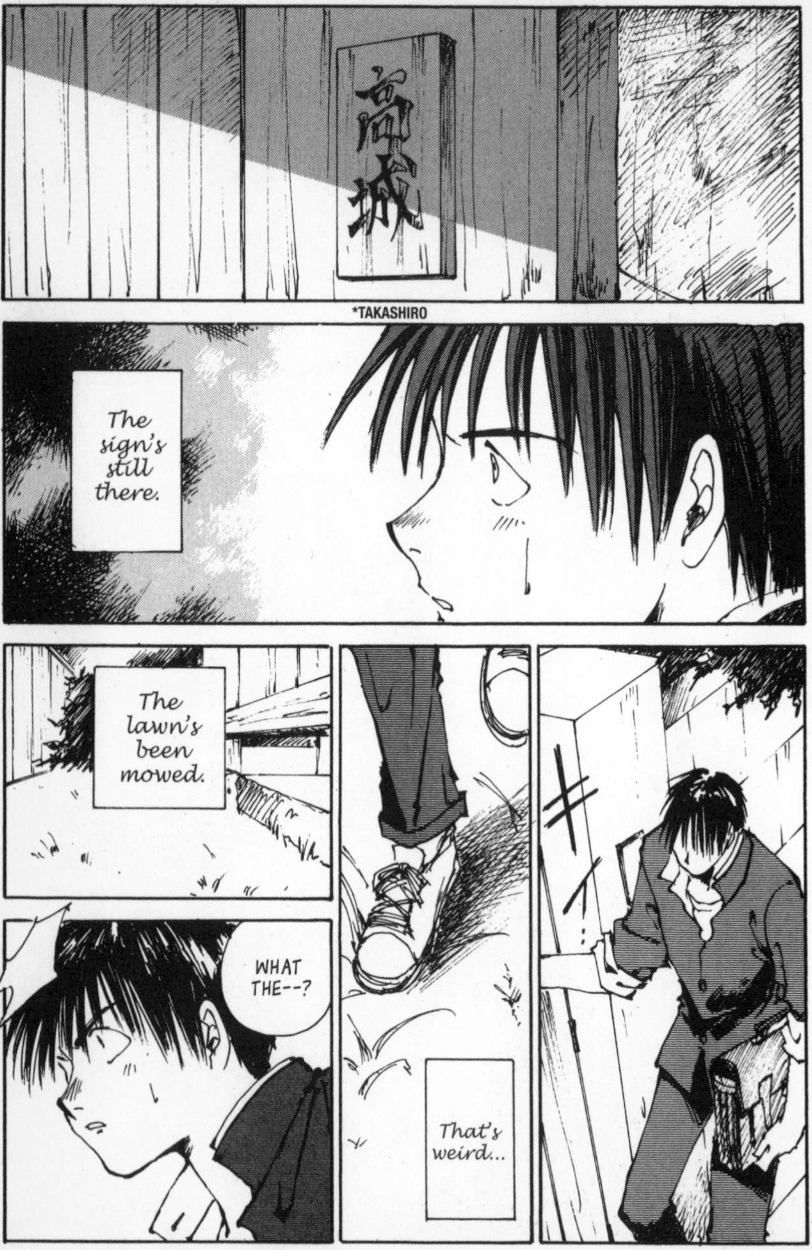
高城
*TAKASHIRO
The sign's still there.
That's weird...
The lawn's been mowed.
WHAT THE--?

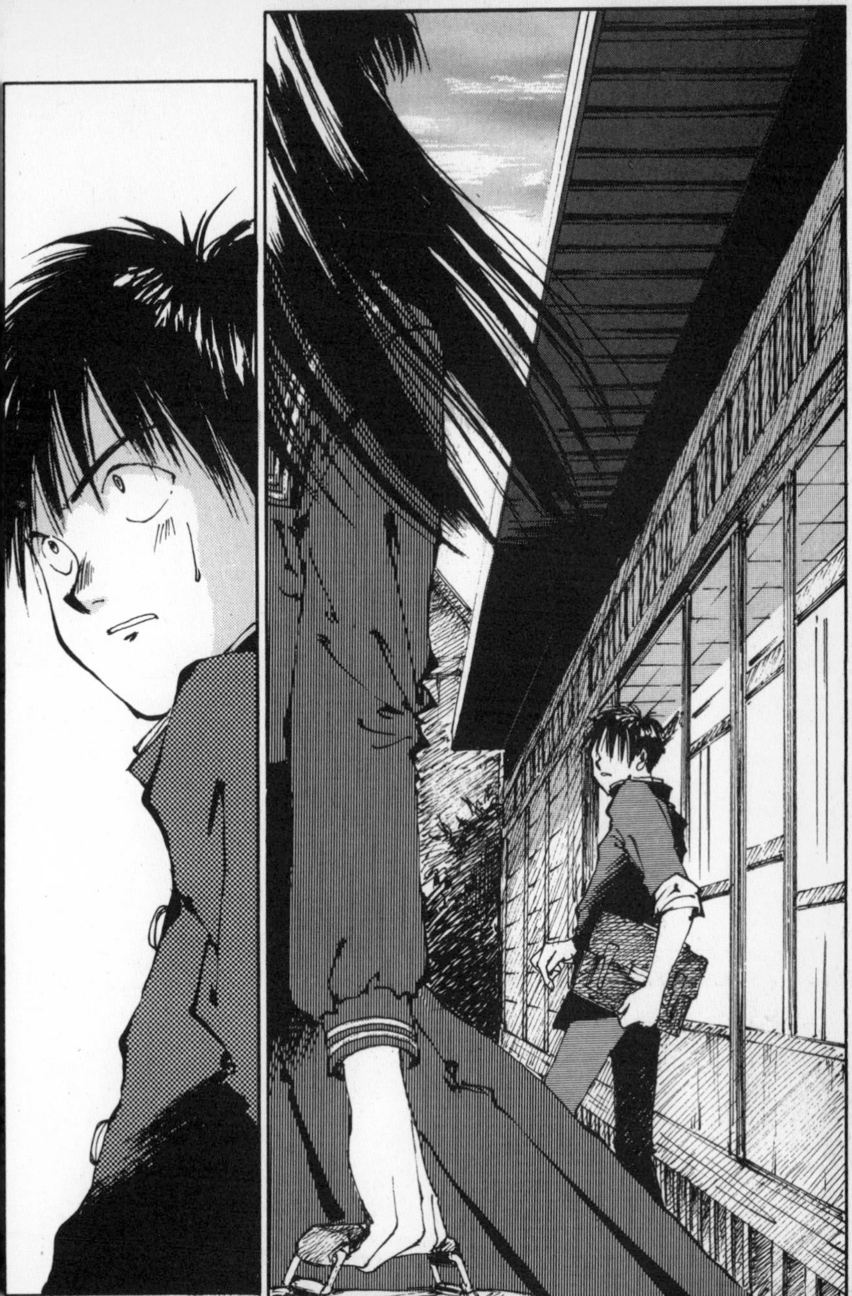

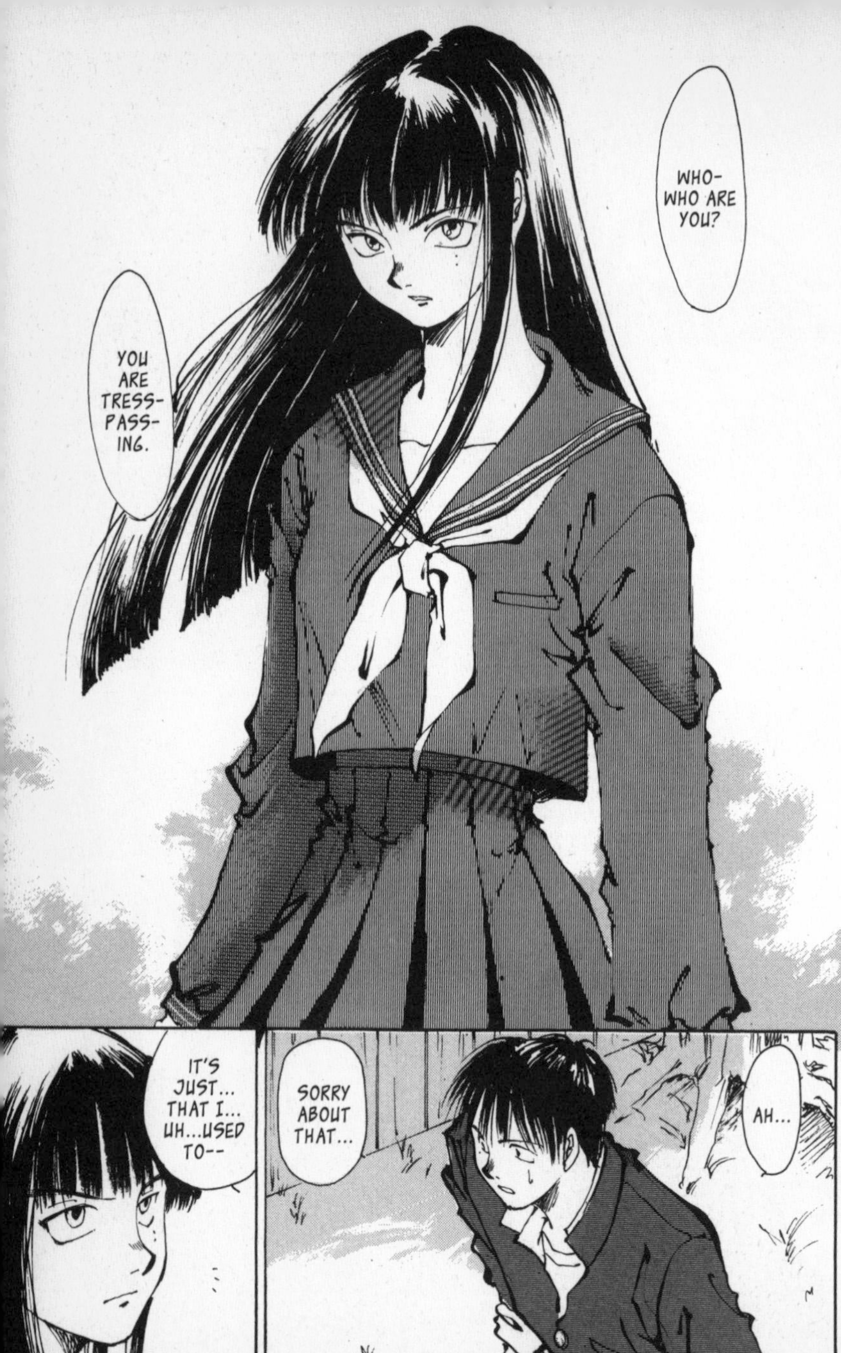
WHO- WHO ARE YOU?
YOU ARE TRESS-PASSING.
AH...
SORRY ABOUT THAT...
IT'S JUST... THAT I... UH...USED TO--

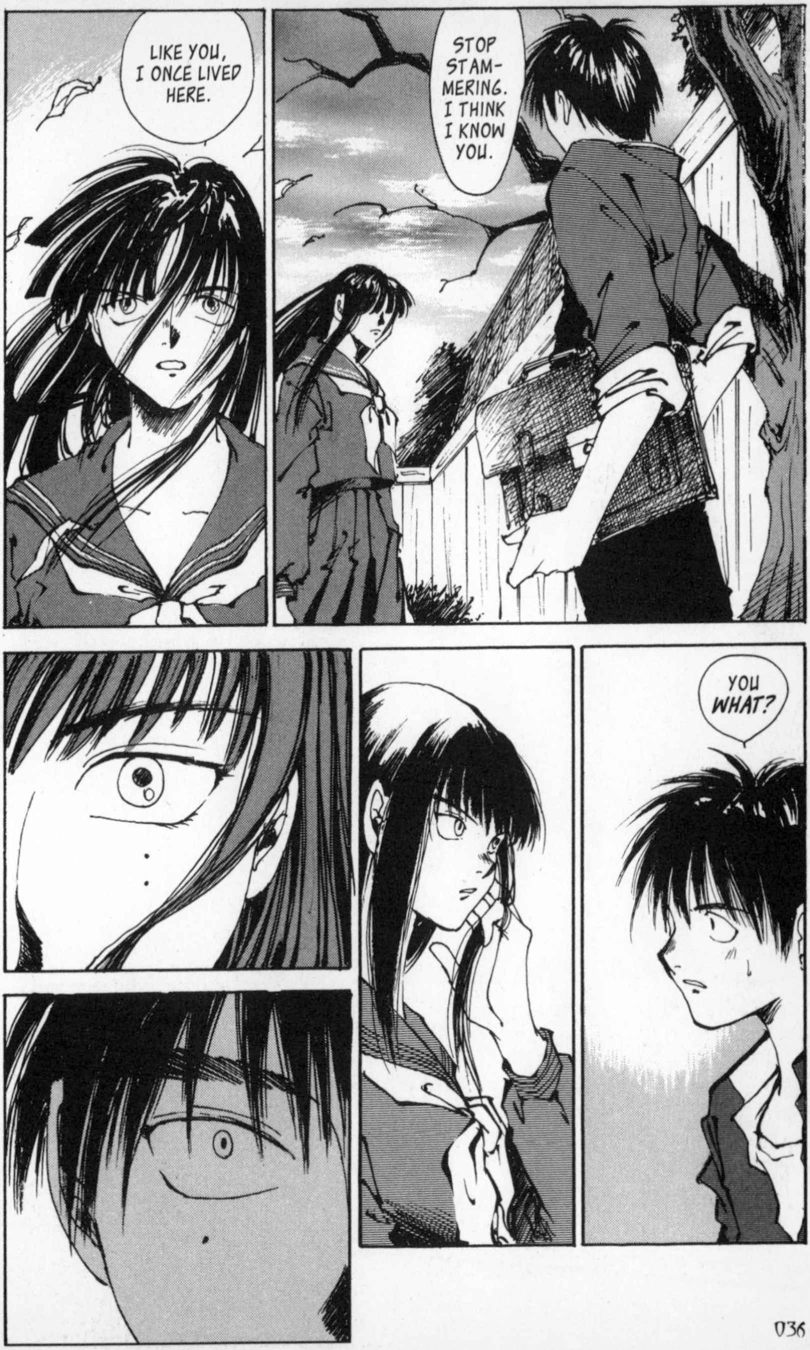
STOP STAM-MERING. I THINK I KNOW YOU.
LIKE YOU, I ONCE LIVED HERE.
YOU WHAT?

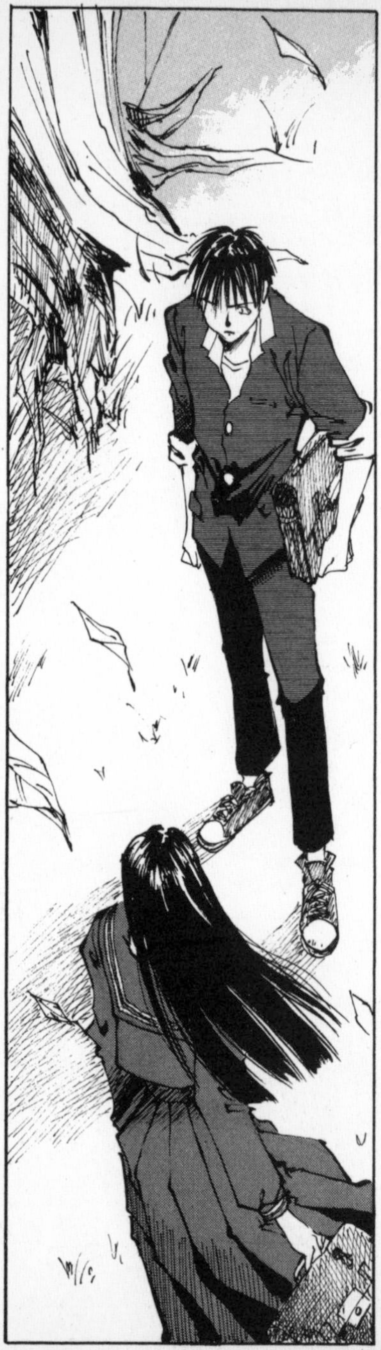

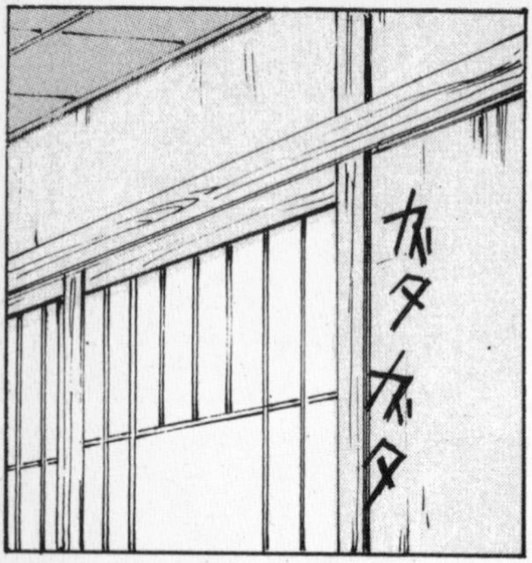
ガタガタ

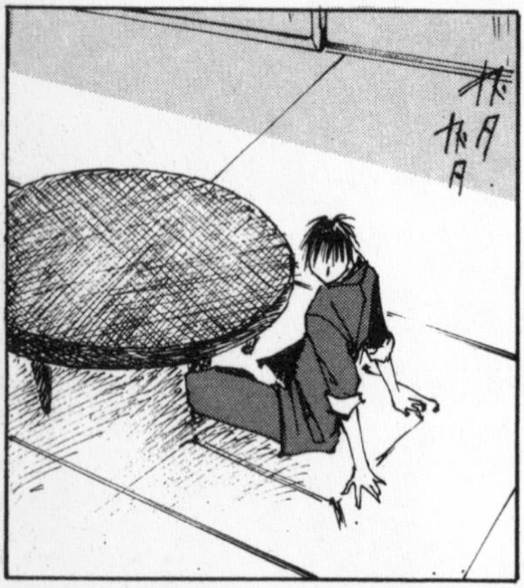
ガタ
ガタ

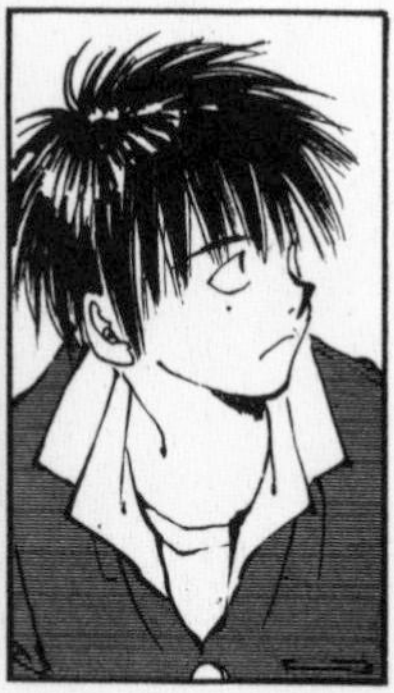

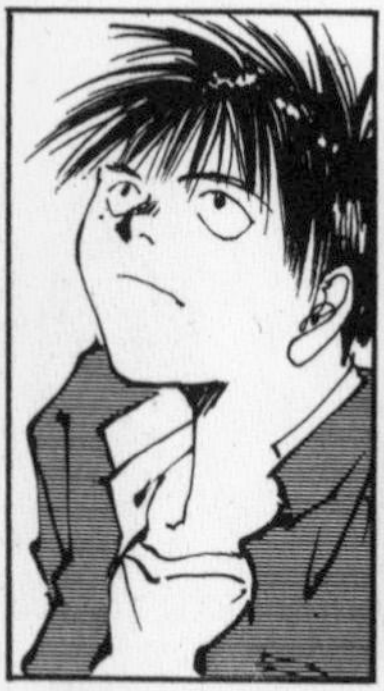

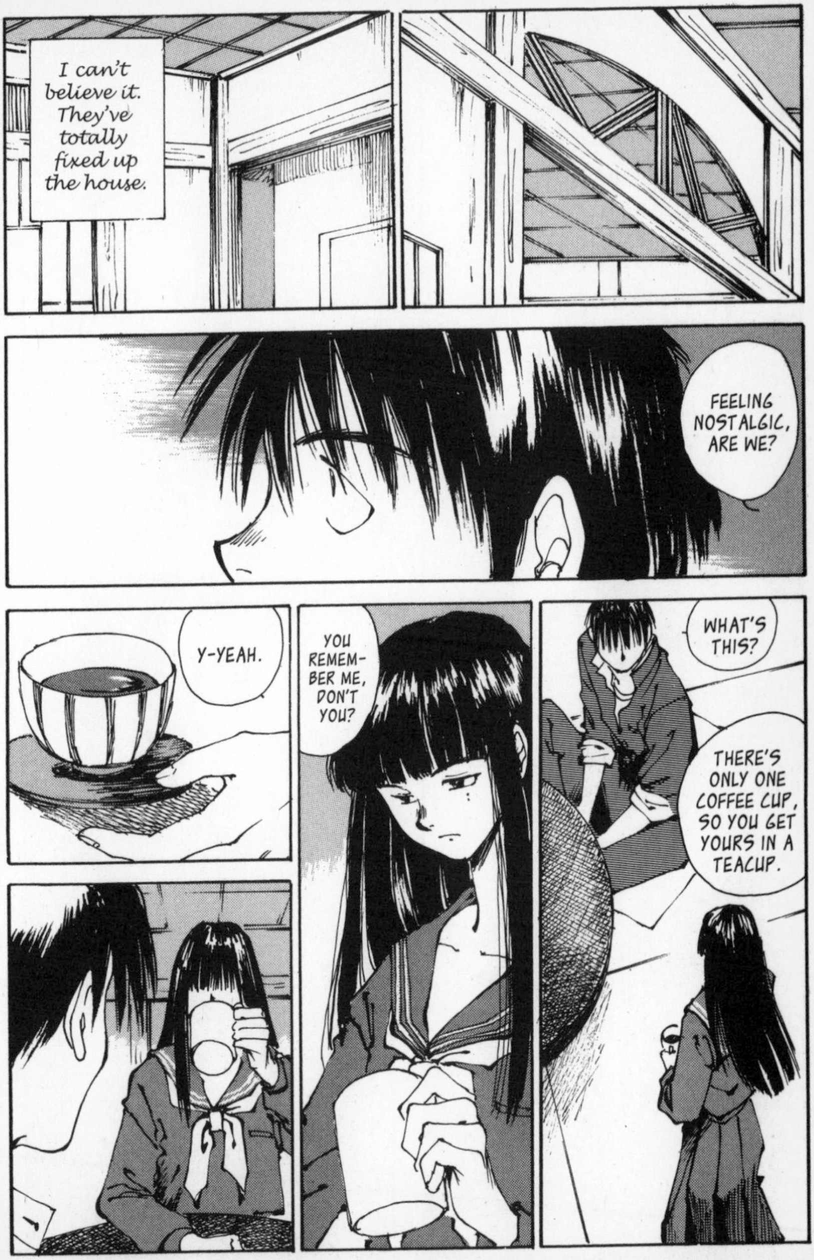
I can't believe it. They've totally fixed up the house.
FEELING NOSTALGIC, ARE WE?
WHAT'S THIS?
THERE'S ONLY ONE COFFEE CUP, SO YOU GET YOURS IN A TEACUP.
YOU REMEMBER ME, DON'T YOU?
Y-YEAH.

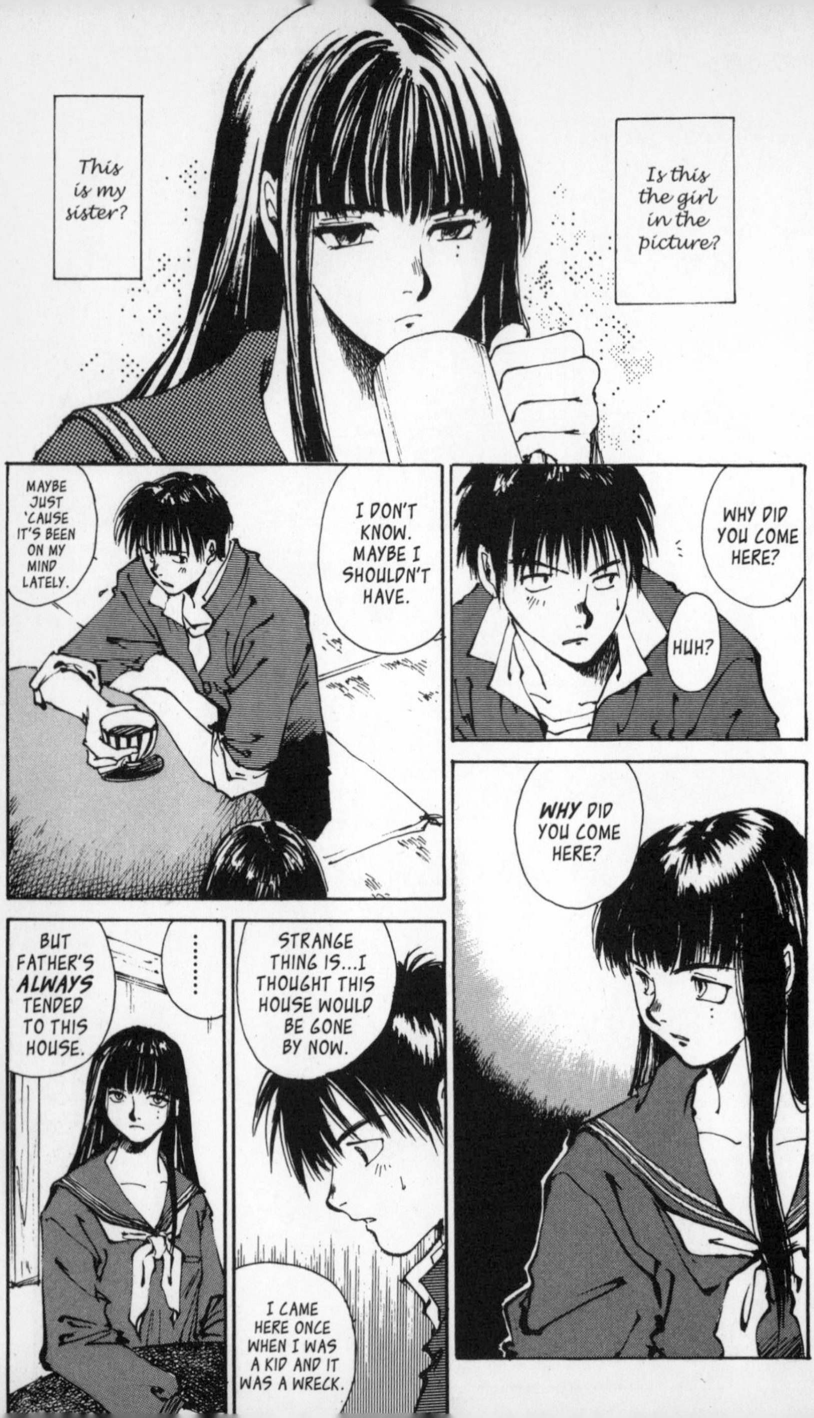
Is this the girl in the picture?
This is my sister?
WHY DID YOU COME HERE?
HUH?
I DON'T KNOW. MAYBE I SHOULDN'T HAVE.
MAYBE JUST 'CAUSE IT'S BEEN ON MY MIND LATELY.
WHY DID YOU COME HERE?
STRANGE THING IS...I THOUGHT THIS HOUSE WOULD BE GONE BY NOW.
I CAME HERE ONCE WHEN I WAS A KID AND IT WAS A WRECK.
......
BUT FATHER'S ALWAYS TENDED TO THIS HOUSE.

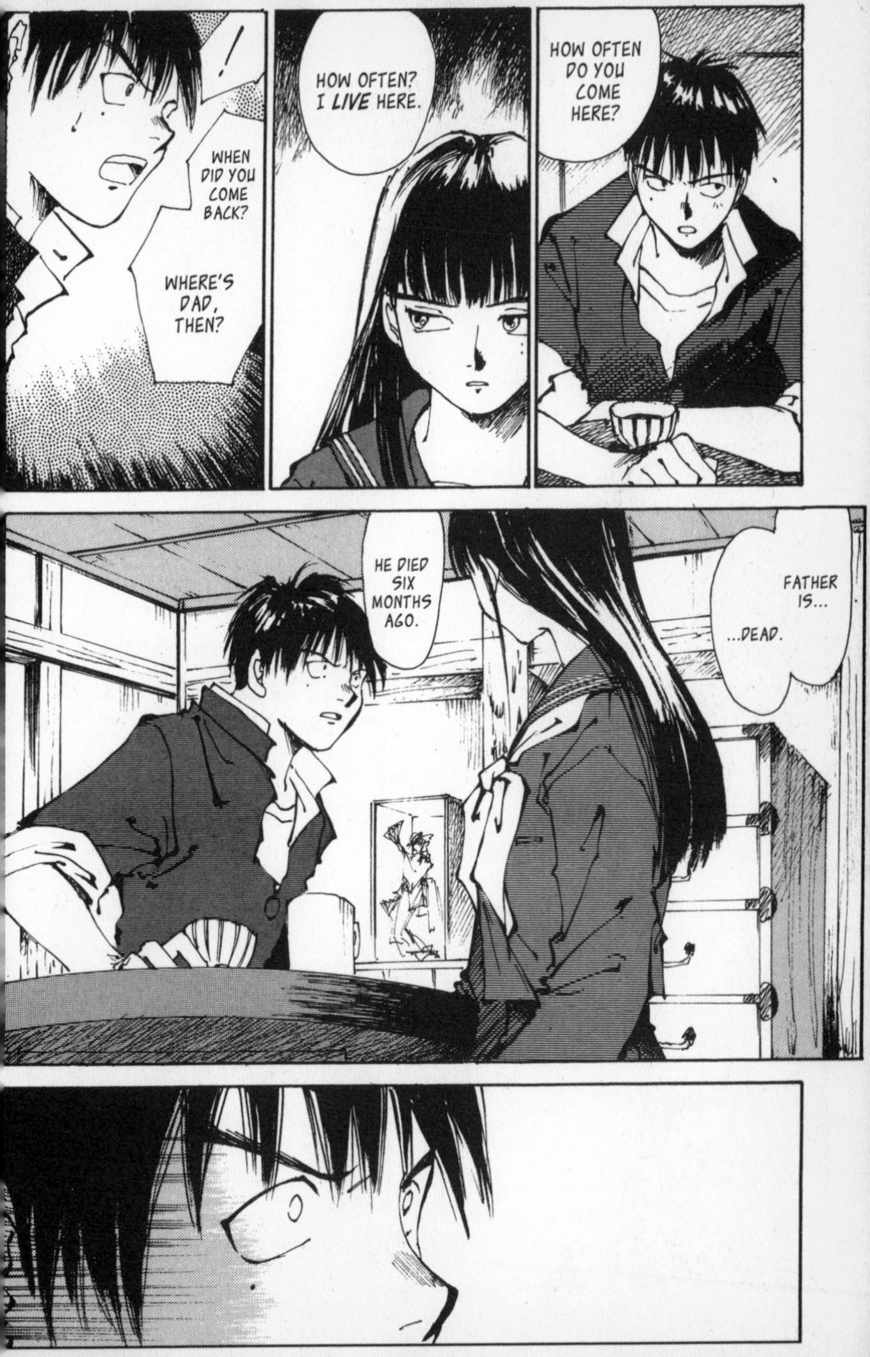
HOW OFTEN DO YOU COME HERE?
HOW OFTEN? I *LIVE* HERE.
!
WHEN DID YOU COME BACK?
WHERE'S DAD, THEN?
FATHER IS...
...DEAD.
HE DIED SIX MONTHS AGO.

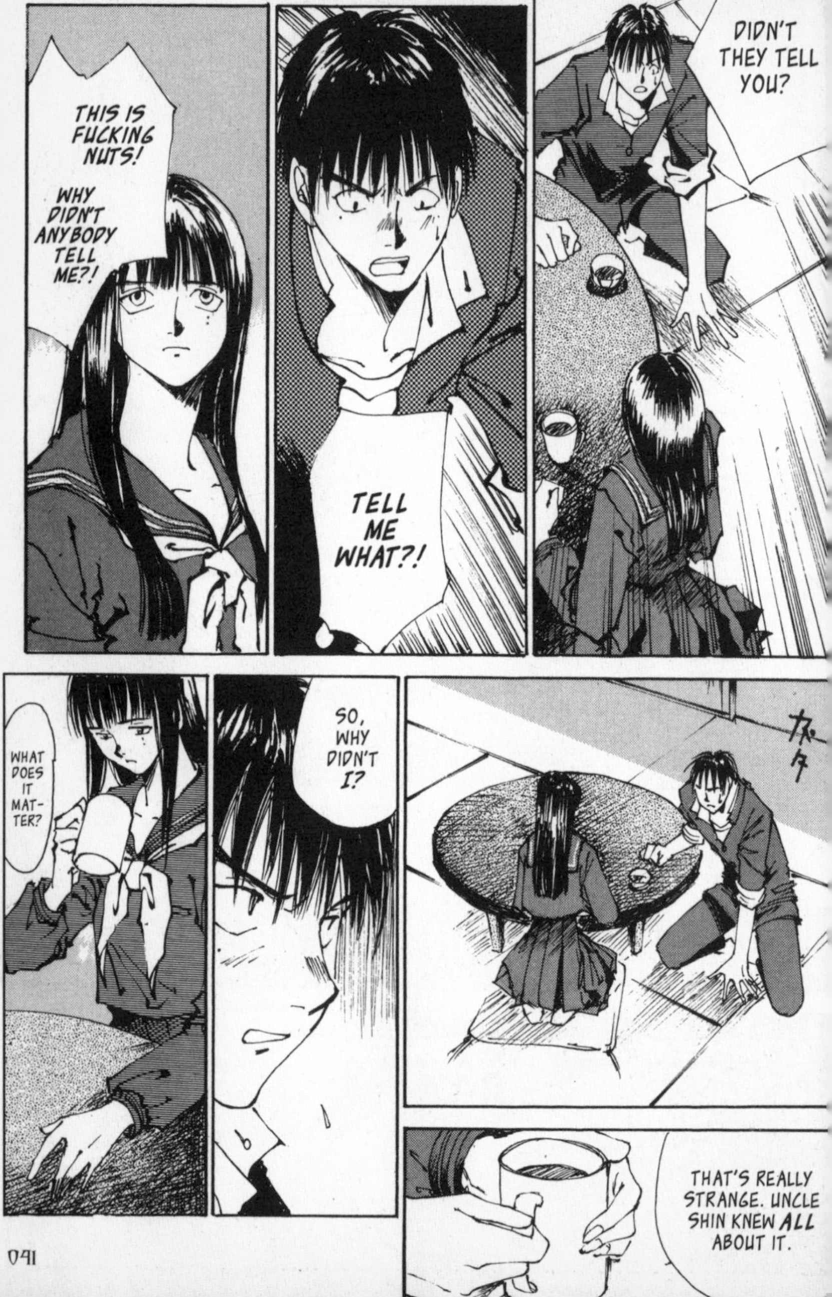
DIDN'T THEY TELL YOU?
TELL ME WHAT?!
THIS IS FUCKING NUTS!
WHY DIDN'T ANYBODY TELL ME?!
ガタ
THAT'S REALLY STRANGE. UNCLE SHIN KNEW **ALL** ABOUT IT.
SO, WHY DIDN'T *I?*
WHAT DOES IT MAT-TER?

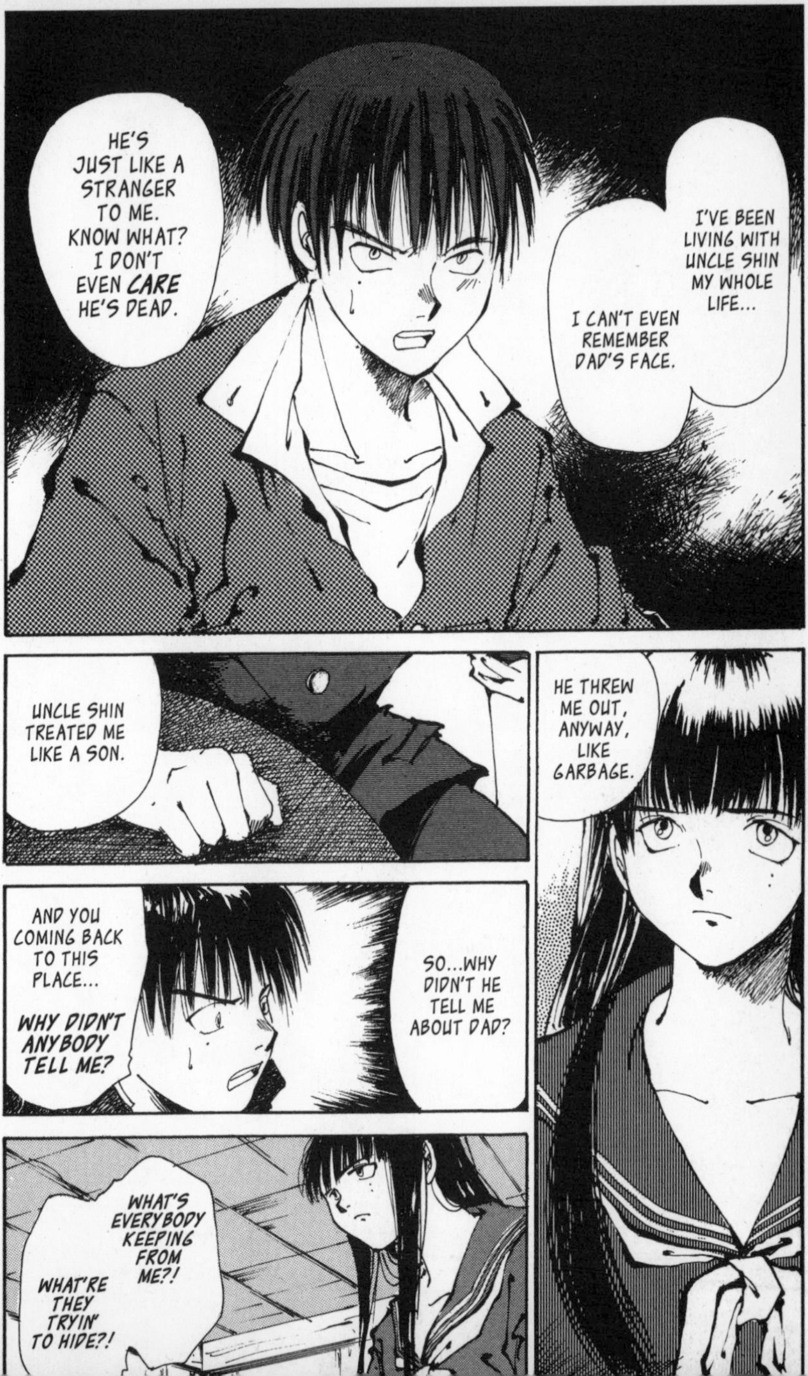
I'VE BEEN LIVING WITH UNCLE SHIN MY WHOLE LIFE...
I CAN'T EVEN REMEMBER DAD'S FACE.
HE'S JUST LIKE A STRANGER TO ME. KNOW WHAT? I DON'T EVEN *CARE* HE'S DEAD.
HE THREW ME OUT, ANYWAY, LIKE GARBAGE.
UNCLE SHIN TREATED ME LIKE A SON.
SO...WHY DIDN'T HE TELL ME ABOUT DAD?
AND YOU COMING BACK TO THIS PLACE...
WHY DIDN'T ANYBODY TELL ME?
WHAT'S EVERYBODY KEEPING FROM ME?!
WHAT'RE THEY TRYIN' TO HIDE?!

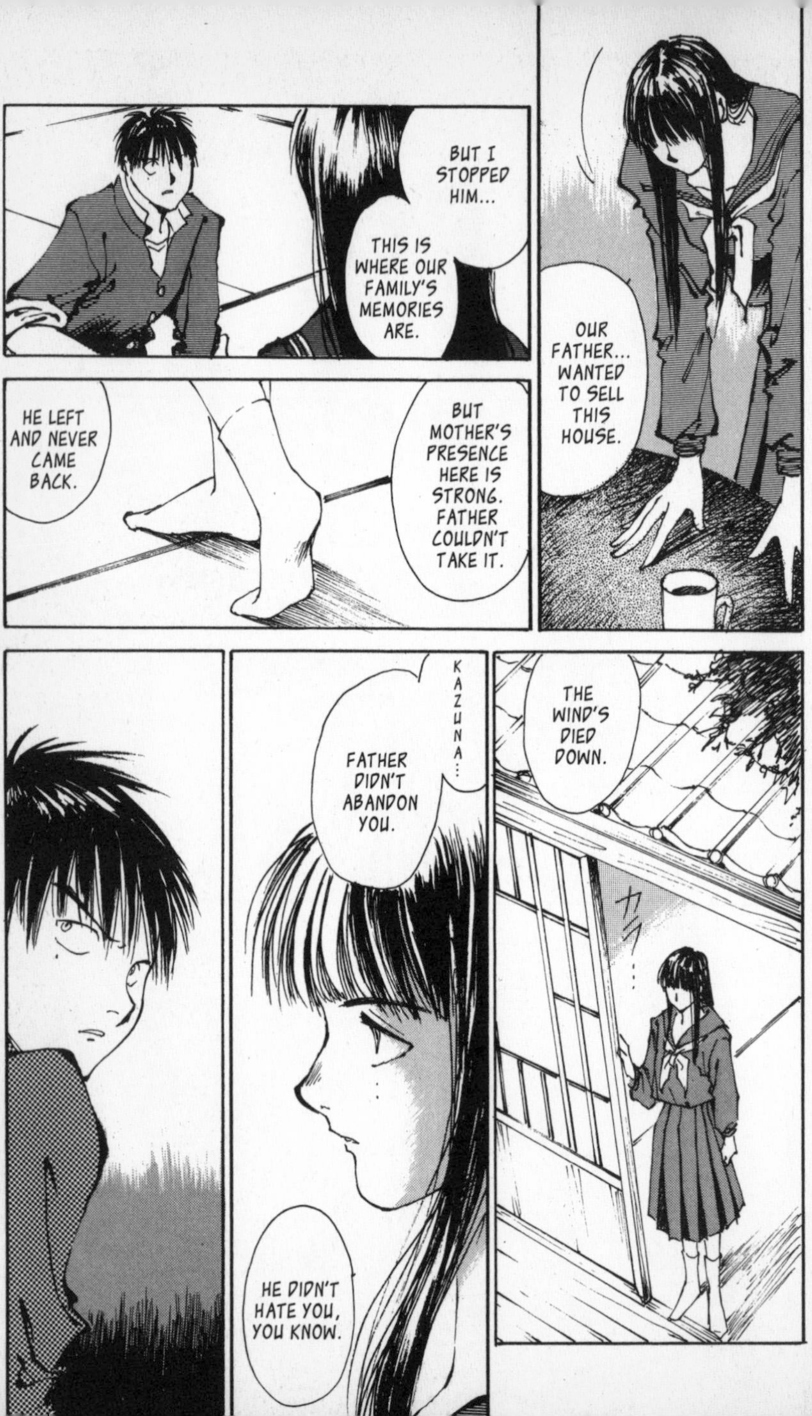
OUR FATHER... WANTED TO SELL THIS HOUSE.
BUT I STOPPED HIM...
THIS IS WHERE OUR FAMILY'S MEMORIES ARE.
BUT MOTHER'S PRESENCE HERE IS STRONG. FATHER COULDN'T TAKE IT.
HE LEFT AND NEVER CAME BACK.
THE WIND'S DIED DOWN.
KAZUNA...
FATHER DIDN'T ABANDON YOU.
HE DIDN'T HATE YOU, YOU KNOW.

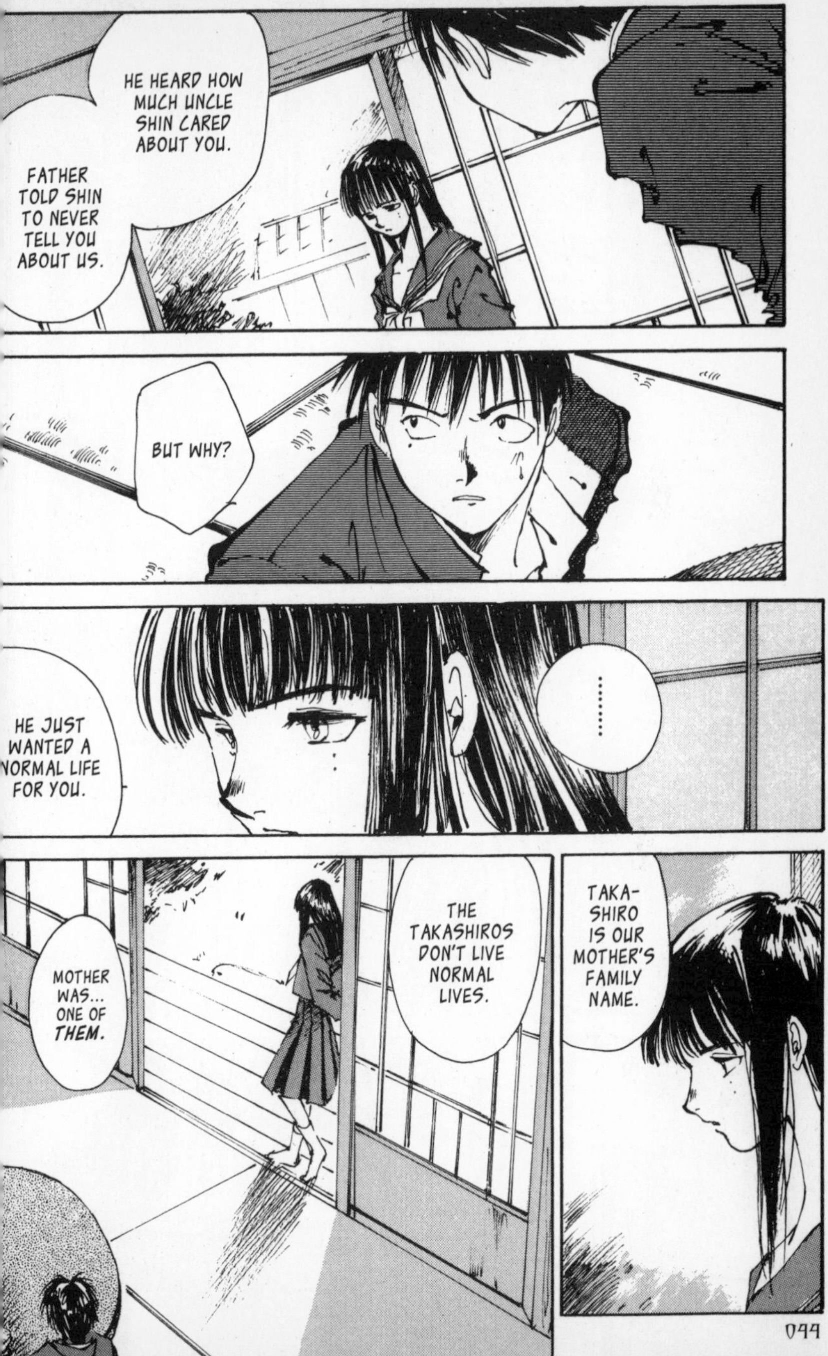
HE HEARD HOW MUCH UNCLE SHIN CARED ABOUT YOU.
FATHER TOLD SHIN TO NEVER TELL YOU ABOUT US.
BUT WHY?
......
HE JUST WANTED A NORMAL LIFE FOR YOU.
TAKA-SHIRO IS OUR MOTHER'S FAMILY NAME.
THE TAKASHIROS DON'T LIVE NORMAL LIVES.
MOTHER WAS... ONE OF *THEM*.

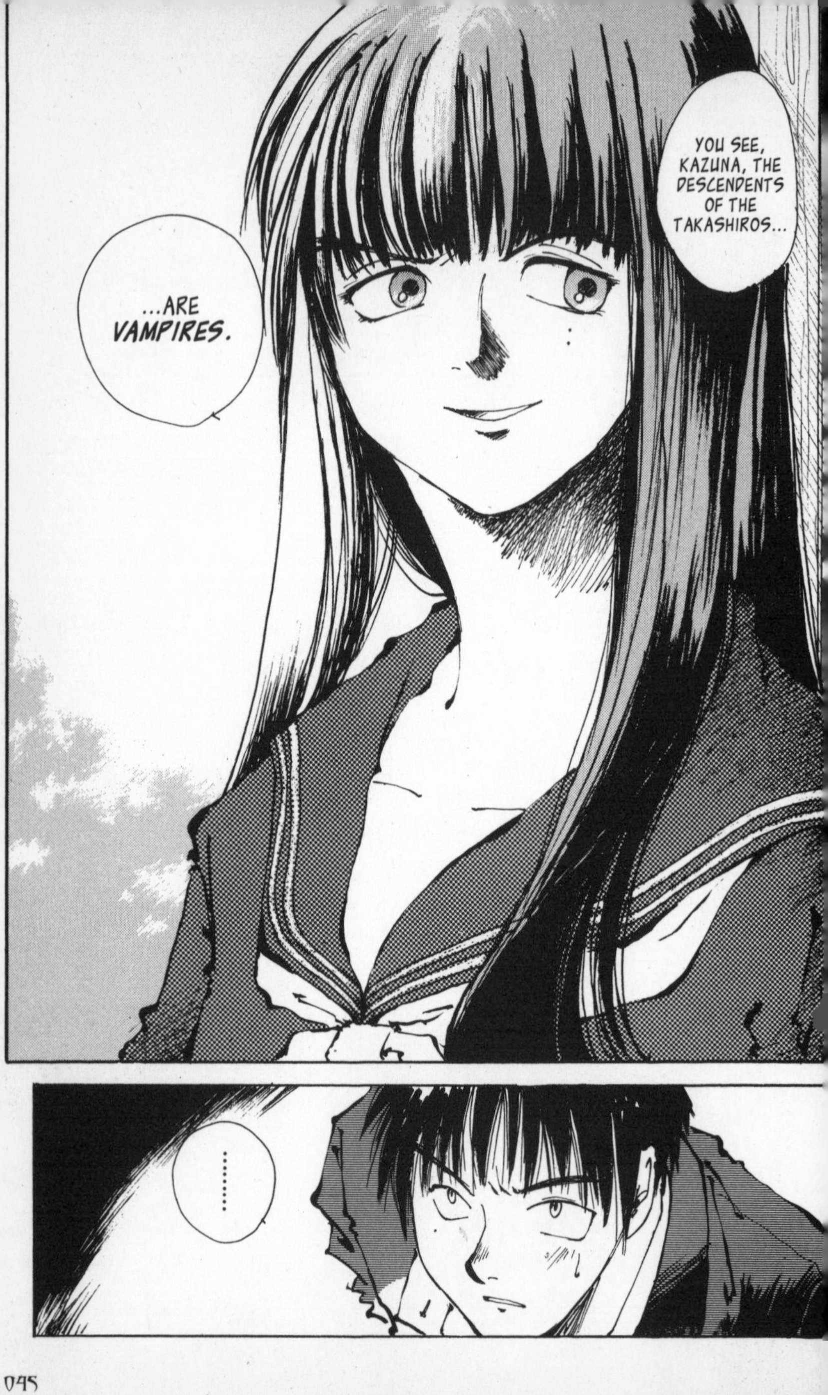
YOU SEE, KAZUNA, THE DESCENDENTS OF THE TAKASHIROS...
...ARE VAMPIRES.
......

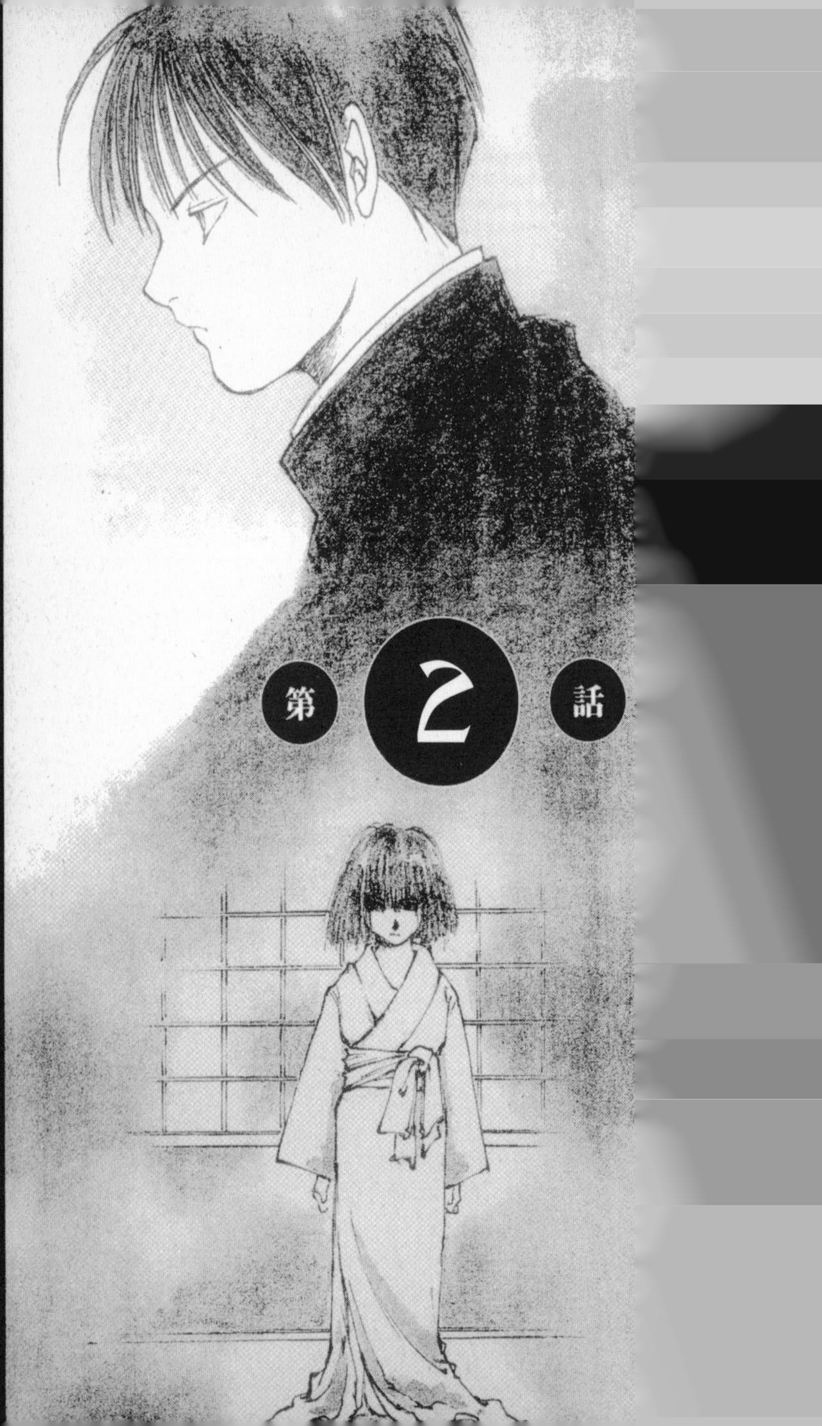
第2話

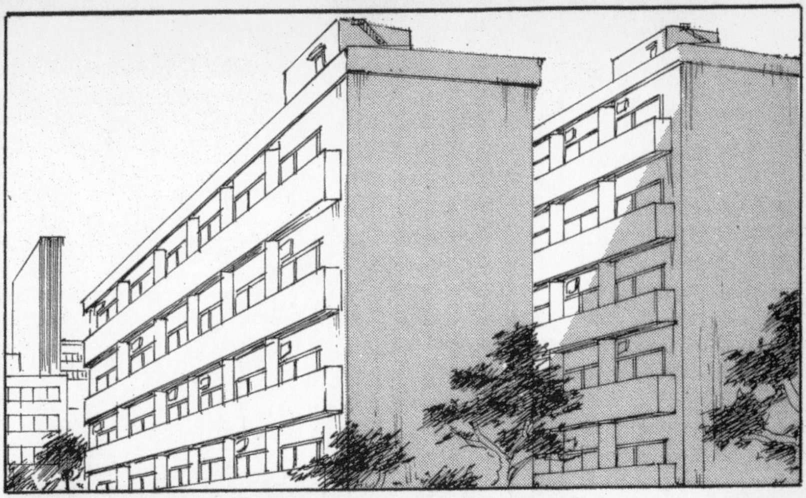
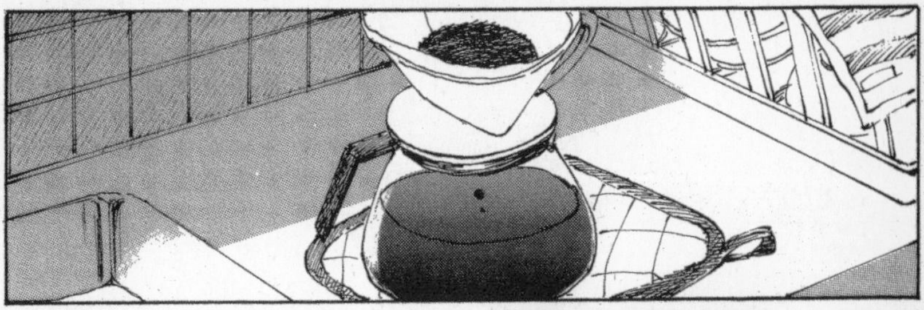
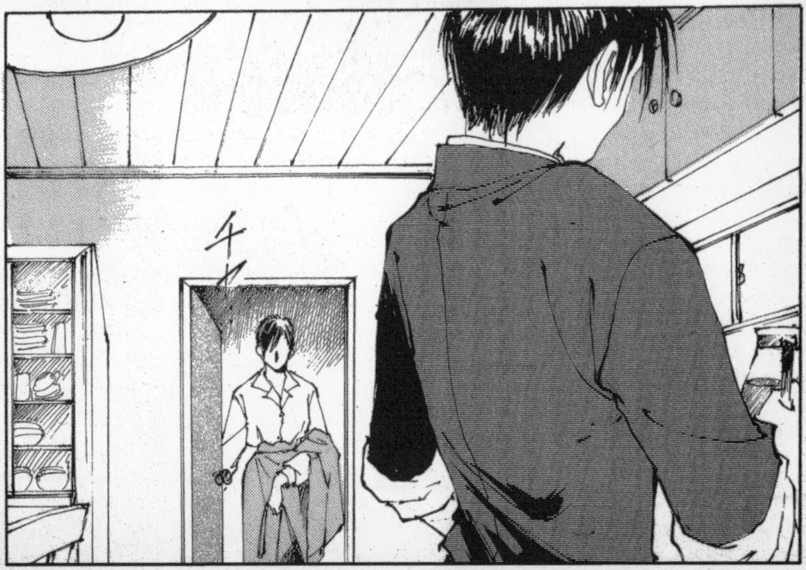
チャ

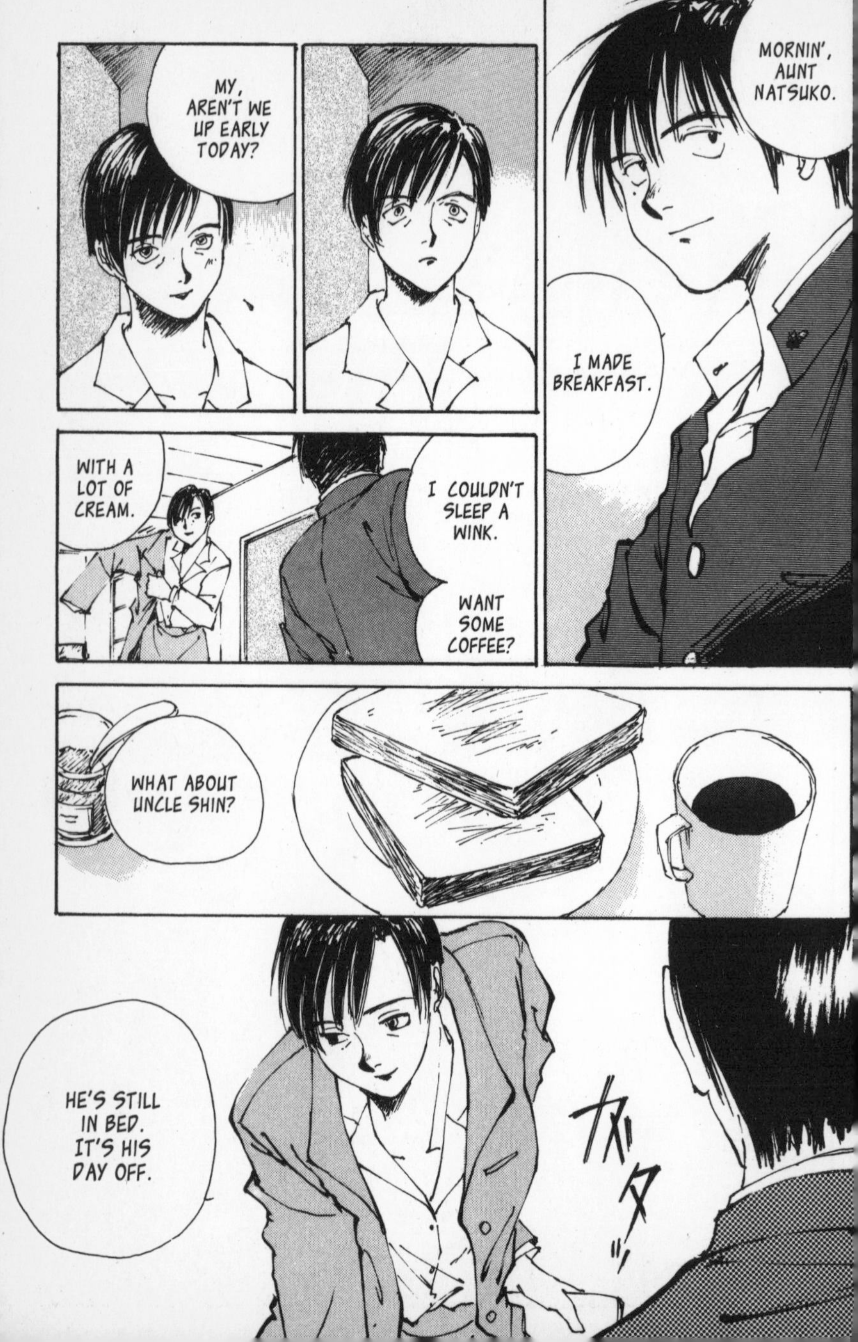
MORNIN', AUNT NATSUKO.
I MADE BREAKFAST.
MY, AREN'T WE UP EARLY TODAY?
I COULDN'T SLEEP A WINK.
WANT SOME COFFEE?
WITH A LOT OF CREAM.
WHAT ABOUT UNCLE SHIN?
HE'S STILL IN BED. IT'S HIS DAY OFF.

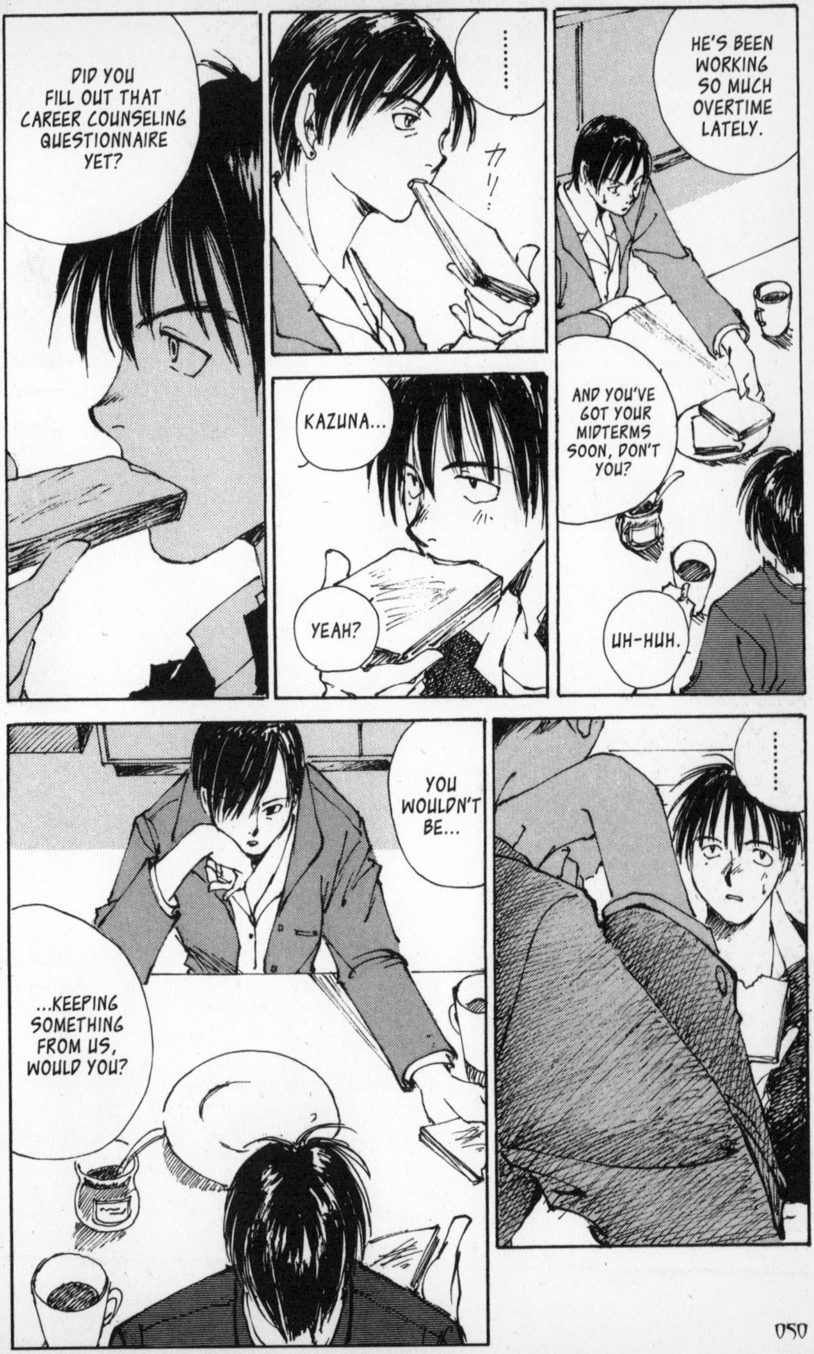
HE'S BEEN WORKING SO MUCH OVERTIME LATELY.
AND YOU'VE GOT YOUR MIDTERMS SOON, DON'T YOU?
UH-HUH.
......
カリッ
KAZUNA...
YEAH?
DID YOU FILL OUT THAT CAREER COUNSELING QUESTIONNAIRE YET?
......
YOU WOULDN'T BE...
...KEEPING SOMETHING FROM US, WOULD YOU?

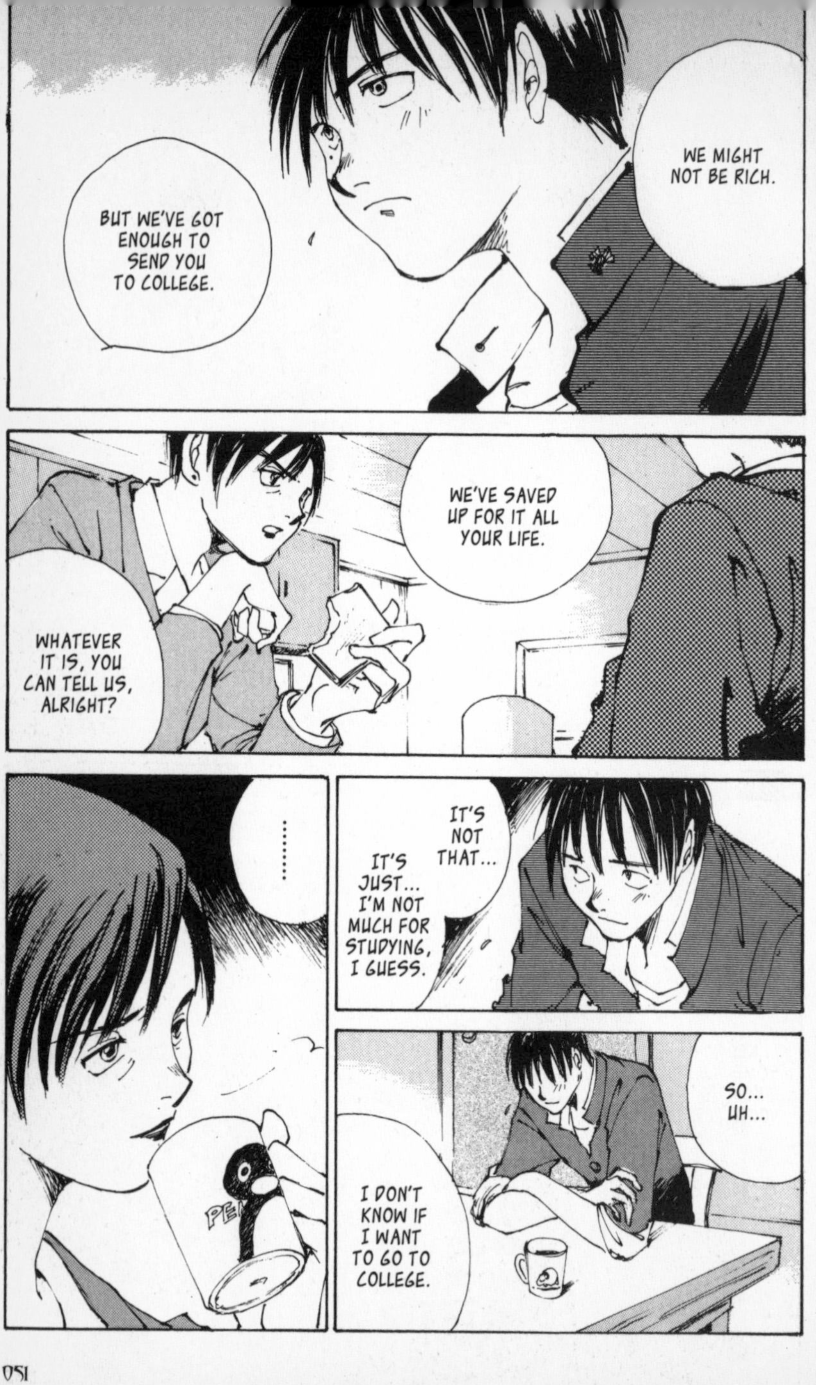
WE MIGHT NOT BE RICH.
BUT WE'VE GOT ENOUGH TO SEND YOU TO COLLEGE.
WE'VE SAVED UP FOR IT ALL YOUR LIFE.
WHATEVER IT IS, YOU CAN TELL US, ALRIGHT?
IT'S NOT THAT...
IT'S JUST... I'M NOT MUCH FOR STUDYING, I GUESS.
SO... UH...
I DON'T KNOW IF I WANT TO GO TO COLLEGE.
......

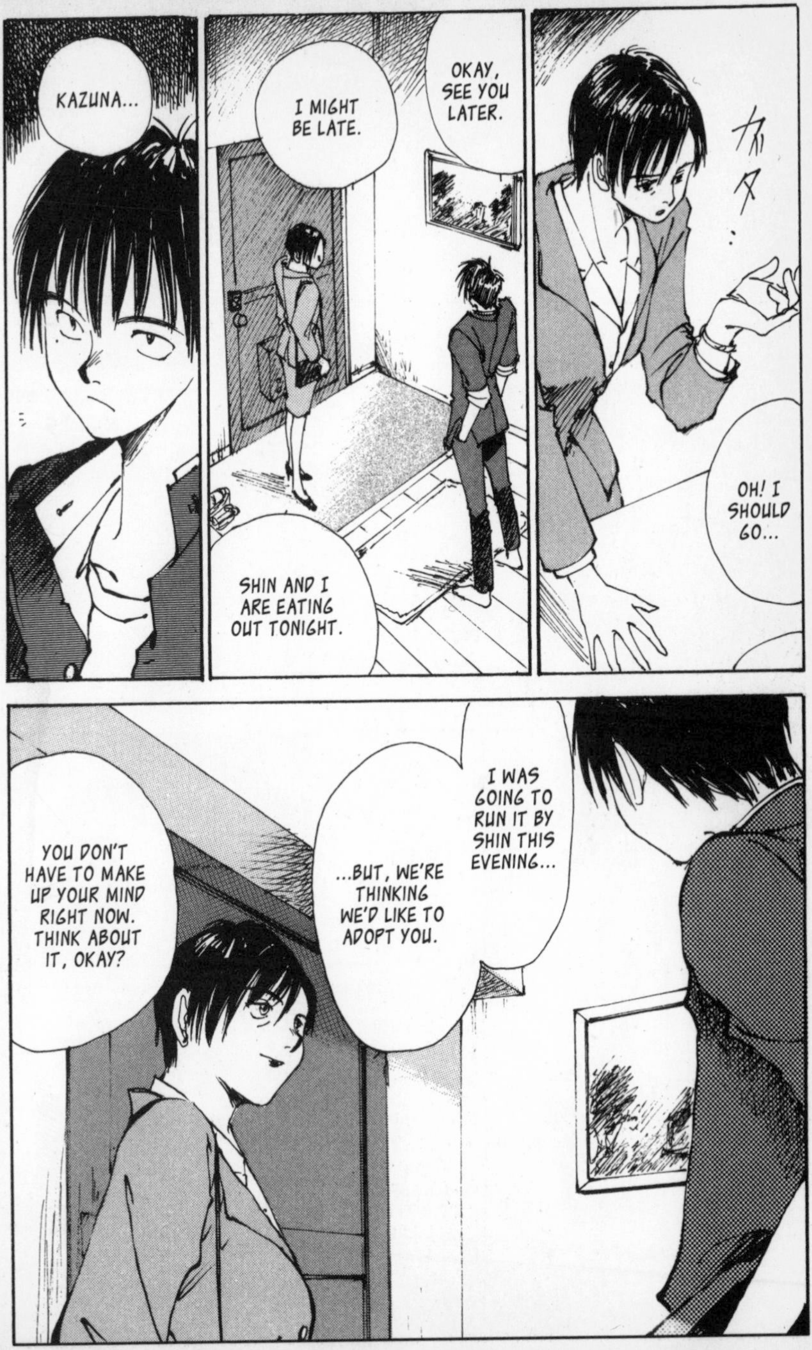
ガタ
OH! I SHOULD GO...
OKAY, SEE YOU LATER.
I MIGHT BE LATE.
SHIN AND I ARE EATING OUT TONIGHT.
KAZUNA...
I WAS GOING TO RUN IT BY SHIN THIS EVENING...
...BUT, WE'RE THINKING WE'D LIKE TO ADOPT YOU.
YOU DON'T HAVE TO MAKE UP YOUR MIND RIGHT NOW. THINK ABOUT IT, OKAY?

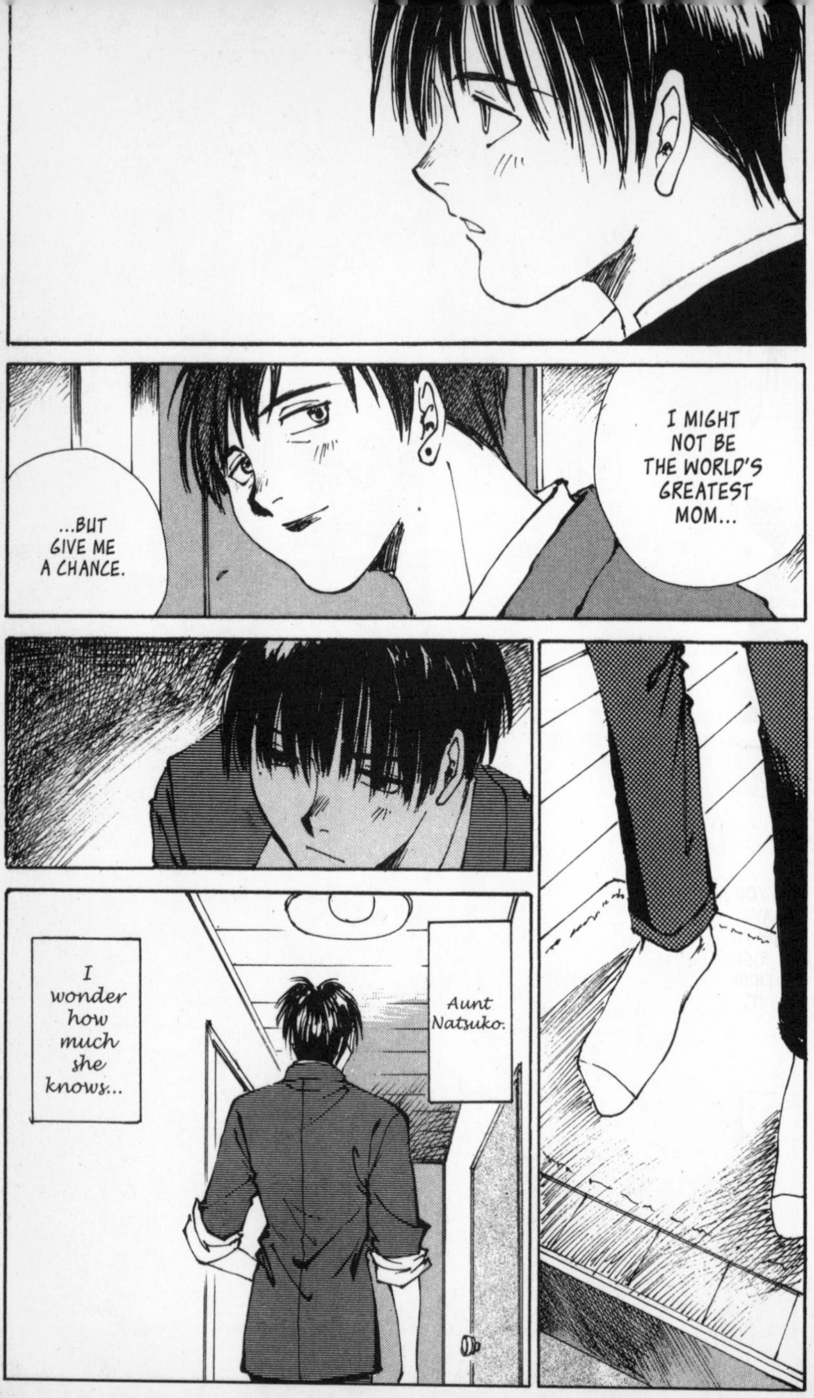
I MIGHT NOT BE THE WORLD'S GREATEST MOM...
...BUT GIVE ME A CHANCE.
Aunt Natsuko.
I wonder how much she knows...

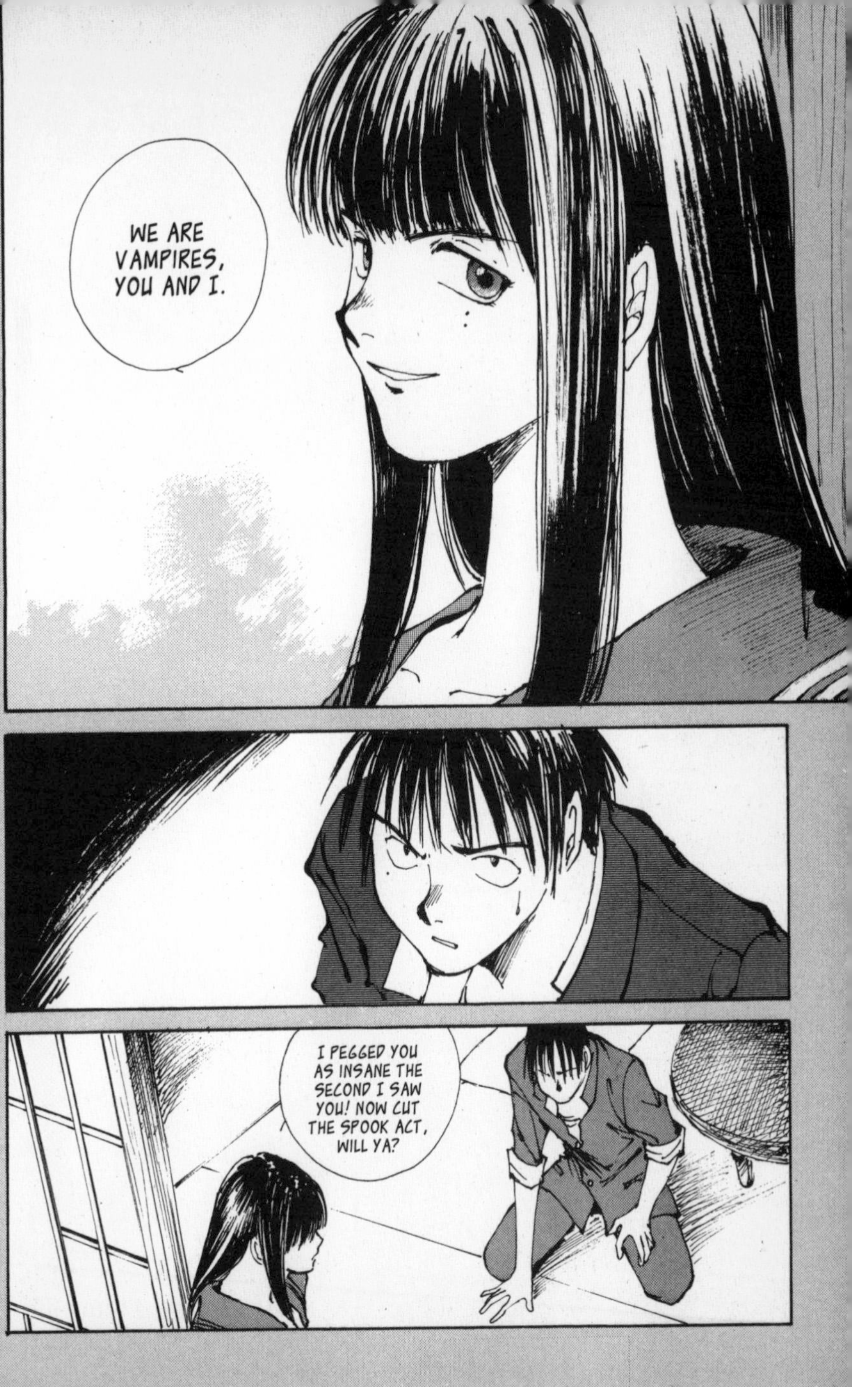
WE ARE VAMPIRES, YOU AND I.
I PEGGED YOU AS INSANE THE SECOND I SAW YOU! NOW CUT THE SPOOK ACT, WILL YA?

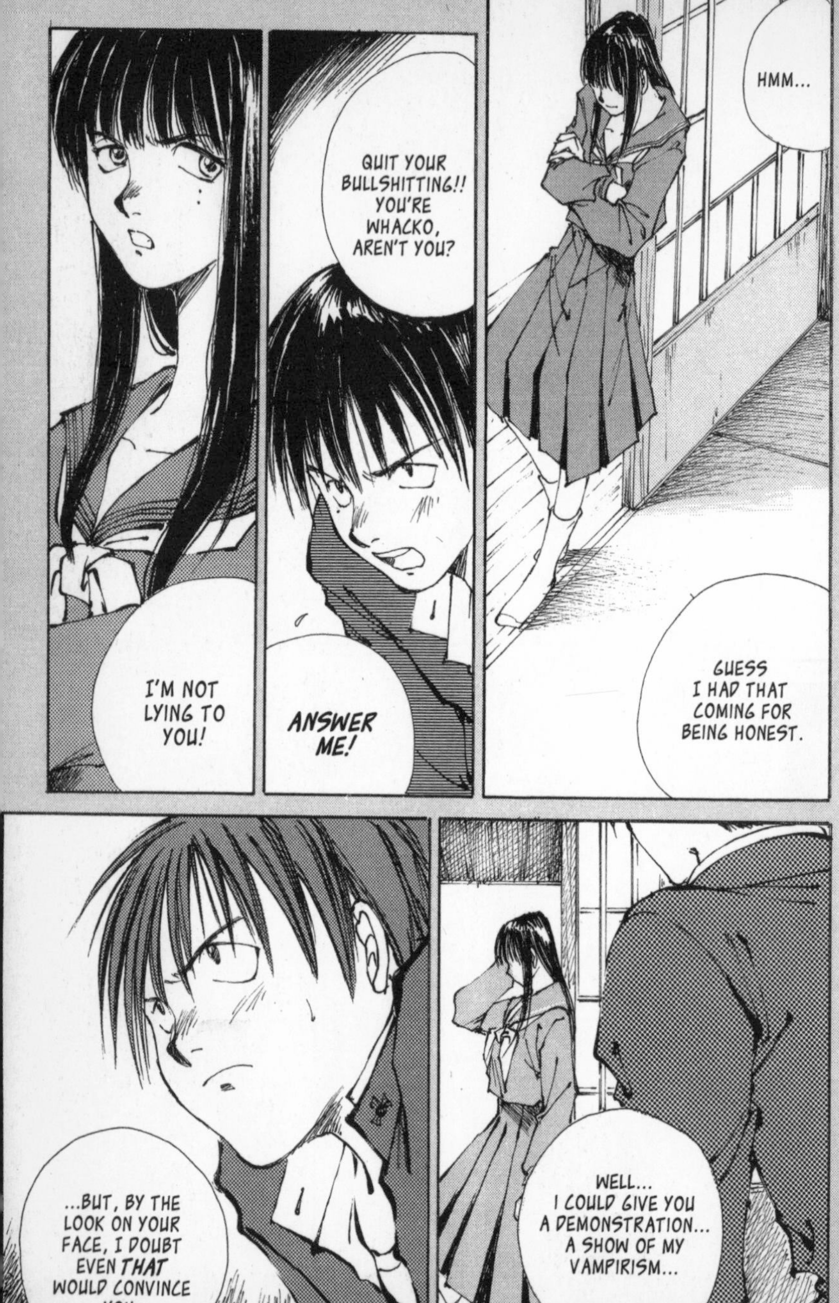
HMM...
GUESS I HAD THAT COMING FOR BEING HONEST.
QUIT YOUR BULLSHITTING!! YOU'RE WHACKO, AREN'T YOU?
ANSWER ME!
I'M NOT LYING TO YOU!
WELL... I COULD GIVE YOU A DEMONSTRATION... A SHOW OF MY VAMPIRISM...
...BUT, BY THE LOOK ON YOUR FACE, I DOUBT EVEN THAT WOULD CONVINCE YOU.

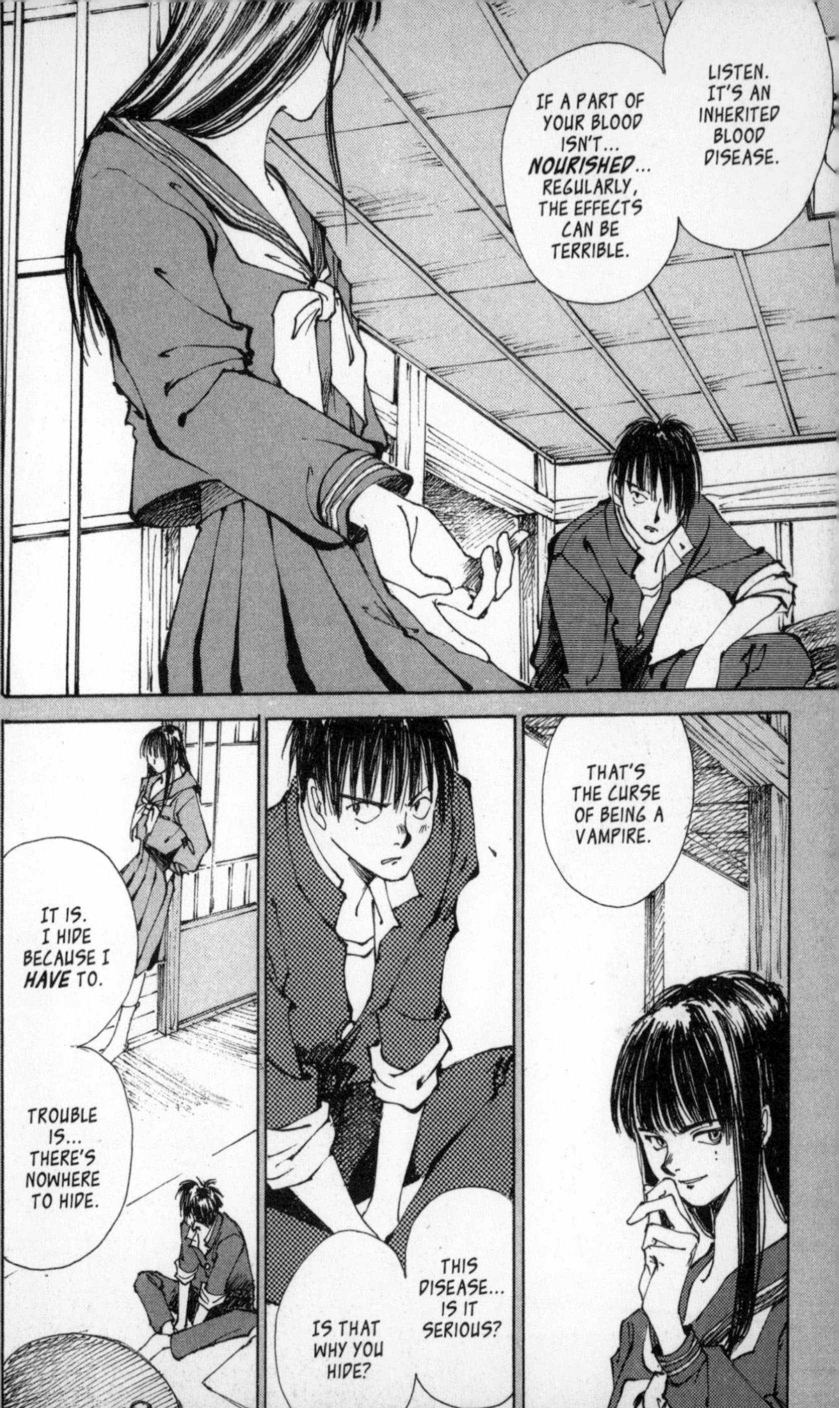
LISTEN. IT'S AN INHERITED BLOOD DISEASE.
IF A PART OF YOUR BLOOD ISN'T... **NOURISHED**... REGULARLY, THE EFFECTS CAN BE TERRIBLE.
THAT'S THE CURSE OF BEING A VAMPIRE.
THIS DISEASE... IS IT SERIOUS?
IS THAT WHY YOU HIDE?
IT IS. I HIDE BECAUSE I **HAVE** TO.
TROUBLE IS... THERE'S NOWHERE TO HIDE.

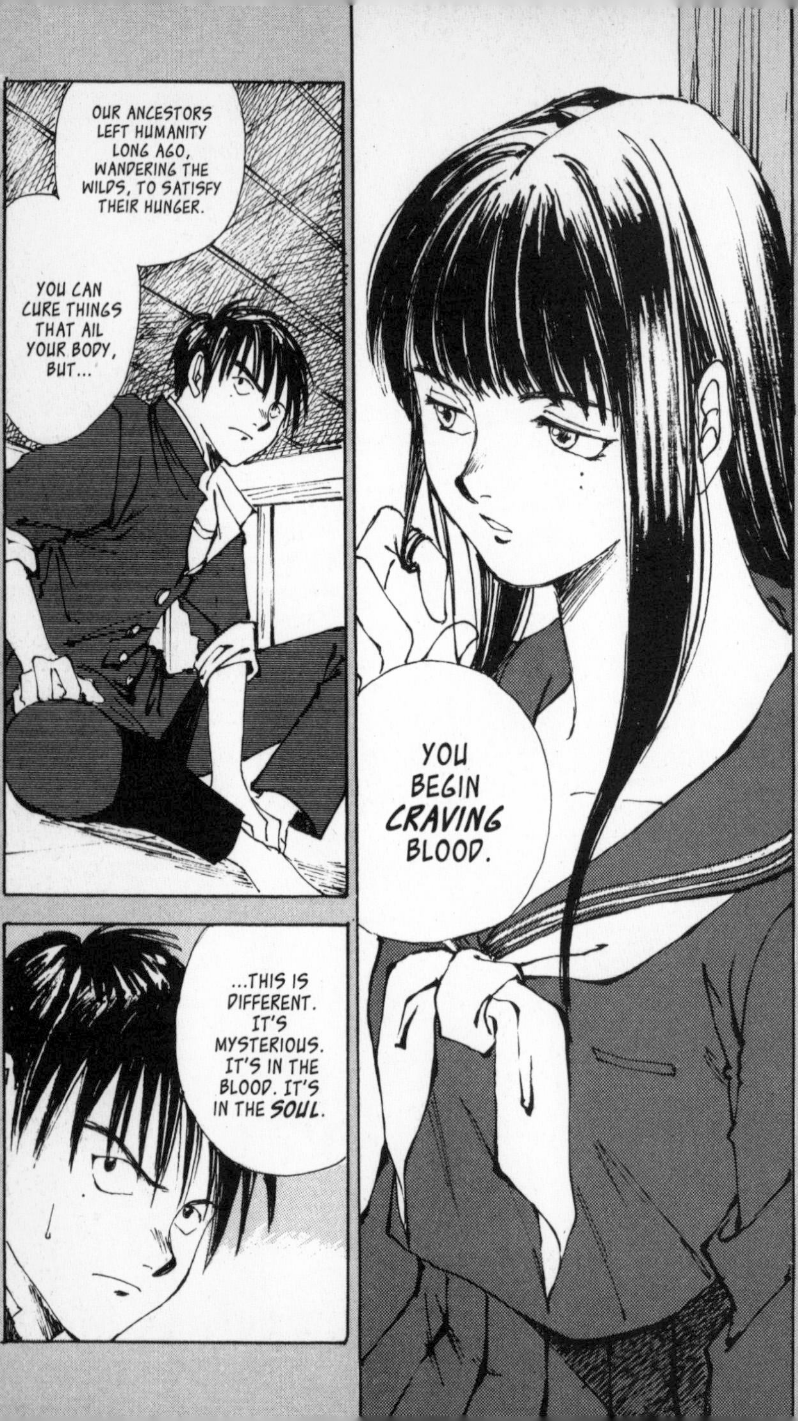
YOU BEGIN *CRAVING* BLOOD.
OUR ANCESTORS LEFT HUMANITY LONG AGO, WANDERING THE WILDS, TO SATISFY THEIR HUNGER.
YOU CAN CURE THINGS THAT AIL YOUR BODY, BUT...
...THIS IS DIFFERENT. IT'S MYSTERIOUS. IT'S IN THE BLOOD. IT'S IN THE *SOUL*.

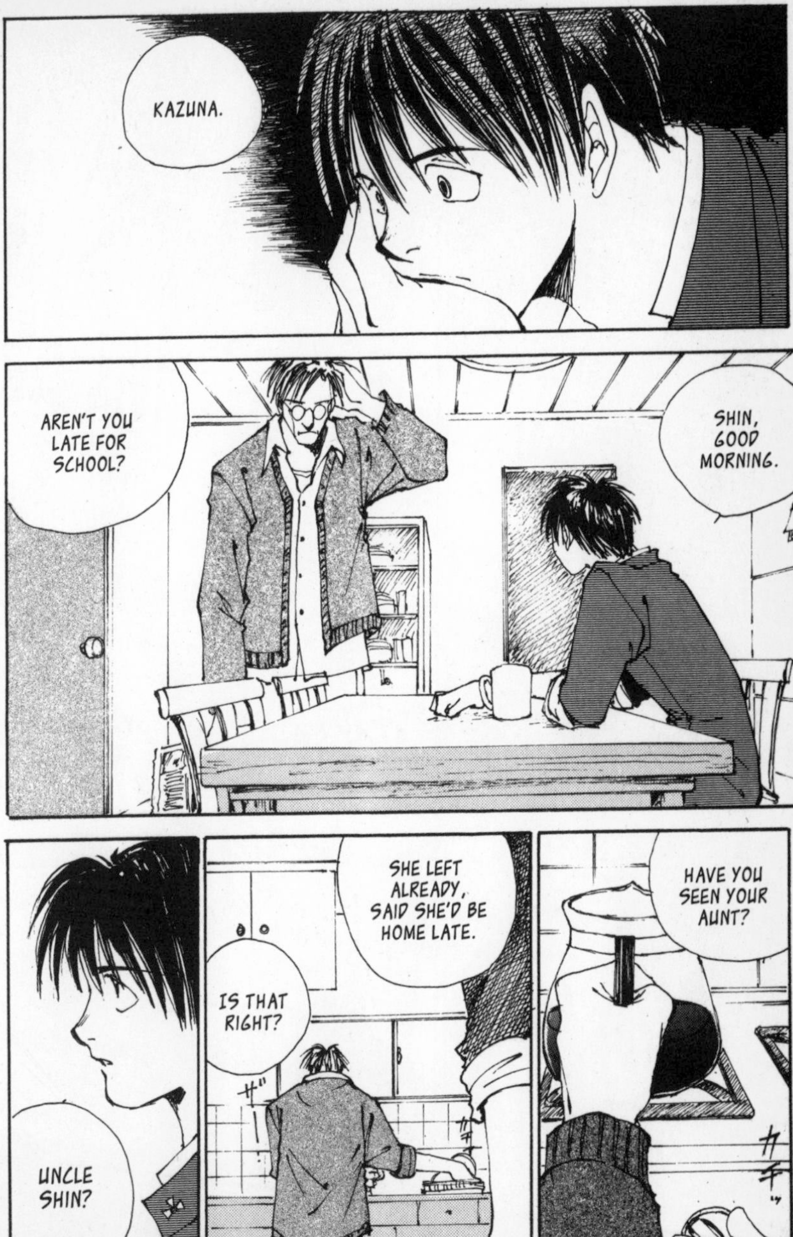
KAZUNA.
SHIN, GOOD MORNING.
AREN'T YOU LATE FOR SCHOOL?
HAVE YOU SEEN YOUR AUNT?
SHE LEFT ALREADY, SAID SHE'D BE HOME LATE.
IS THAT RIGHT?
UNCLE SHIN?

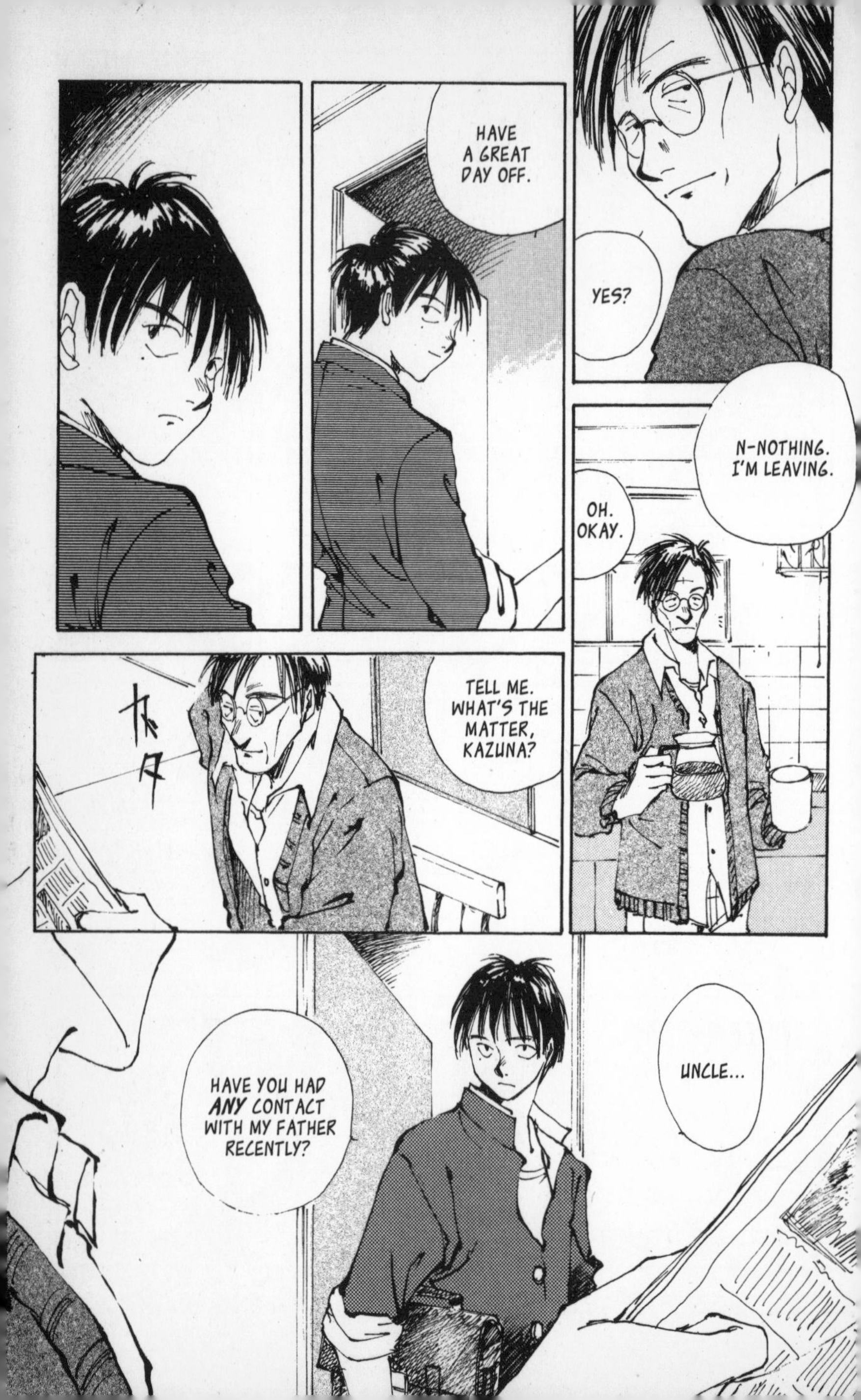
YES?
HAVE A GREAT DAY OFF.
N-NOTHING. I'M LEAVING.
OH. OKAY.
TELL ME. WHAT'S THE MATTER, KAZUNA?
ガタ
UNCLE...
HAVE YOU HAD *ANY* CONTACT WITH MY FATHER RECENTLY?

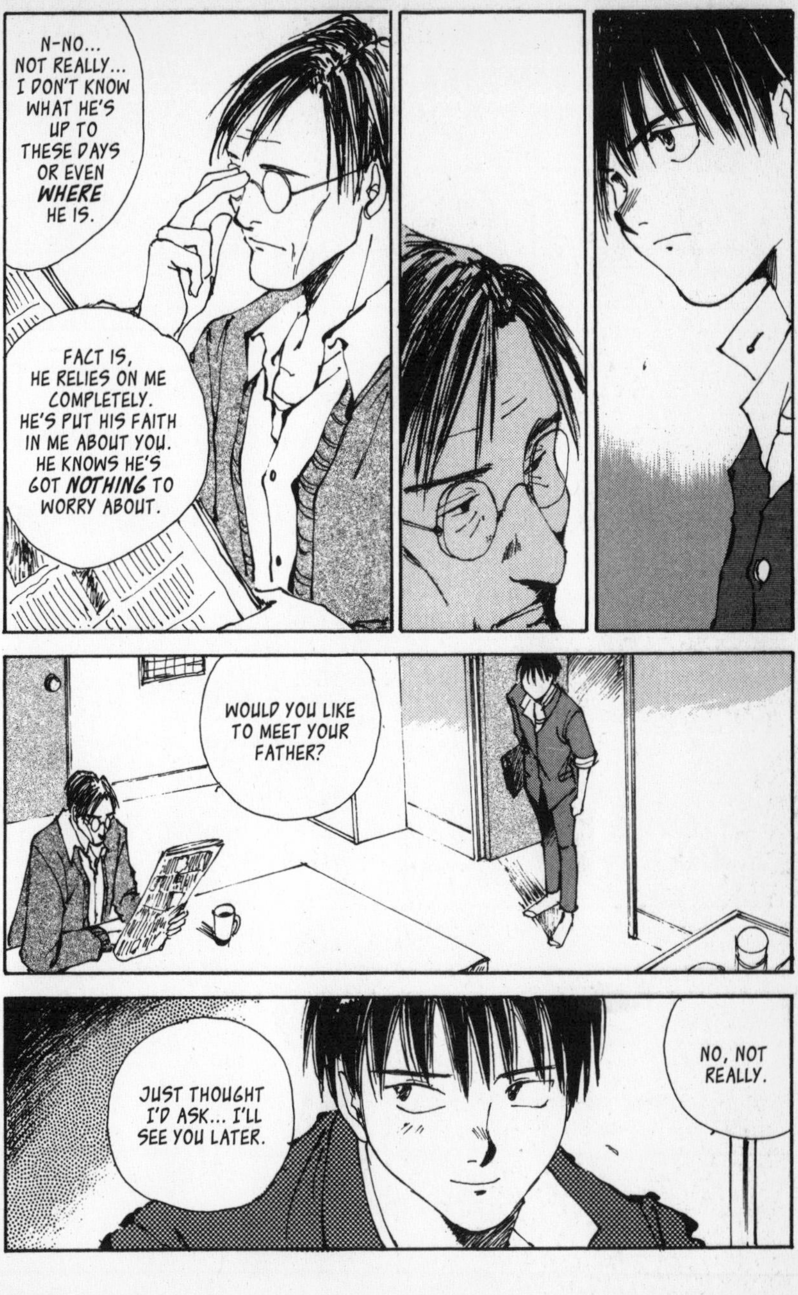
N-NO... NOT REALLY... I DON'T KNOW WHAT HE'S UP TO THESE DAYS OR EVEN ***WHERE*** HE IS.
FACT IS, HE RELIES ON ME COMPLETELY. HE'S PUT HIS FAITH IN ME ABOUT YOU. HE KNOWS HE'S GOT ***NOTHING*** TO WORRY ABOUT.
WOULD YOU LIKE TO MEET YOUR FATHER?
NO, NOT REALLY.
JUST THOUGHT I'D ASK... I'LL SEE YOU LATER.

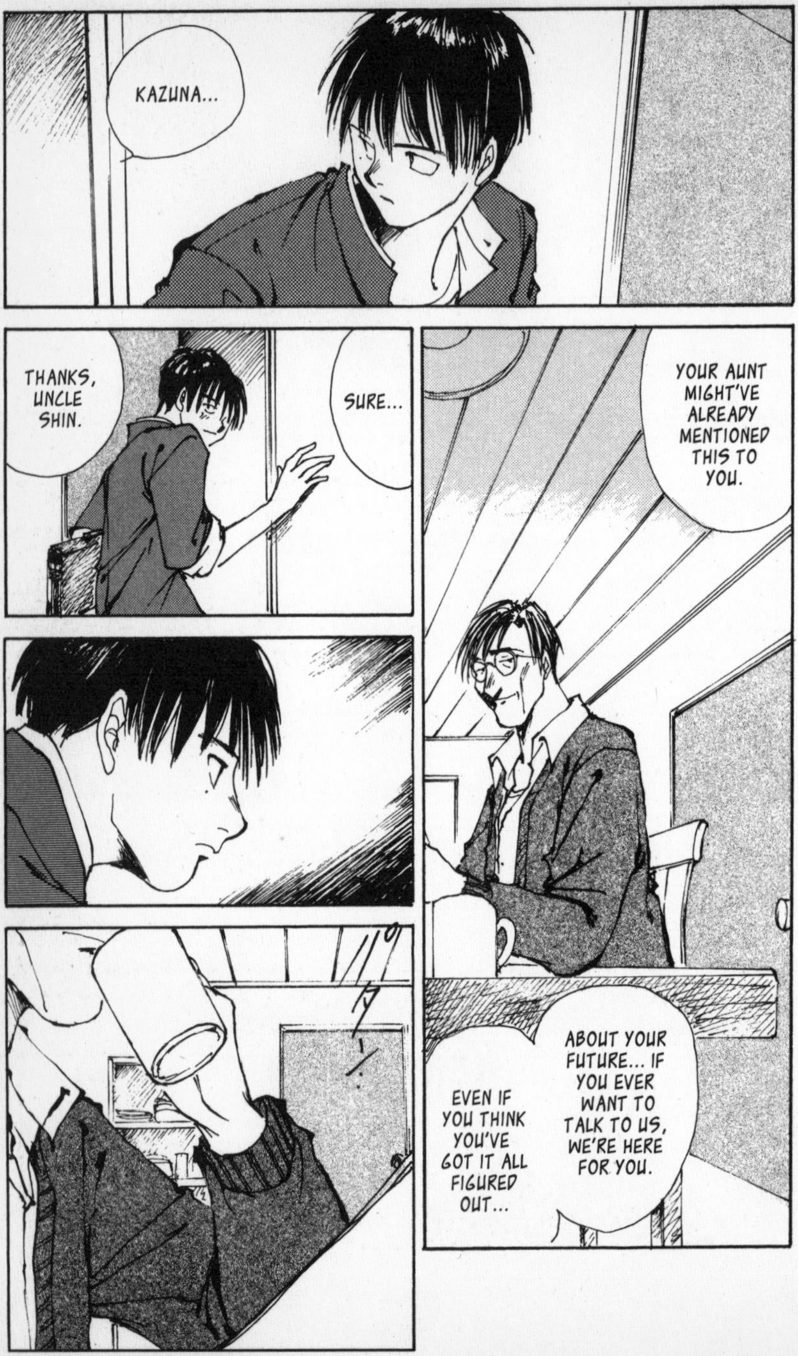
KAZUNA...
YOUR AUNT MIGHT'VE ALREADY MENTIONED THIS TO YOU.
SURE...
THANKS, UNCLE SHIN.
ABOUT YOUR FUTURE... IF YOU EVER WANT TO TALK TO US, WE'RE HERE FOR YOU.
EVEN IF YOU THINK YOU'VE GOT IT ALL FIGURED OUT...

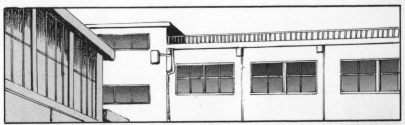

Uncle Shin lied to me...

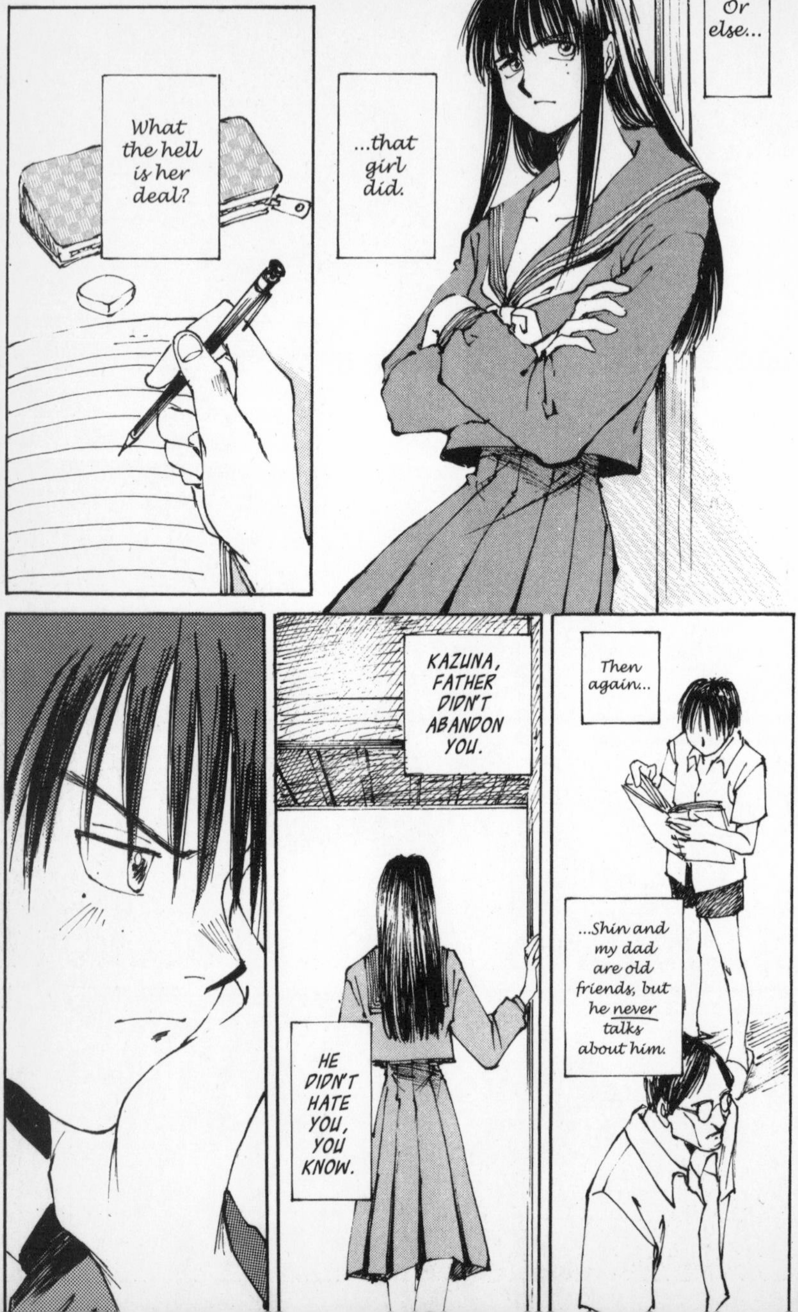
Or else...
...that girl did.
What the hell is her deal?
Then again...
...Shin and my dad are old friends, but he never talks about him.
KAZUNA, FATHER DIDN'T ABANDON YOU.
HE DIDN'T HATE YOU, YOU KNOW.

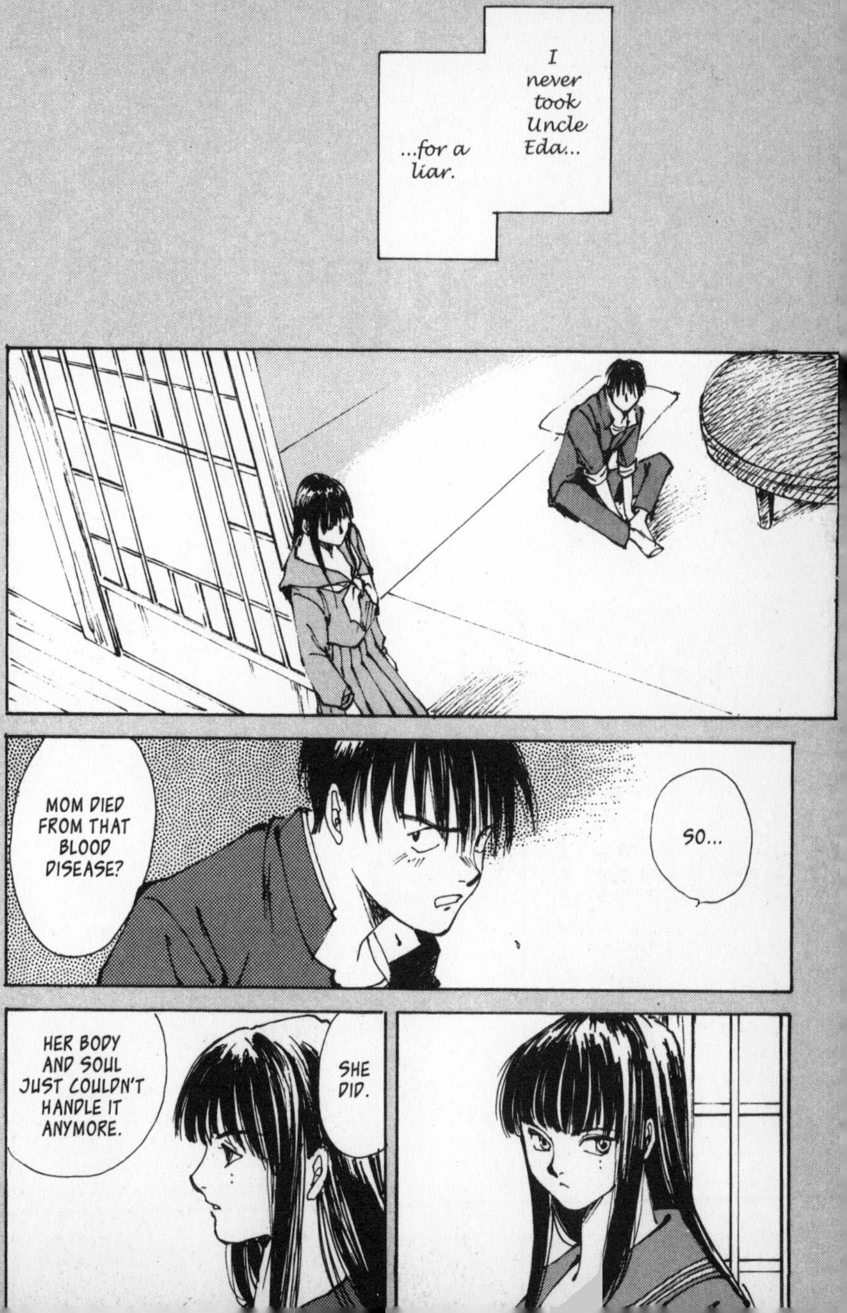
I never took Uncle Eda...
...for a liar.
SO...
MOM DIED FROM THAT BLOOD DISEASE?
SHE DID.
HER BODY AND SOUL JUST COULDN'T HANDLE IT ANYMORE.

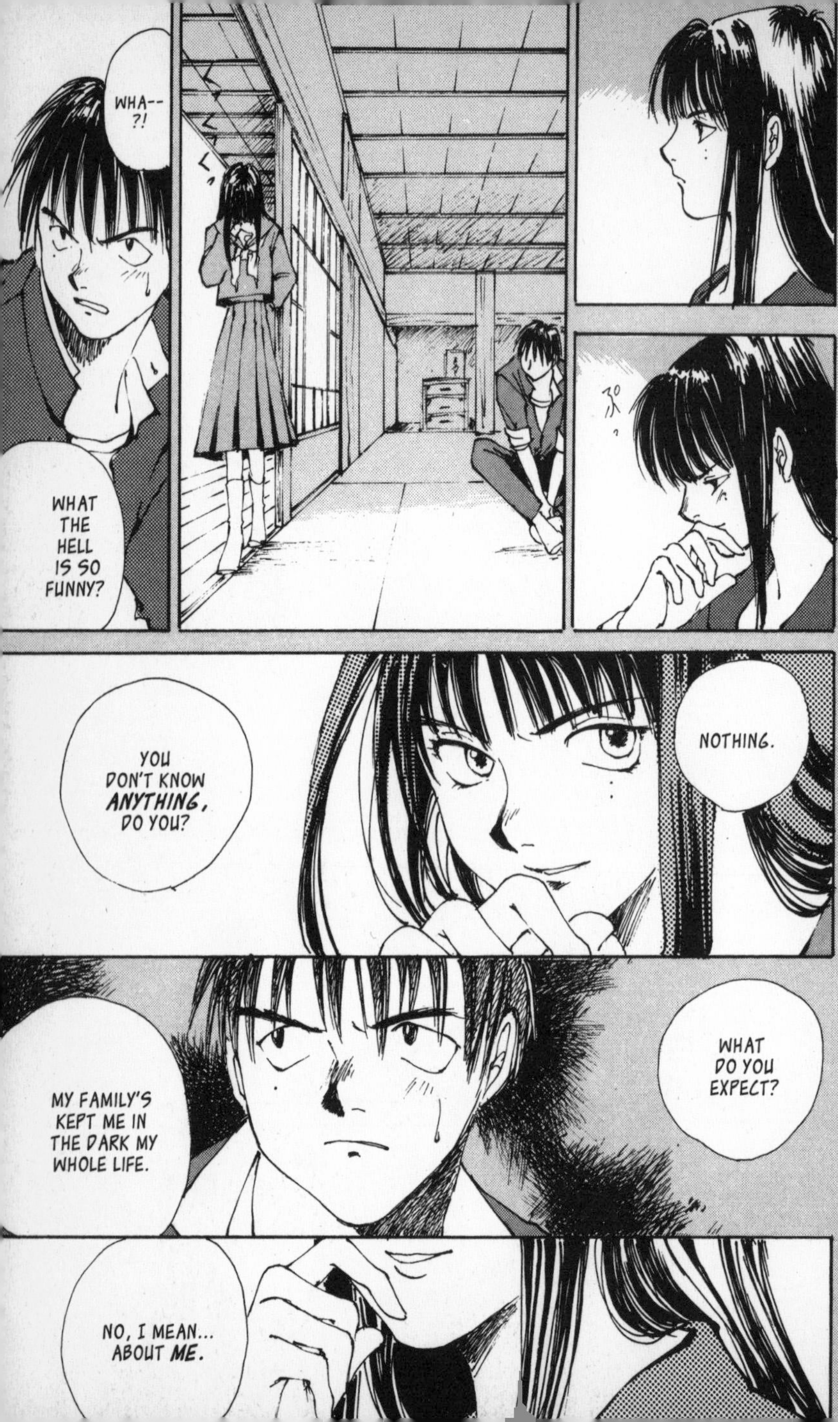

ぷっ
くっ
WHA--?!
WHAT THE HELL IS SO FUNNY?
NOTHING.
YOU DON'T KNOW ANYTHING, DO YOU?
WHAT DO YOU EXPECT?
MY FAMILY'S KEPT ME IN THE DARK MY WHOLE LIFE.
NO, I MEAN... ABOUT ME.

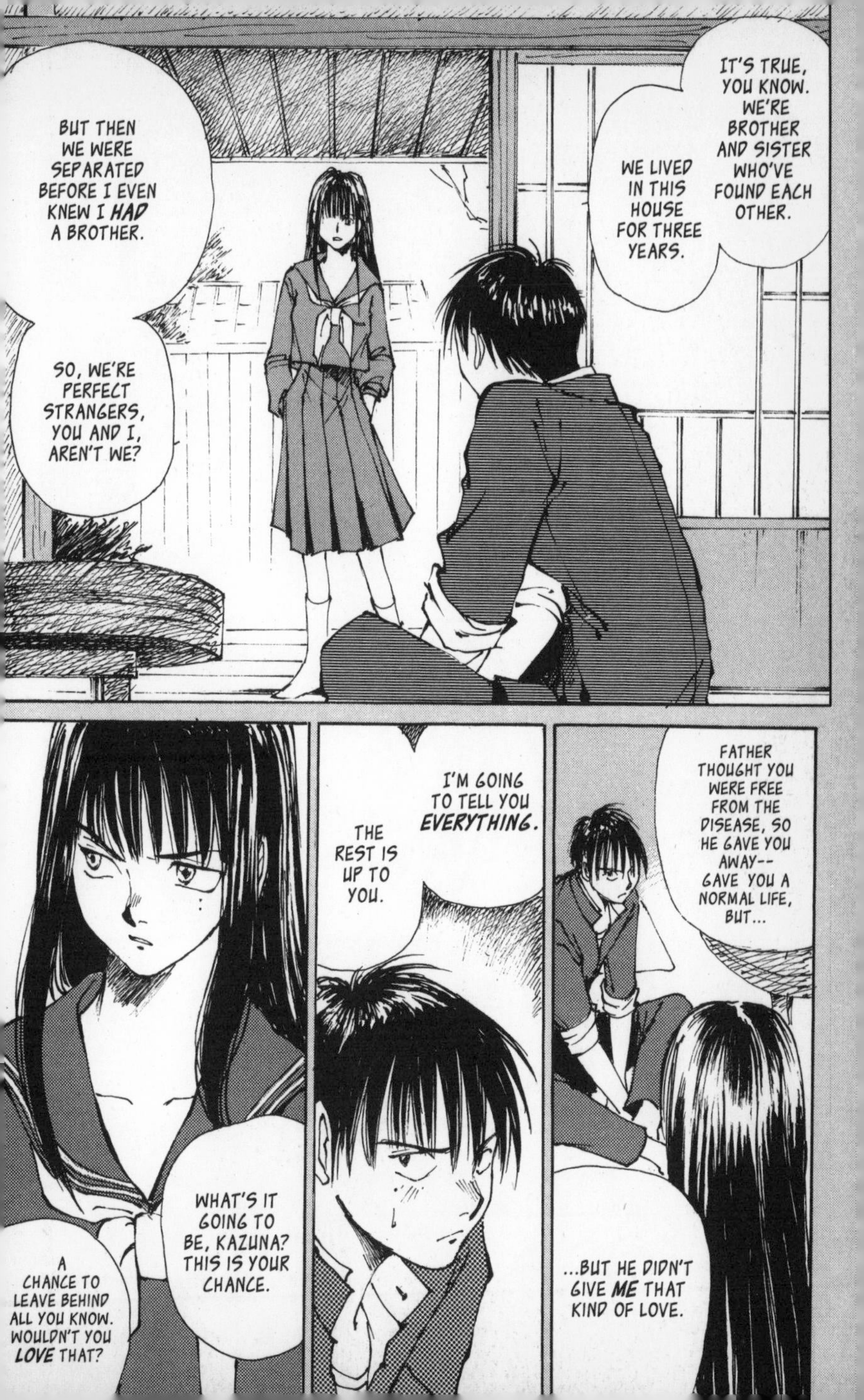
IT'S TRUE, YOU KNOW. WE'RE BROTHER AND SISTER WHO'VE FOUND EACH OTHER.
WE LIVED IN THIS HOUSE FOR THREE YEARS.
BUT THEN WE WERE SEPARATED BEFORE I EVEN KNEW I *HAD* A BROTHER.
SO, WE'RE PERFECT STRANGERS, YOU AND I, AREN'T WE?
FATHER THOUGHT YOU WERE FREE FROM THE DISEASE, SO HE GAVE YOU AWAY-- GAVE YOU A NORMAL LIFE, BUT...
...BUT HE DIDN'T GIVE *ME* THAT KIND OF LOVE.
I'M GOING TO TELL YOU ***EVERYTHING***.
THE REST IS UP TO YOU.
WHAT'S IT GOING TO BE, KAZUNA? THIS IS YOUR CHANCE.
A CHANCE TO LEAVE BEHIND ALL YOU KNOW. WOULDN'T YOU *LOVE* THAT?

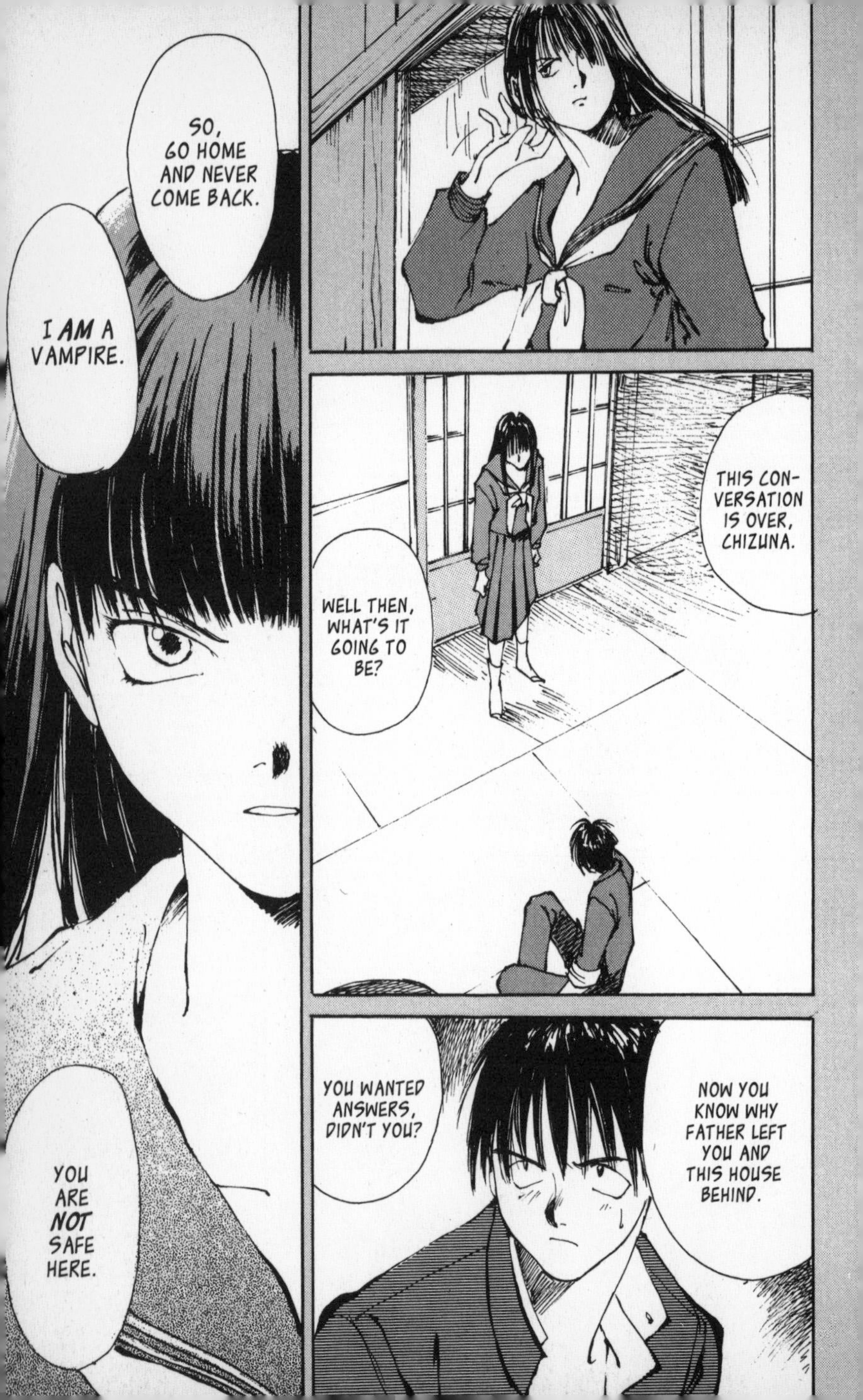
THIS CON-VERSATION IS OVER, CHIZUNA.
WELL THEN, WHAT'S IT GOING TO BE?
NOW YOU KNOW WHY FATHER LEFT YOU AND THIS HOUSE BEHIND.
YOU WANTED ANSWERS, DIDN'T YOU?
SO, GO HOME AND NEVER COME BACK.
I *AM* A VAMPIRE.
YOU ARE ***NOT*** SAFE HERE.

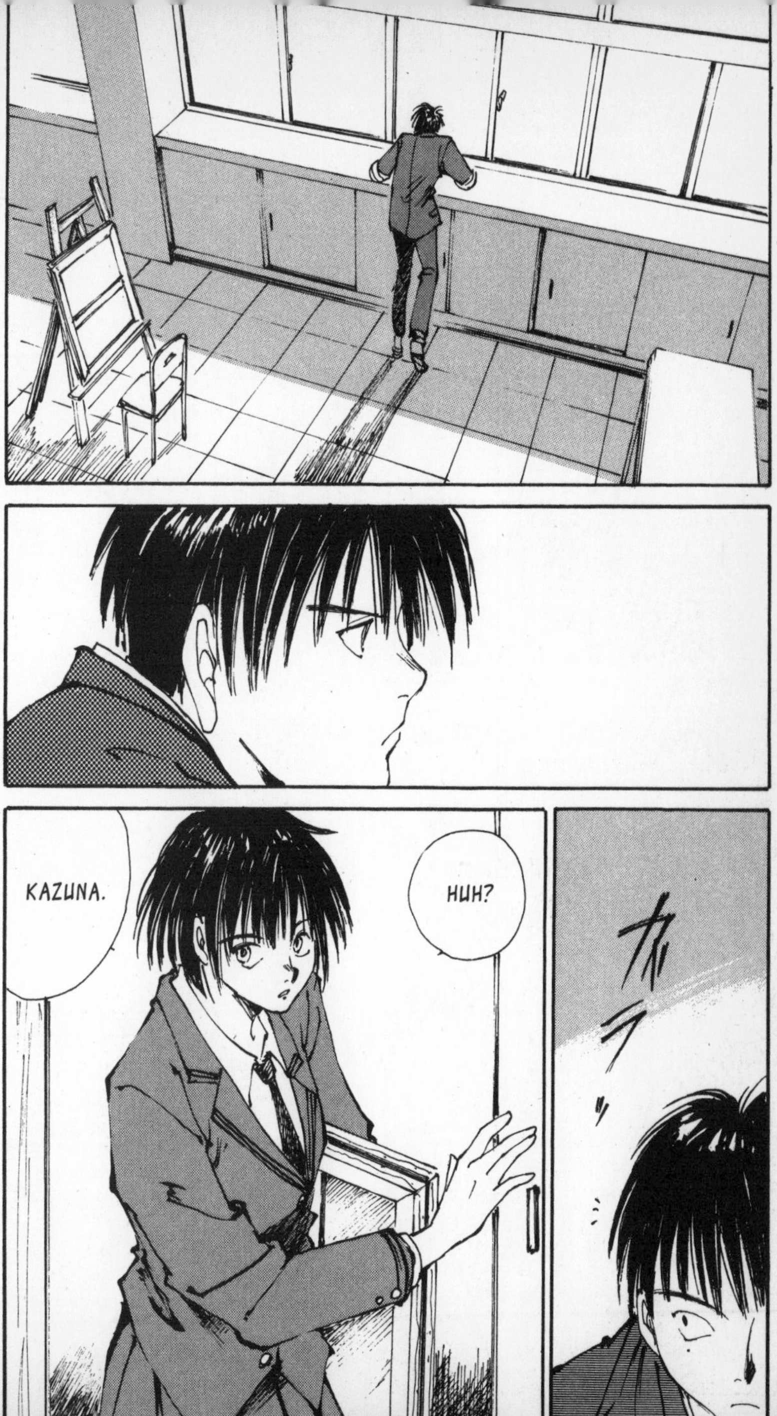
ガラッ
KAZUNA.
HUH?

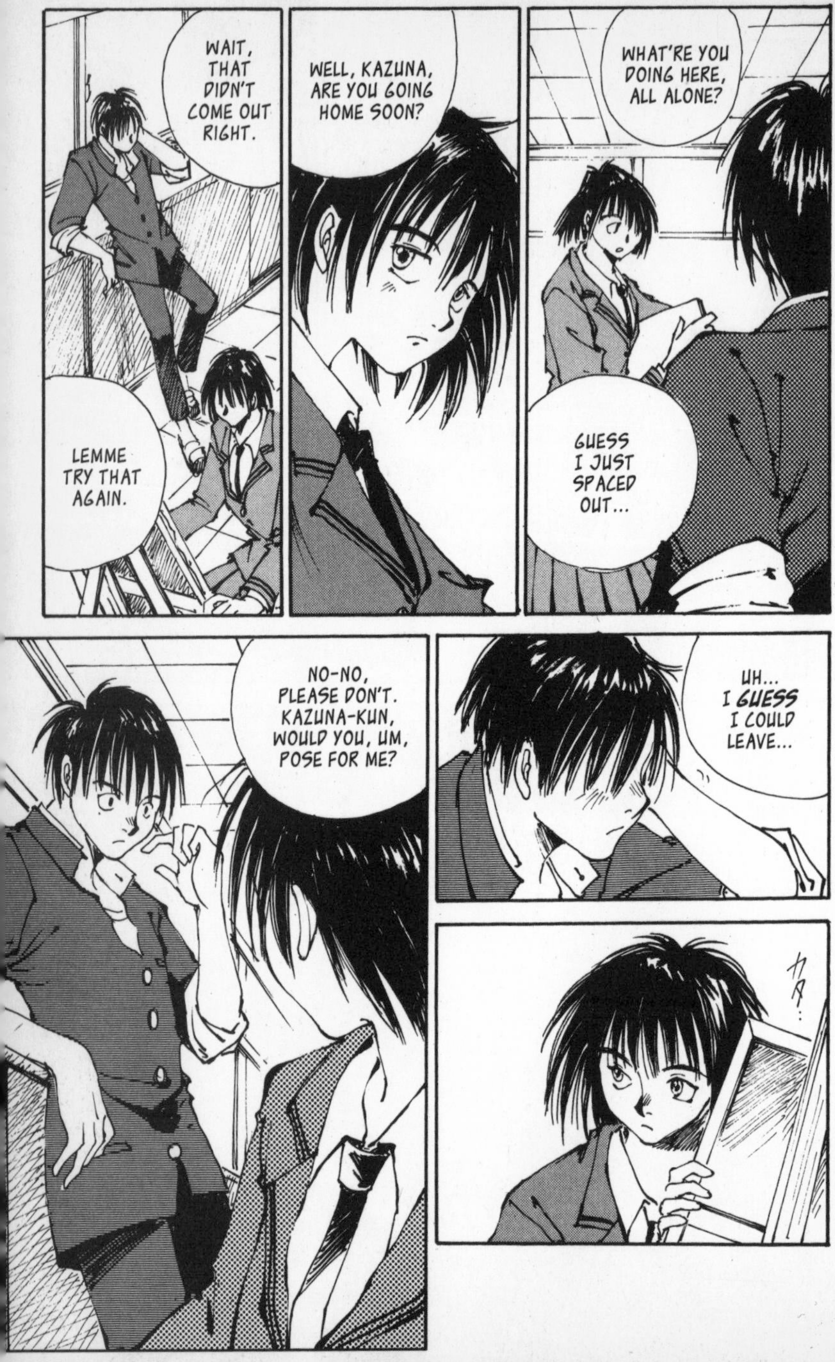
WHAT'RE YOU DOING HERE, ALL ALONE?
GUESS I JUST SPACED OUT...
WELL, KAZUNA, ARE YOU GOING HOME SOON?
WAIT, THAT DIDN'T COME OUT RIGHT.
LEMME TRY THAT AGAIN.
UH... I **GUESS** I COULD LEAVE...
NO-NO, PLEASE DON'T. KAZUNA-KUN, WOULD YOU, UM, POSE FOR ME?

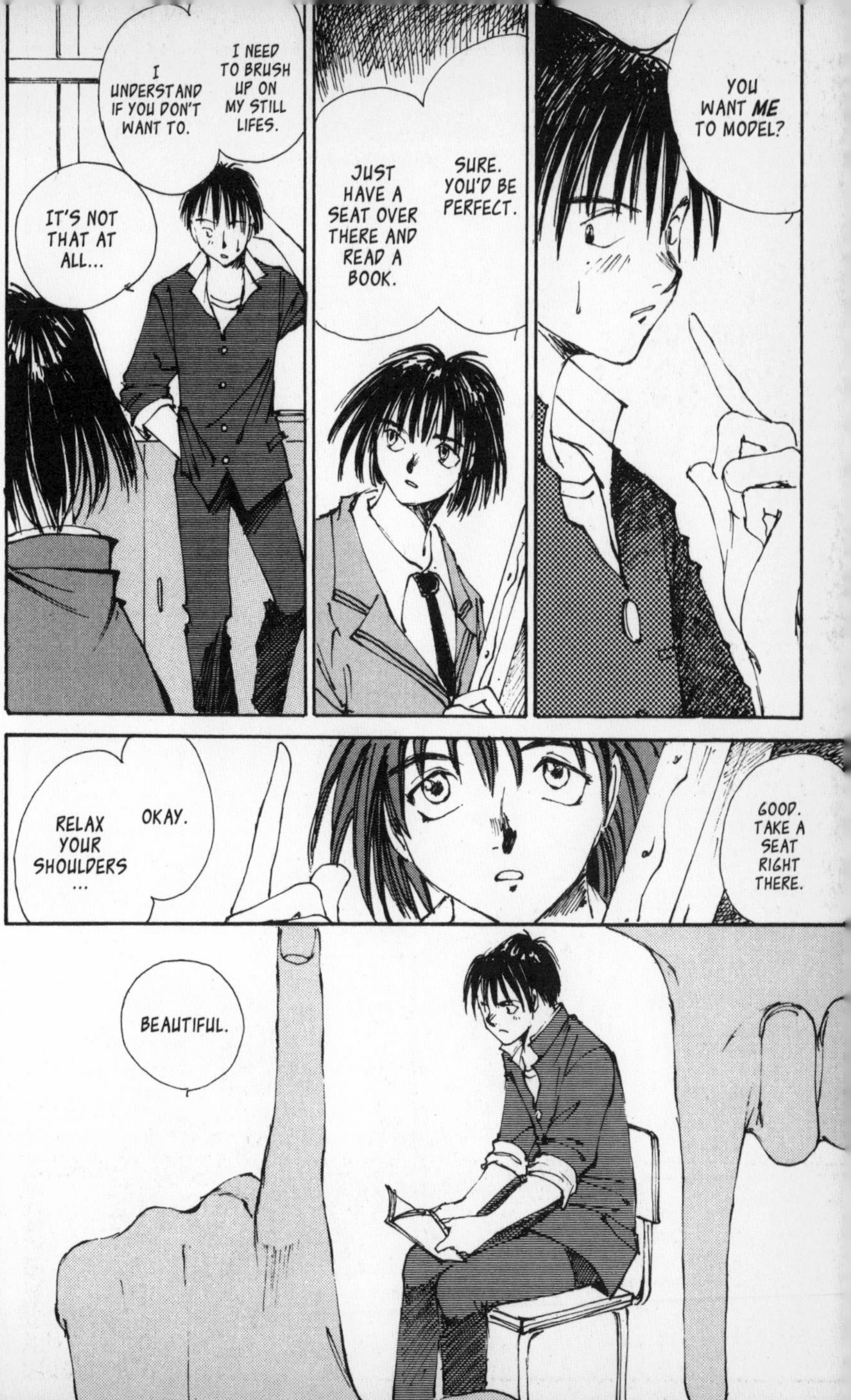
YOU WANT *ME* TO MODEL?
SURE. YOU'D BE PERFECT.
JUST HAVE A SEAT OVER THERE AND READ A BOOK.
I NEED TO BRUSH UP ON MY STILL LIFES.
I UNDERSTAND IF YOU DON'T WANT TO.
IT'S NOT THAT AT ALL...
GOOD. TAKE A SEAT RIGHT THERE.
OKAY.
RELAX YOUR SHOULDERS ...
BEAUTIFUL.

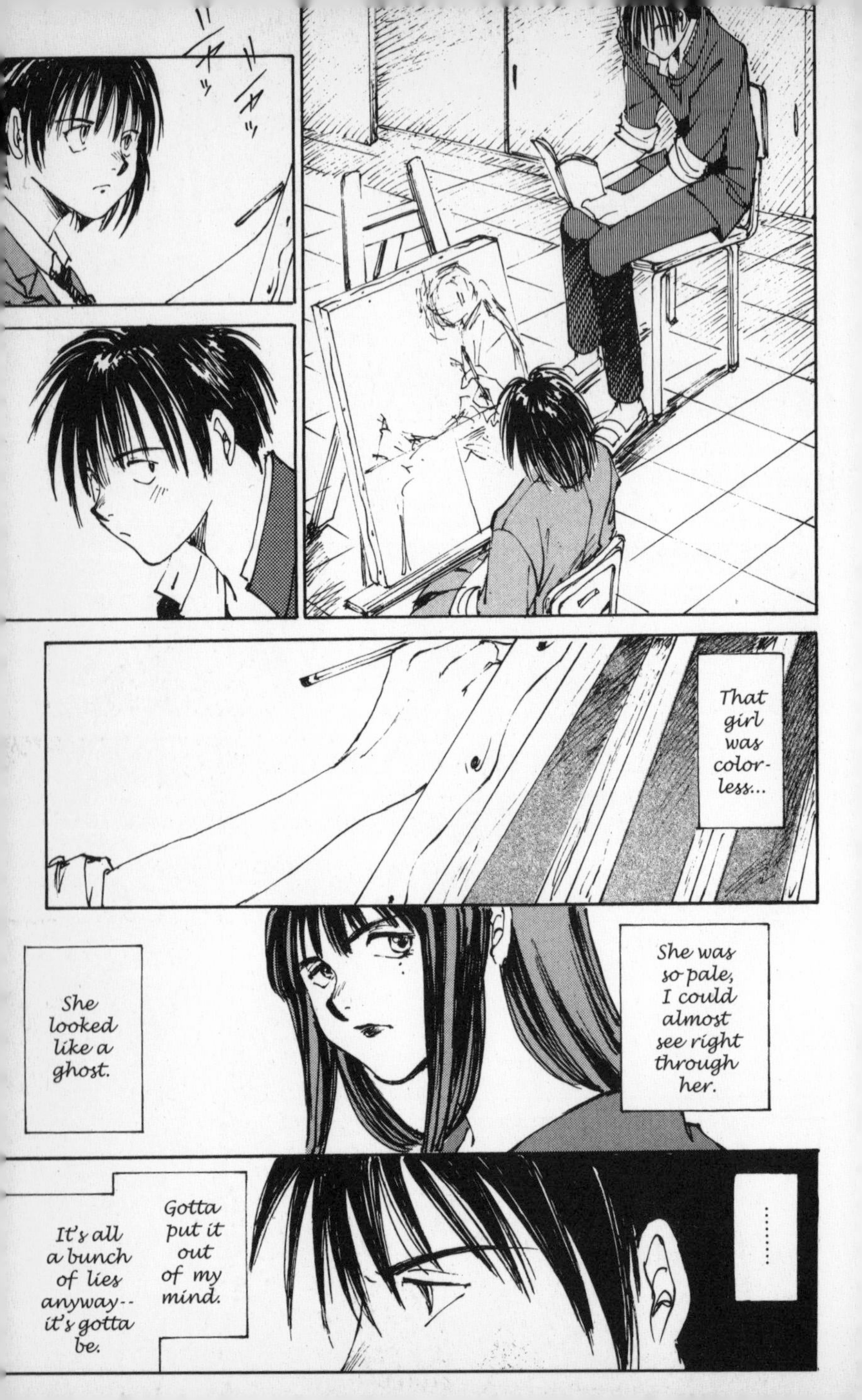
That girl was colorless...
She was so pale, I could almost see right through her.
She looked like a ghost.
......
Gotta put it out of my mind.
It's all a bunch of lies anyway-- it's gotta be.

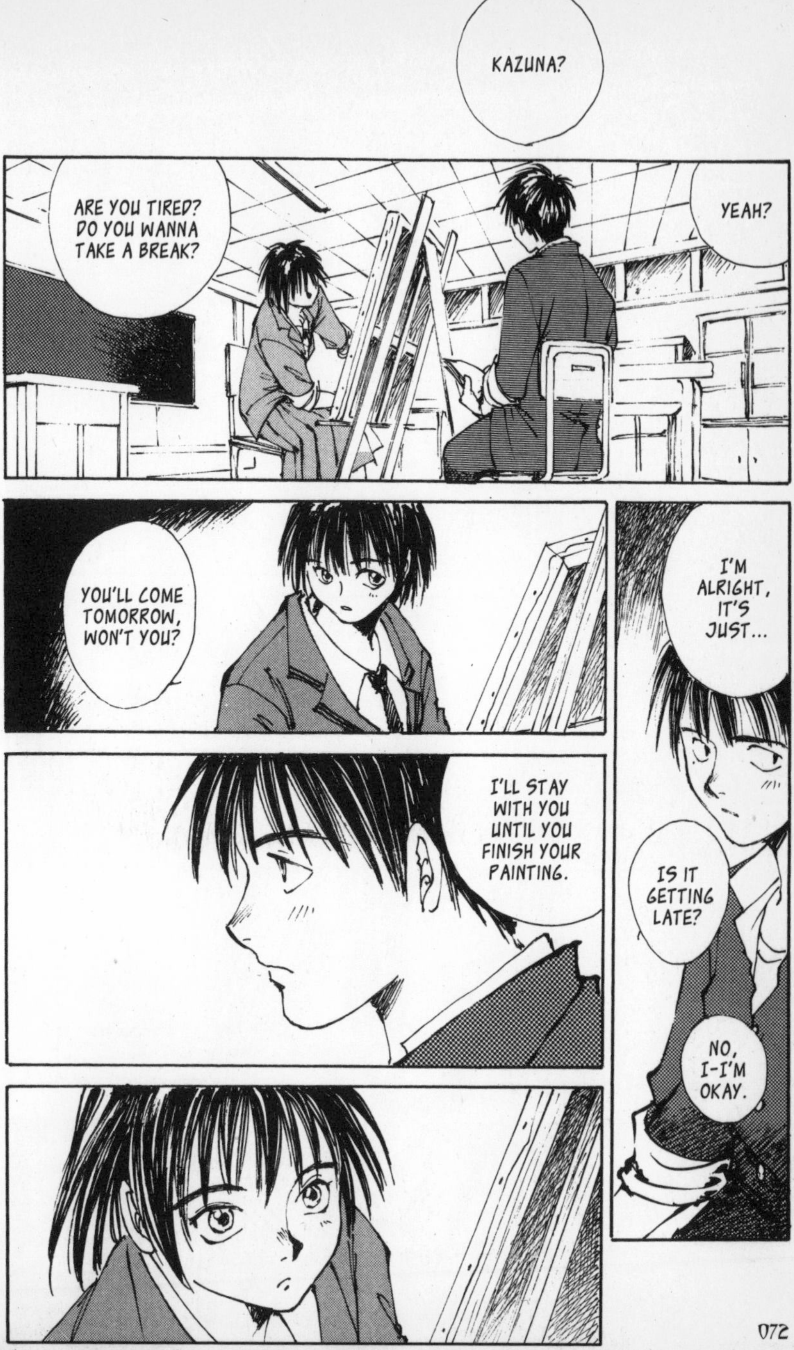
KAZUNA?
YEAH?
ARE YOU TIRED? DO YOU WANNA TAKE A BREAK?
I'M ALRIGHT, IT'S JUST...
IS IT GETTING LATE?
NO, I-I'M OKAY.
YOU'LL COME TOMORROW, WON'T YOU?
I'LL STAY WITH YOU UNTIL YOU FINISH YOUR PAINTING.

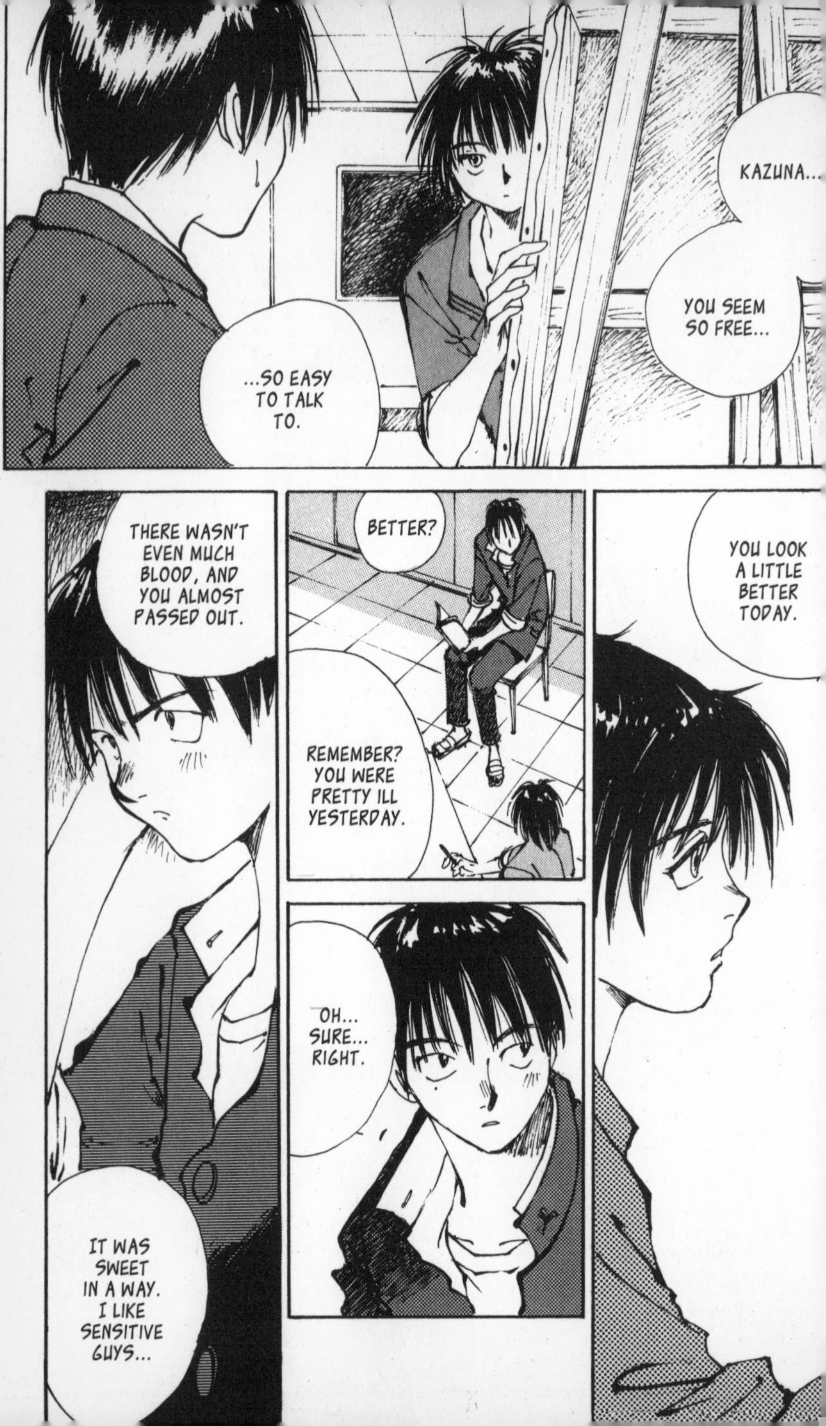
KAZUNA...
YOU SEEM SO FREE...
...SO EASY TO TALK TO.
YOU LOOK A LITTLE BETTER TODAY.
BETTER?
REMEMBER? YOU WERE PRETTY ILL YESTERDAY.
OH... SURE... RIGHT.
THERE WASN'T EVEN MUCH BLOOD, AND YOU ALMOST PASSED OUT.
IT WAS SWEET IN A WAY. I LIKE SENSITIVE GUYS...

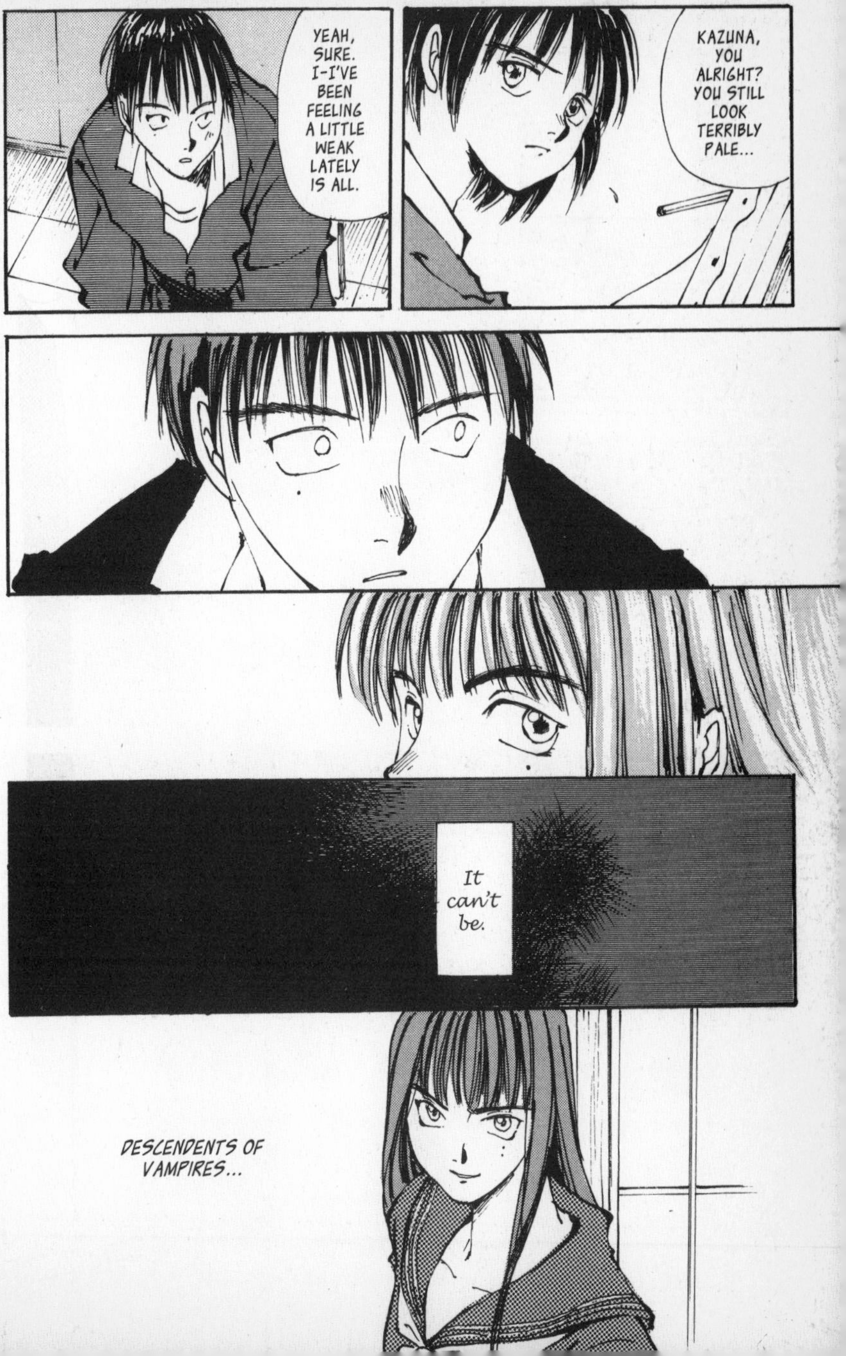
KAZUNA, YOU ALRIGHT? YOU STILL LOOK TERRIBLY PALE...
YEAH, SURE. I-I'VE BEEN FEELING A LITTLE WEAK LATELY IS ALL.
It can't be.
DESCENDENTS OF VAMPIRES...

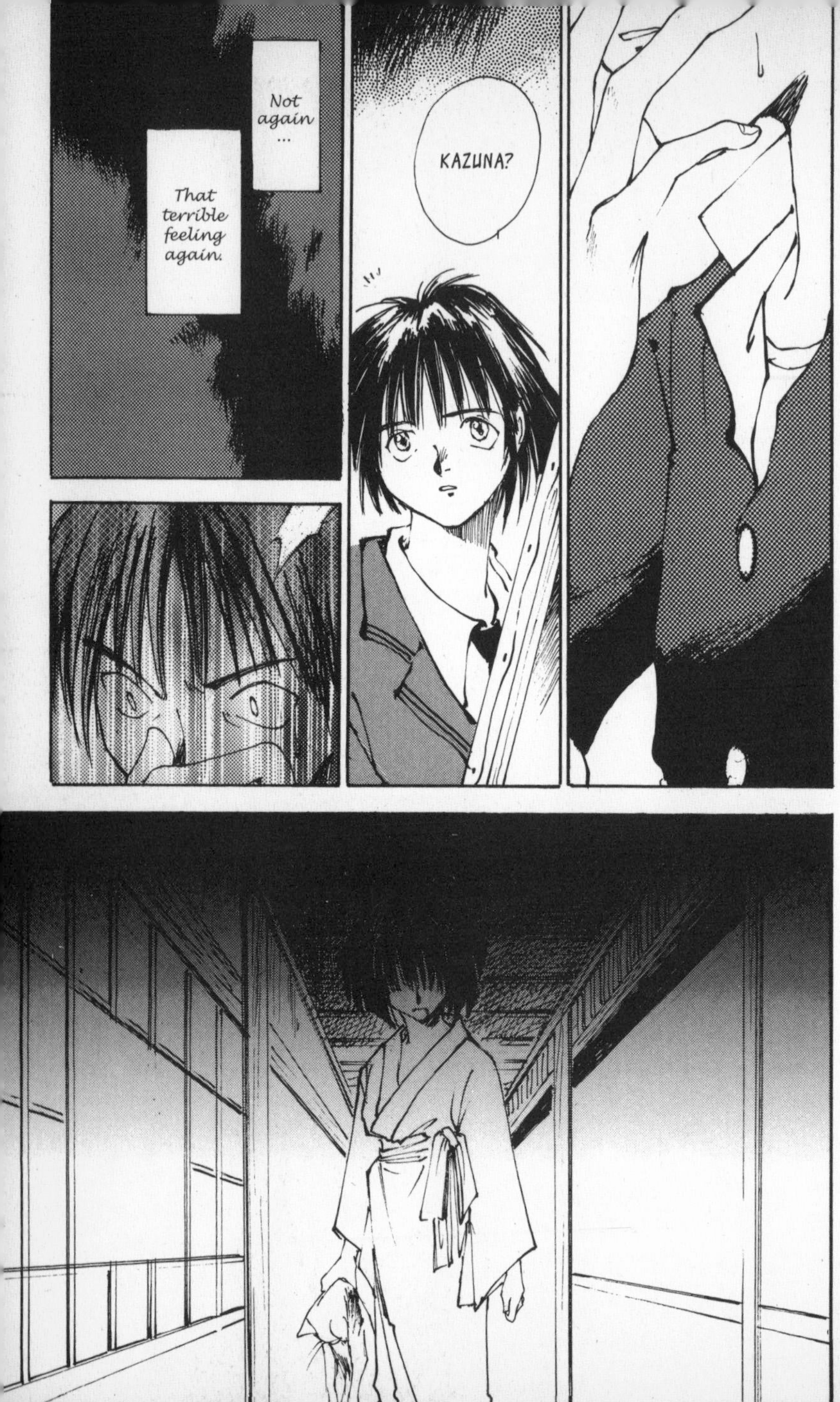
KAZUNA?
Not again ...
That terrible feeling again.

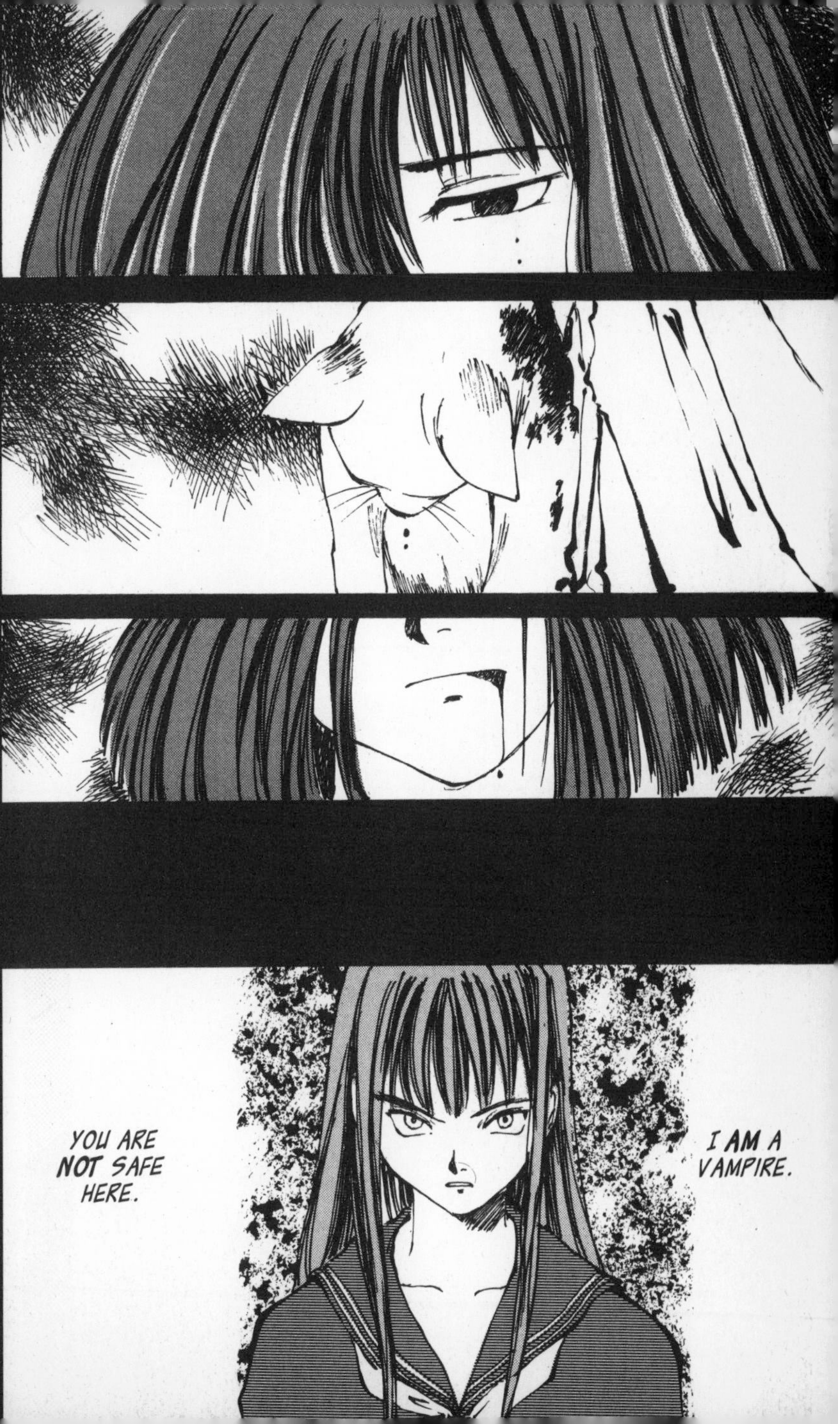
I AM A VAMPIRE.
YOU ARE NOT SAFE HERE.

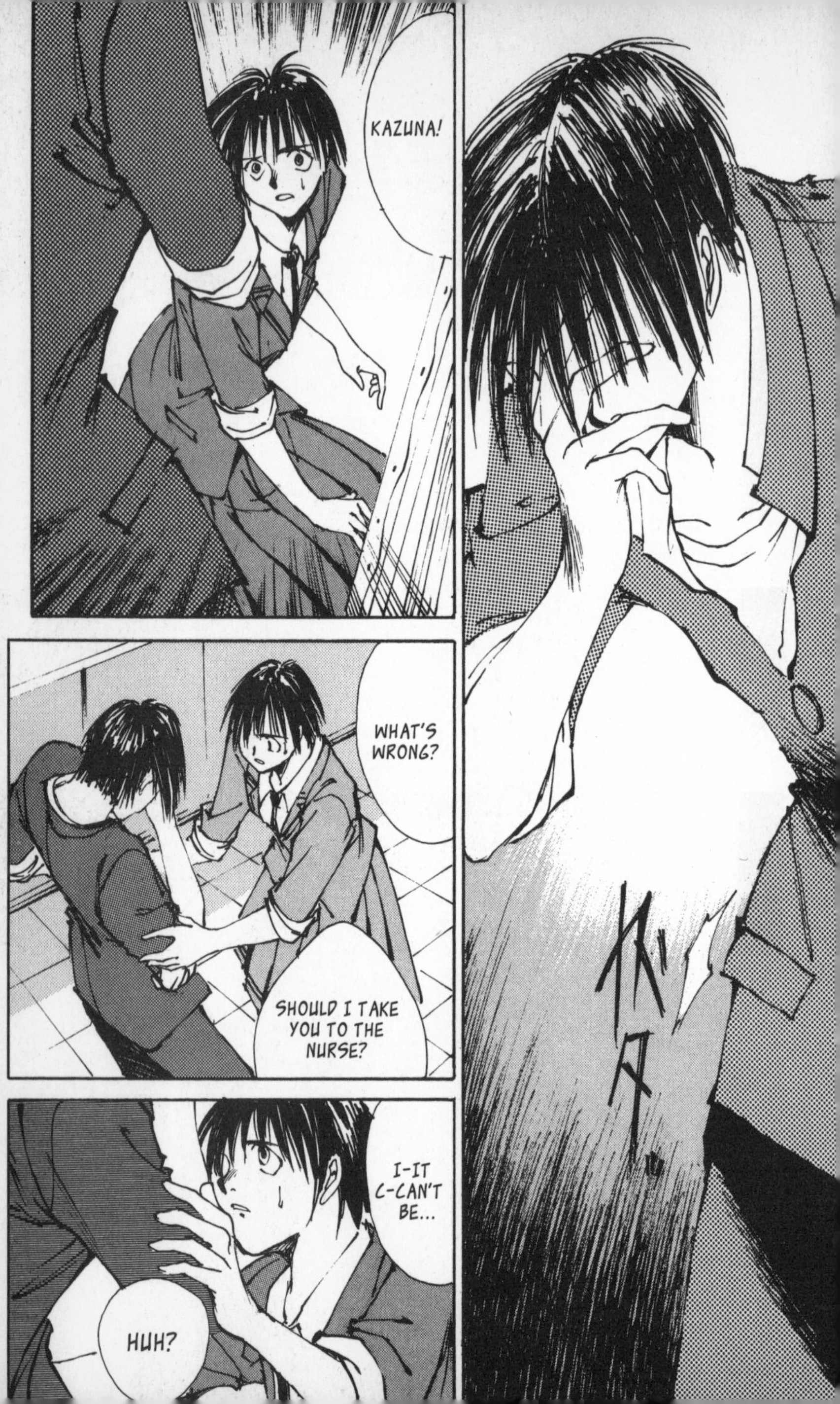
KAZUNA!
WHAT'S WRONG?
SHOULD I TAKE YOU TO THE NURSE?
I-IT C-CAN'T BE...
HUH?

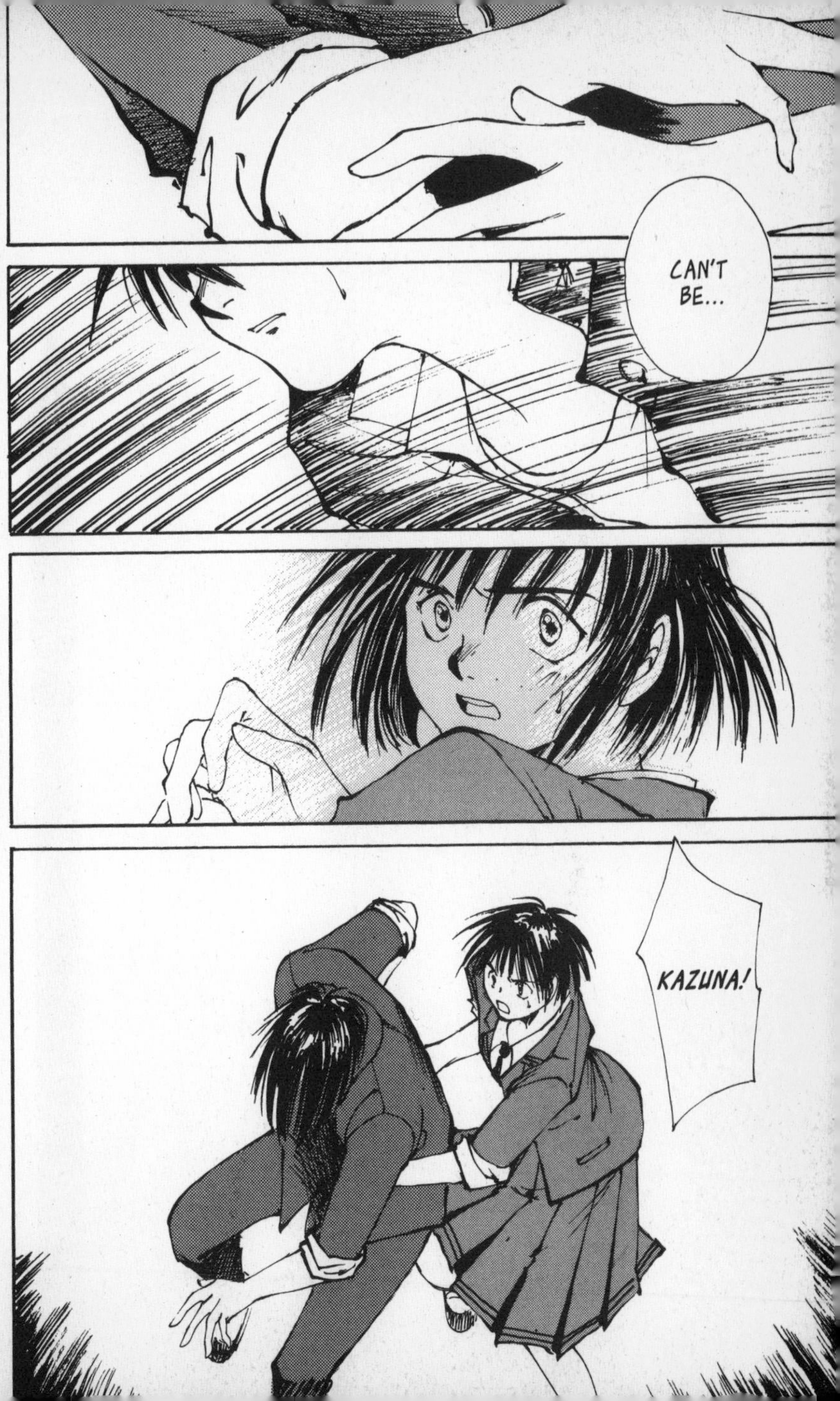
CAN'T BE...
KAZUNA!

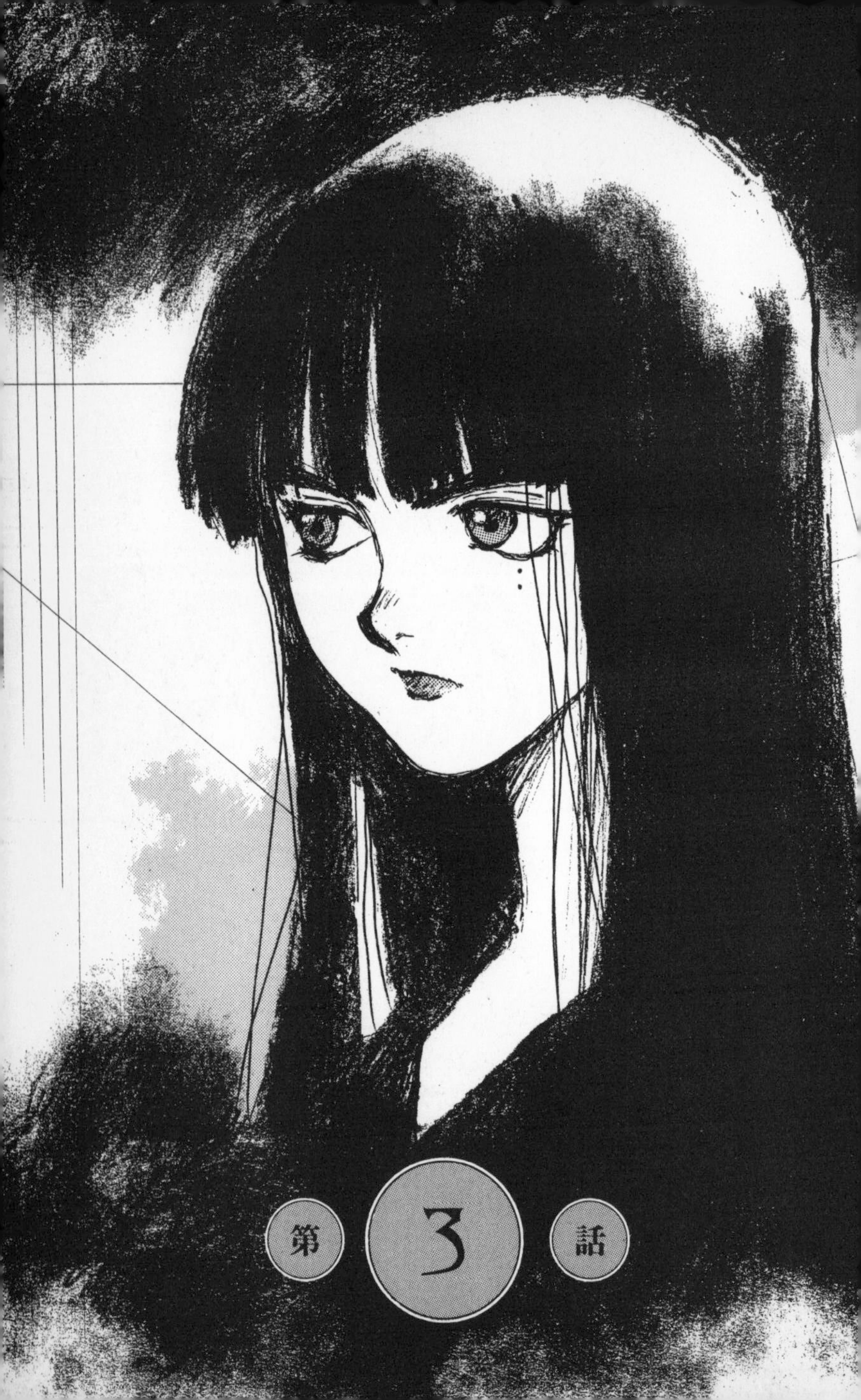
第
3
話

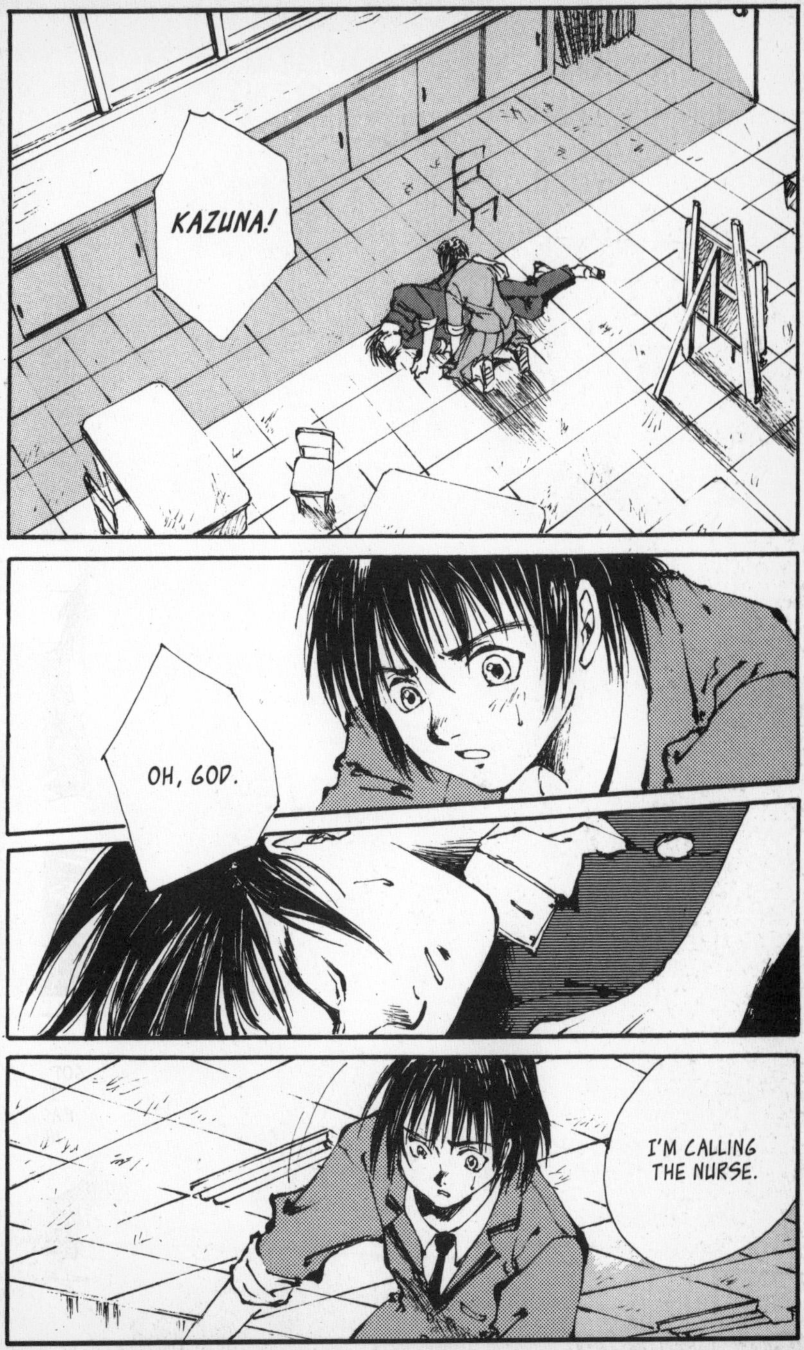
KAZUNA!
OH, GOD.
I'M CALLING THE NURSE.

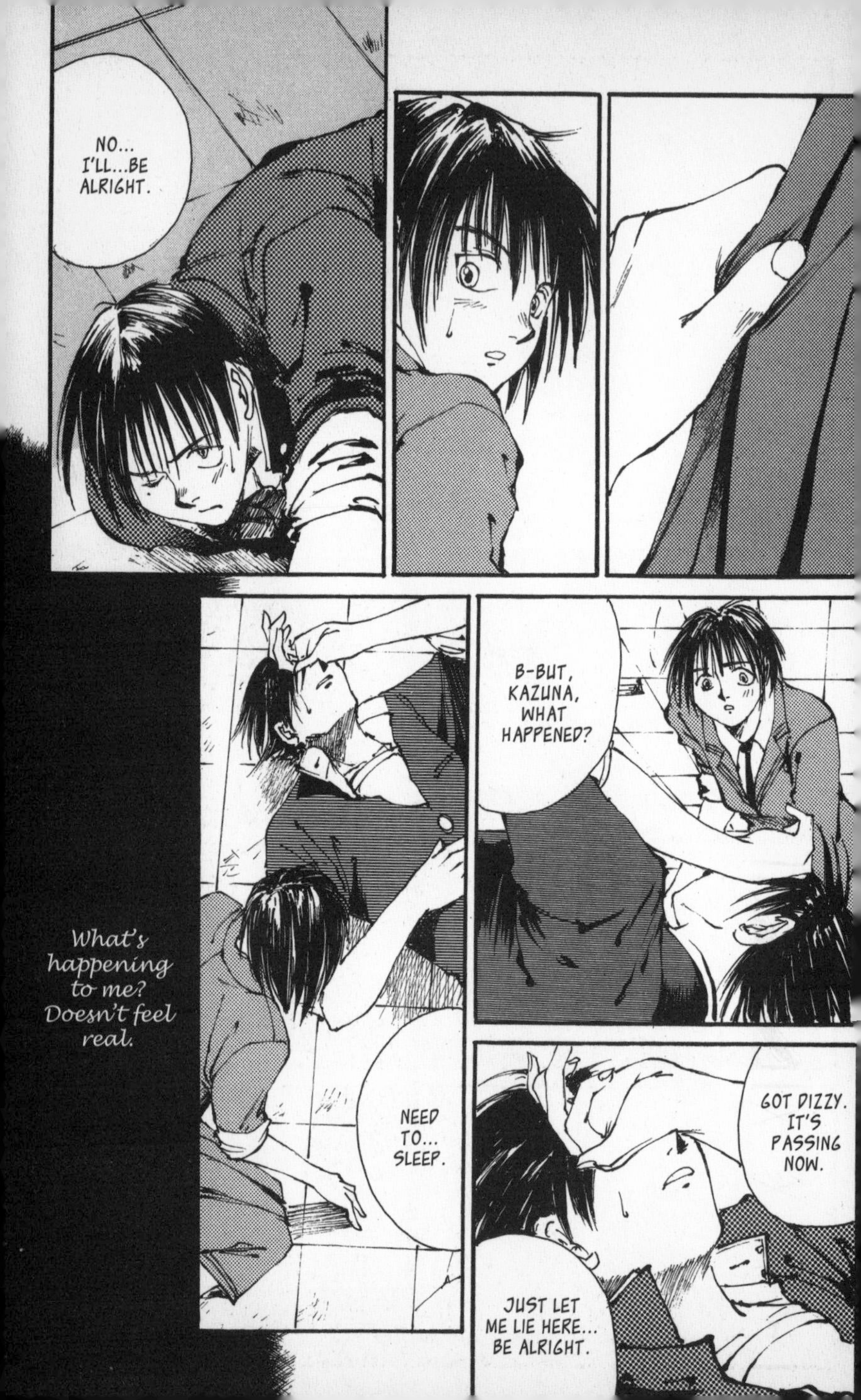
NO... I'LL...BE ALRIGHT.
B-BUT, KAZUNA, WHAT HAPPENED?
GOT DIZZY. IT'S PASSING NOW.
JUST LET ME LIE HERE... BE ALRIGHT.
NEED TO... SLEEP.
What's happening to me? Doesn't feel real.

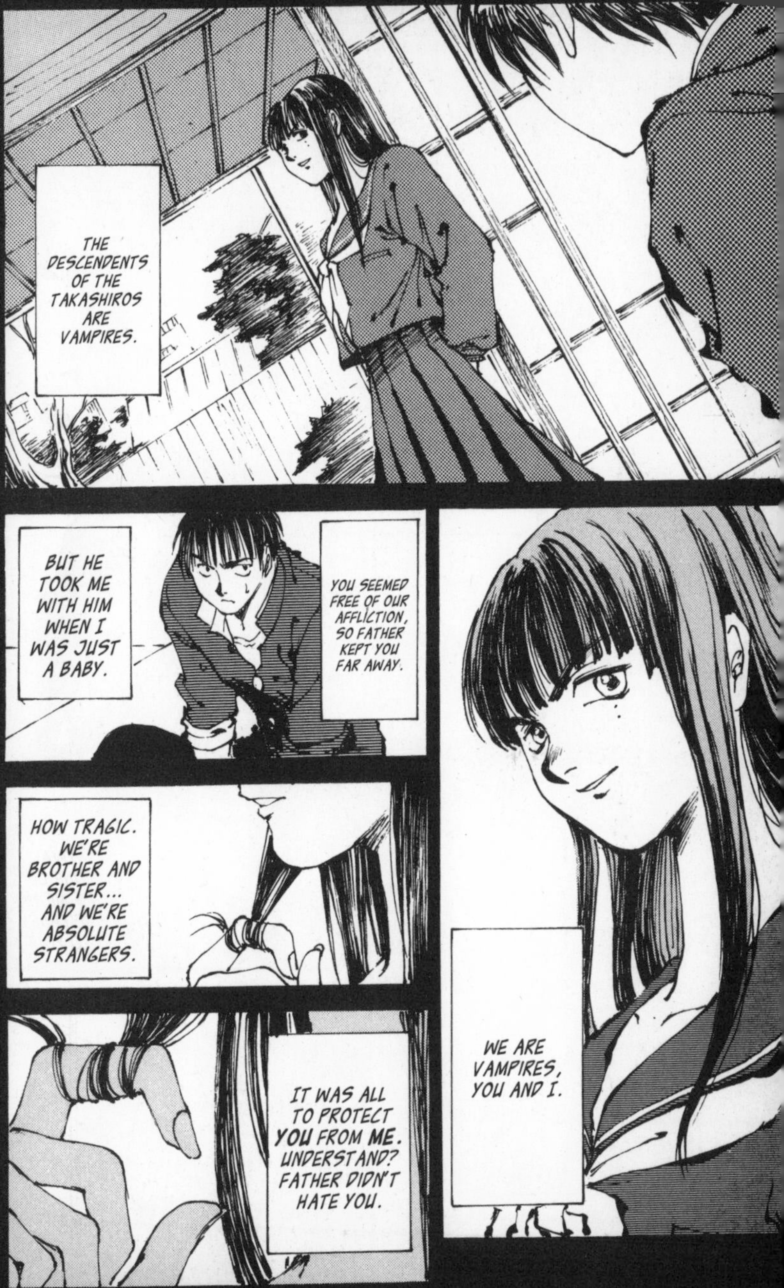
THE DESCENDENTS OF THE TAKASHIROS ARE VAMPIRES.
WE ARE VAMPIRES, YOU AND I.
YOU SEEMED FREE OF OUR AFFLICTION, SO FATHER KEPT YOU FAR AWAY.
BUT HE TOOK ME WITH HIM WHEN I WAS JUST A BABY.
HOW TRAGIC. WE'RE BROTHER AND SISTER... AND WE'RE ABSOLUTE STRANGERS.
IT WAS ALL TO PROTECT YOU FROM ME. UNDERSTAND? FATHER DIDN'T HATE YOU.

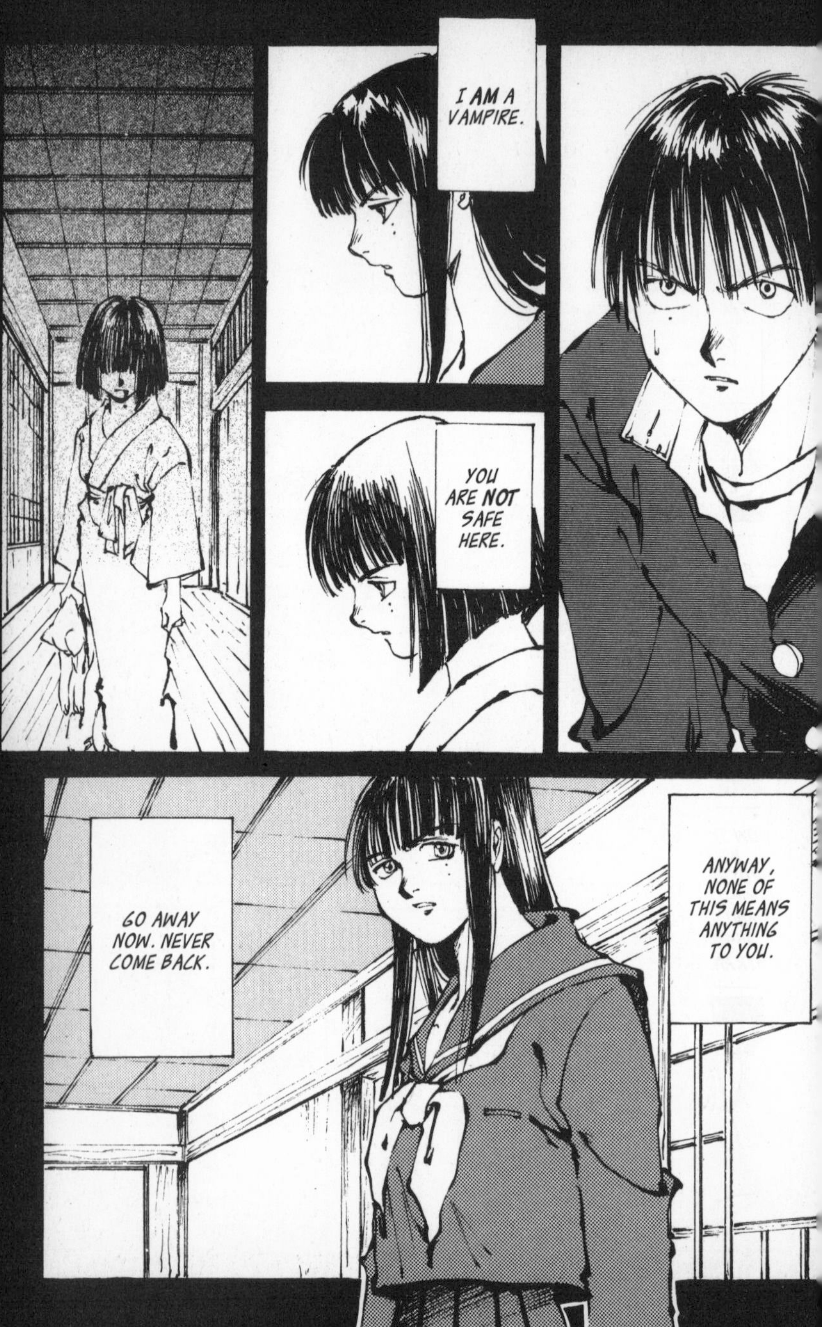
I AM A VAMPIRE.
YOU ARE NOT SAFE HERE.
ANYWAY, NONE OF THIS MEANS ANYTHING TO YOU.
GO AWAY NOW. NEVER COME BACK.

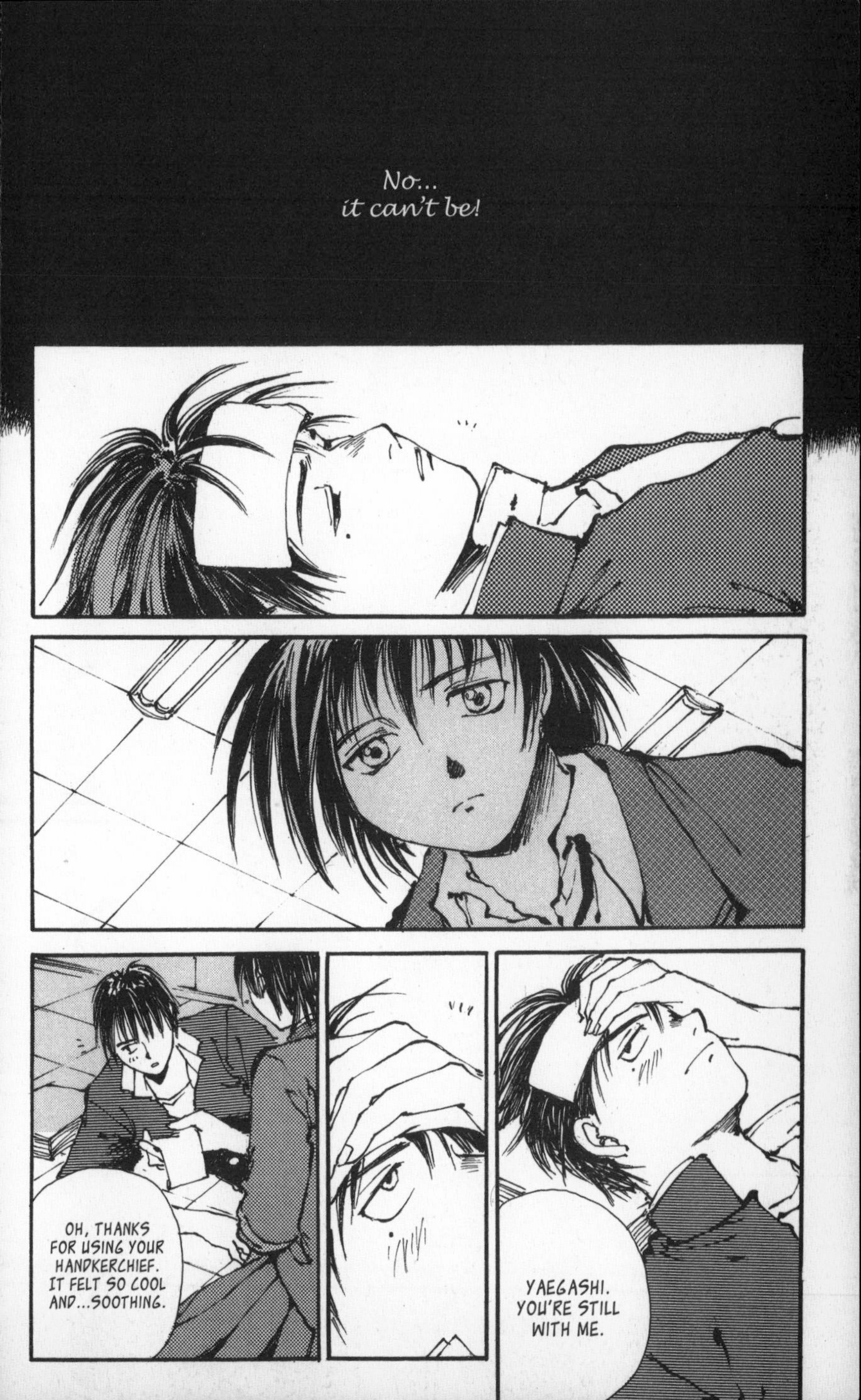
No...
it can't be!
YAEGASHI. YOU'RE STILL WITH ME.
OH, THANKS FOR USING YOUR HANDKERCHIEF. IT FELT SO COOL AND...SOOTHING.

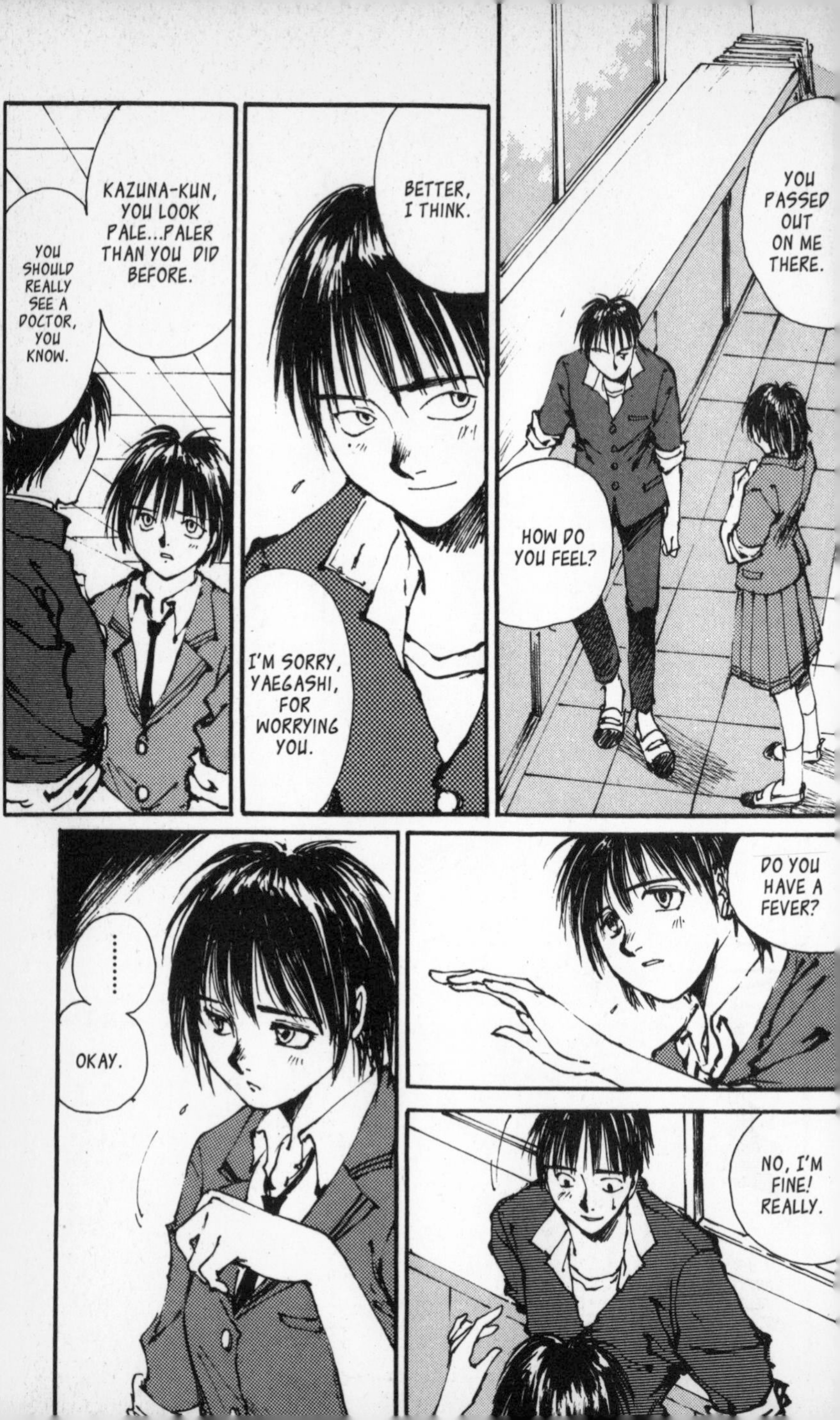
YOU PASSED OUT ON ME THERE.
HOW DO YOU FEEL?
BETTER, I THINK.
I'M SORRY, YAEGASHI, FOR WORRYING YOU.
KAZUNA-KUN, YOU LOOK PALE...PALER THAN YOU DID BEFORE.
YOU SHOULD REALLY SEE A DOCTOR, YOU KNOW.
DO YOU HAVE A FEVER?
NO, I'M FINE! REALLY.
......
OKAY.

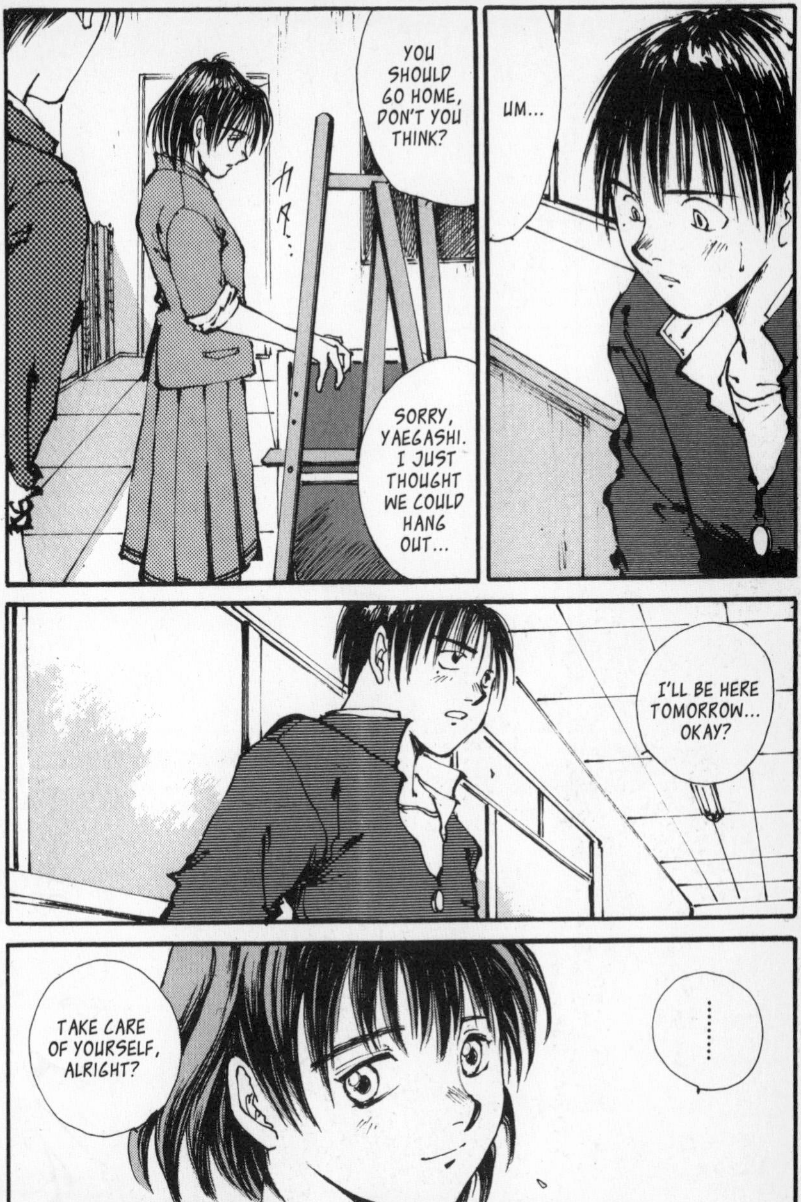
UM...
YOU SHOULD GO HOME, DON'T YOU THINK?
カタ...
SORRY, YAEGASHI. I JUST THOUGHT WE COULD HANG OUT...
I'LL BE HERE TOMORROW... OKAY?
......
TAKE CARE OF YOURSELF, ALRIGHT?

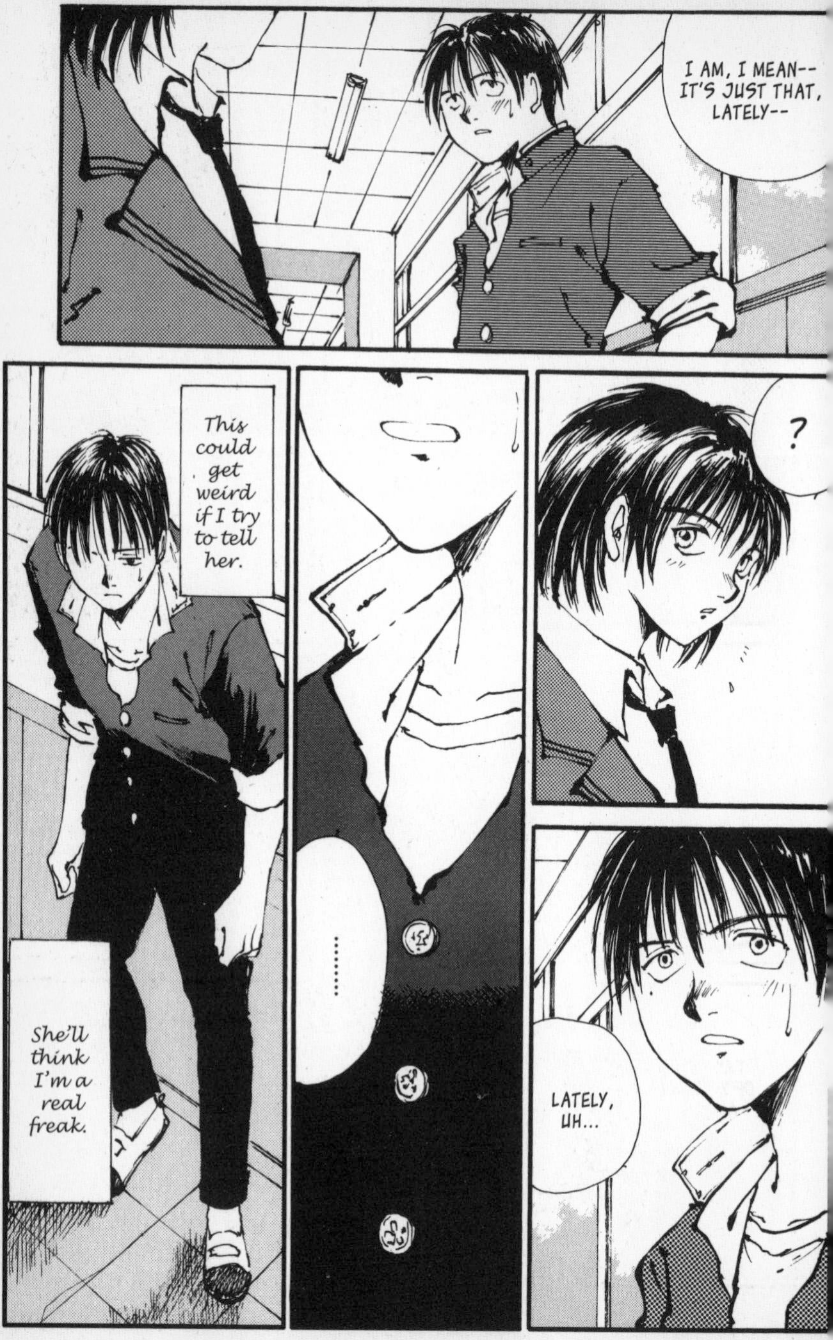
I AM, I MEAN-- IT'S JUST THAT, LATELY--
?
LATELY, UH...
......
This could get weird if I try to tell her.
She'll think I'm a real freak.

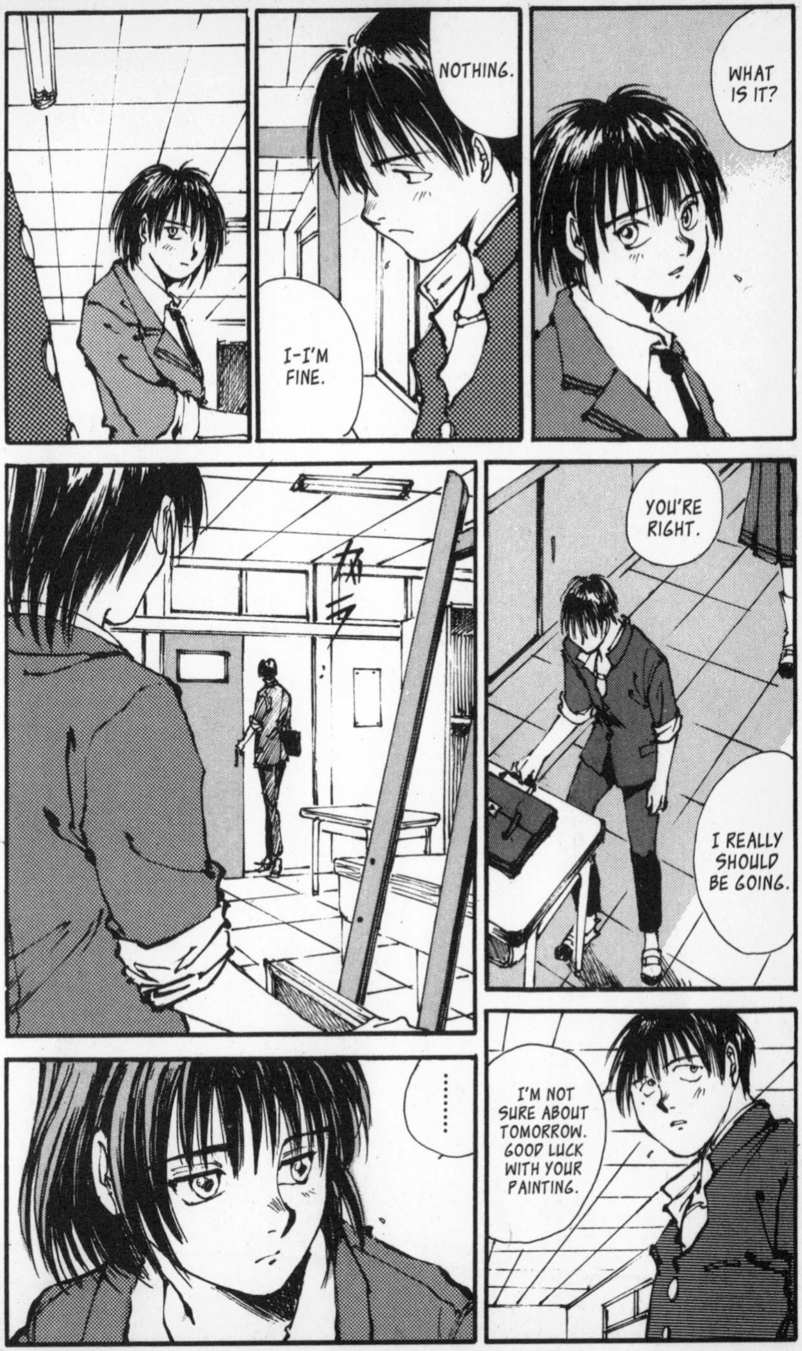
WHAT IS IT?
NOTHING.
I-I'M FINE.
YOU'RE RIGHT.
I REALLY SHOULD BE GOING.
I'M NOT SURE ABOUT TOMORROW. GOOD LUCK WITH YOUR PAINTING.
......

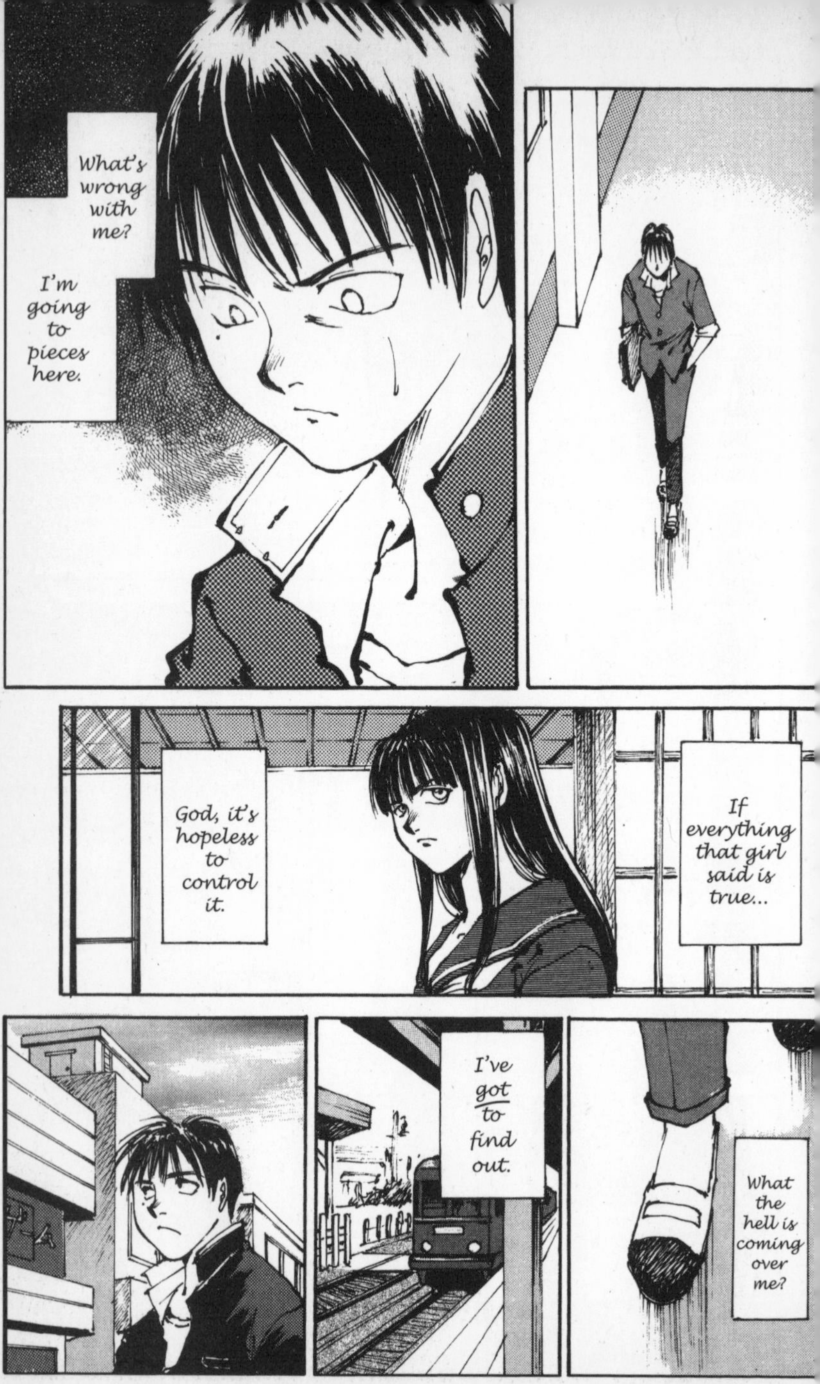
What's wrong with me?
I'm going to pieces here.
If everything that girl said is true...
God, it's hopeless to control it.
What the hell is coming over me?
I've got to find out.

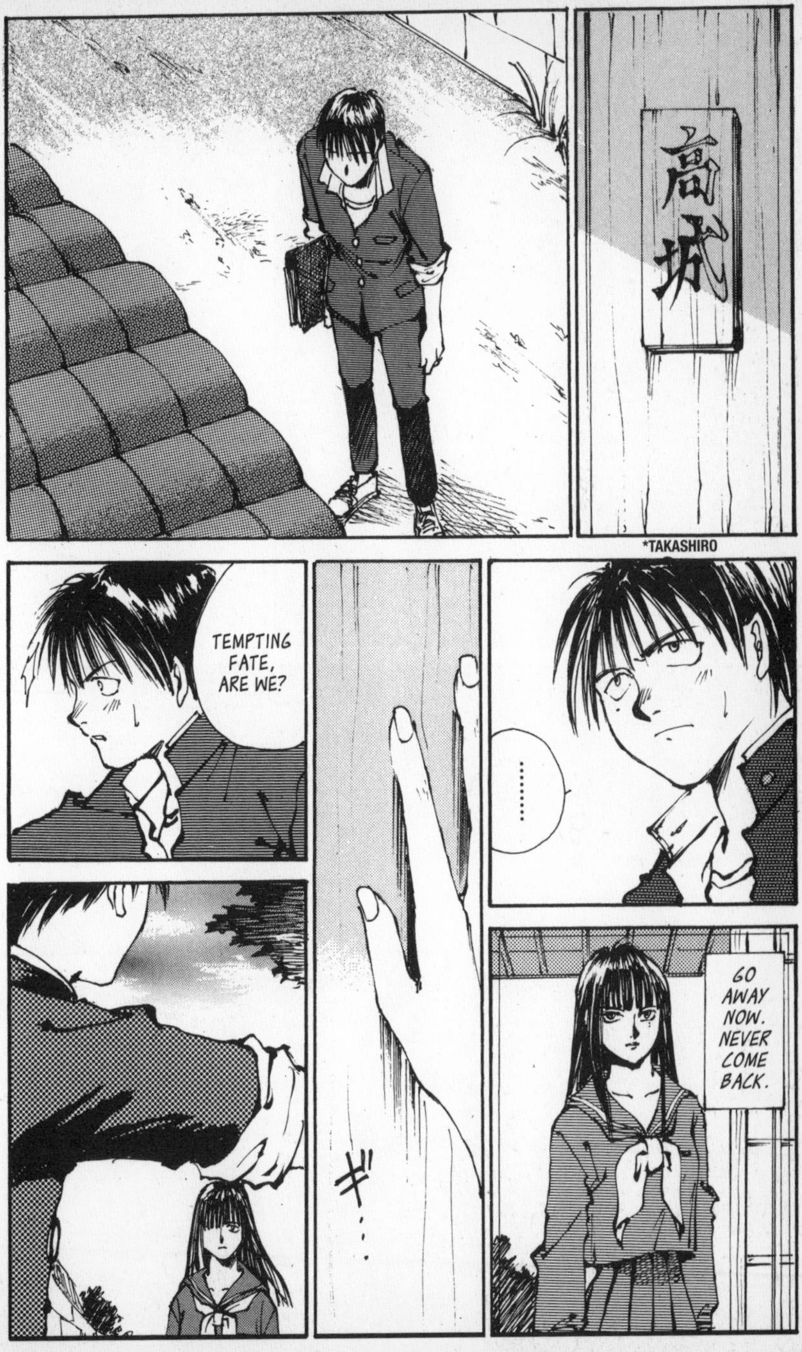
高城
*TAKASHIRO
……
GO AWAY NOW. NEVER COME BACK.
ギ…
TEMPTING FATE, ARE WE?

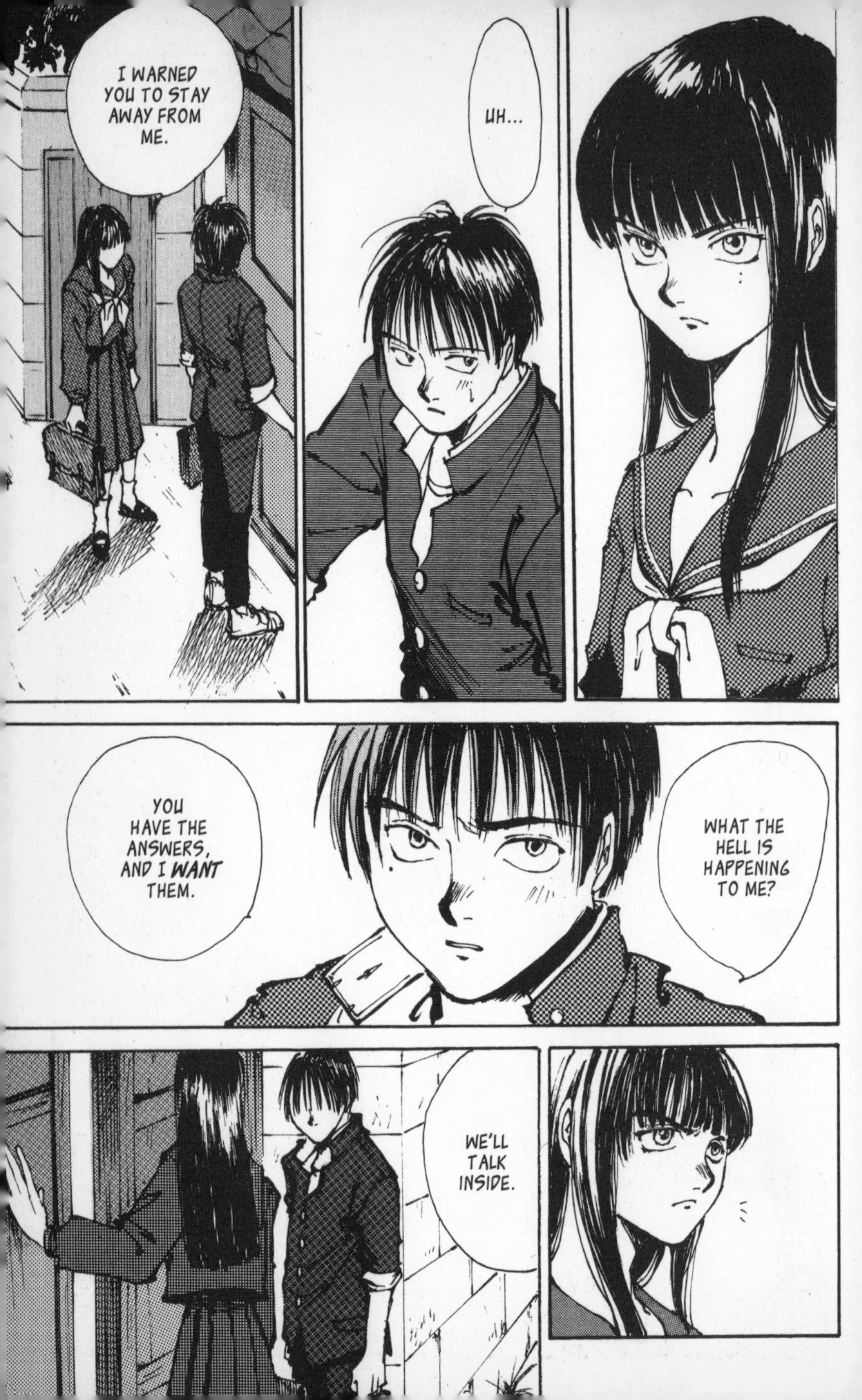
UH...
I WARNED YOU TO STAY AWAY FROM ME.
WHAT THE HELL IS HAPPENING TO ME?
YOU HAVE THE ANSWERS, AND I *WANT* THEM.
WE'LL TALK INSIDE.

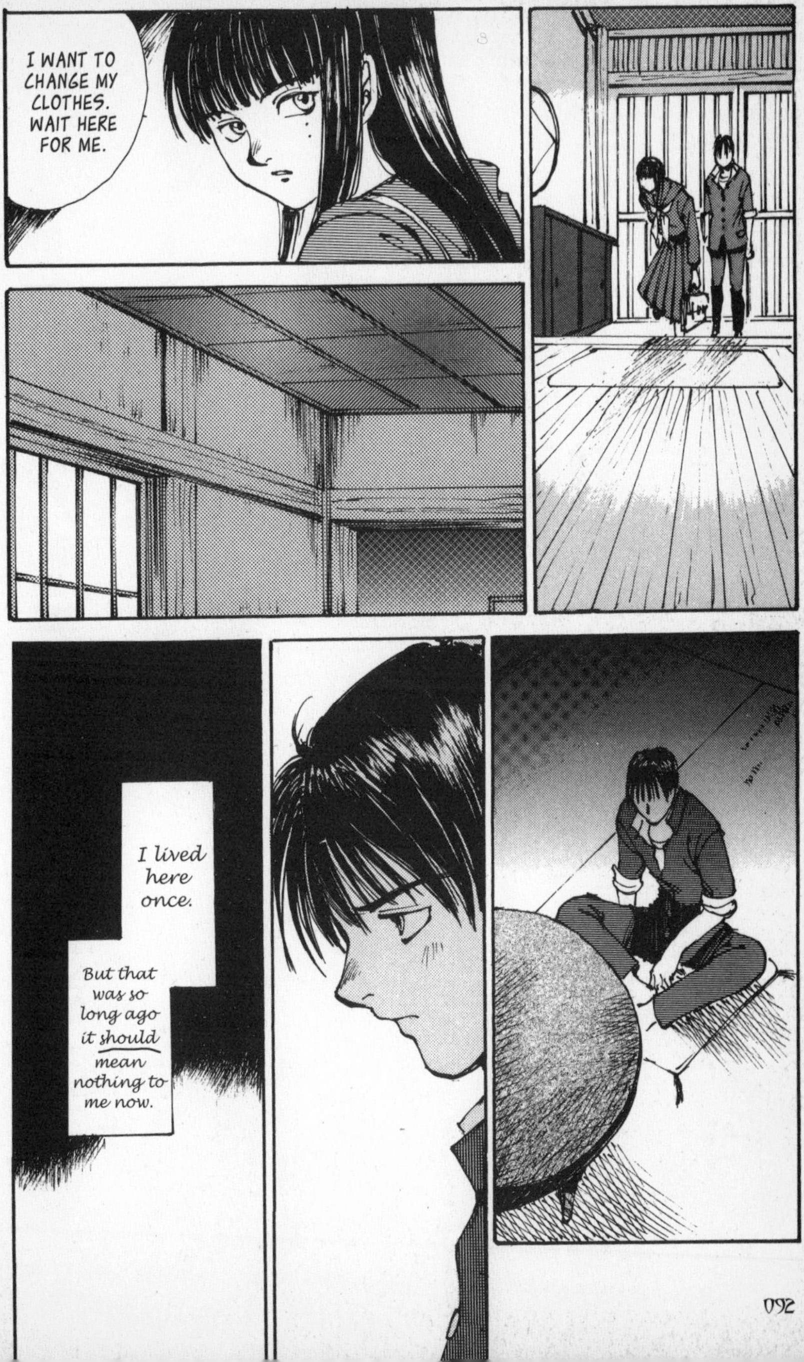
I WANT TO CHANGE MY CLOTHES. WAIT HERE FOR ME.
I lived here once.
But that was so long ago it should mean nothing to me now.

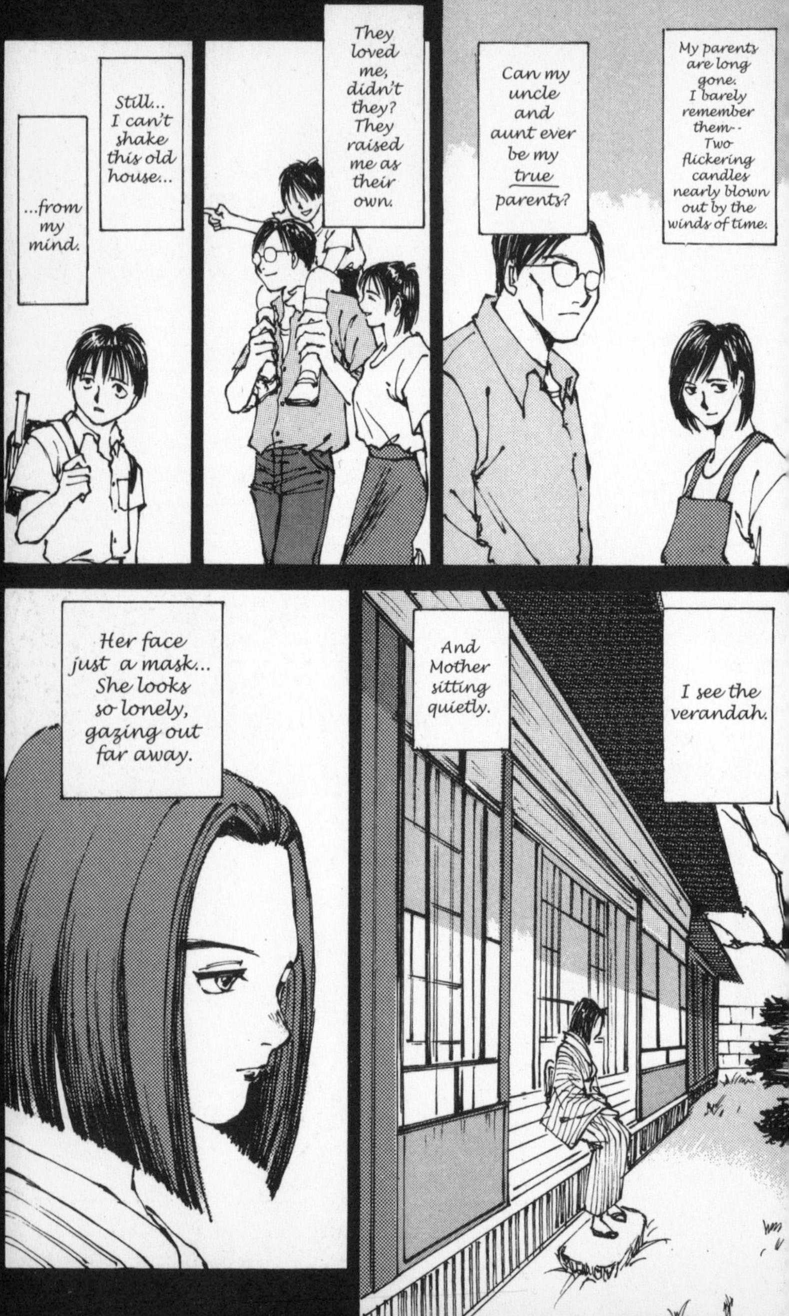
My parents are long gone. I barely remember them-- Two flickering candles nearly blown out by the winds of time.
Can my uncle and aunt ever be my true parents?
They loved me, didn't they? They raised me as their own.
Still... I can't shake this old house...
...from my mind.
I see the verandah.
And Mother sitting quietly.
Her face just a mask... She looks so lonely, gazing out far away.

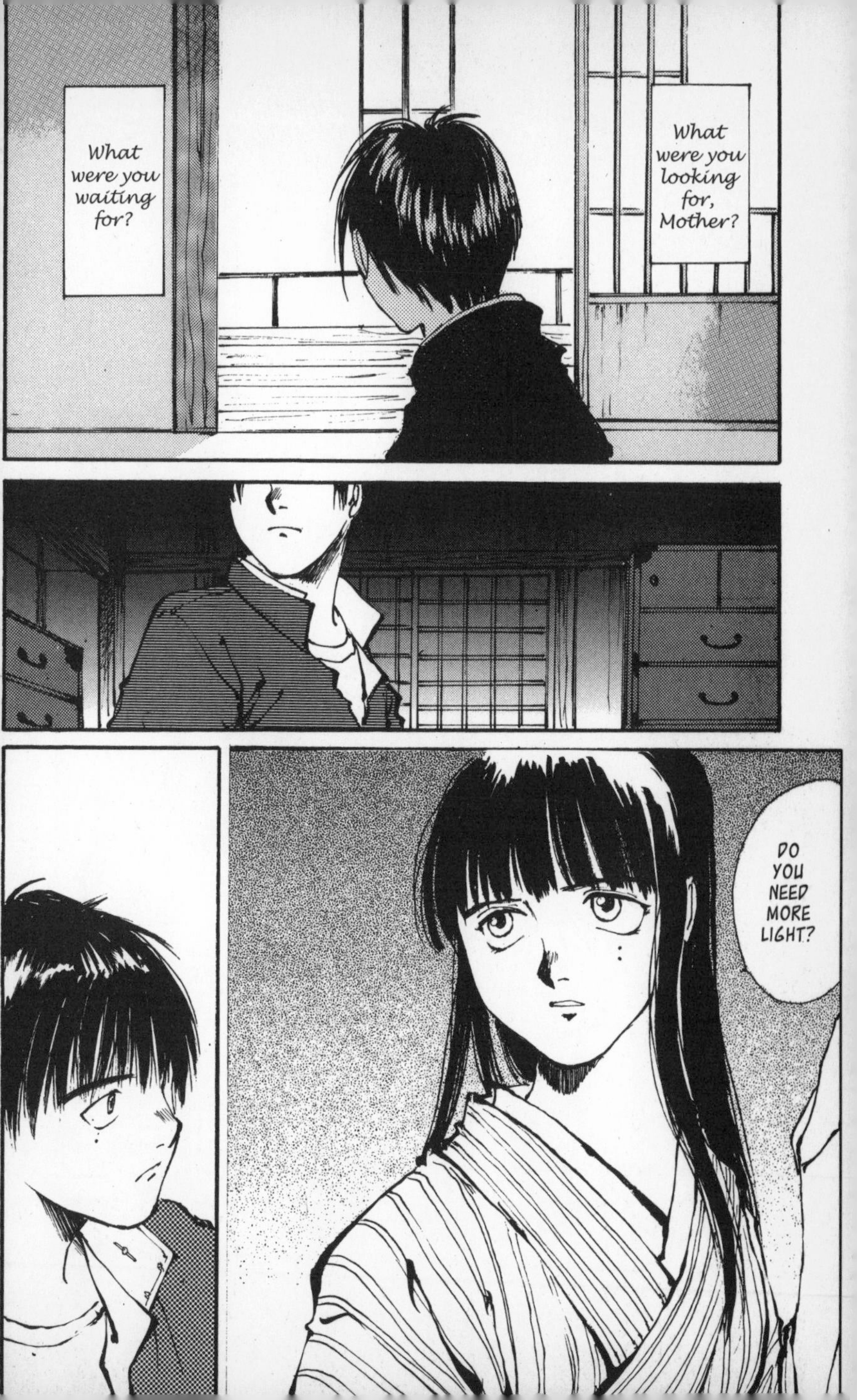
What were you looking for, Mother?
What were you waiting for?
DO YOU NEED MORE LIGHT?

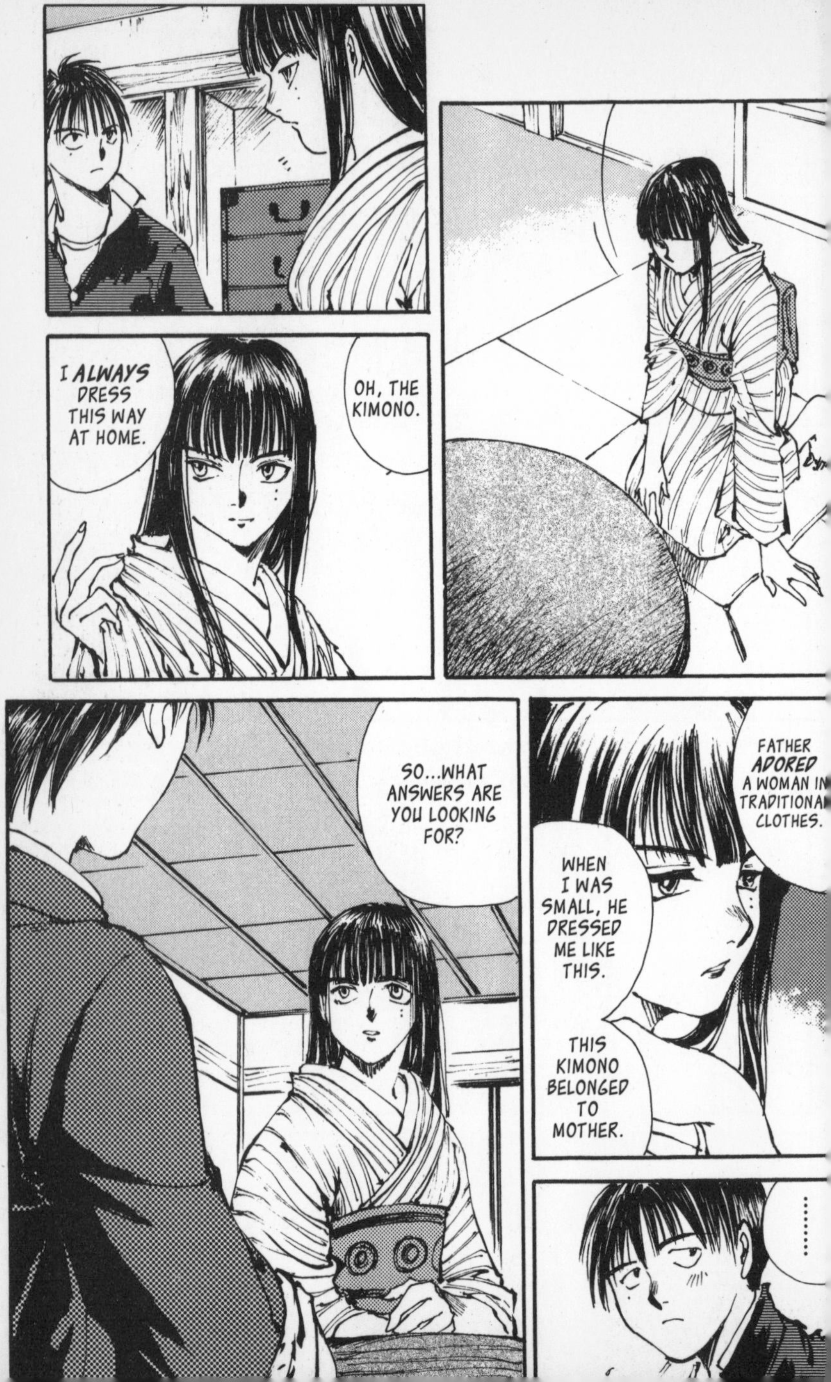
OH, THE KIMONO.
I ALWAYS DRESS THIS WAY AT HOME.
FATHER ADORED A WOMAN IN TRADITIONA CLOTHES.
WHEN I WAS SMALL, HE DRESSED ME LIKE THIS.
THIS KIMONO BELONGED TO MOTHER.
......
SO...WHAT ANSWERS ARE YOU LOOKING FOR?

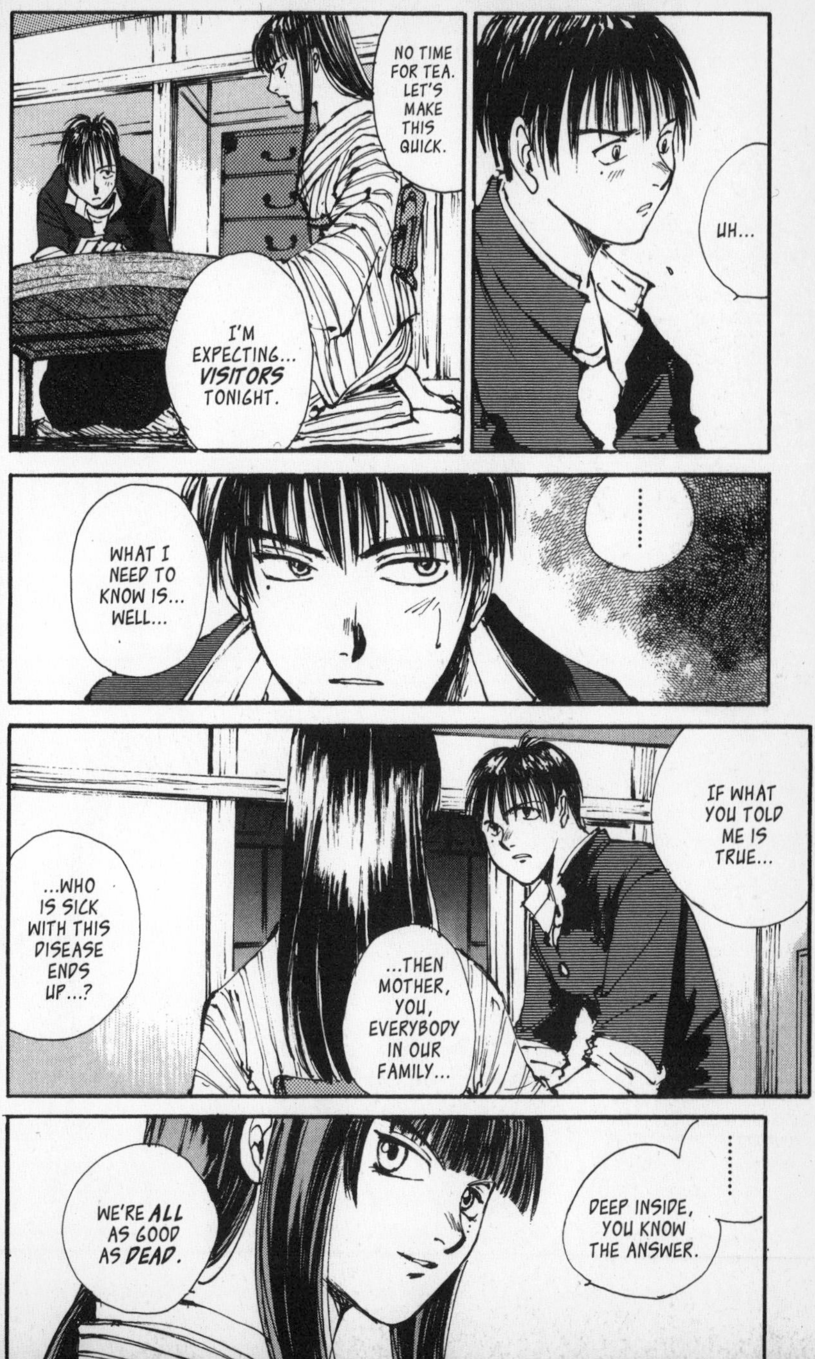
UH...
NO TIME FOR TEA. LET'S MAKE THIS QUICK.
I'M EXPECTING... VISITORS TONIGHT.
......
WHAT I NEED TO KNOW IS... WELL...
IF WHAT YOU TOLD ME IS TRUE...
...THEN MOTHER, YOU, EVERYBODY IN OUR FAMILY...
...WHO IS SICK WITH THIS DISEASE ENDS UP...?
......
DEEP INSIDE, YOU KNOW THE ANSWER.
WE'RE ALL AS GOOD AS DEAD.

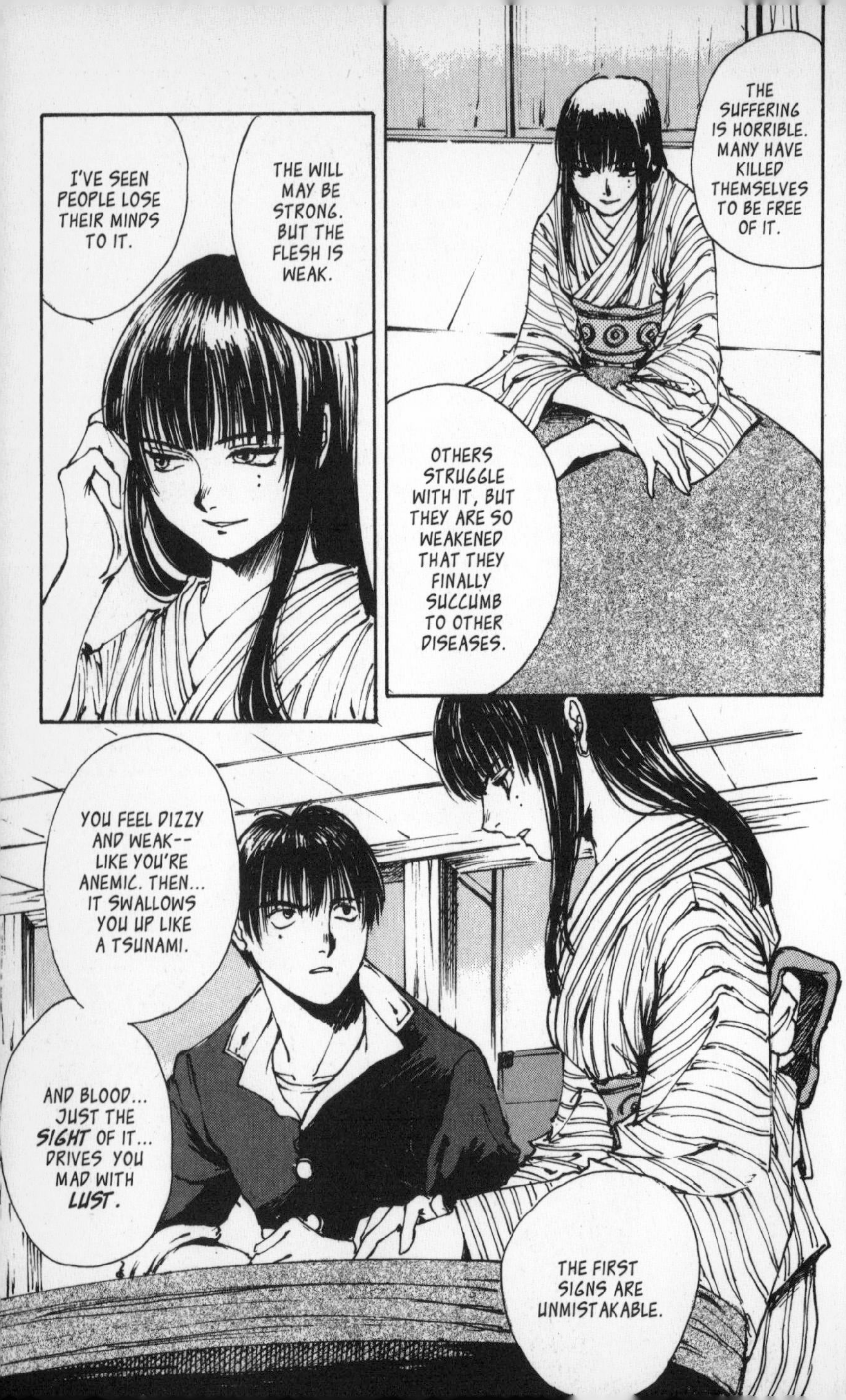
THE SUFFERING IS HORRIBLE. MANY HAVE KILLED THEMSELVES TO BE FREE OF IT.
OTHERS STRUGGLE WITH IT, BUT THEY ARE SO WEAKENED THAT THEY FINALLY SUCCUMB TO OTHER DISEASES.
THE WILL MAY BE STRONG. BUT THE FLESH IS WEAK.
I'VE SEEN PEOPLE LOSE THEIR MINDS TO IT.
THE FIRST SIGNS ARE UNMISTAKABLE.
YOU FEEL DIZZY AND WEAK-- LIKE YOU'RE ANEMIC. THEN... IT SWALLOWS YOU UP LIKE A TSUNAMI.
AND BLOOD... JUST THE SIGHT OF IT... DRIVES YOU MAD WITH LUST.

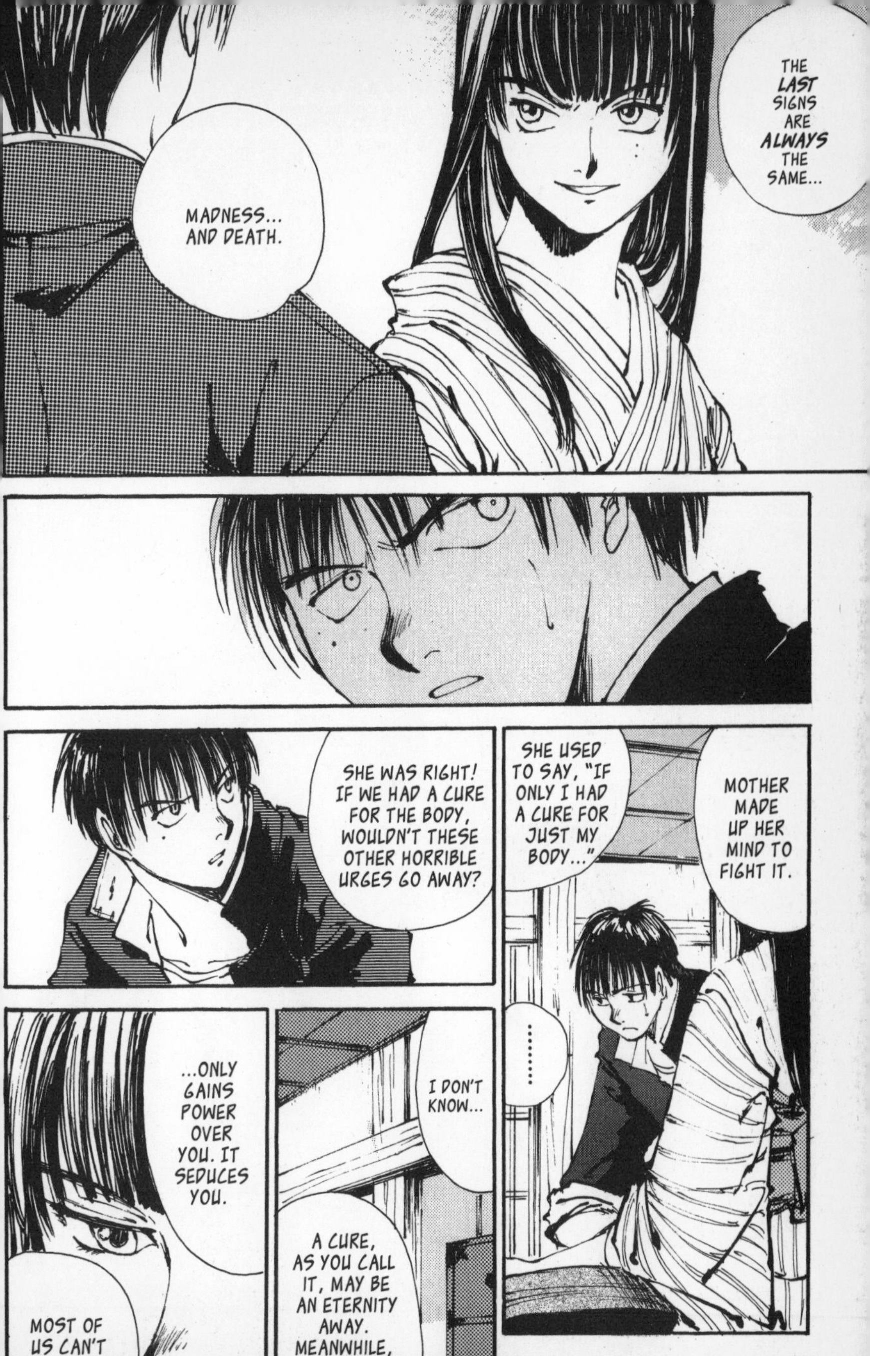
THE LAST SIGNS ARE ALWAYS THE SAME...
MADNESS... AND DEATH.
MOTHER MADE UP HER MIND TO FIGHT IT.
SHE USED TO SAY, "IF ONLY I HAD A CURE FOR JUST MY BODY..."
......
SHE WAS RIGHT! IF WE HAD A CURE FOR THE BODY, WOULDN'T THESE OTHER HORRIBLE URGES GO AWAY?
I DON'T KNOW...
A CURE, AS YOU CALL IT, MAY BE AN ETERNITY AWAY. MEANWHILE, THE DISEASE...
...ONLY GAINS POWER OVER YOU. IT SEDUCES YOU.
MOST OF US CAN'T RESIST IT.

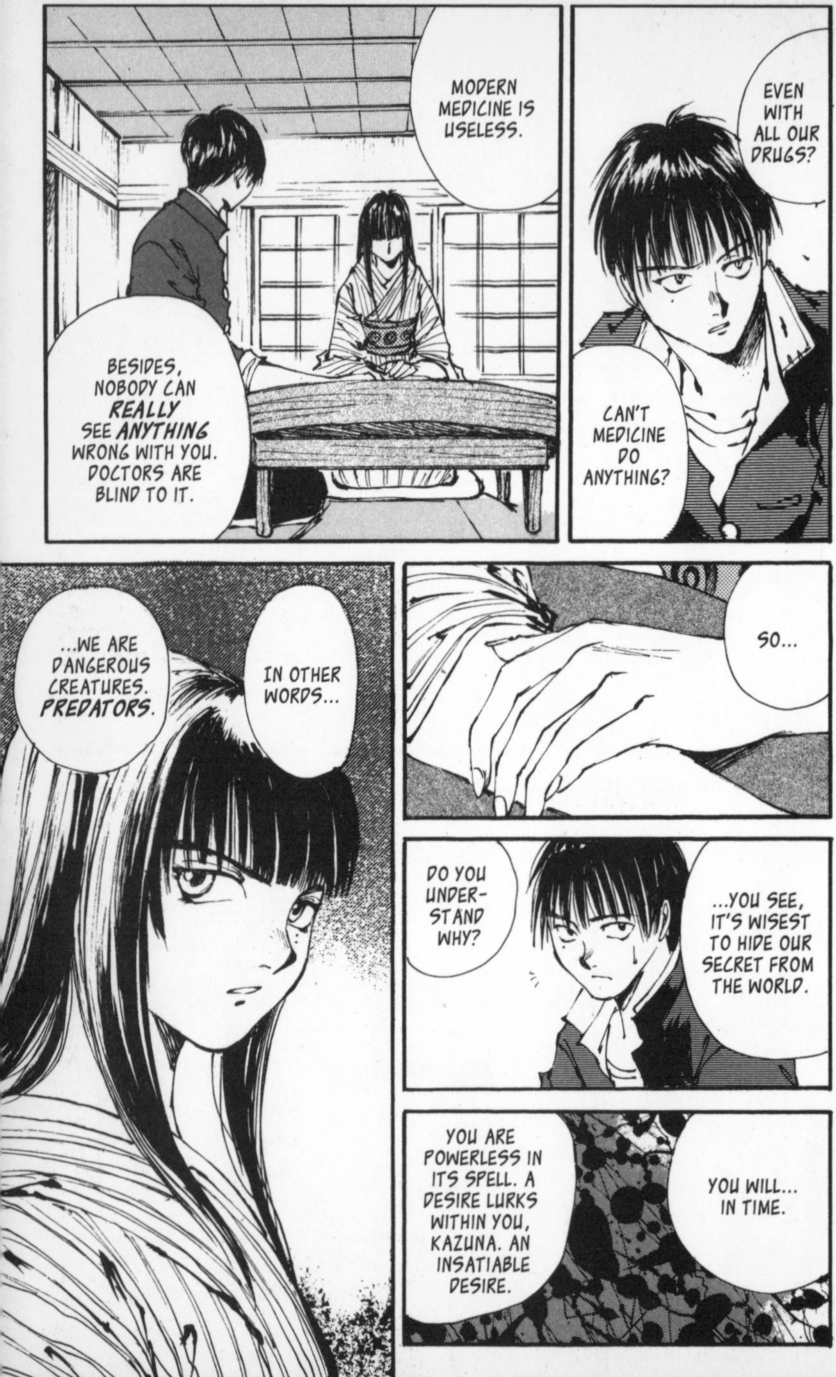
EVEN WITH ALL OUR DRUGS?
CAN'T MEDICINE DO ANYTHING?
MODERN MEDICINE IS USELESS.
BESIDES, NOBODY CAN **REALLY** SEE **ANYTHING** WRONG WITH YOU. DOCTORS ARE BLIND TO IT.
SO...
...YOU SEE, IT'S WISEST TO HIDE OUR SECRET FROM THE WORLD.
DO YOU UNDER-STAND WHY?
YOU WILL... IN TIME.
YOU ARE POWERLESS IN ITS SPELL. A DESIRE LURKS WITHIN YOU, KAZUNA. AN INSATIABLE DESIRE.
IN OTHER WORDS...
...WE ARE DANGEROUS CREATURES. **PREDATORS**.

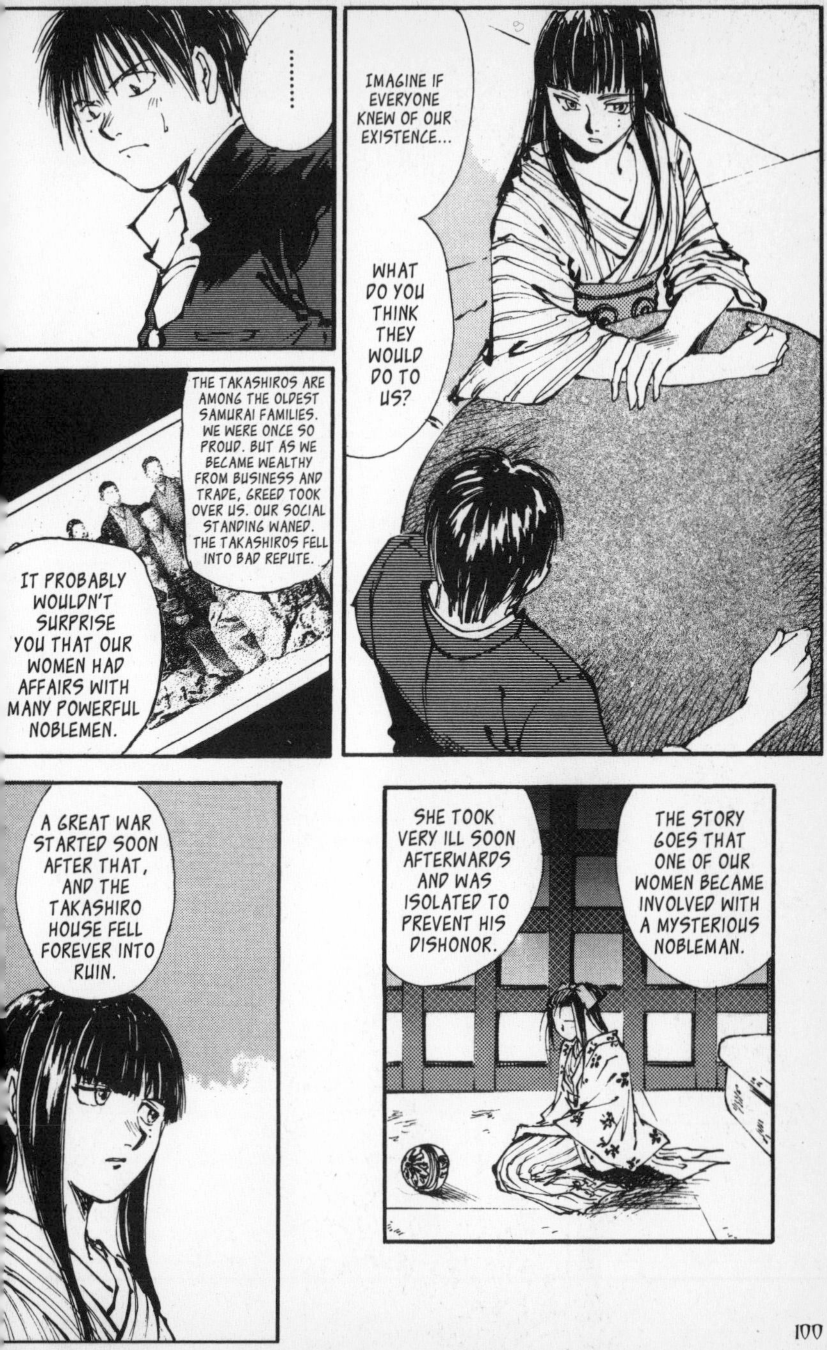
IMAGINE IF EVERYONE KNEW OF OUR EXISTENCE...
WHAT DO YOU THINK THEY WOULD DO TO US?
......
THE TAKASHIROS ARE AMONG THE OLDEST SAMURAI FAMILIES. WE WERE ONCE SO PROUD. BUT AS WE BECAME WEALTHY FROM BUSINESS AND TRADE, GREED TOOK OVER US. OUR SOCIAL STANDING WANED. THE TAKASHIROS FELL INTO BAD REPUTE.
IT PROBABLY WOULDN'T SURPRISE YOU THAT OUR WOMEN HAD AFFAIRS WITH MANY POWERFUL NOBLEMEN.
THE STORY GOES THAT ONE OF OUR WOMEN BECAME INVOLVED WITH A MYSTERIOUS NOBLEMAN.
SHE TOOK VERY ILL SOON AFTERWARDS AND WAS ISOLATED TO PREVENT HIS DISHONOR.
A GREAT WAR STARTED SOON AFTER THAT, AND THE TAKASHIRO HOUSE FELL FOREVER INTO RUIN.

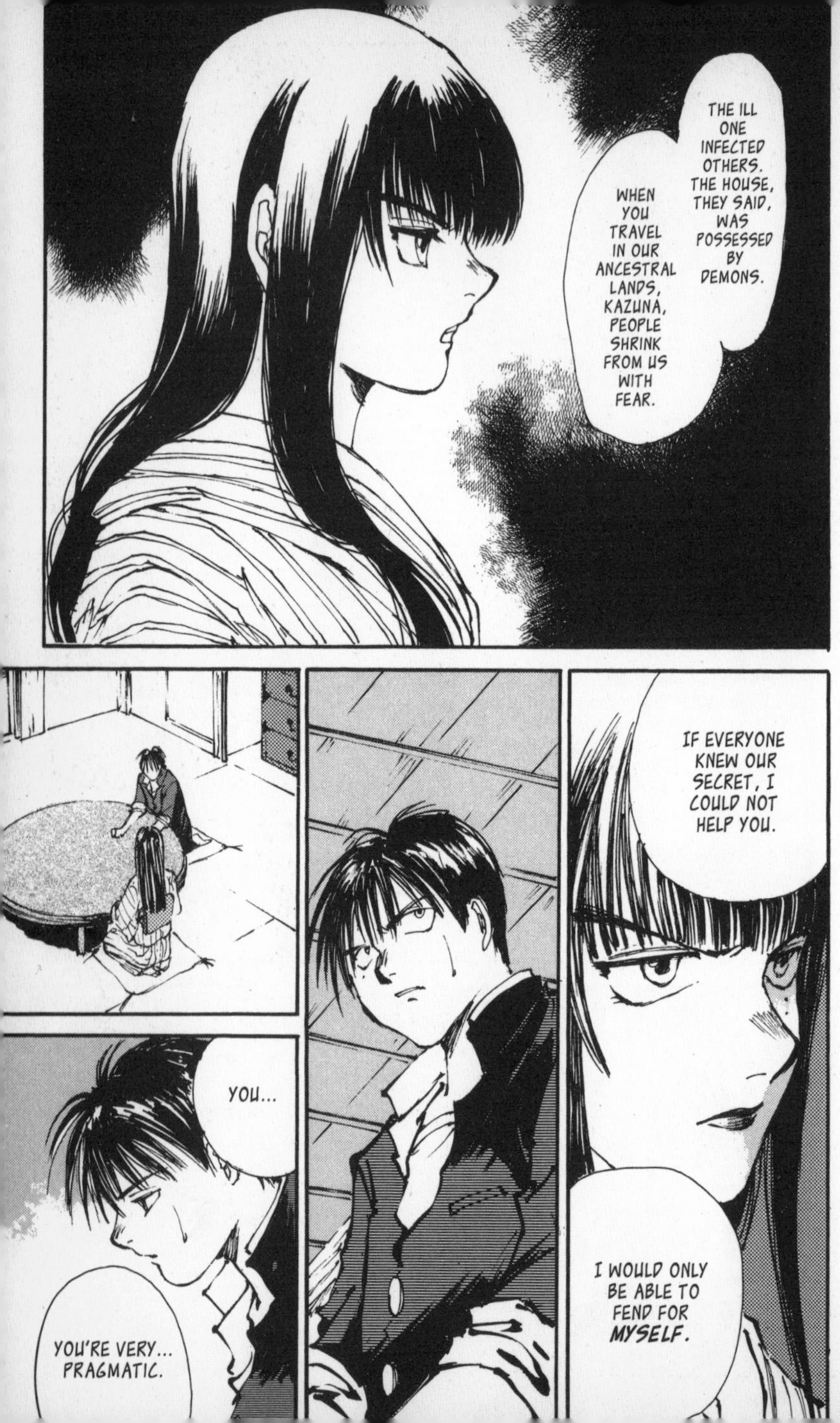
THE ILL ONE INFECTED OTHERS. THE HOUSE, THEY SAID, WAS POSSESSED BY DEMONS.
WHEN YOU TRAVEL IN OUR ANCESTRAL LANDS, KAZUNA, PEOPLE SHRINK FROM US WITH FEAR.
IF EVERYONE KNEW OUR SECRET, I COULD NOT HELP YOU.
I WOULD ONLY BE ABLE TO FEND FOR ***MYSELF***.
YOU...
YOU'RE VERY... PRAGMATIC.

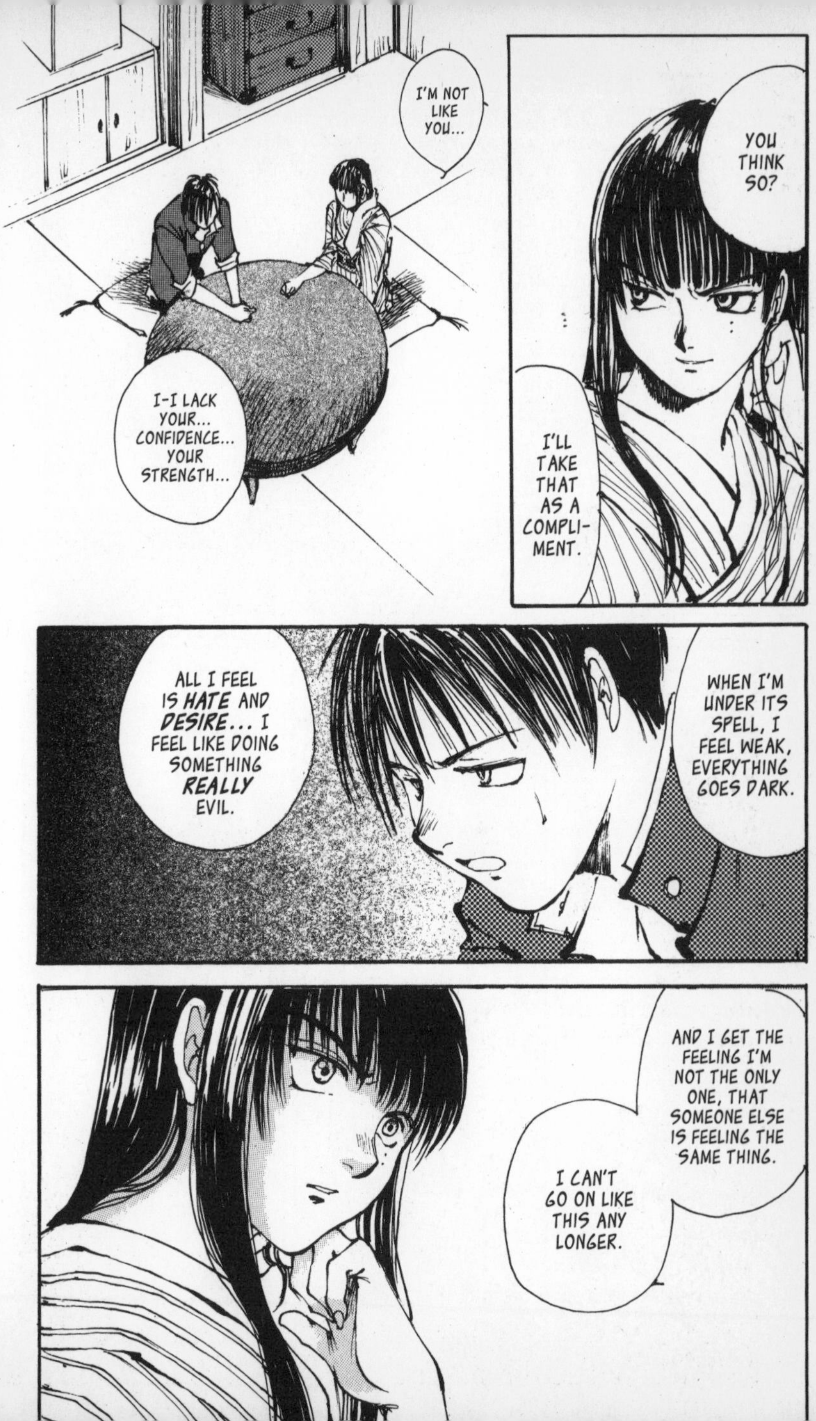
I'M NOT LIKE YOU...
I-I LACK YOUR... CONFIDENCE... YOUR STRENGTH...
YOU THINK SO?
I'LL TAKE THAT AS A COMPLI-MENT.
ALL I FEEL IS HATE AND DESIRE... I FEEL LIKE DOING SOMETHING REALLY EVIL.
WHEN I'M UNDER ITS SPELL, I FEEL WEAK, EVERYTHING GOES DARK.
AND I GET THE FEELING I'M NOT THE ONLY ONE, THAT SOMEONE ELSE IS FEELING THE SAME THING.
I CAN'T GO ON LIKE THIS ANY LONGER.

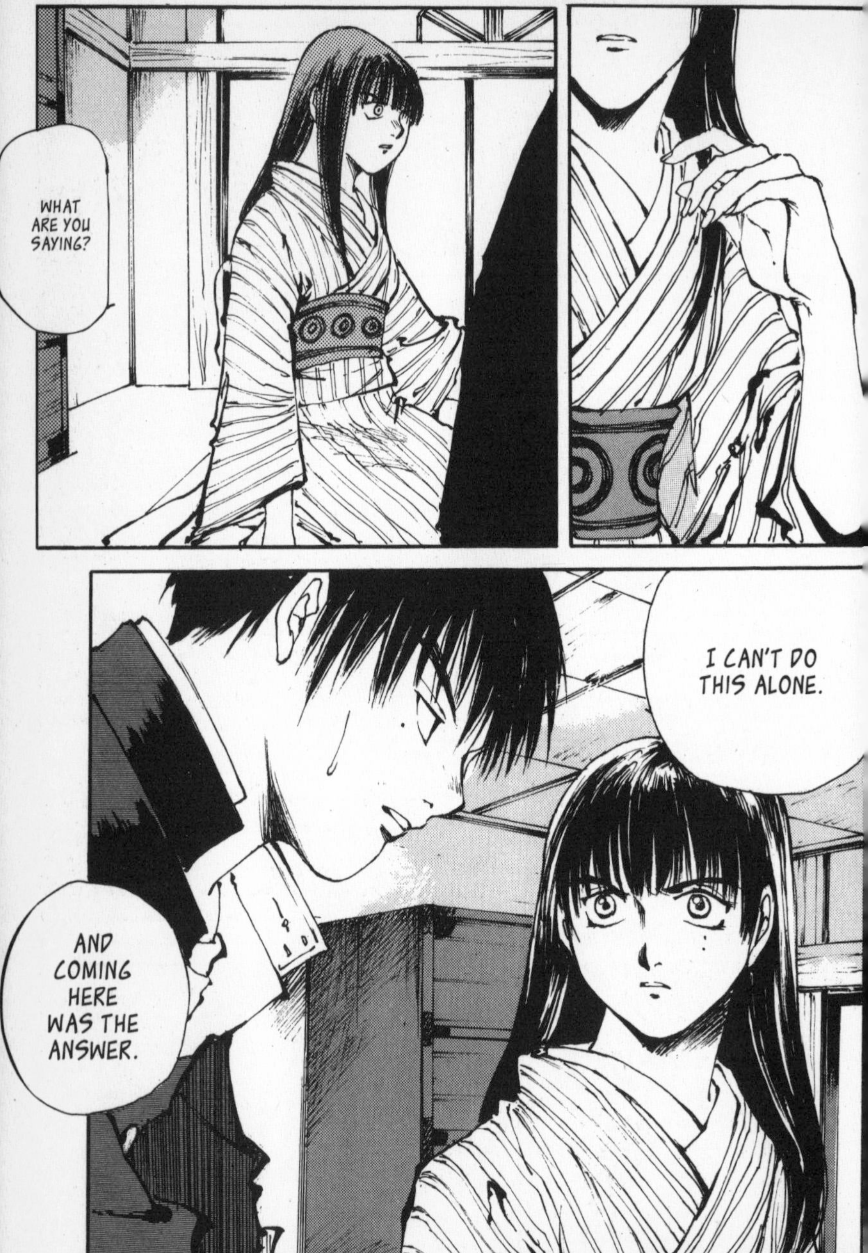
WHAT ARE YOU SAYING?
I CAN'T DO THIS ALONE.
AND COMING HERE WAS THE ANSWER.

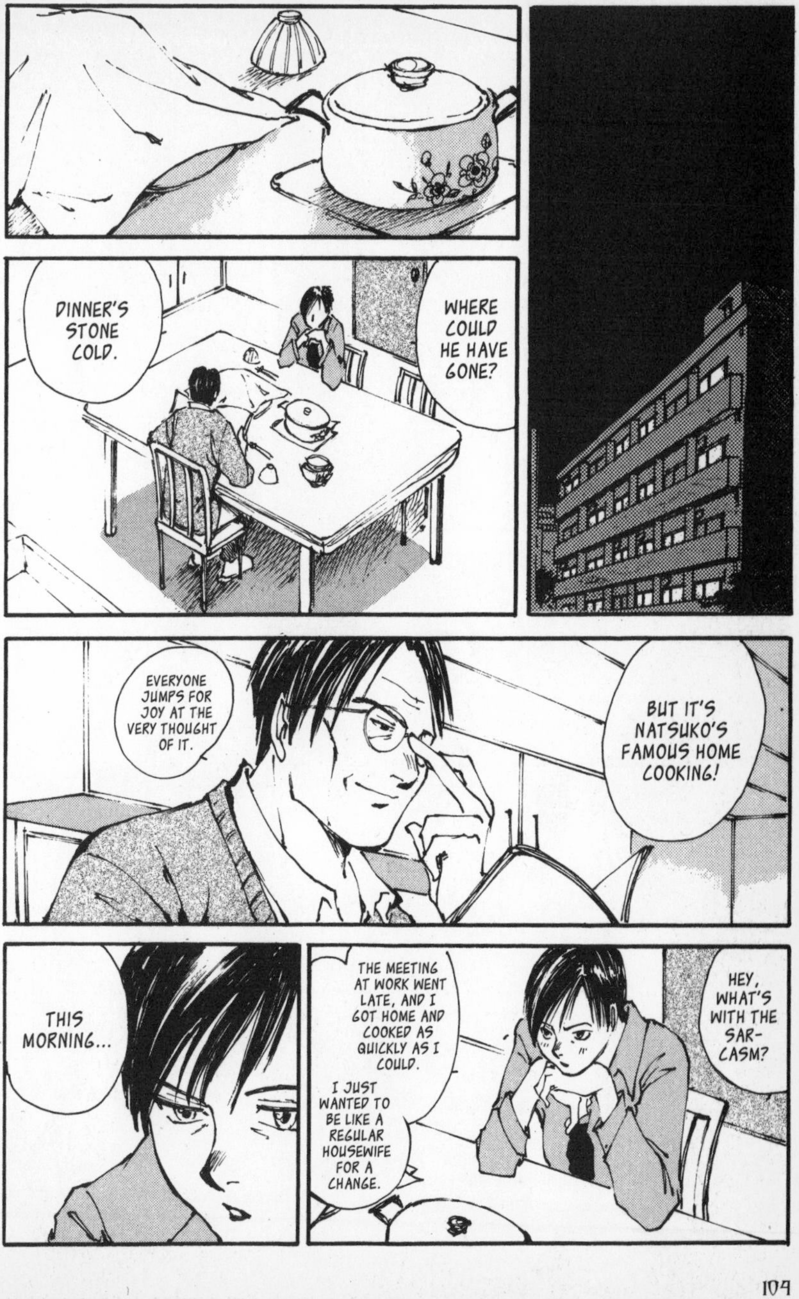
WHERE COULD HE HAVE GONE?
DINNER'S STONE COLD.
BUT IT'S NATSUKO'S FAMOUS HOME COOKING!
EVERYONE JUMPS FOR JOY AT THE VERY THOUGHT OF IT.
HEY, WHAT'S WITH THE SAR-CASM?
THE MEETING AT WORK WENT LATE, AND I GOT HOME AND COOKED AS QUICKLY AS I COULD.
I JUST WANTED TO BE LIKE A REGULAR HOUSEWIFE FOR A CHANGE.
THIS MORNING...

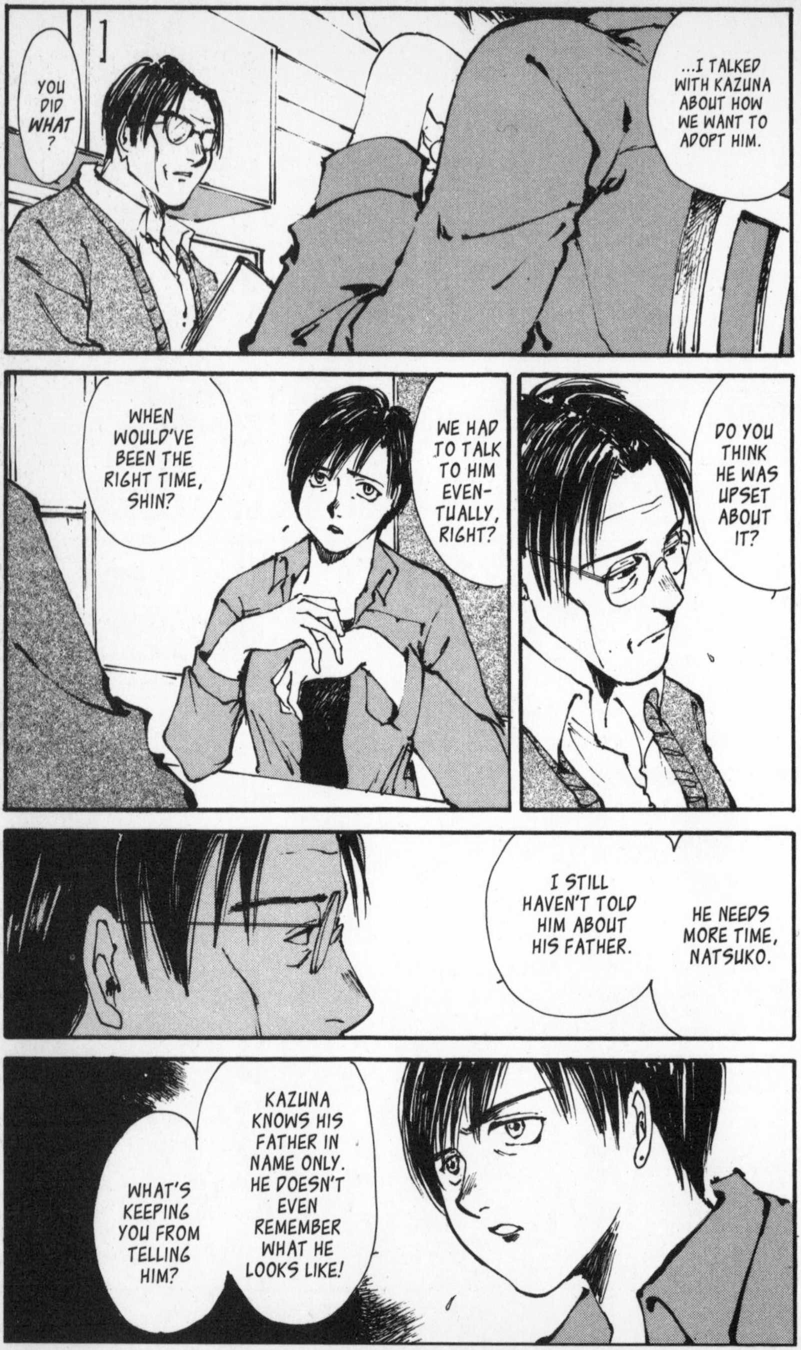
...I TALKED WITH KAZUNA ABOUT HOW WE WANT TO ADOPT HIM.
YOU DID *WHAT*?
DO YOU THINK HE WAS UPSET ABOUT IT?
WE HAD TO TALK TO HIM EVENTUALLY, RIGHT?
WHEN WOULD'VE BEEN THE RIGHT TIME, SHIN?
I STILL HAVEN'T TOLD HIM ABOUT HIS FATHER.
HE NEEDS MORE TIME, NATSUKO.
KAZUNA KNOWS HIS FATHER IN NAME ONLY. HE DOESN'T EVEN REMEMBER WHAT HE LOOKS LIKE!
WHAT'S KEEPING YOU FROM TELLING HIM?

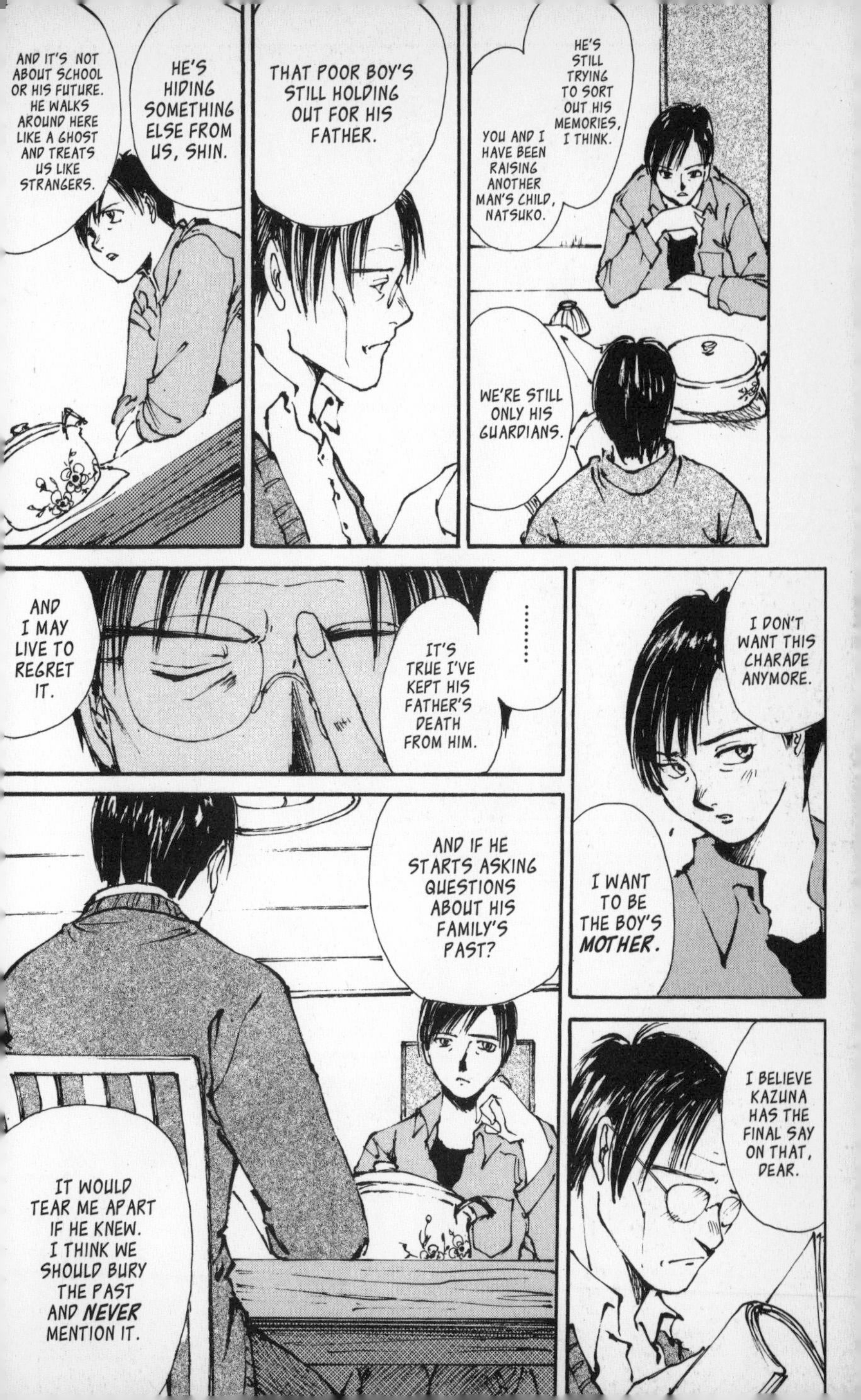

HE'S STILL TRYING TO SORT OUT HIS MEMORIES, I THINK.
YOU AND I HAVE BEEN RAISING ANOTHER MAN'S CHILD, NATSUKO.
WE'RE STILL ONLY HIS GUARDIANS.
THAT POOR BOY'S STILL HOLDING OUT FOR HIS FATHER.
HE'S HIDING SOMETHING ELSE FROM US, SHIN.
AND IT'S NOT ABOUT SCHOOL OR HIS FUTURE. HE WALKS AROUND HERE LIKE A GHOST AND TREATS US LIKE STRANGERS.
I DON'T WANT THIS CHARADE ANYMORE.
I WANT TO BE THE BOY'S MOTHER.
......
IT'S TRUE I'VE KEPT HIS FATHER'S DEATH FROM HIM.
AND I MAY LIVE TO REGRET IT.
I BELIEVE KAZUNA HAS THE FINAL SAY ON THAT, DEAR.
AND IF HE STARTS ASKING QUESTIONS ABOUT HIS FAMILY'S PAST?
IT WOULD TEAR ME APART IF HE KNEW. I THINK WE SHOULD BURY THE PAST AND NEVER MENTION IT.

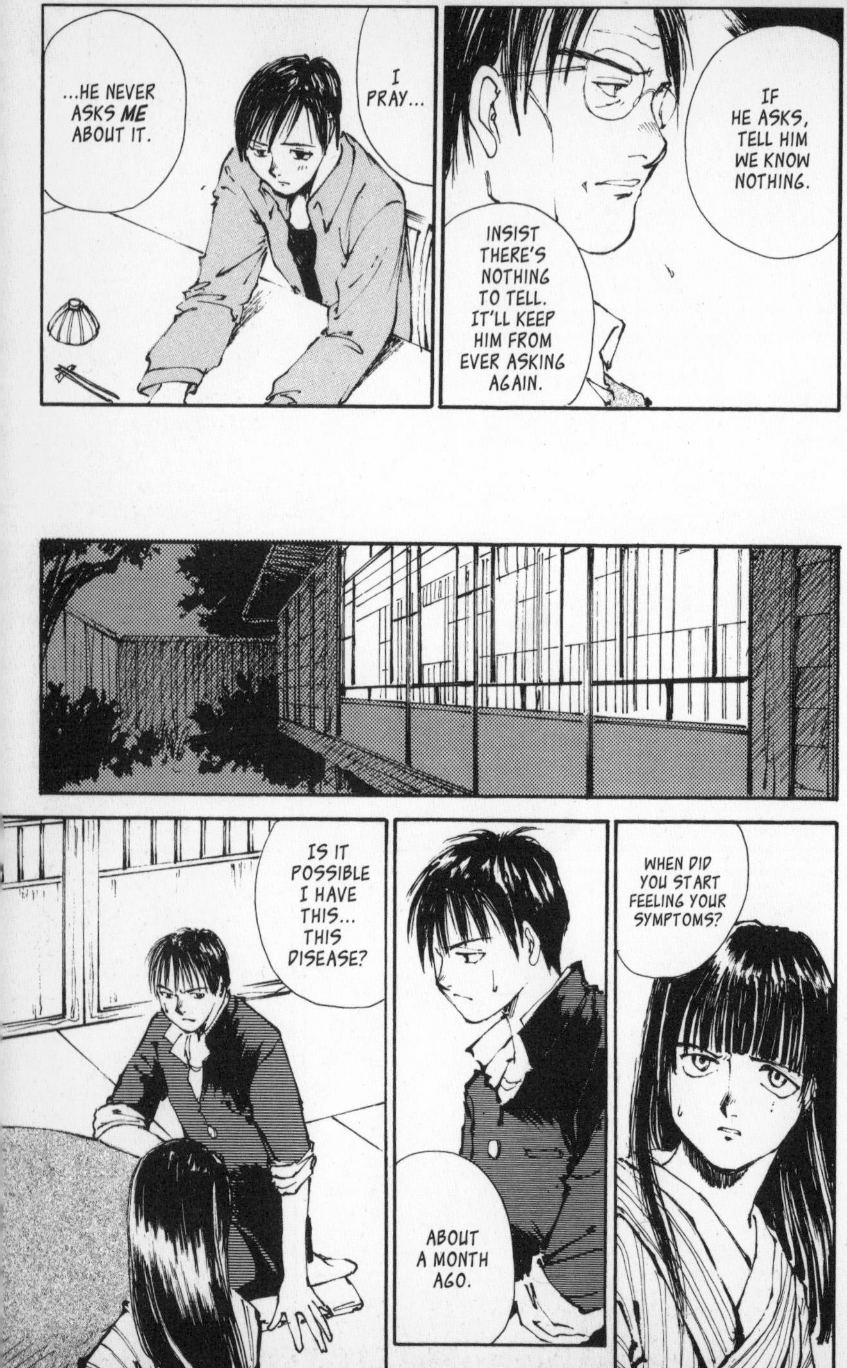
IF HE ASKS, TELL HIM WE KNOW NOTHING.
INSIST THERE'S NOTHING TO TELL. IT'LL KEEP HIM FROM EVER ASKING AGAIN.
I PRAY...
...HE NEVER ASKS *ME* ABOUT IT.
WHEN DID YOU START FEELING YOUR SYMPTOMS?
ABOUT A MONTH AGO.
IS IT POSSIBLE I HAVE THIS... THIS DISEASE?

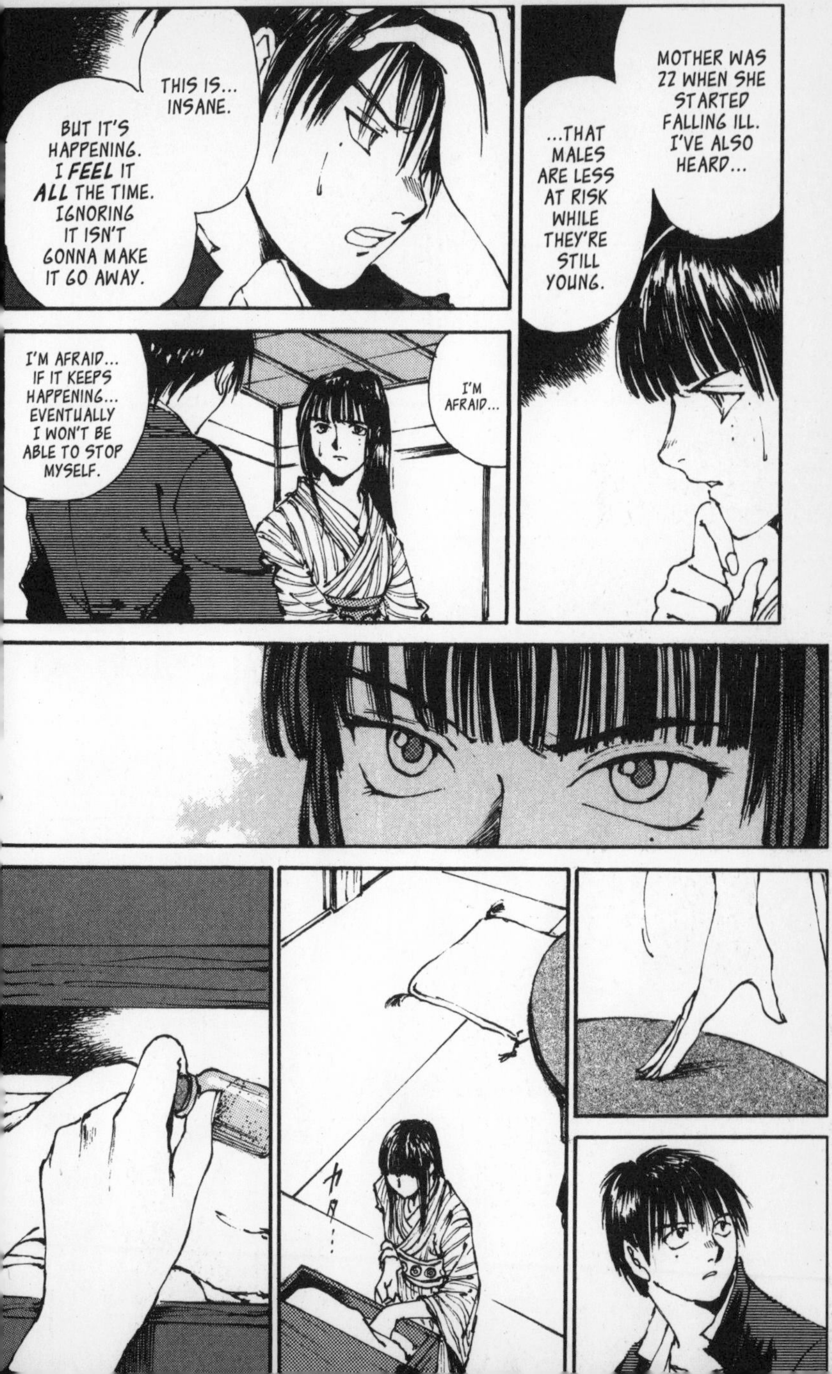
MOTHER WAS 22 WHEN SHE STARTED FALLING ILL. I'VE ALSO HEARD...
...THAT MALES ARE LESS AT RISK WHILE THEY'RE STILL YOUNG.
THIS IS... INSANE.
BUT IT'S HAPPENING. I FEEL IT ALL THE TIME. IGNORING IT ISN'T GONNA MAKE IT GO AWAY.
I'M AFRAID...
I'M AFRAID... IF IT KEEPS HAPPENING... EVENTUALLY I WON'T BE ABLE TO STOP MYSELF.

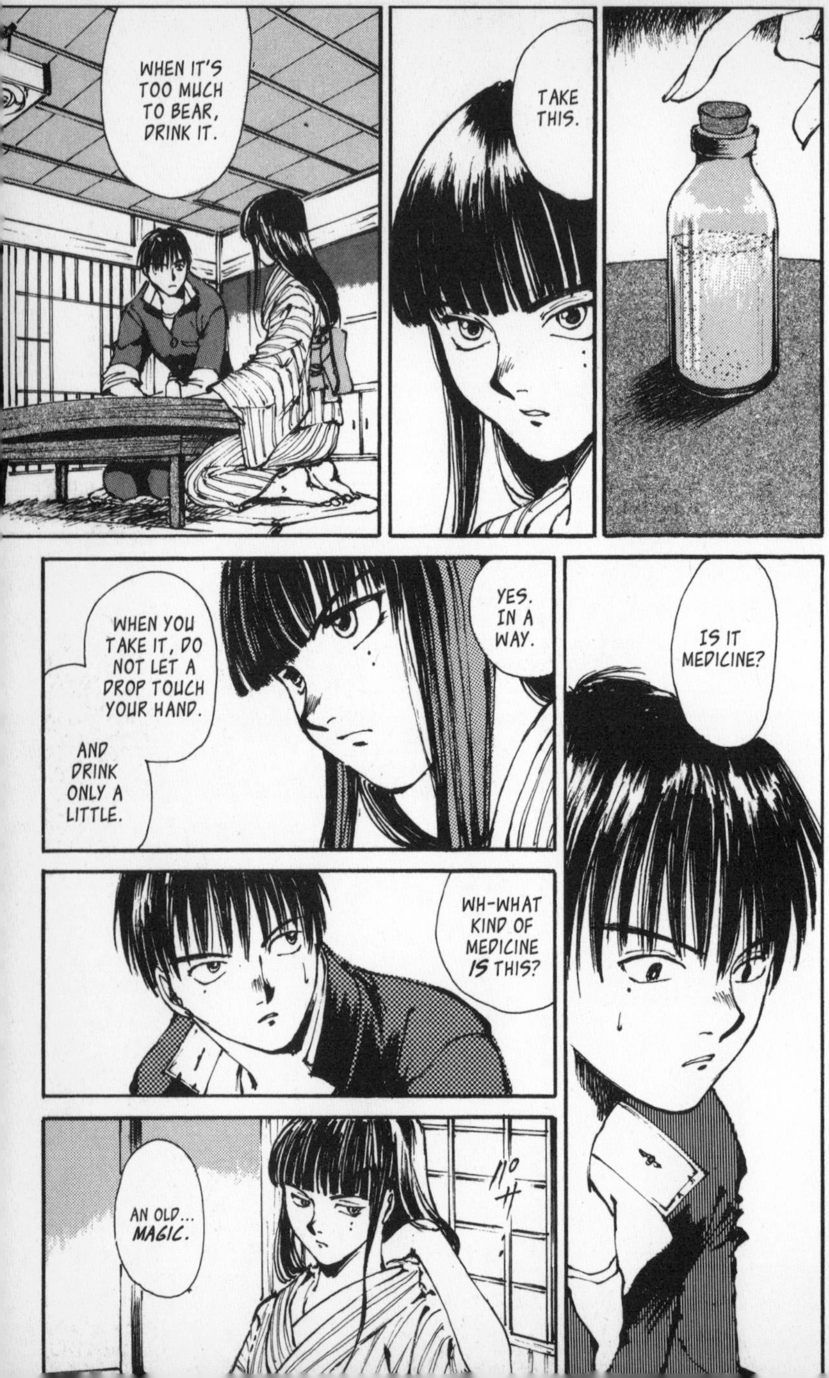
TAKE THIS.
WHEN IT'S TOO MUCH TO BEAR, DRINK IT.
IS IT MEDICINE?
YES. IN A WAY.
WHEN YOU TAKE IT, DO NOT LET A DROP TOUCH YOUR HAND.
AND DRINK ONLY A LITTLE.
WH-WHAT KIND OF MEDICINE *IS* THIS?
AN OLD... **MAGIC.**

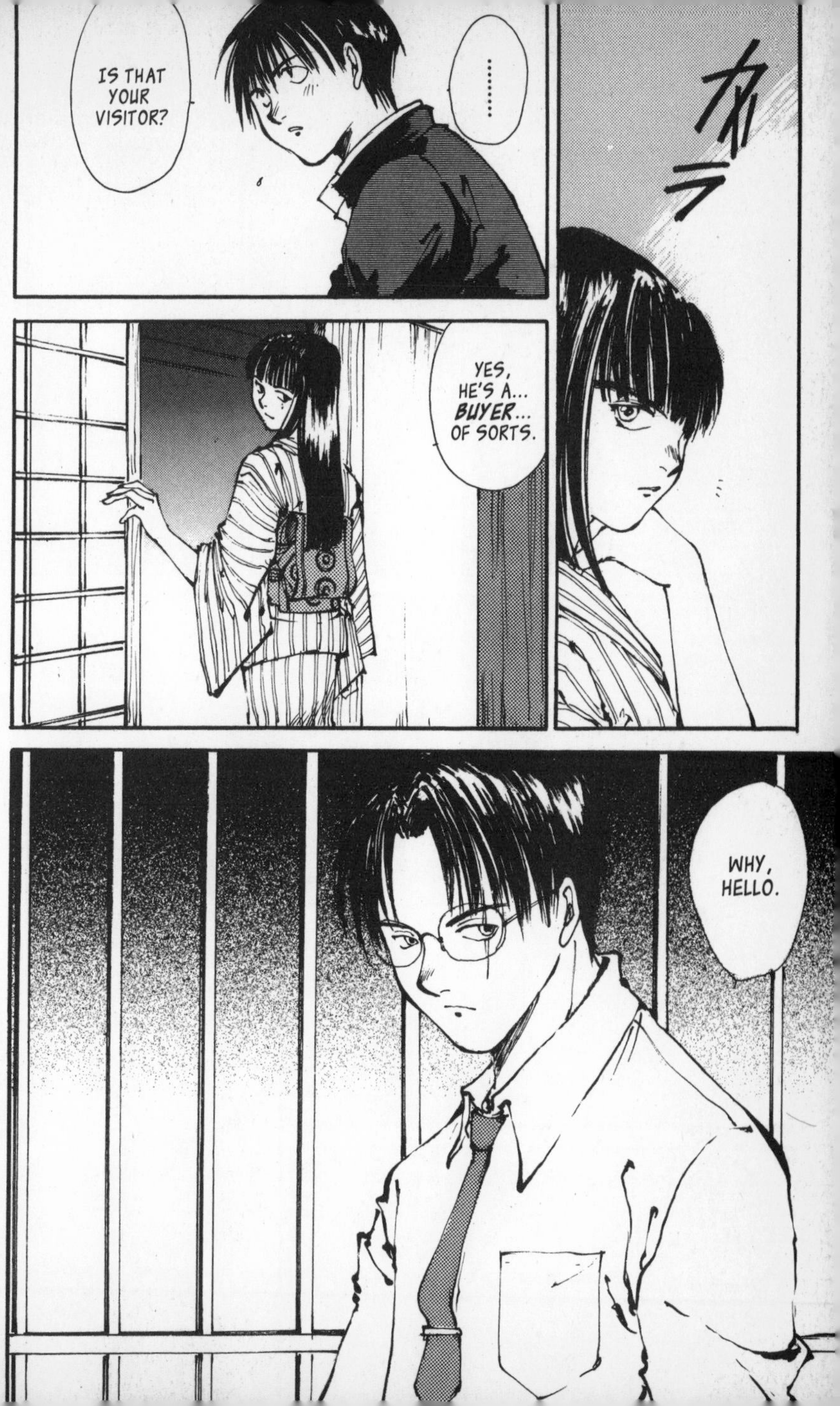

カラ
....
IS THAT YOUR VISITOR?
YES, HE'S A... ***BUYER***... OF SORTS.
WHY, HELLO.

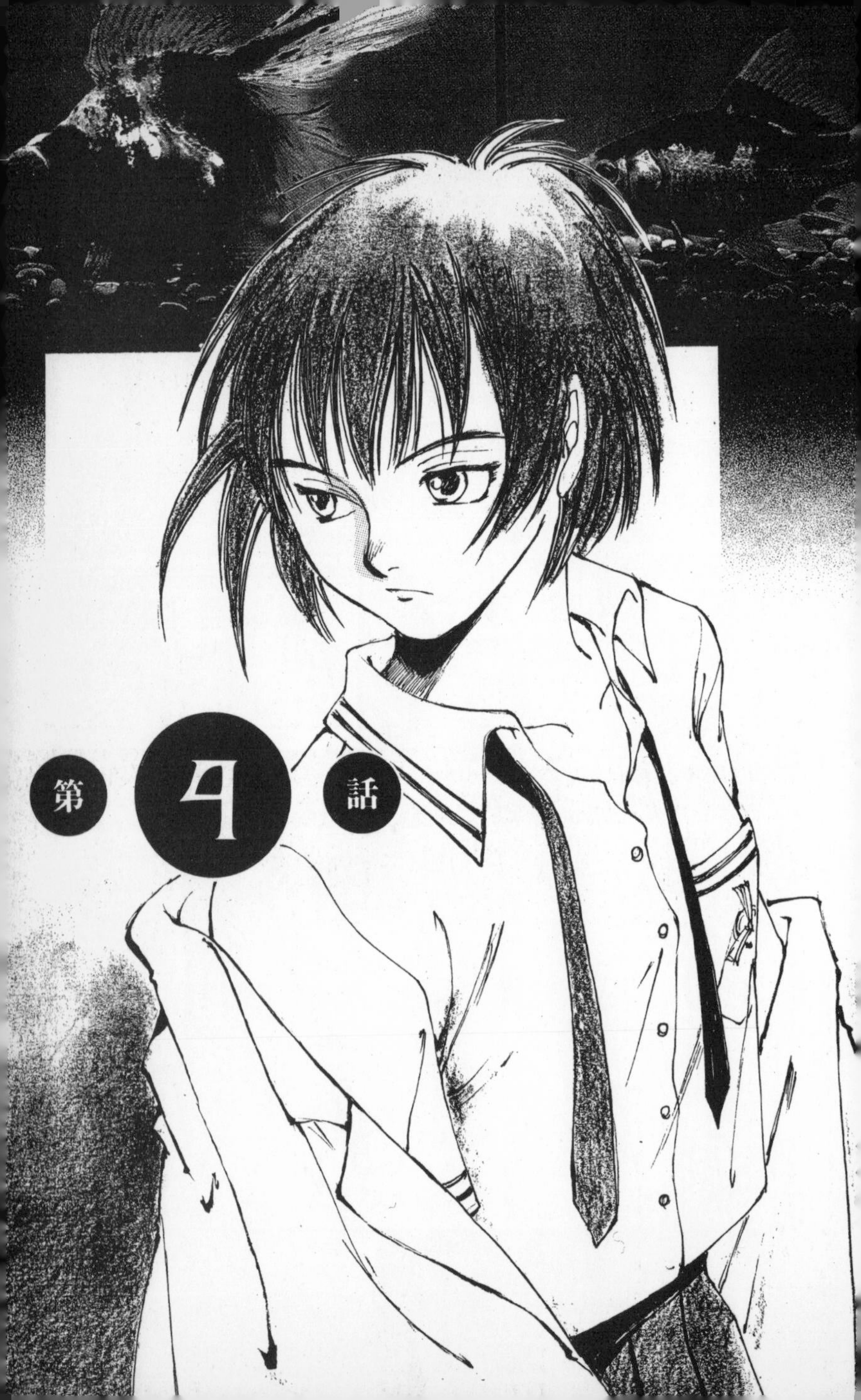
第4話

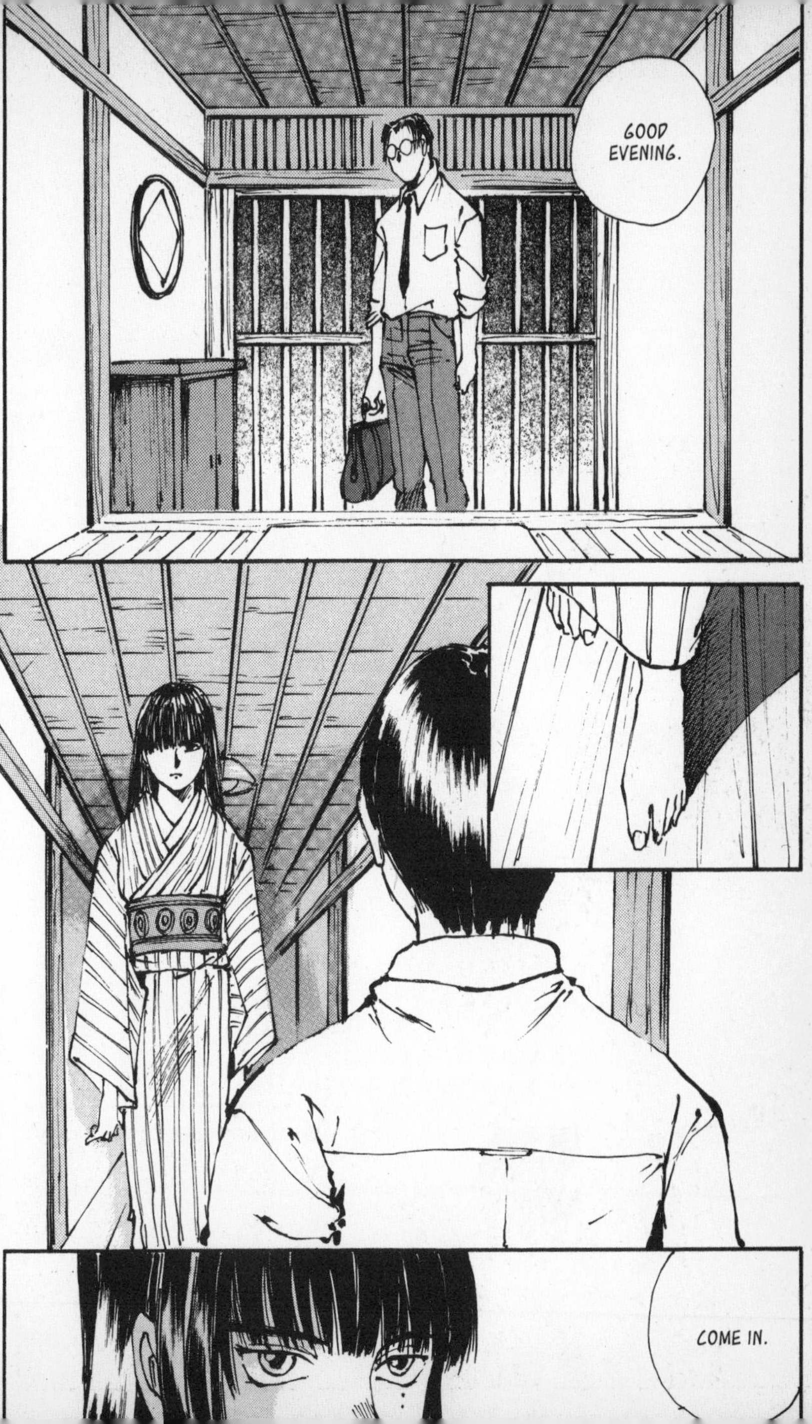
GOOD EVENING.
COME IN.

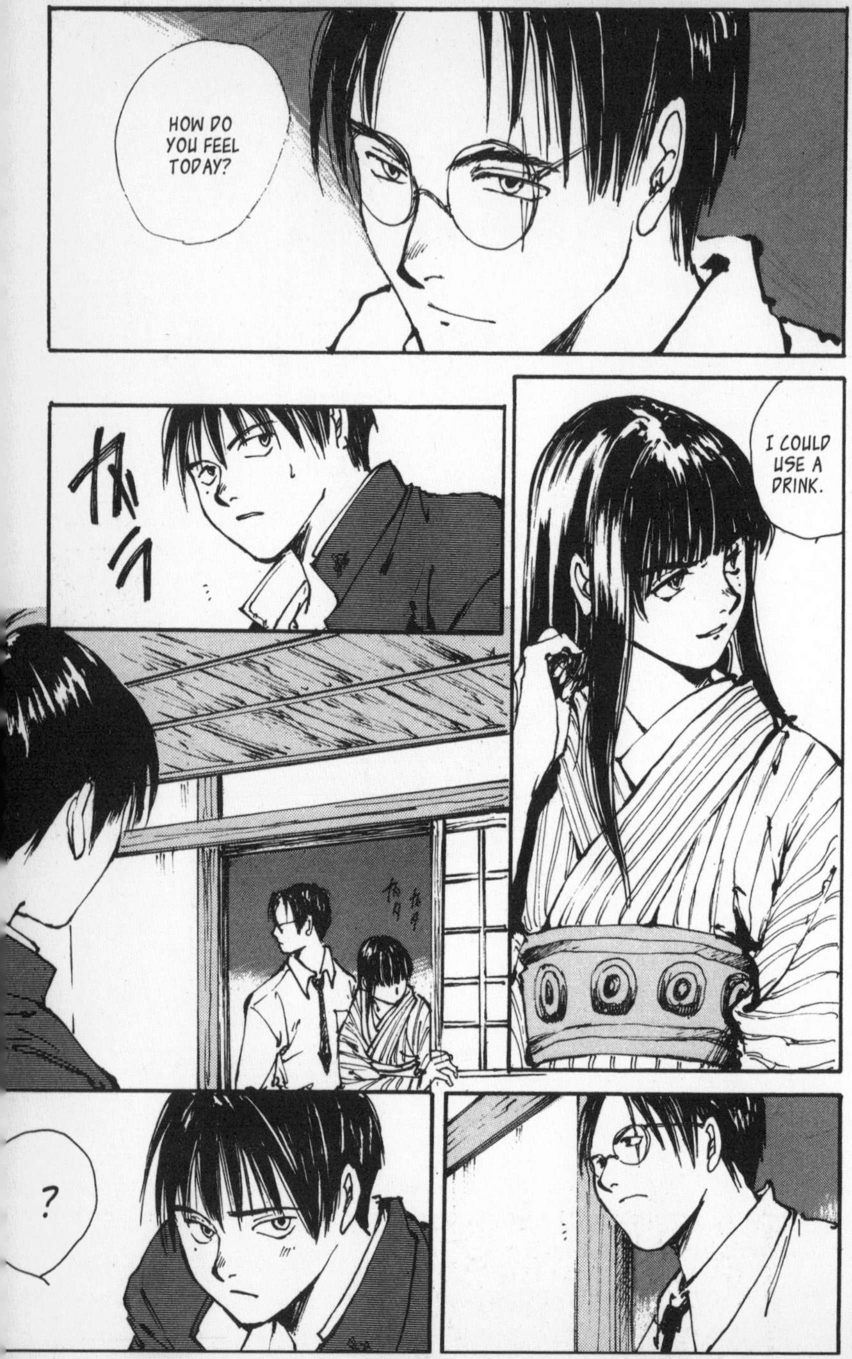
HOW DO YOU FEEL TODAY?
I COULD USE A DRINK.
?

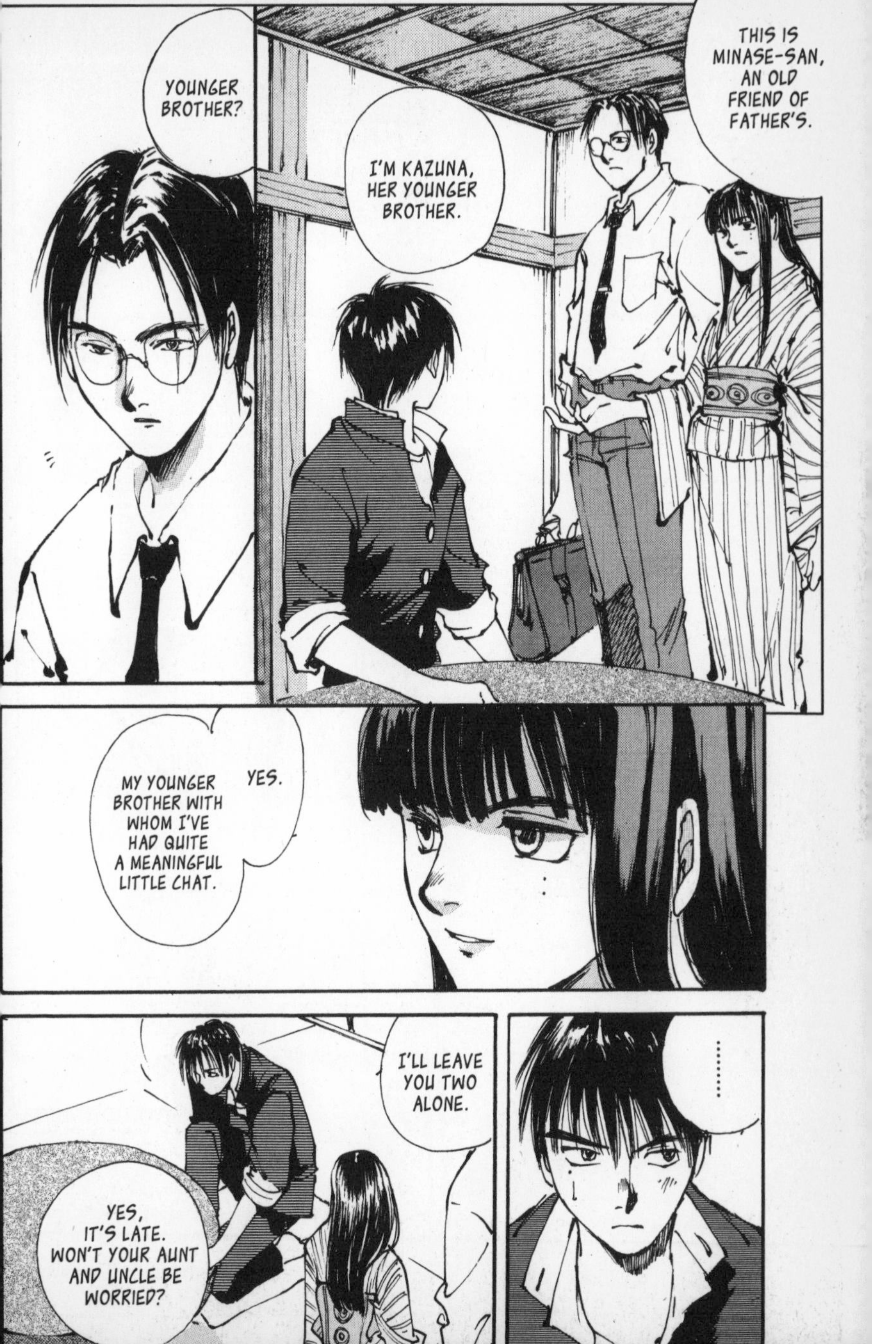
THIS IS MINASE-SAN, AN OLD FRIEND OF FATHER'S.
I'M KAZUNA, HER YOUNGER BROTHER.
YOUNGER BROTHER?
YES.
MY YOUNGER BROTHER WITH WHOM I'VE HAD QUITE A MEANINGFUL LITTLE CHAT.
......
I'LL LEAVE YOU TWO ALONE.
YES, IT'S LATE. WON'T YOUR AUNT AND UNCLE BE WORRIED?

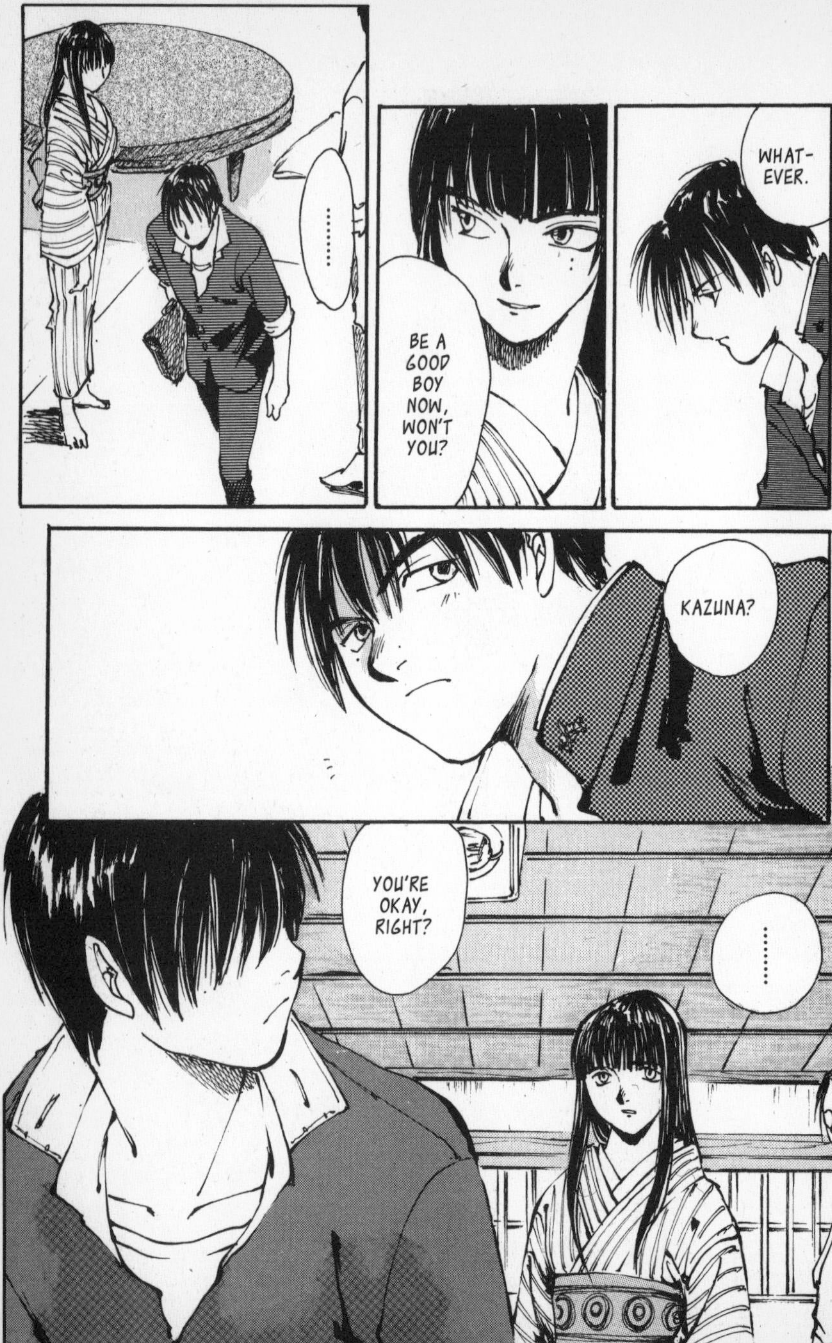
WHAT-EVER.
BE A GOOD BOY NOW, WON'T YOU?
......
KAZUNA?
YOU'RE OKAY, RIGHT?
......

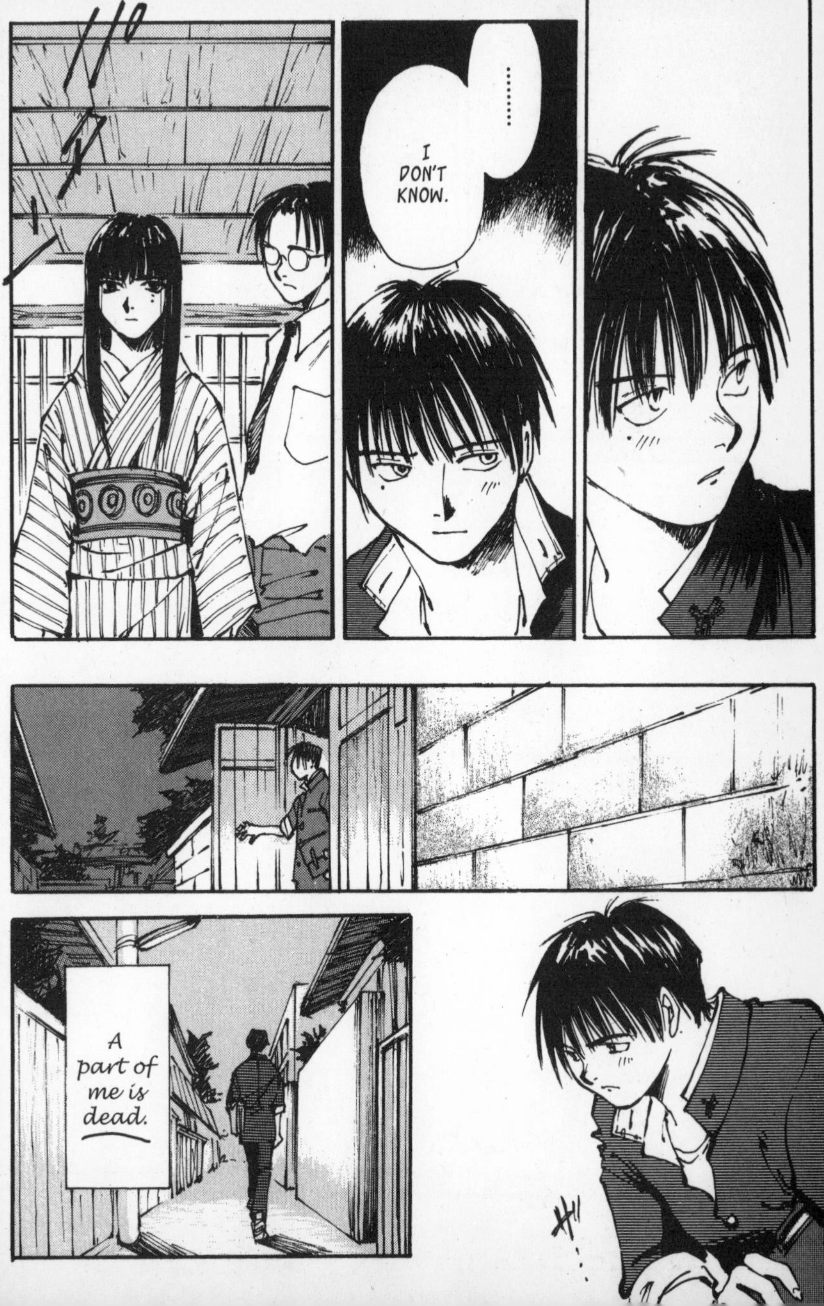

......
I DON'T KNOW.
A part of me is dead.

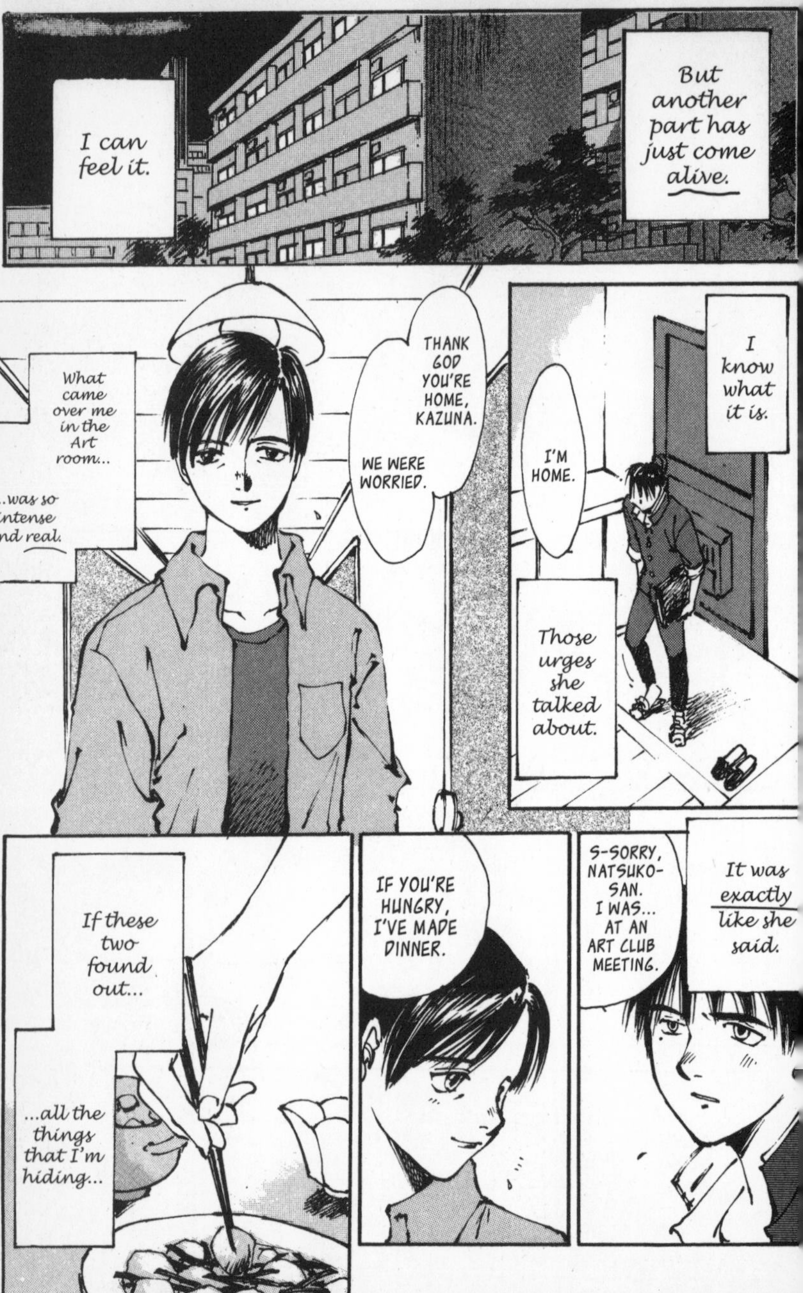

But another part has just come alive.
I can feel it.
I know what it is.
I'M HOME.
Those urges she talked about.
THANK GOD YOU'RE HOME, KAZUNA.
WE WERE WORRIED.
What came over me in the Art room...
...was so intense and real.
It was exactly like she said.
S-SORRY, NATSUKO-SAN. I WAS... AT AN ART CLUB MEETING.
IF YOU'RE HUNGRY, I'VE MADE DINNER.
If these two found out...
...all the things that I'm hiding...

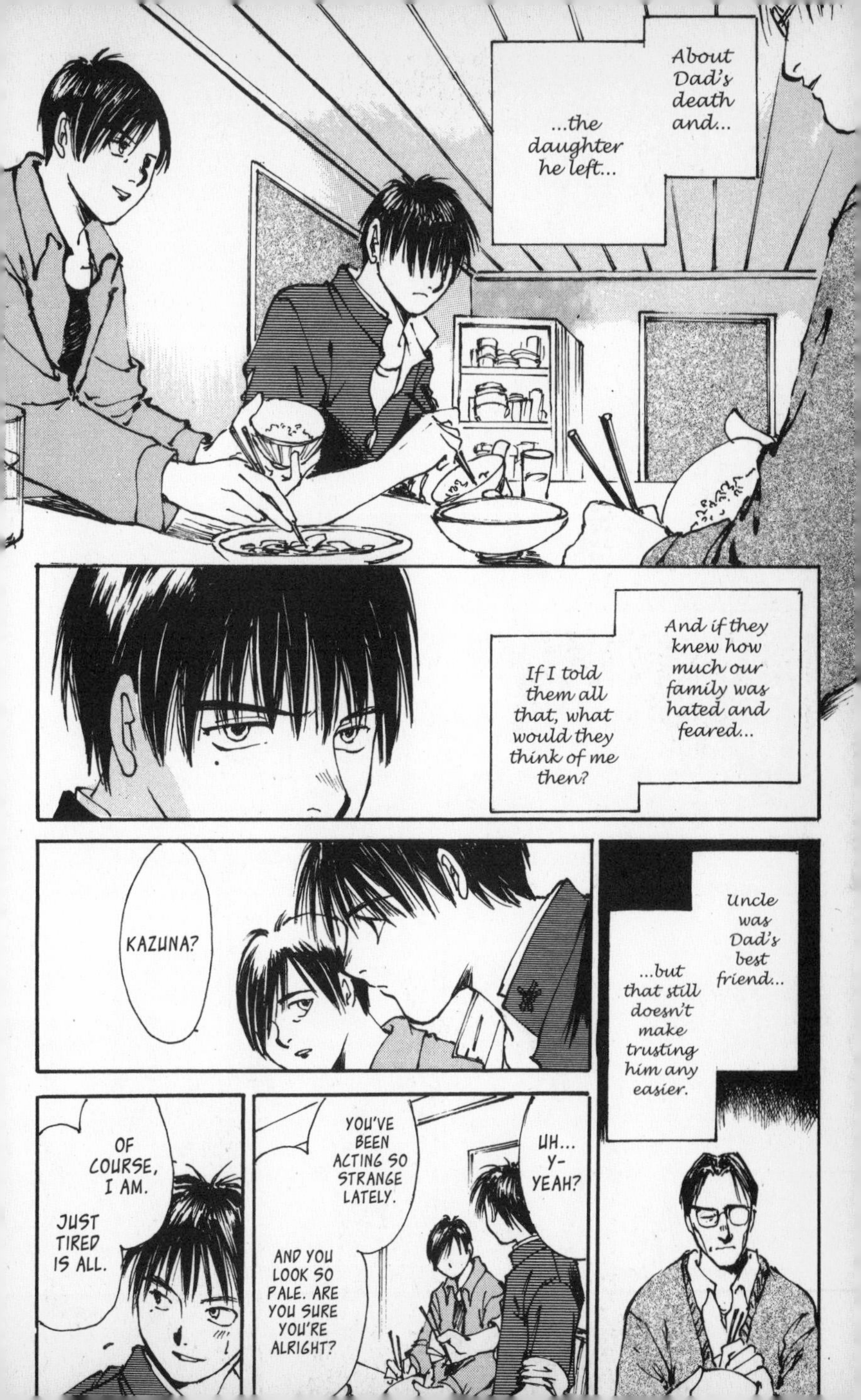
About Dad's death and...
...the daughter he left...
And if they knew how much our family was hated and feared...
If I told them all that, what would they think of me then?
Uncle was Dad's best friend...
...but that still doesn't make trusting him any easier.
KAZUNA?
UH... Y-YEAH?
YOU'VE BEEN ACTING SO STRANGE LATELY.
AND YOU LOOK SO PALE. ARE YOU SURE YOU'RE ALRIGHT?
OF COURSE, I AM.
JUST TIRED IS ALL.

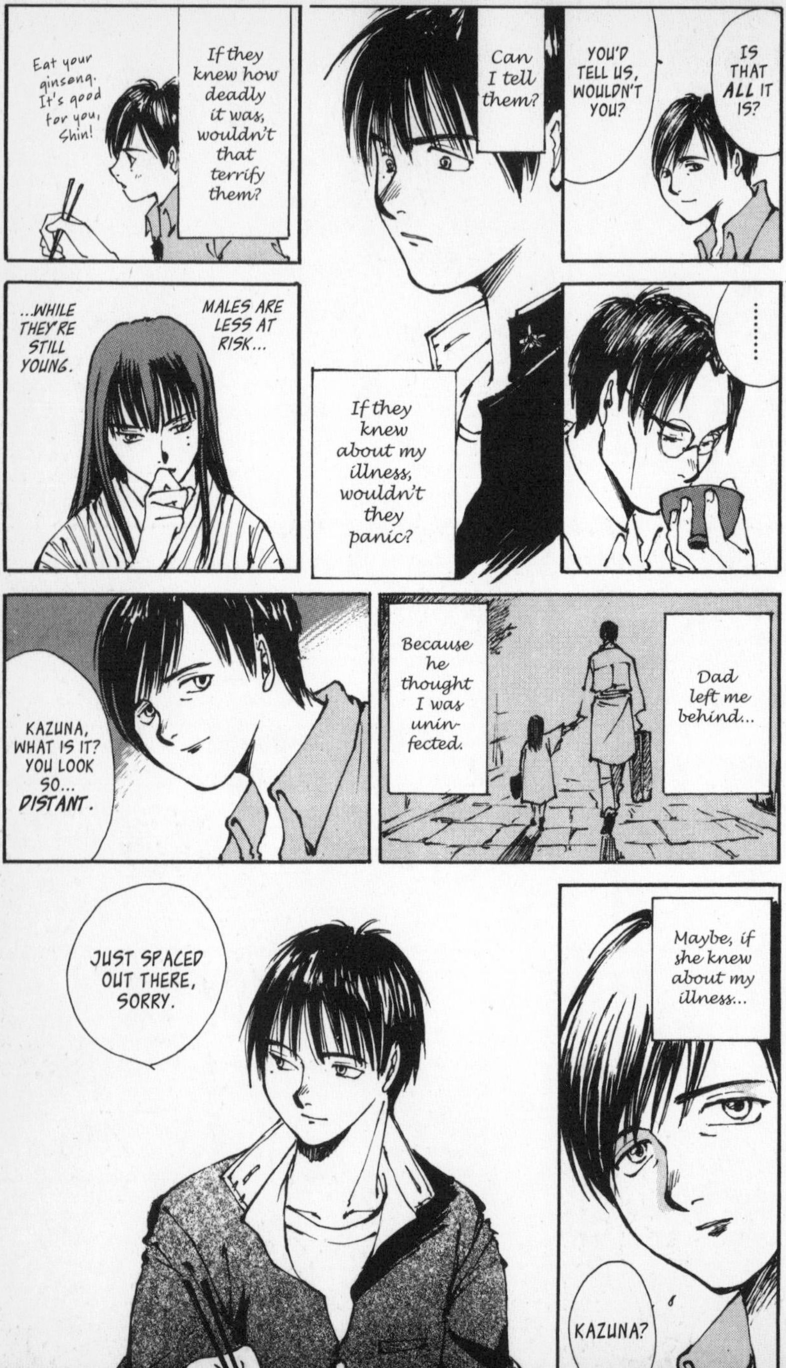
IS THAT ALL IT IS?
YOU'D TELL US, WOULDN'T YOU?
Can I tell them?
If they knew how deadly it was, wouldn't that terrify them?
Eat your ginseng. It's good for you, Shin!
......
If they knew about my illness, wouldn't they panic?
MALES ARE LESS AT RISK...
...WHILE THEY'RE STILL YOUNG.
Dad left me behind...
Because he thought I was unin-fected.
KAZUNA, WHAT IS IT? YOU LOOK SO... DISTANT.
Maybe, if she knew about my illness...
KAZUNA?
JUST SPACED OUT THERE, SORRY.

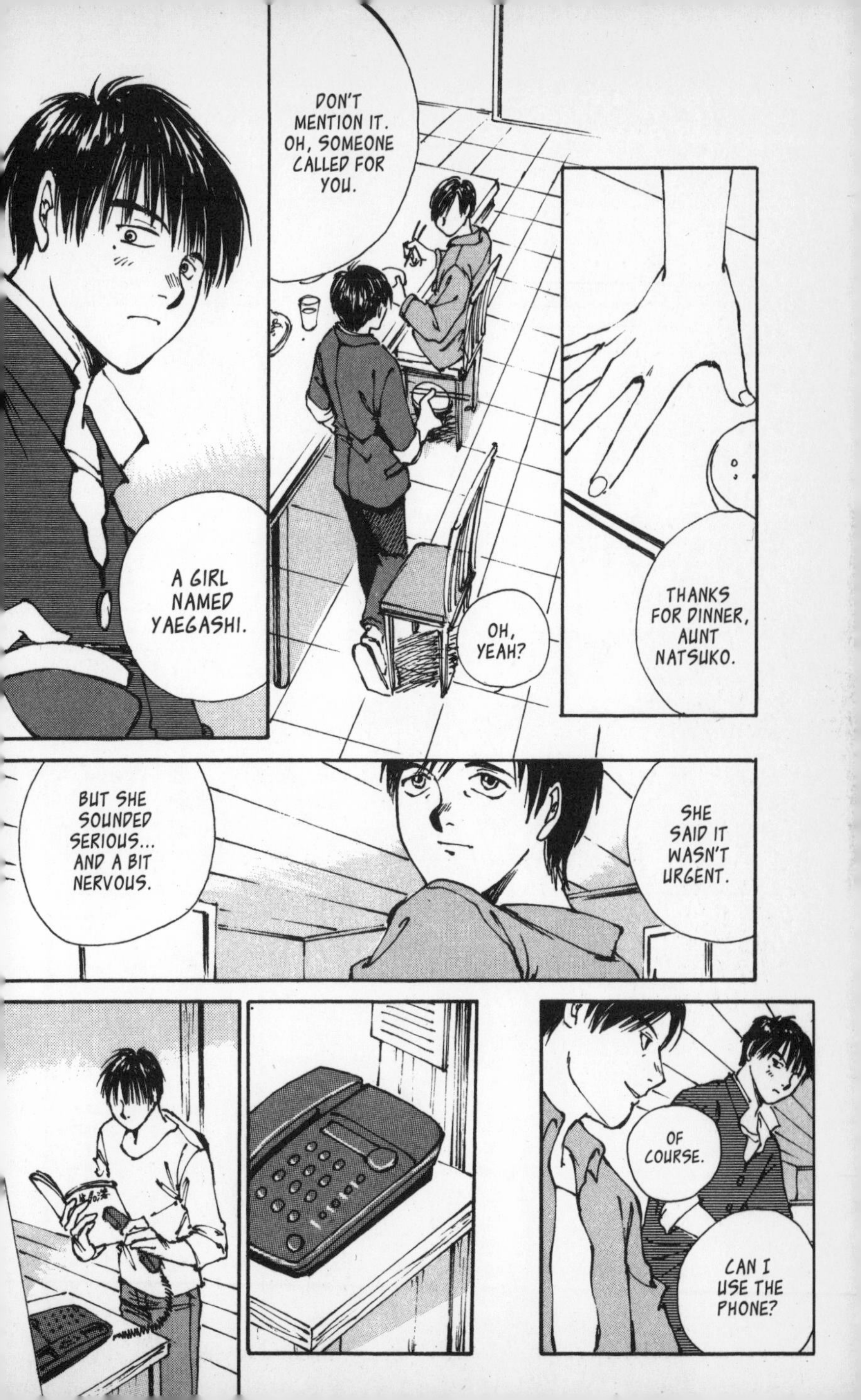
THANKS FOR DINNER, AUNT NATSUKO.
DON'T MENTION IT. OH, SOMEONE CALLED FOR YOU.
OH, YEAH?
A GIRL NAMED YAEGASHI.
SHE SAID IT WASN'T URGENT.
BUT SHE SOUNDED SERIOUS... AND A BIT NERVOUS.
CAN I USE THE PHONE?
OF COURSE.

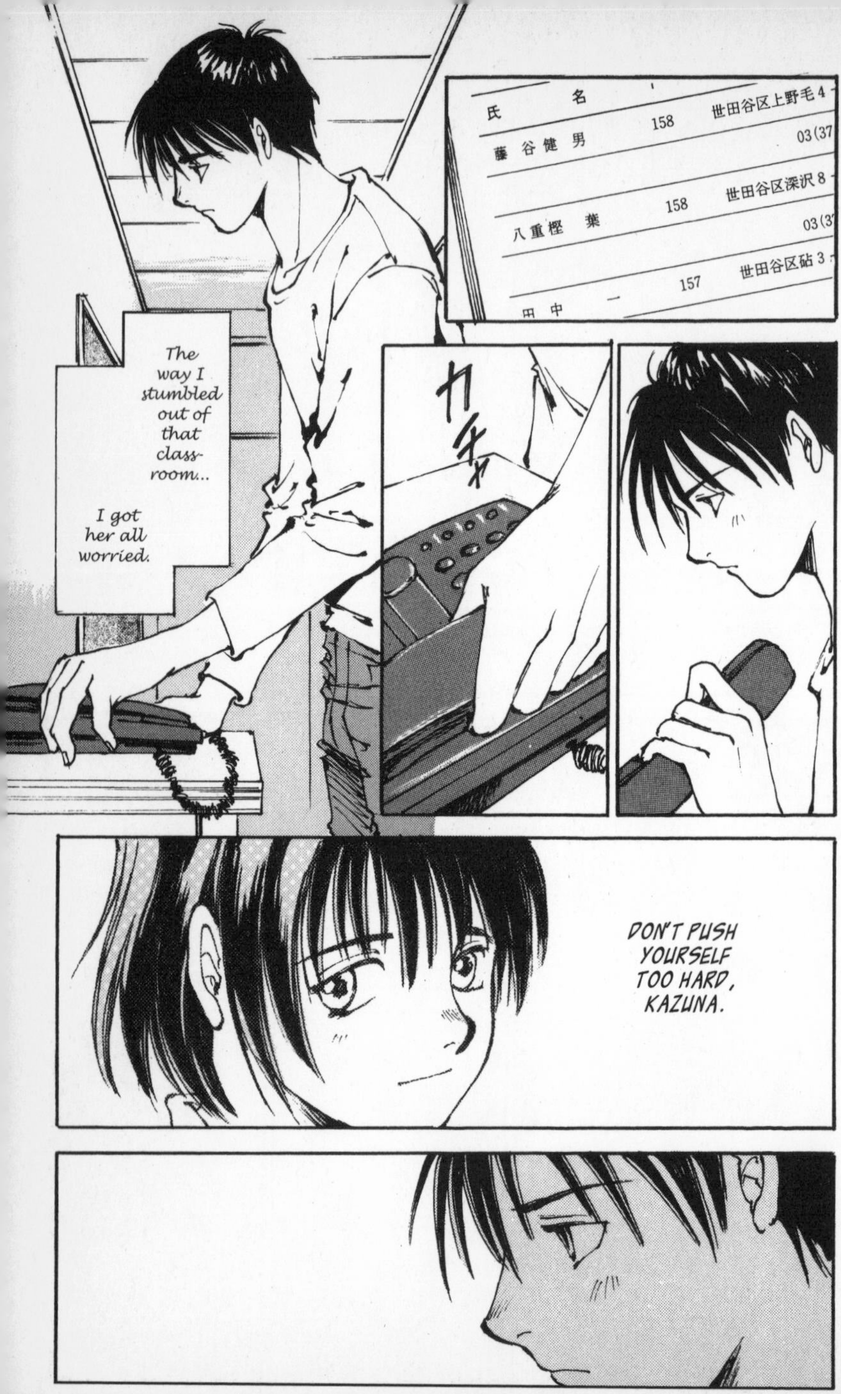
氏名
藤谷健男 158 世田谷区上野毛4-
03(37
八重樫 葉 158 世田谷区深沢8-
03(37
田中 一 157 世田谷区砧3-
カチャ
The way I stumbled out of that classroom...
I got her all worried.
DON'T PUSH YOURSELF TOO HARD, KAZUNA.

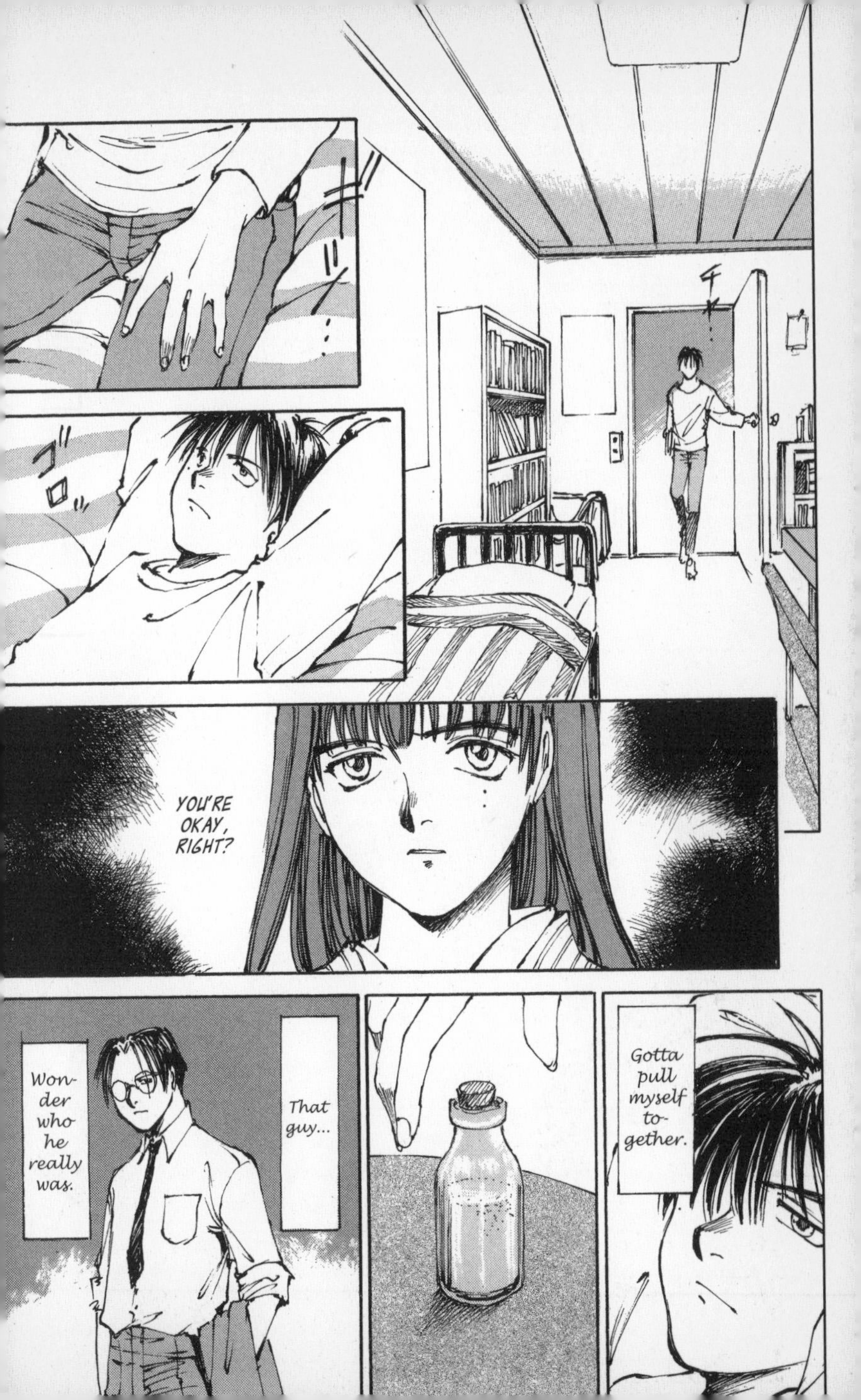
YOU'RE OKAY, RIGHT?
Gotta pull myself to-gether.
That guy...
Won-der who he really was.

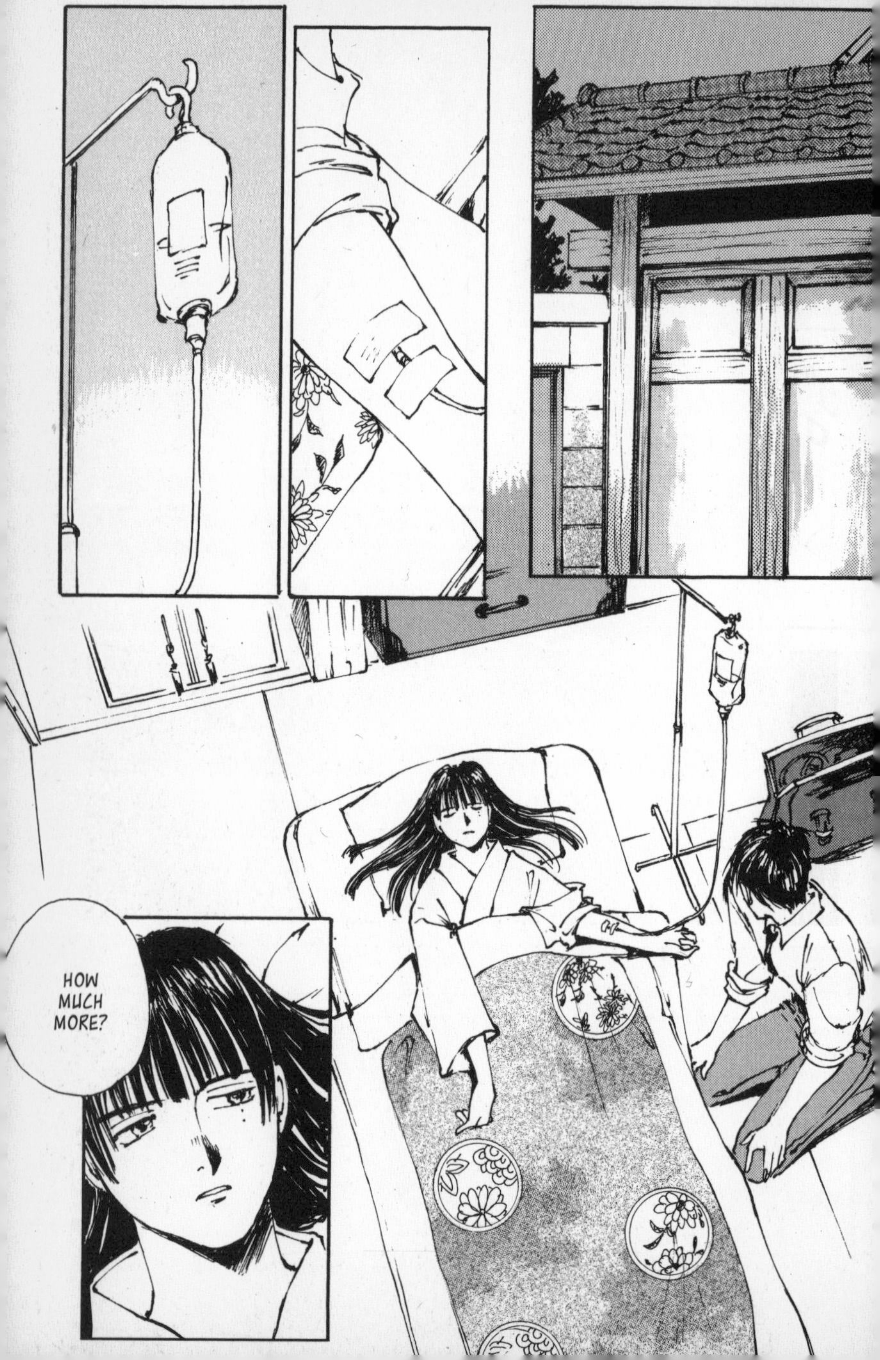
HOW MUCH MORE?

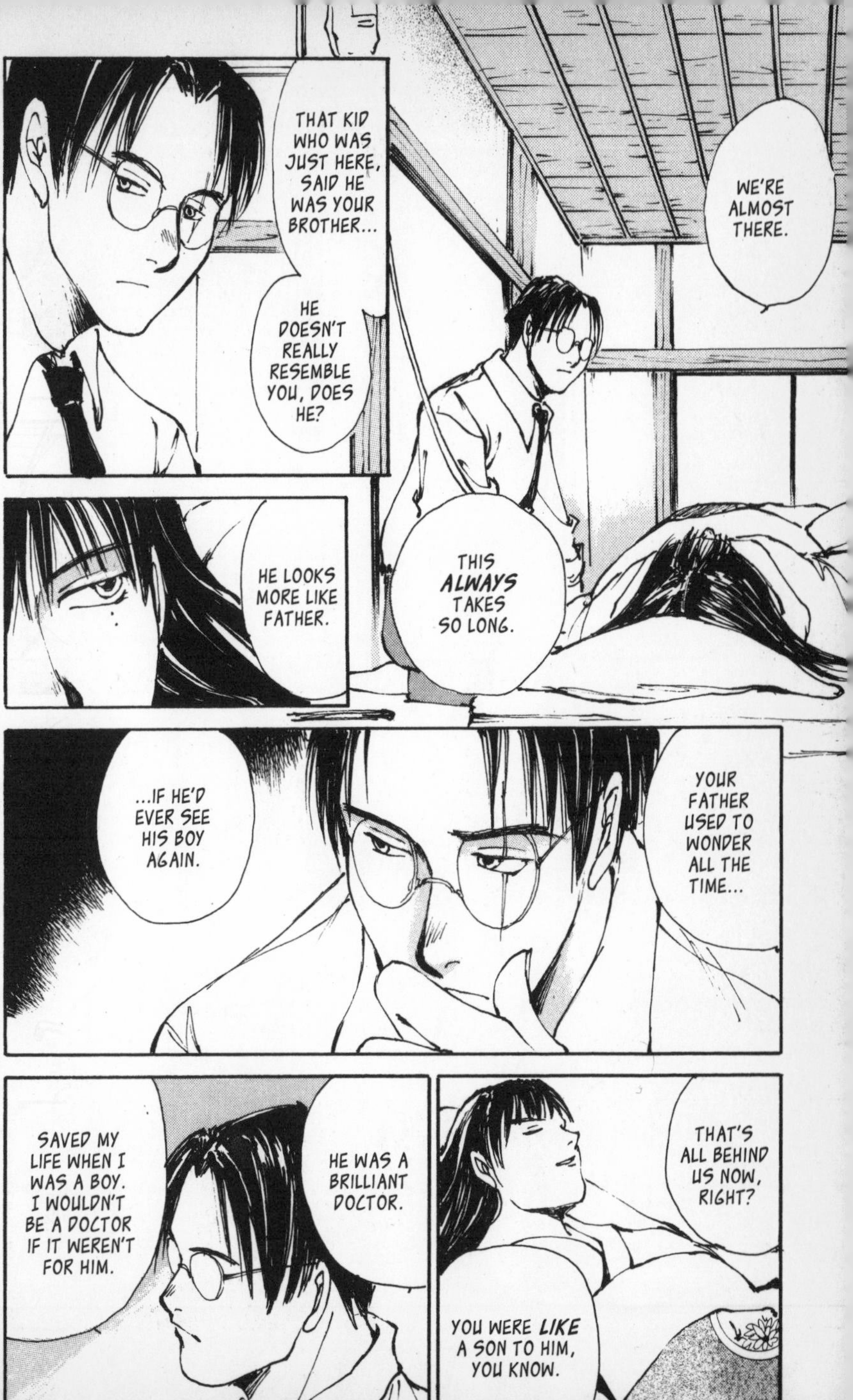
WE'RE ALMOST THERE.
THIS *ALWAYS* TAKES SO LONG.
THAT KID WHO WAS JUST HERE, SAID HE WAS YOUR BROTHER...
HE DOESN'T REALLY RESEMBLE YOU, DOES HE?
HE LOOKS MORE LIKE FATHER.
YOUR FATHER USED TO WONDER ALL THE TIME...
...IF HE'D EVER SEE HIS BOY AGAIN.
THAT'S ALL BEHIND US NOW, RIGHT?
YOU WERE *LIKE* A SON TO HIM, YOU KNOW.
HE WAS A BRILLIANT DOCTOR.
SAVED MY LIFE WHEN I WAS A BOY. I WOULDN'T BE A DOCTOR IF IT WEREN'T FOR HIM.

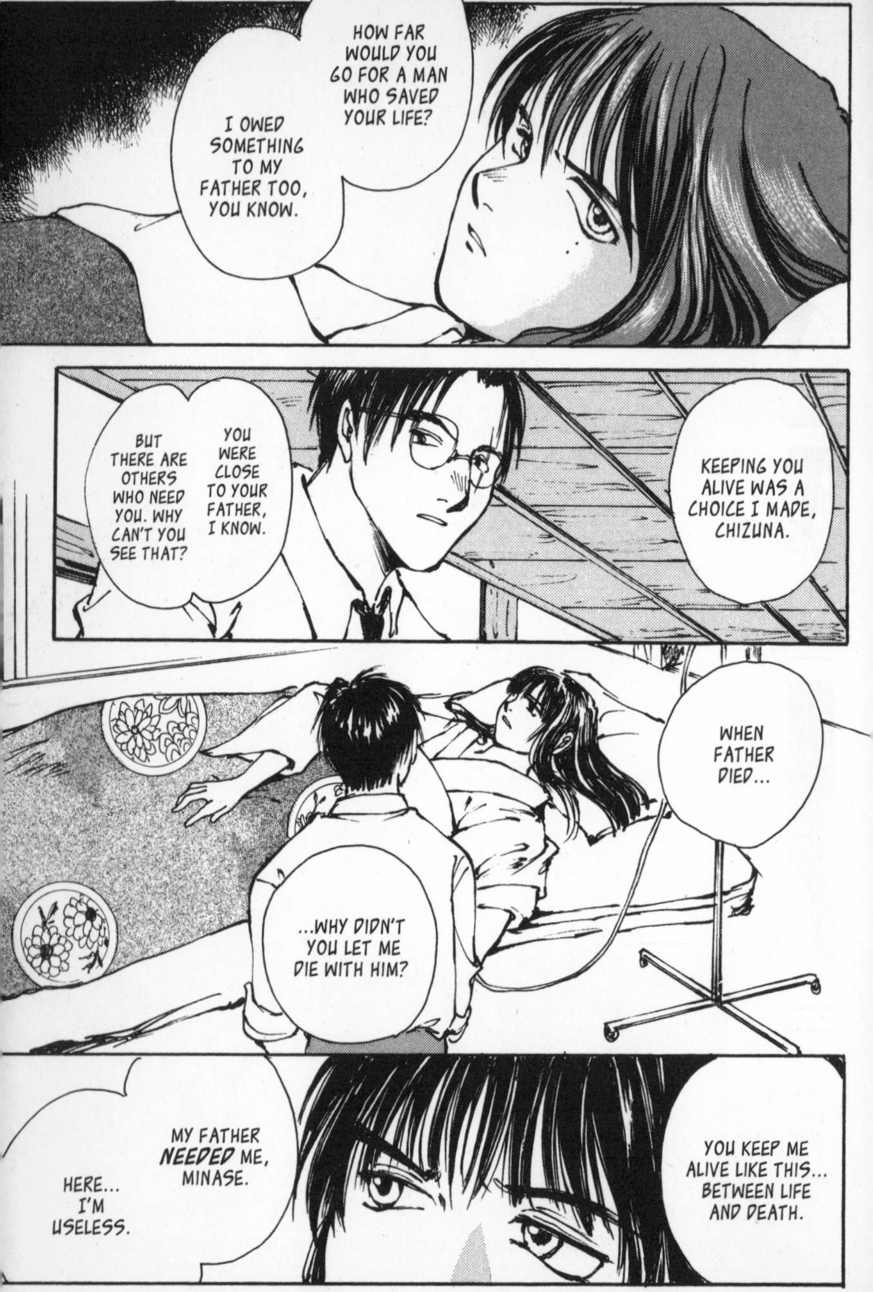
HOW FAR WOULD YOU GO FOR A MAN WHO SAVED YOUR LIFE?
I OWED SOMETHING TO MY FATHER TOO, YOU KNOW.
KEEPING YOU ALIVE WAS A CHOICE I MADE, CHIZUNA.
YOU WERE CLOSE TO YOUR FATHER, I KNOW.
BUT THERE ARE OTHERS WHO NEED YOU. WHY CAN'T YOU SEE THAT?
WHEN FATHER DIED...
...WHY DIDN'T YOU LET ME DIE WITH HIM?
YOU KEEP ME ALIVE LIKE THIS... BETWEEN LIFE AND DEATH.
MY FATHER ***NEEDED*** ME, MINASE.
HERE... I'M USELESS.

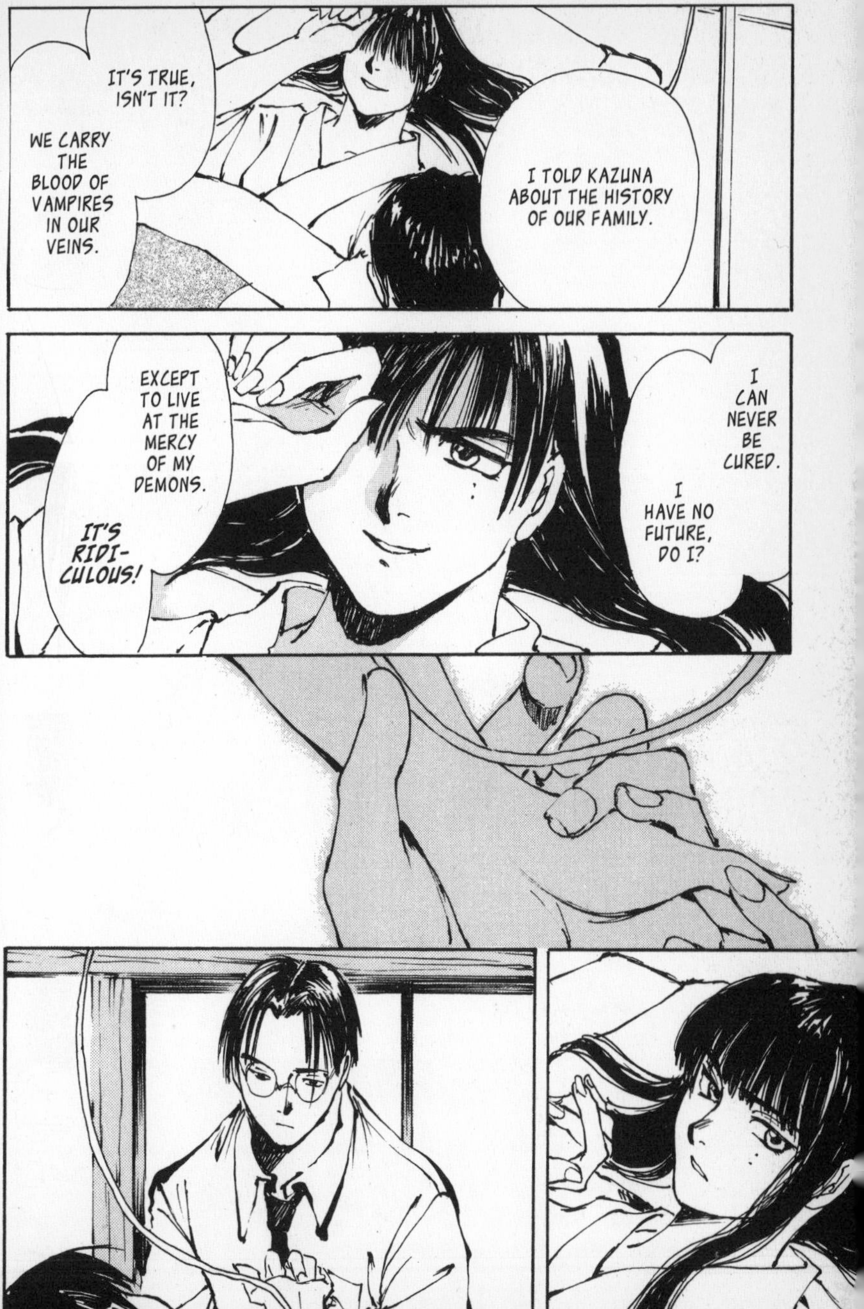
I TOLD KAZUNA ABOUT THE HISTORY OF OUR FAMILY.
IT'S TRUE, ISN'T IT?
WE CARRY THE BLOOD OF VAMPIRES IN OUR VEINS.
I CAN NEVER BE CURED.
I HAVE NO FUTURE, DO I?
EXCEPT TO LIVE AT THE MERCY OF MY DEMONS.
IT'S RIDI-CULOUS!

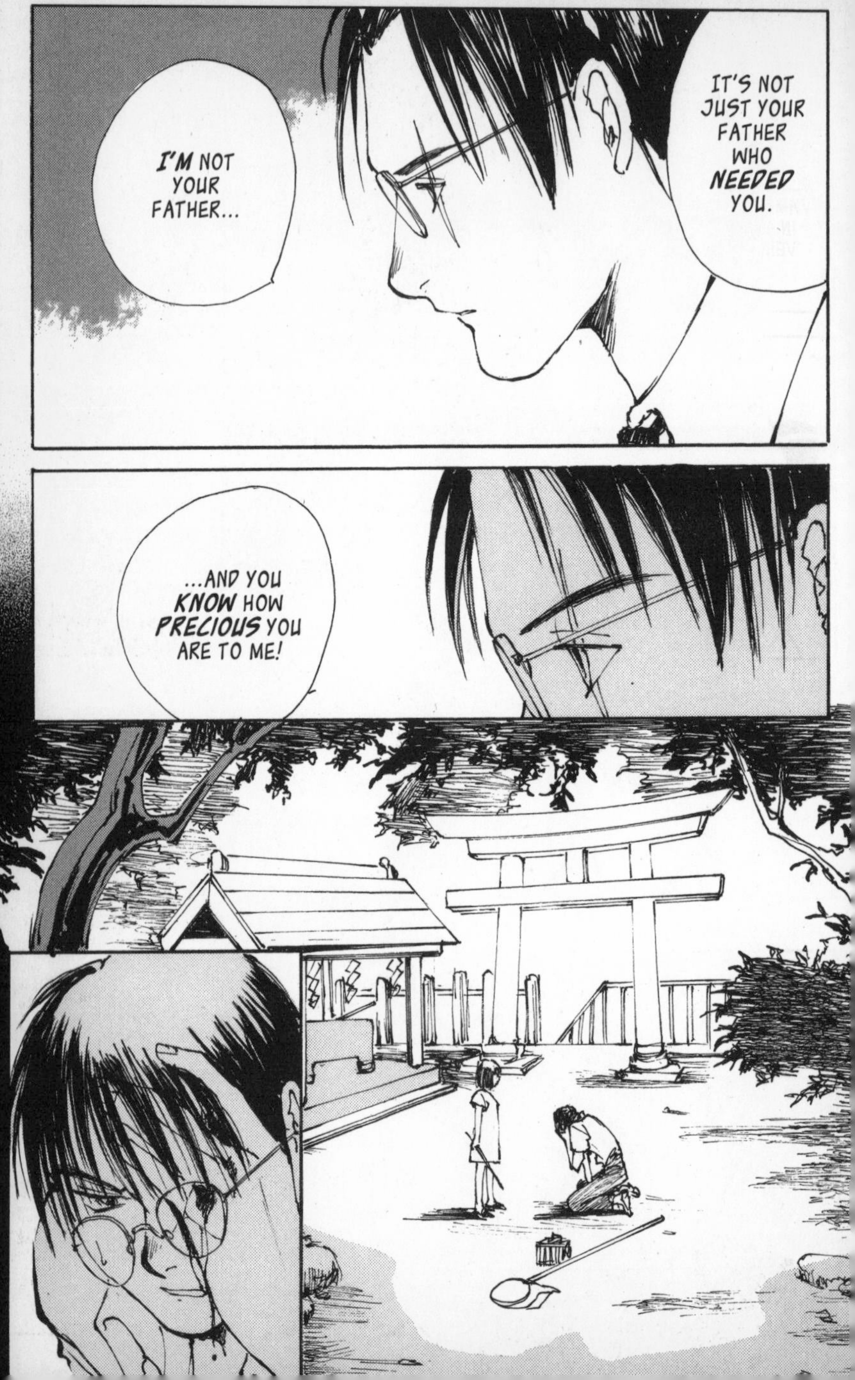
IT'S NOT JUST YOUR FATHER WHO NEEDED YOU.
I'M NOT YOUR FATHER...
...AND YOU KNOW HOW PRECIOUS YOU ARE TO ME!

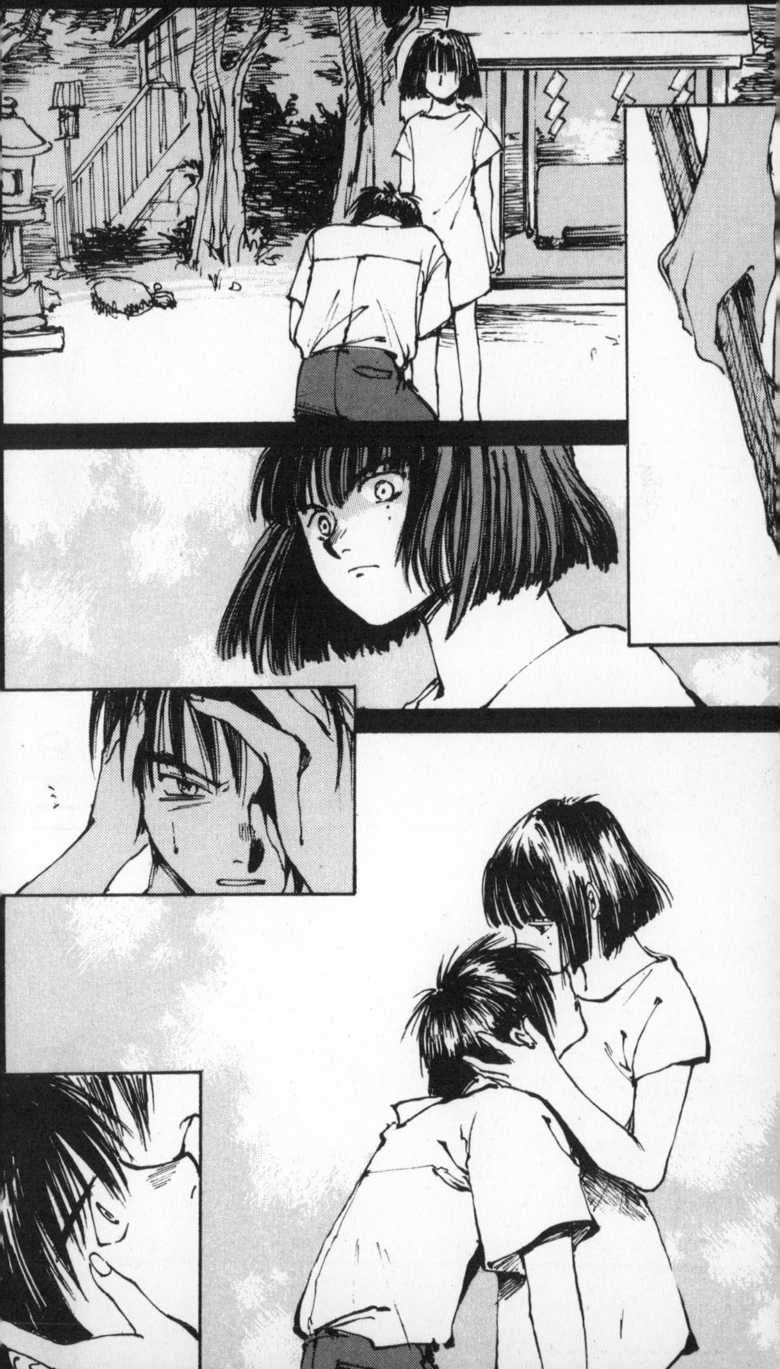

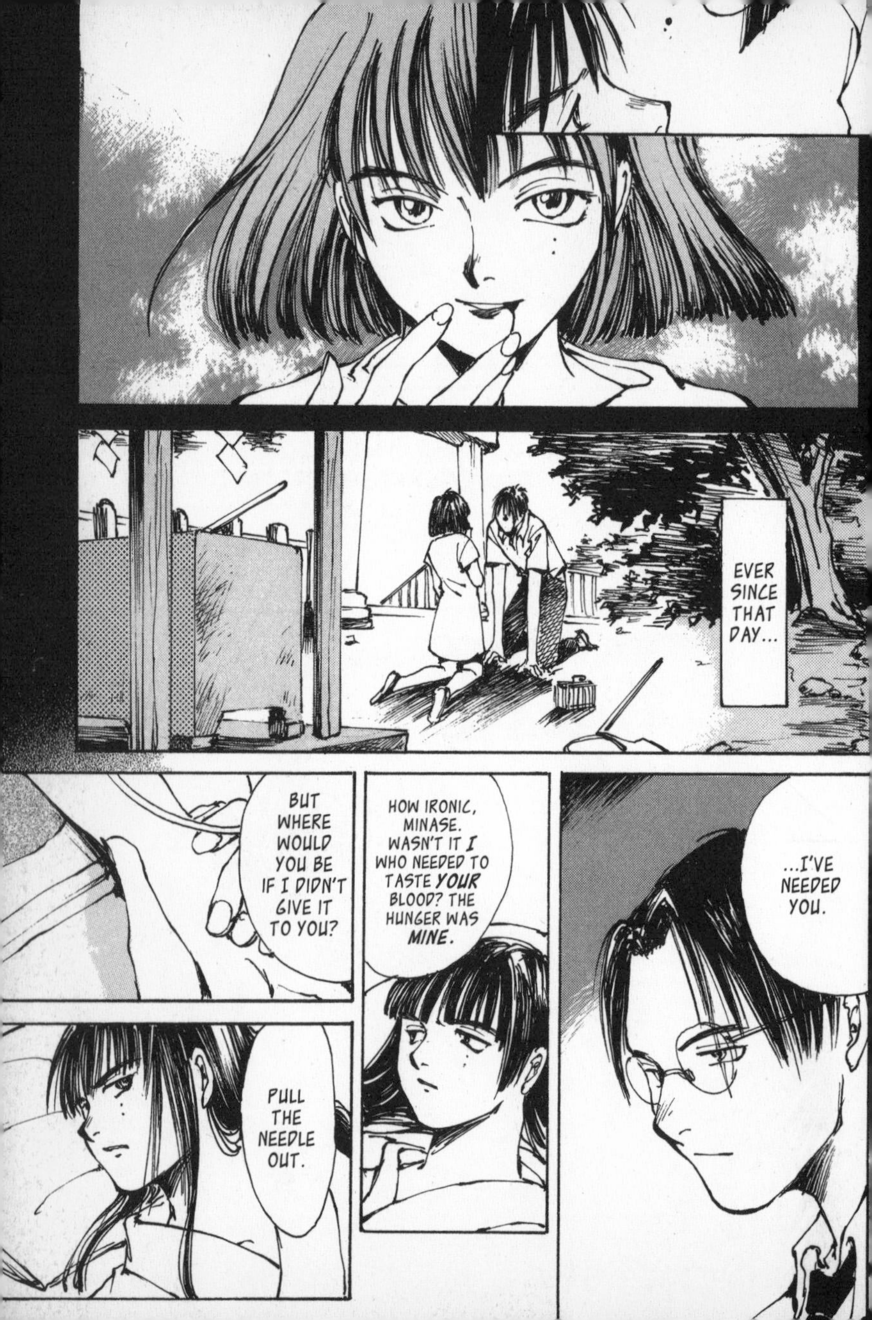
EVER SINCE THAT DAY...
...I'VE NEEDED YOU.
HOW IRONIC, MINASE. WASN'T IT *I* WHO NEEDED TO TASTE *YOUR* BLOOD? THE HUNGER WAS *MINE*.
BUT WHERE WOULD YOU BE IF I DIDN'T GIVE IT TO YOU?
PULL THE NEEDLE OUT.

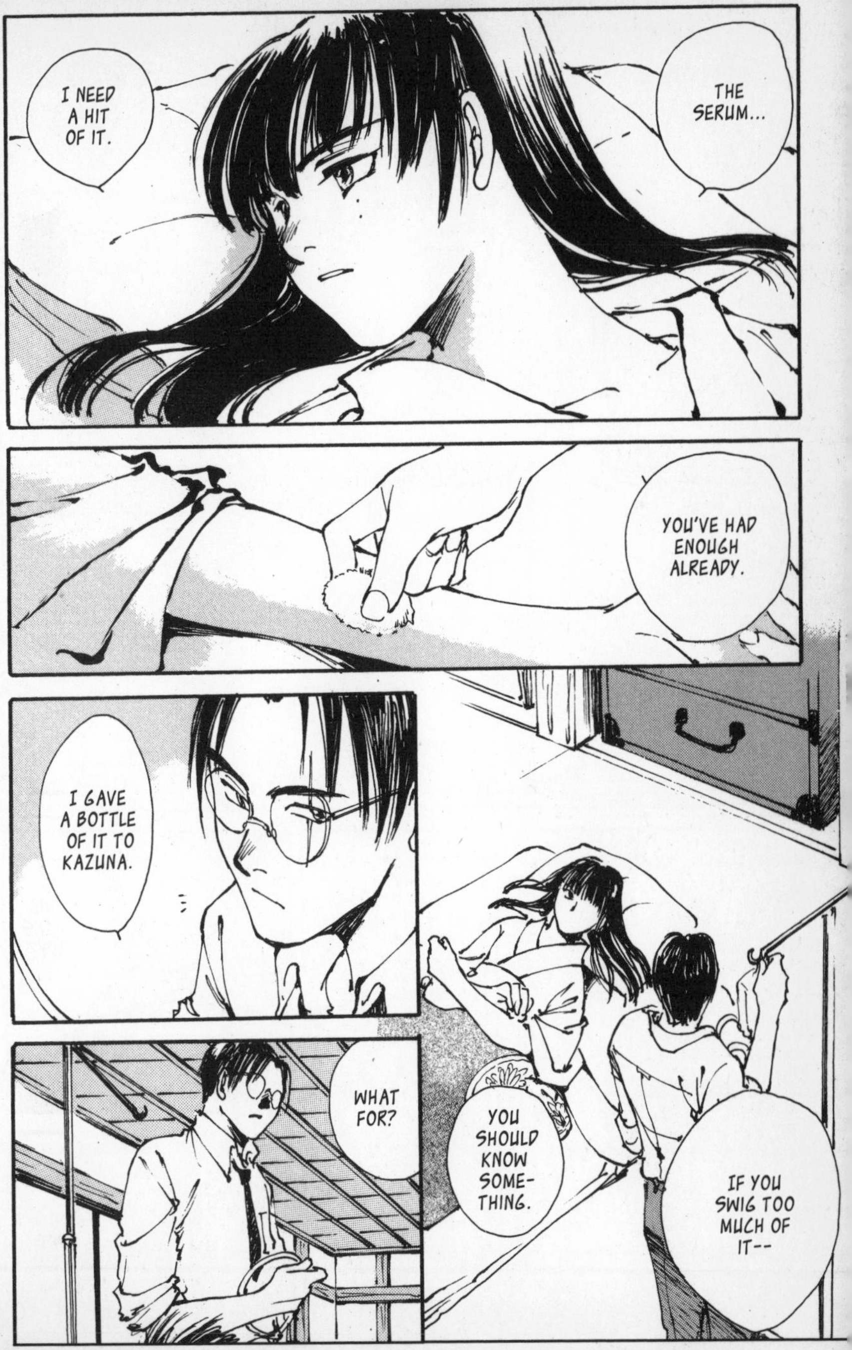
THE SERUM...
I NEED A HIT OF IT.
YOU'VE HAD ENOUGH ALREADY.
I GAVE A BOTTLE OF IT TO KAZUNA.
WHAT FOR?
YOU SHOULD KNOW SOME-THING.
IF YOU SWIG TOO MUCH OF IT--

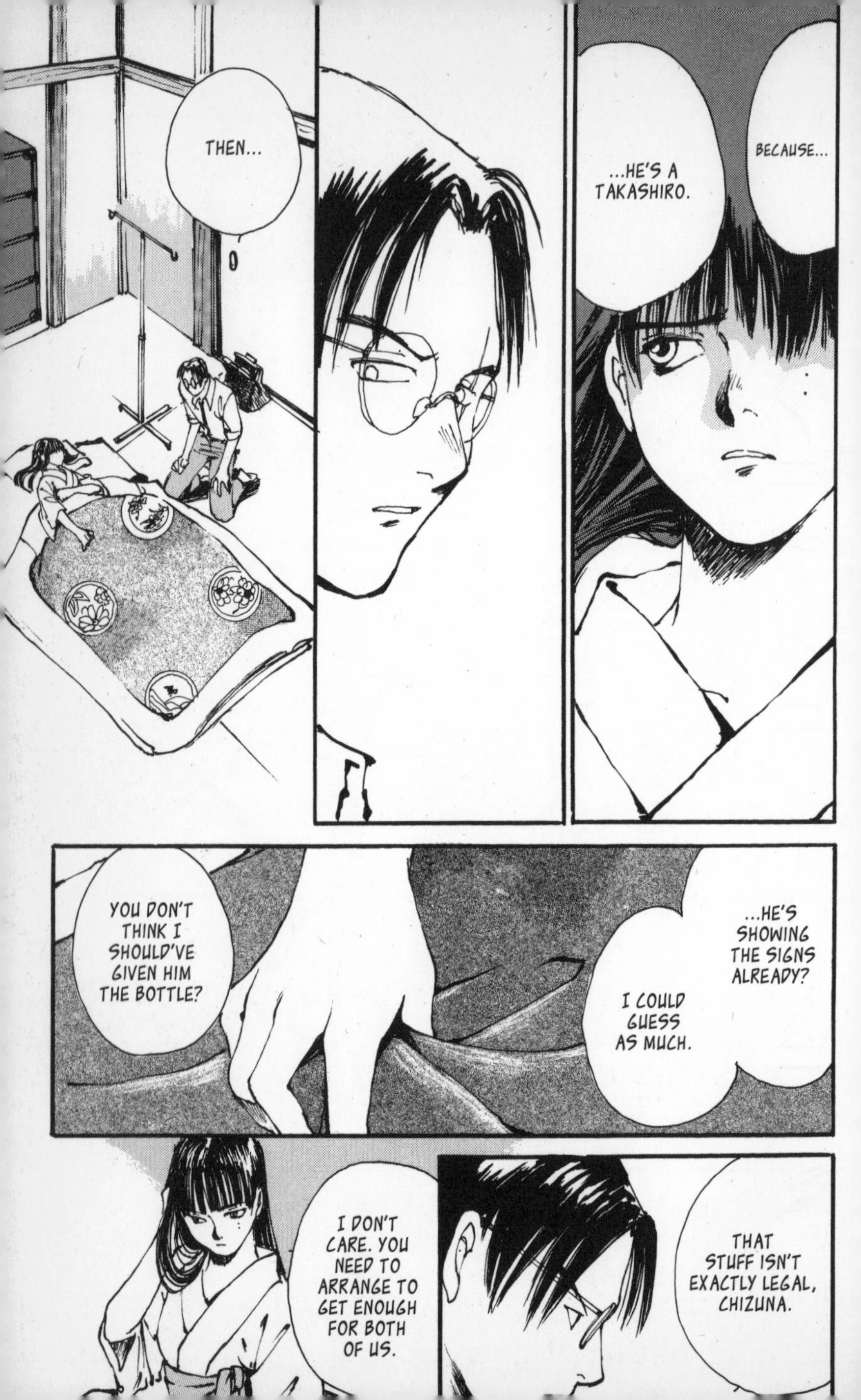
BECAUSE...
...HE'S A TAKASHIRO.
THEN...
...HE'S SHOWING THE SIGNS ALREADY?
I COULD GUESS AS MUCH.
YOU DON'T THINK I SHOULD'VE GIVEN HIM THE BOTTLE?
THAT STUFF ISN'T EXACTLY LEGAL, CHIZUNA.
I DON'T CARE. YOU NEED TO ARRANGE TO GET ENOUGH FOR BOTH OF US.

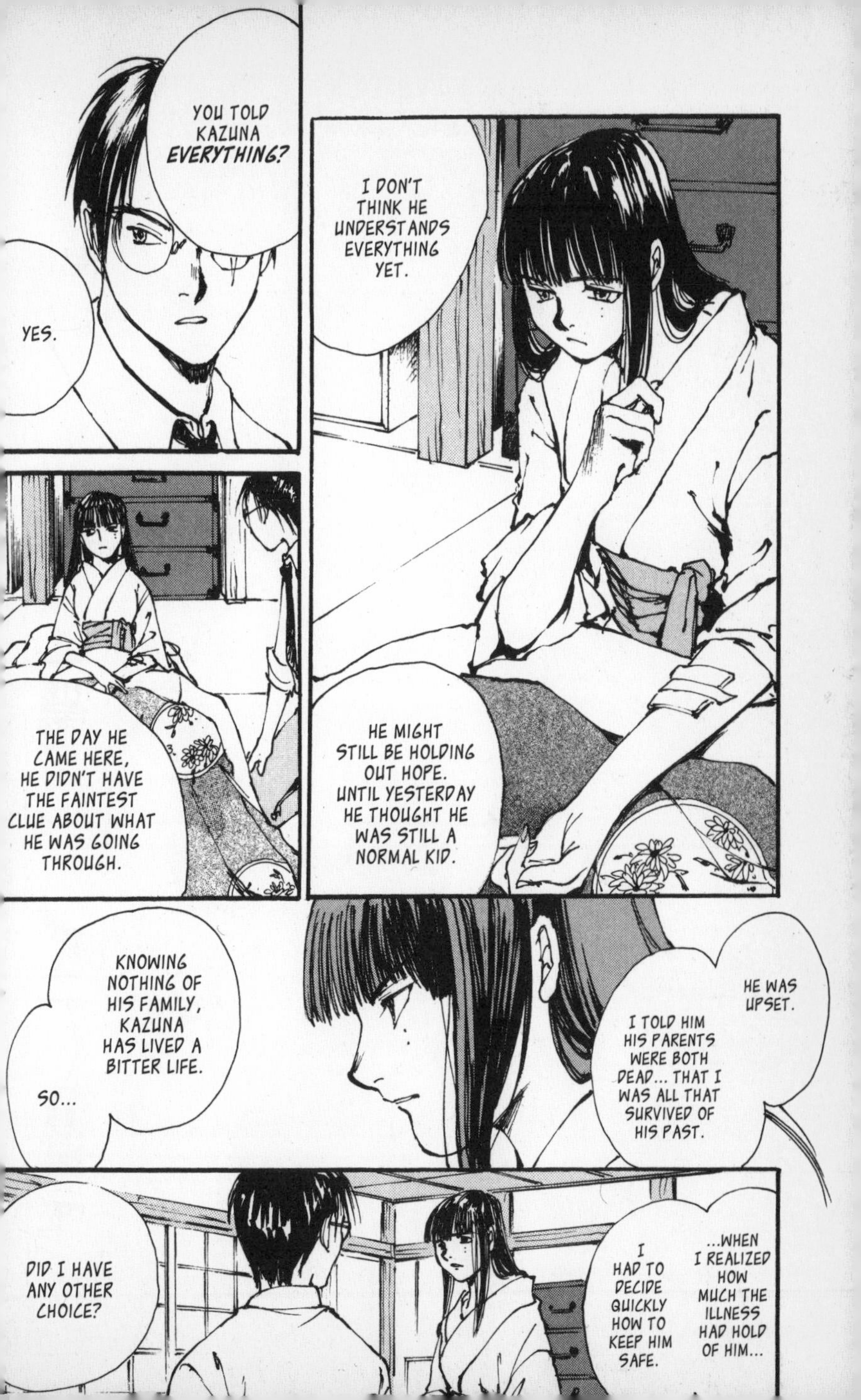

YOU TOLD KAZUNA *EVERYTHING?*
YES.
I DON'T THINK HE UNDERSTANDS EVERYTHING YET.
THE DAY HE CAME HERE, HE DIDN'T HAVE THE FAINTEST CLUE ABOUT WHAT HE WAS GOING THROUGH.
HE MIGHT STILL BE HOLDING OUT HOPE. UNTIL YESTERDAY HE THOUGHT HE WAS STILL A NORMAL KID.
HE WAS UPSET.
I TOLD HIM HIS PARENTS WERE BOTH DEAD... THAT I WAS ALL THAT SURVIVED OF HIS PAST.
KNOWING NOTHING OF HIS FAMILY, KAZUNA HAS LIVED A BITTER LIFE.
SO...
...WHEN I REALIZED HOW MUCH THE ILLNESS HAD HOLD OF HIM...
I HAD TO DECIDE QUICKLY HOW TO KEEP HIM SAFE.
DID I HAVE ANY OTHER CHOICE?

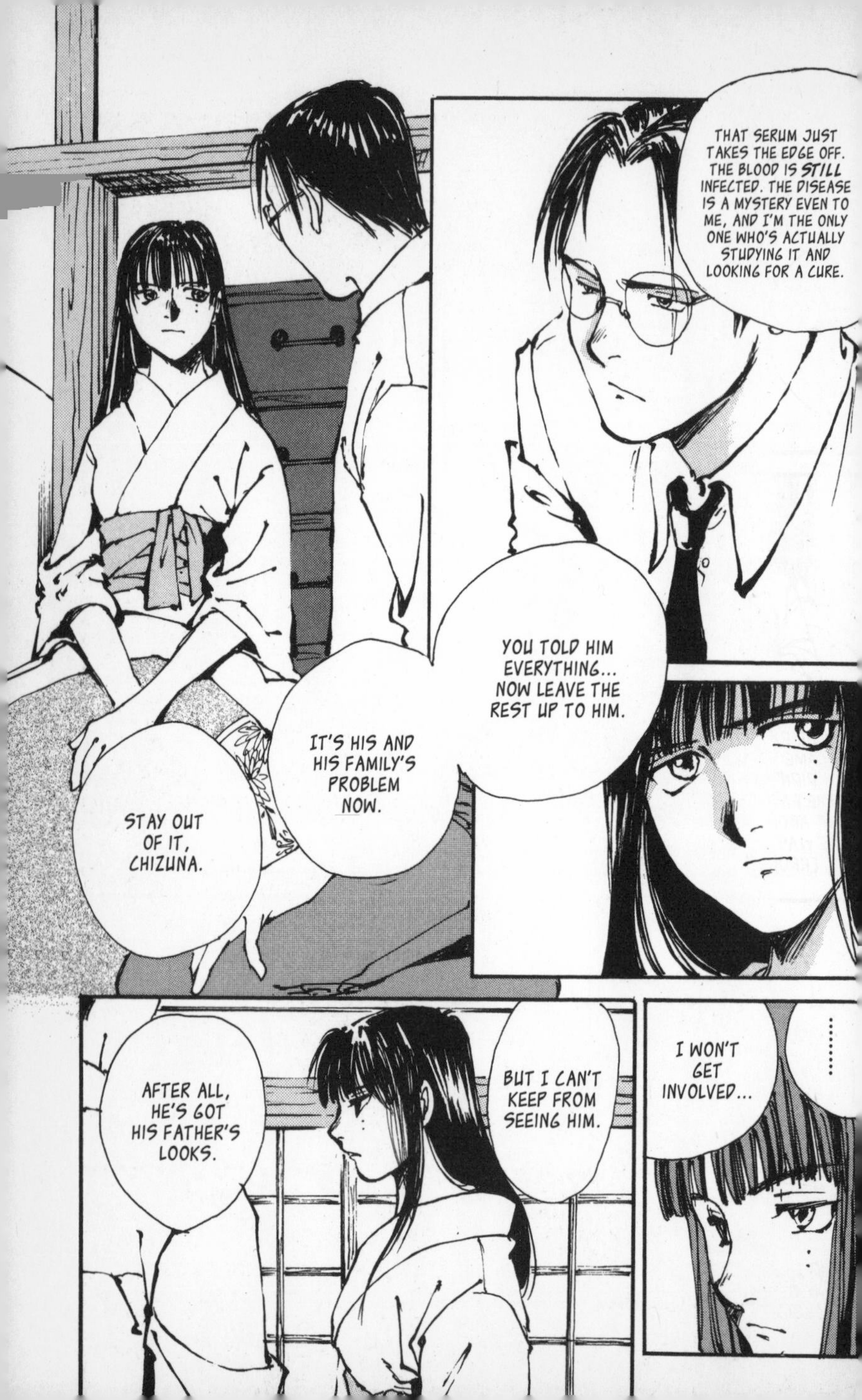
THAT SERUM JUST TAKES THE EDGE OFF. THE BLOOD IS STILL INFECTED. THE DISEASE IS A MYSTERY EVEN TO ME, AND I'M THE ONLY ONE WHO'S ACTUALLY STUDYING IT AND LOOKING FOR A CURE.
YOU TOLD HIM EVERYTHING... NOW LEAVE THE REST UP TO HIM.
IT'S HIS AND HIS FAMILY'S PROBLEM NOW.
STAY OUT OF IT, CHIZUNA.
....
I WON'T GET INVOLVED...
BUT I CAN'T KEEP FROM SEEING HIM.
AFTER ALL, HE'S GOT HIS FATHER'S LOOKS.

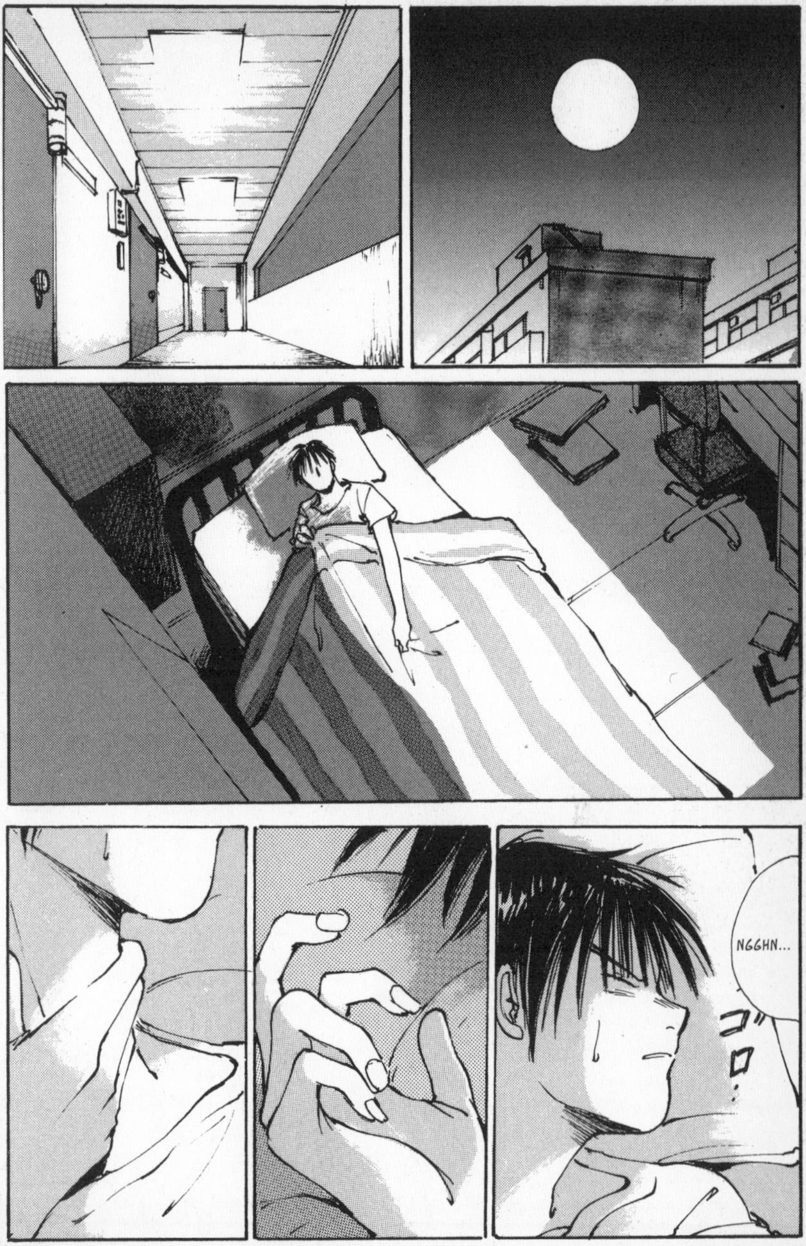
NGGHN...
ゴロ

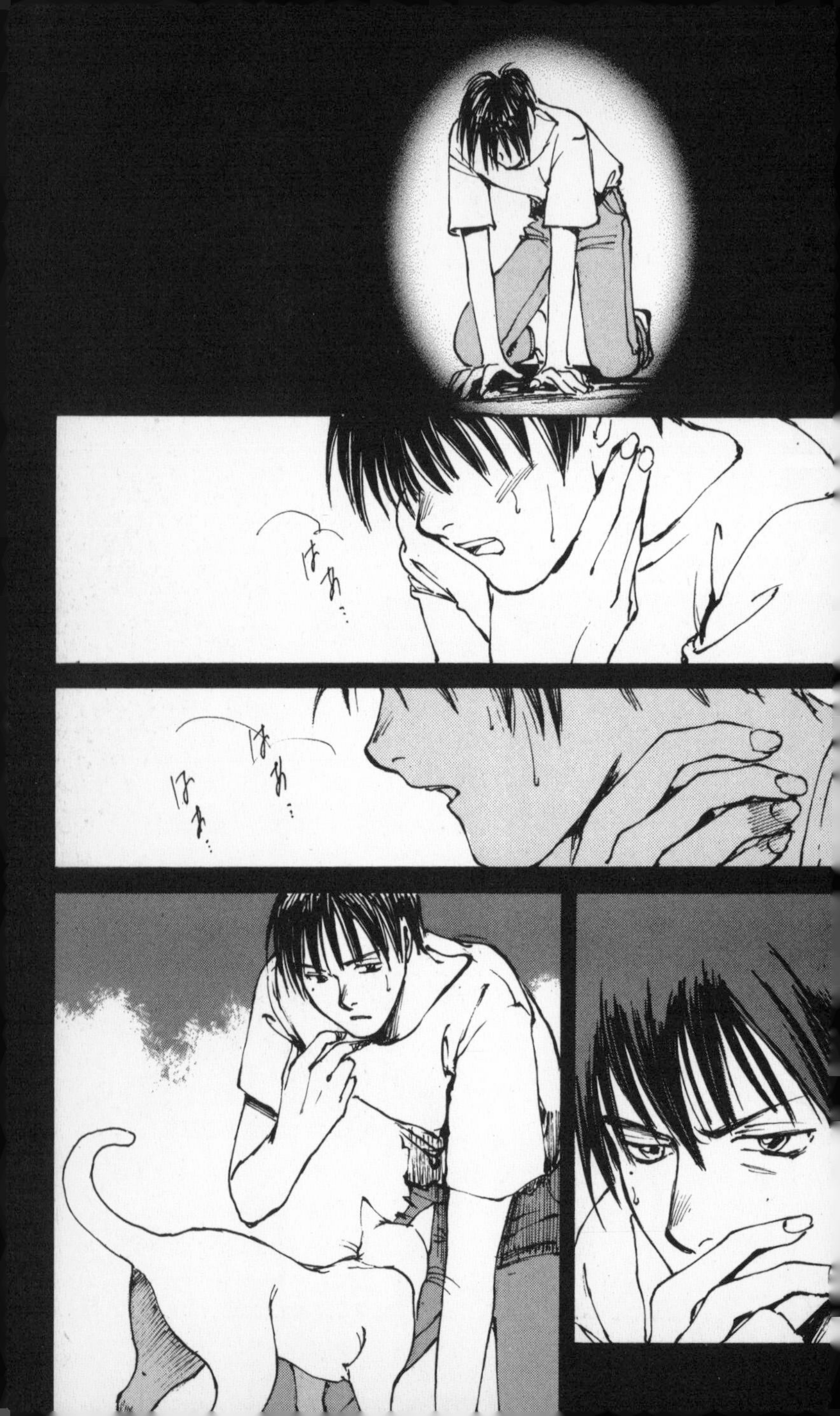
はぁ…
はぁ…
はぁ…

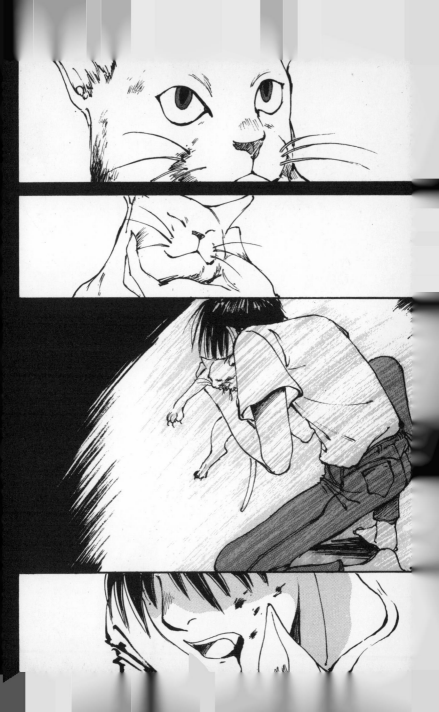

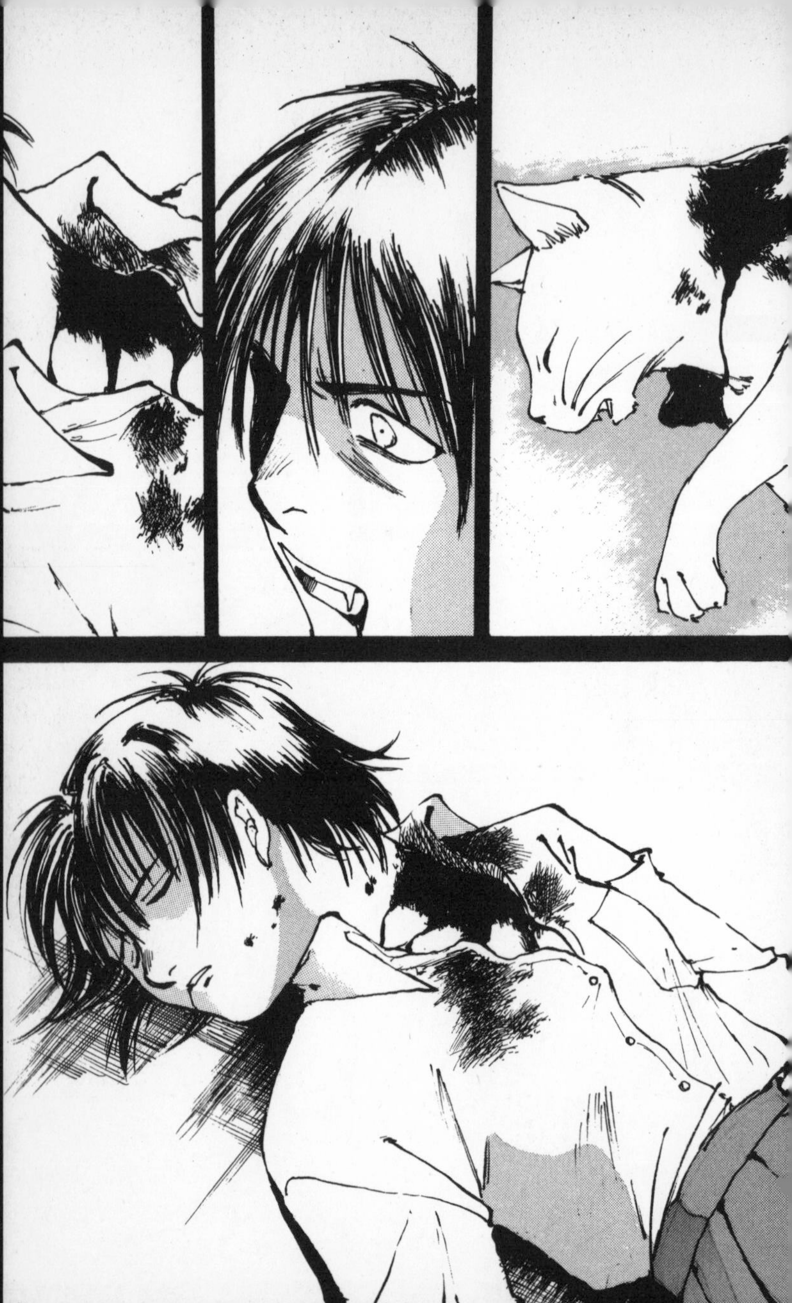

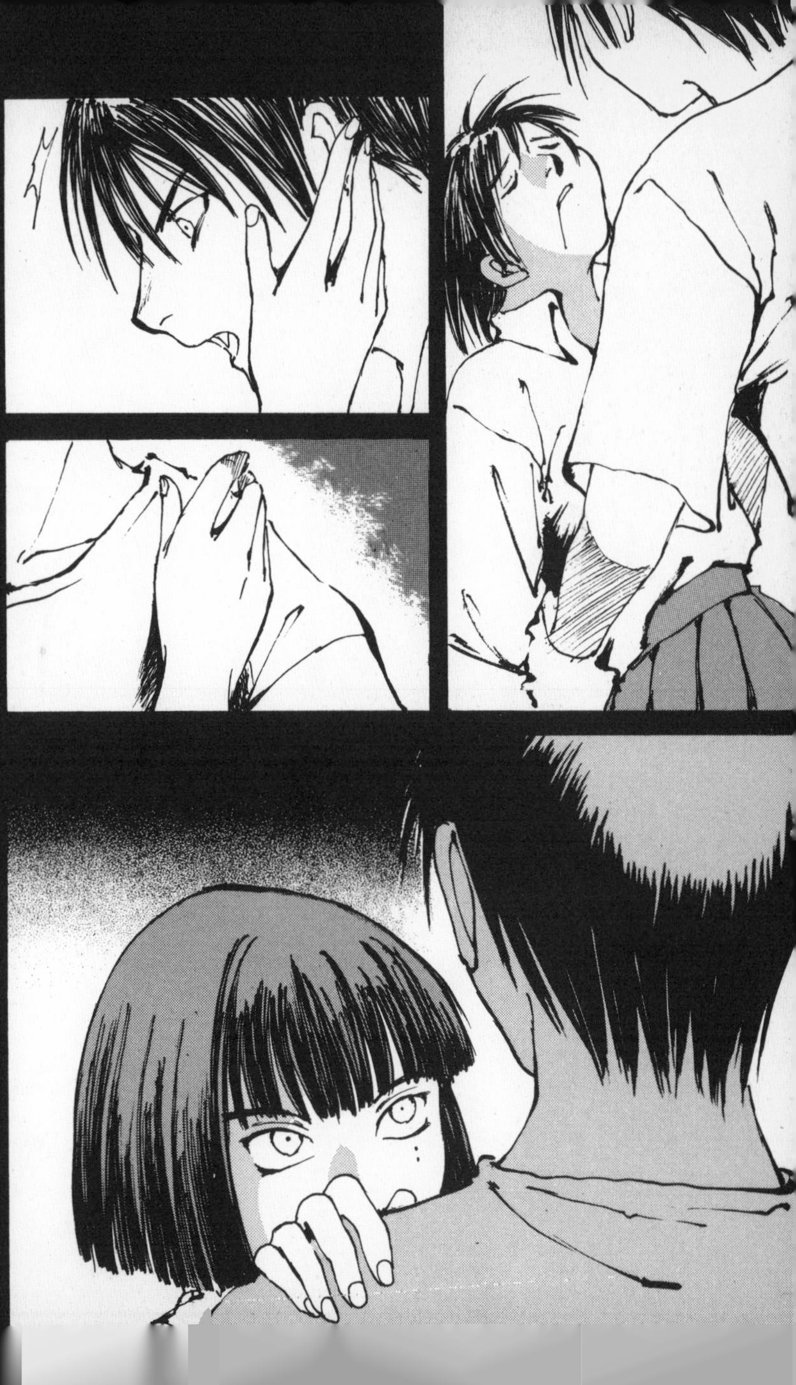

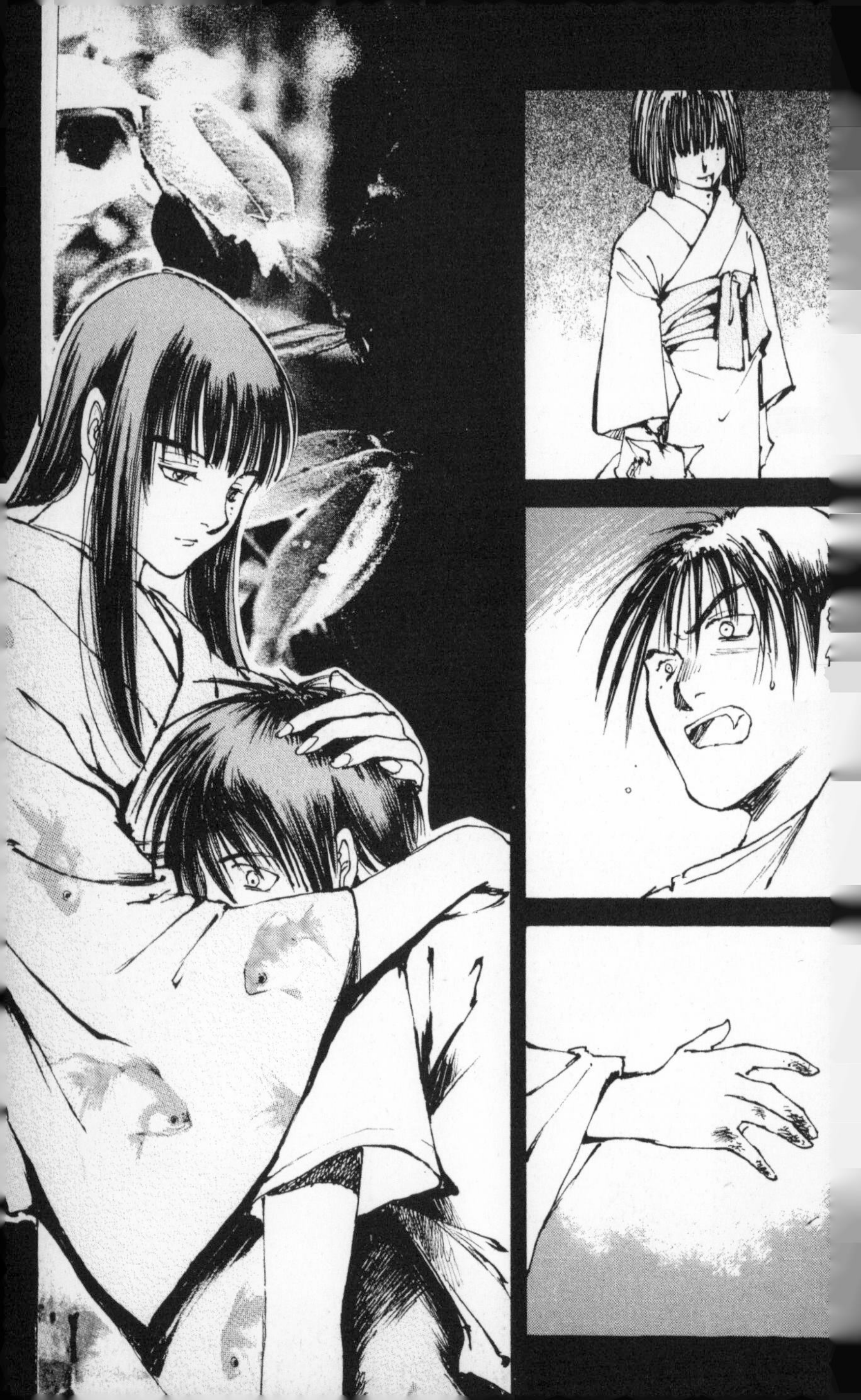

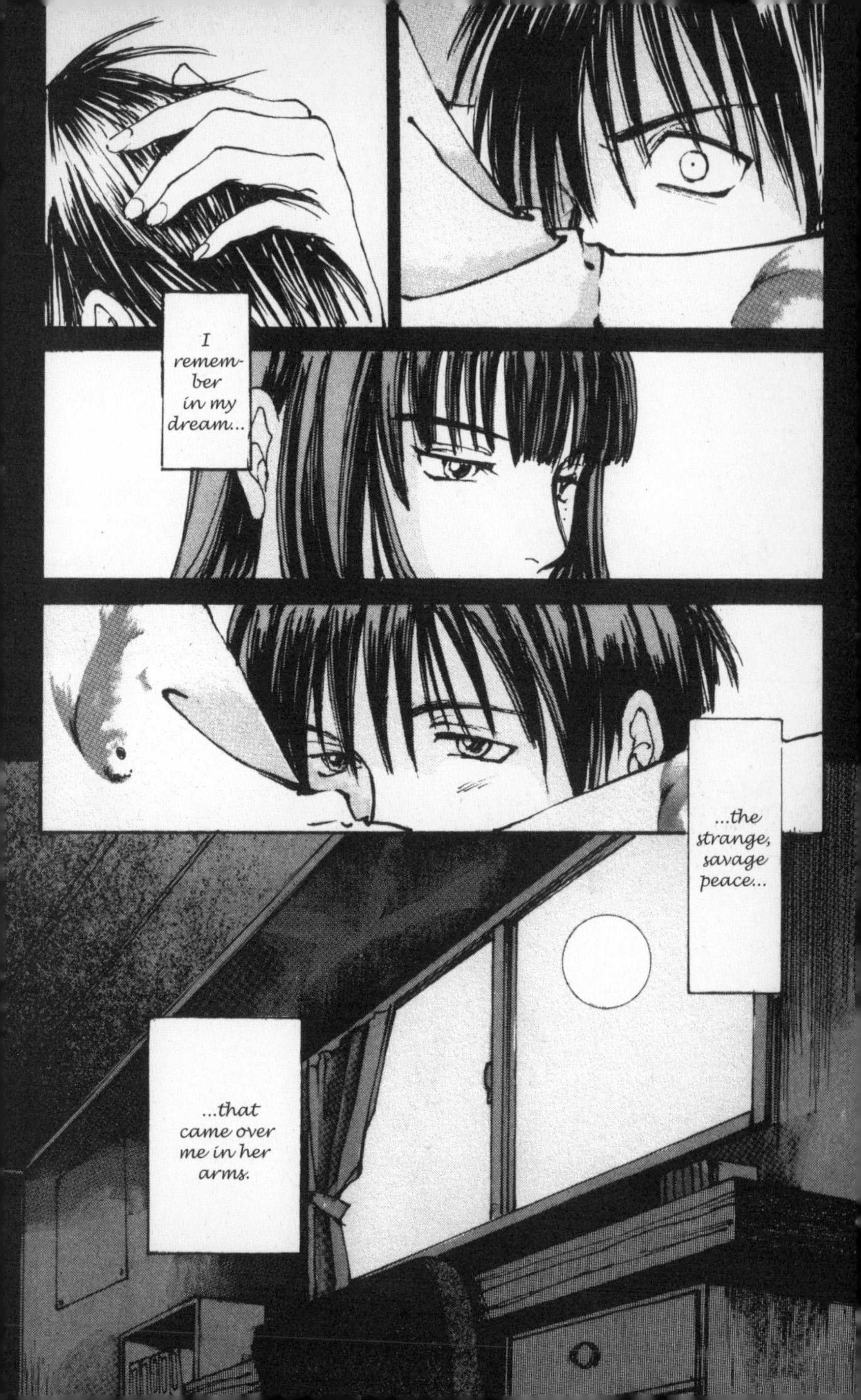
I remember in my dream...
...the strange, savage peace...
...that came over me in her arms.

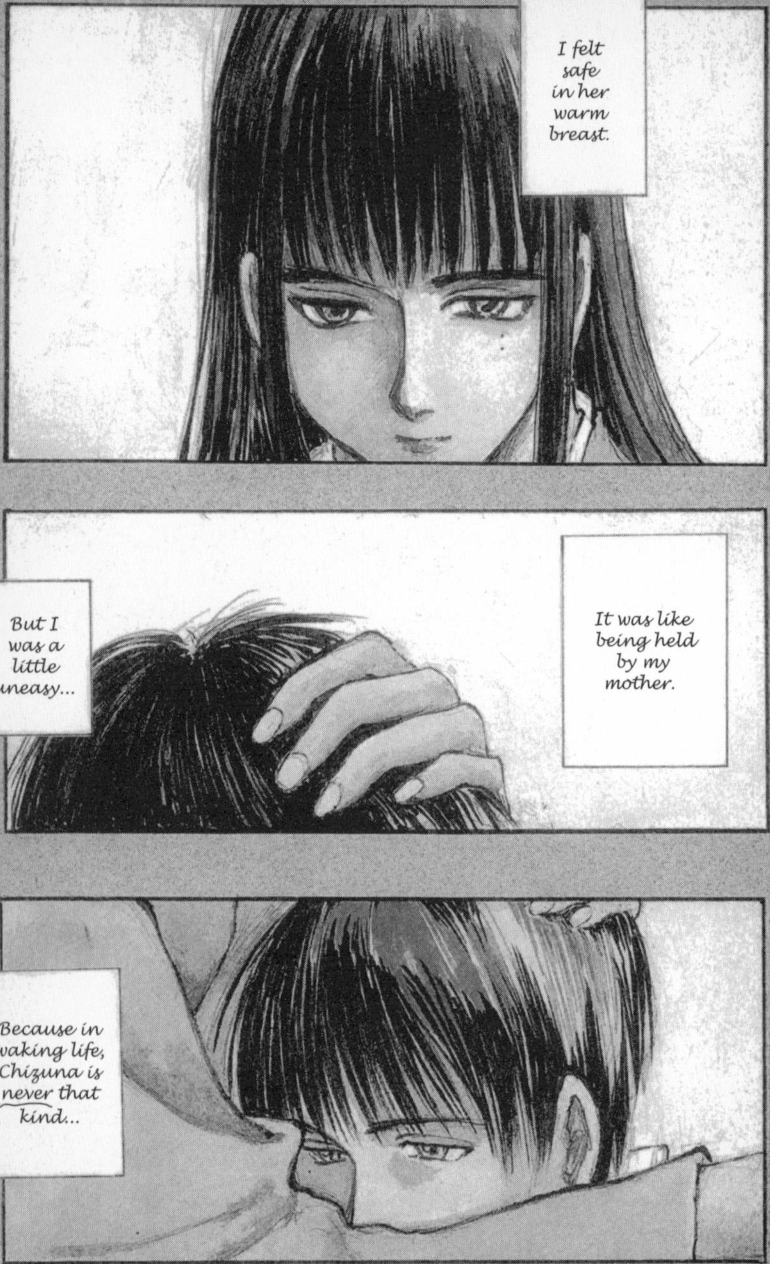
I felt safe in her warm breast.
It was like being held by my mother.
But I was a little uneasy...
Because in waking life, Chizuna is never that kind...

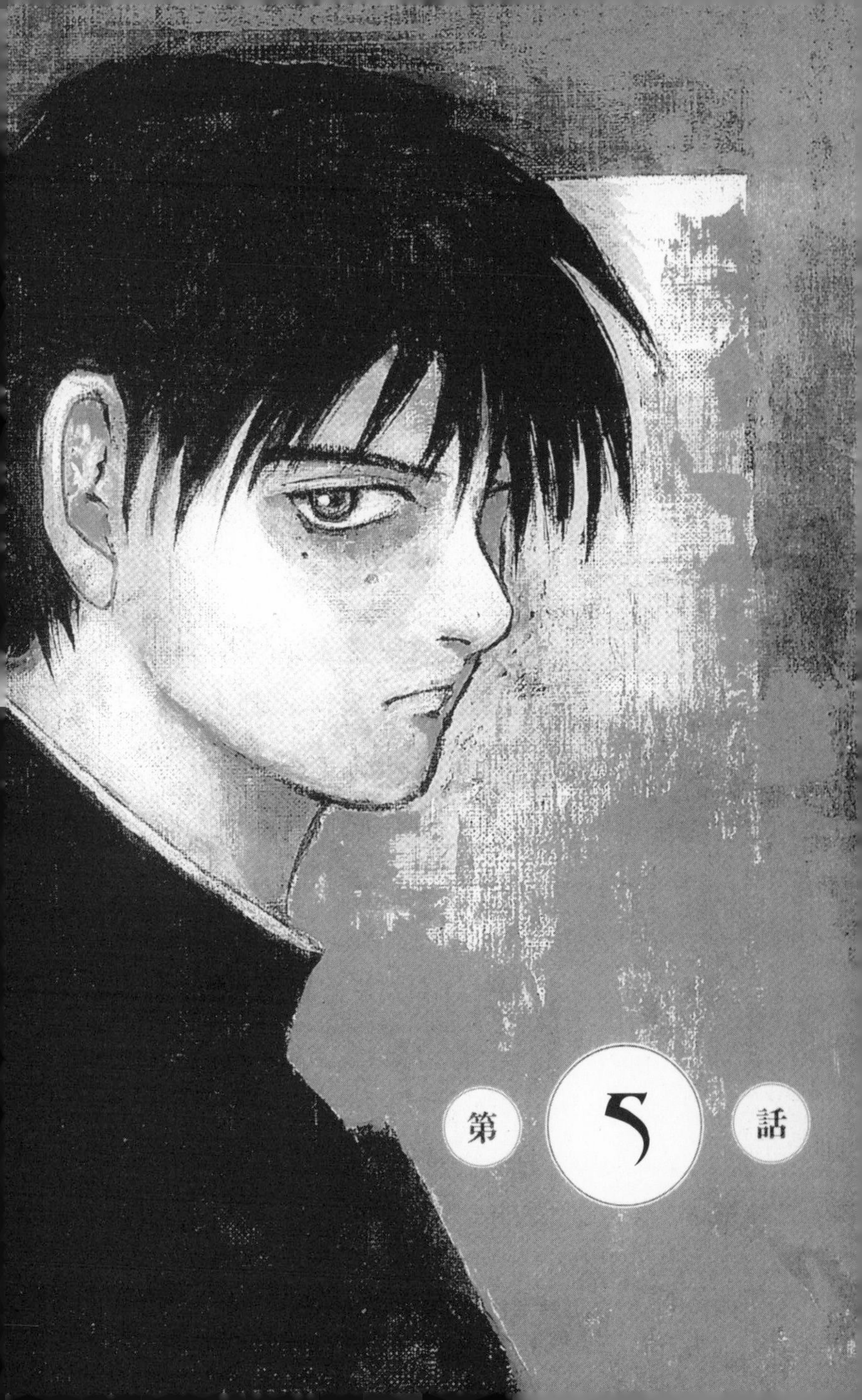
第
5
話

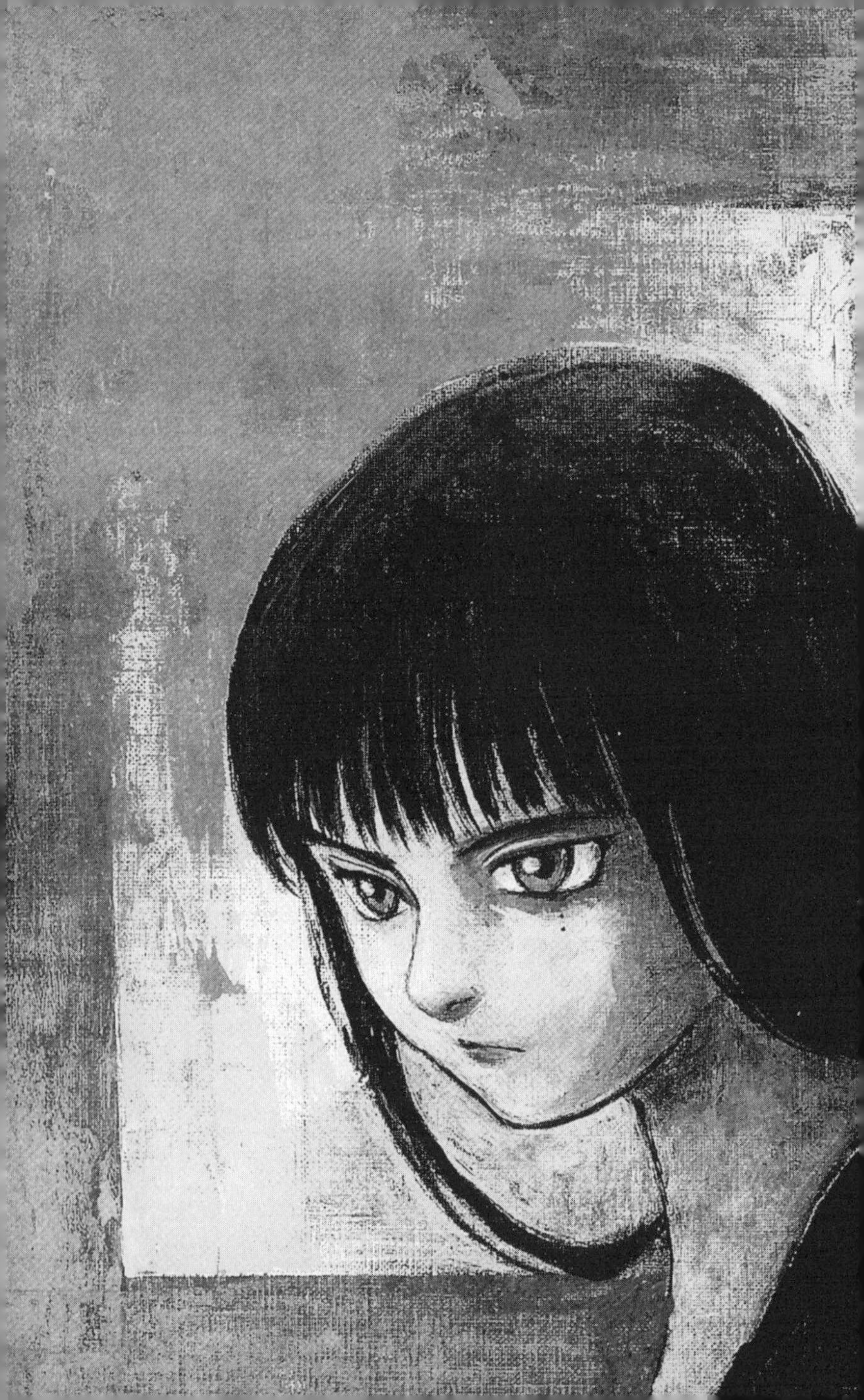

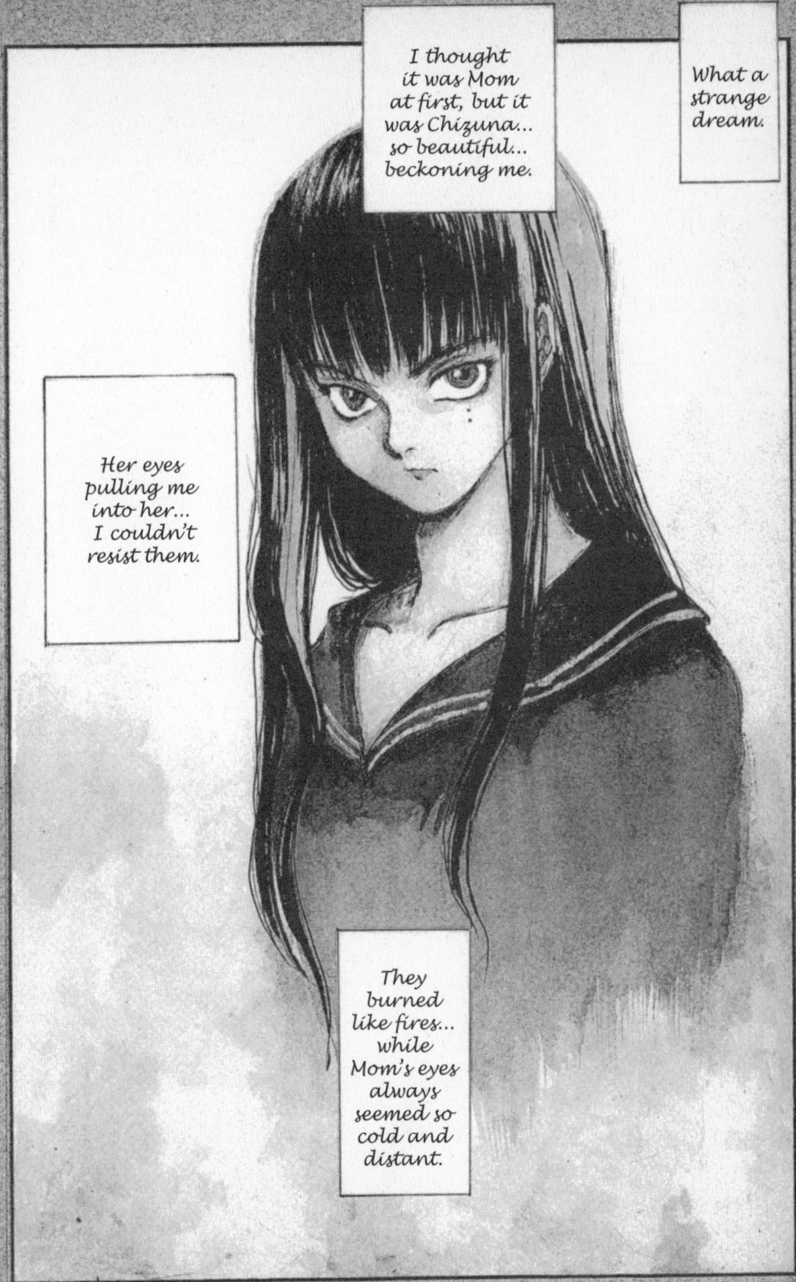
What a strange dream.
I thought it was Mom at first, but it was Chizuna... so beautiful... beckoning me.
Her eyes pulling me into her... I couldn't resist them.
They burned like fires... while Mom's eyes always seemed so cold and distant.

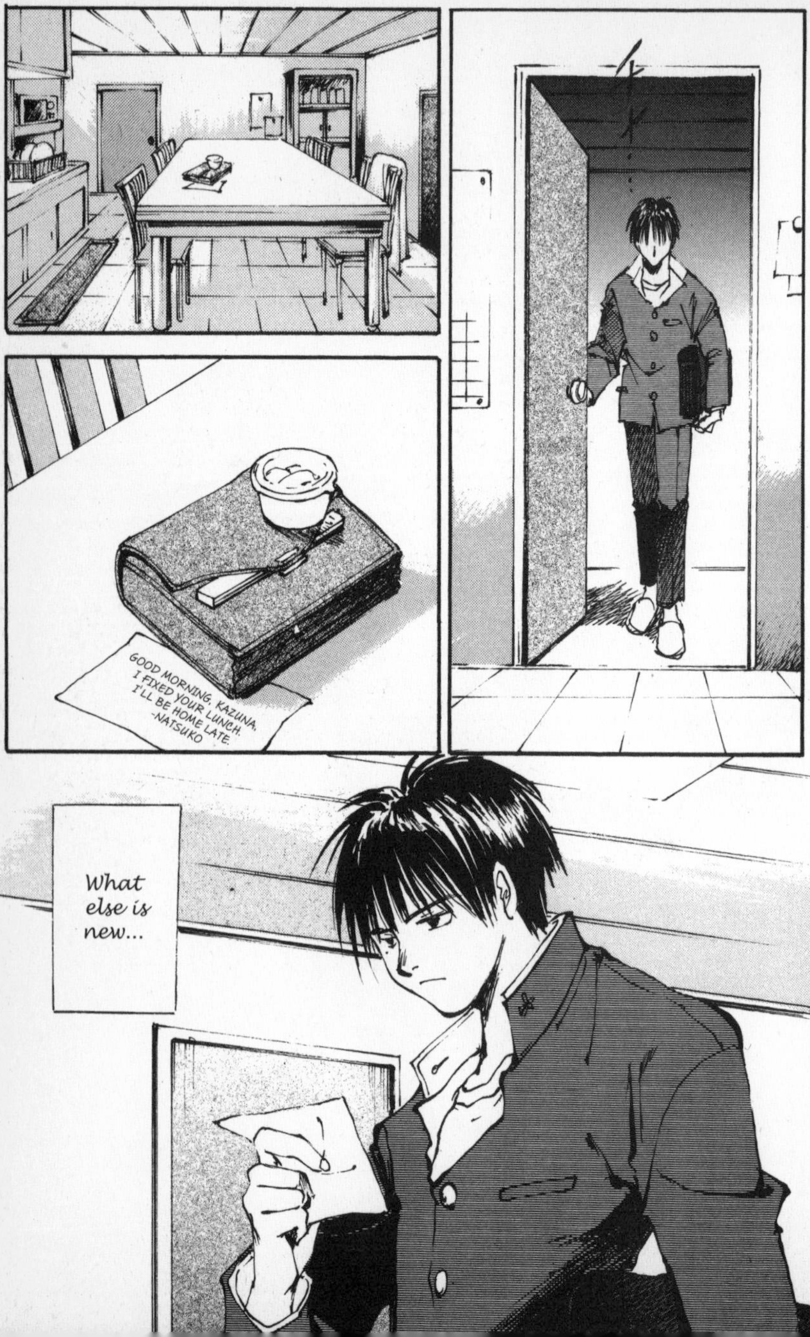
GOOD MORNING, KAZUNA.
I FIXED YOUR LUNCH.
I'LL BE HOME LATE.
-NATSUKO
What else is new...

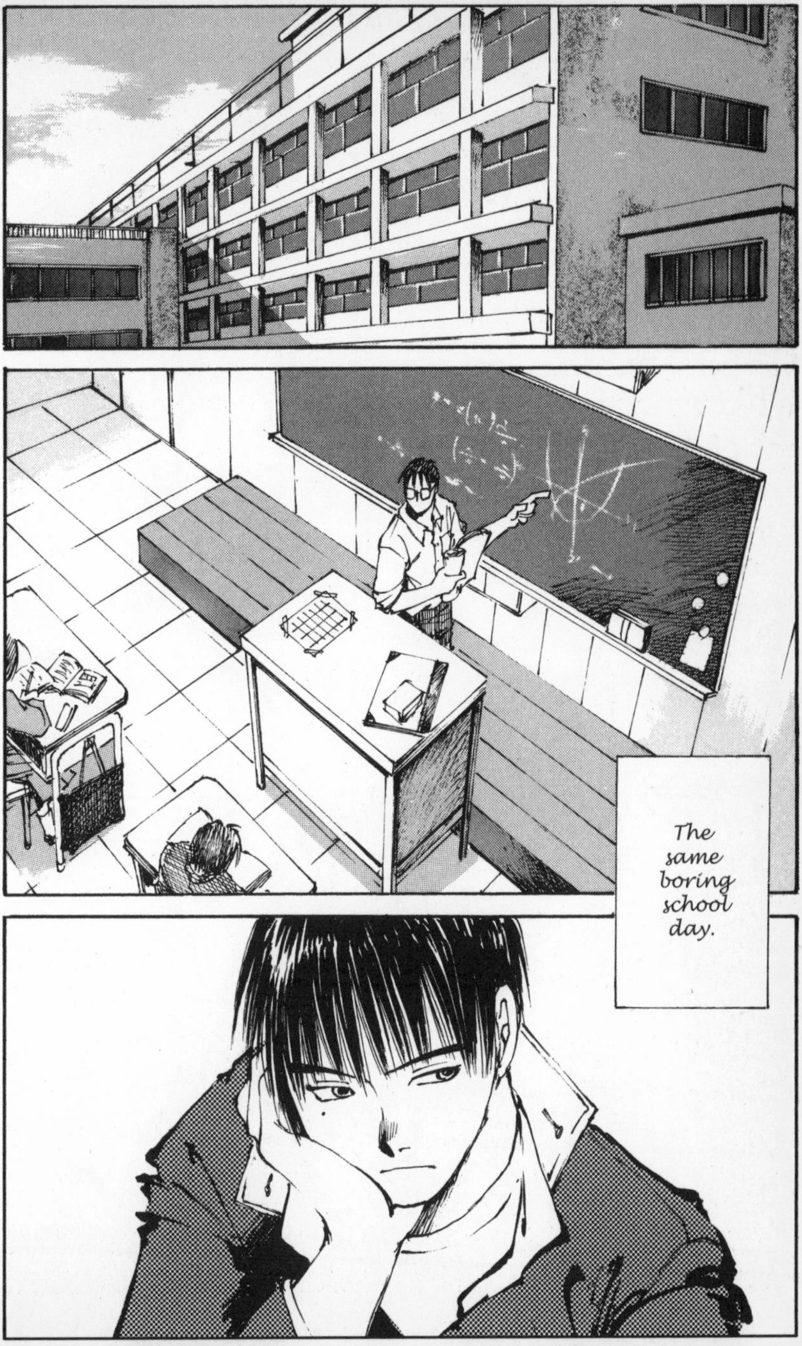
The same boring school day.

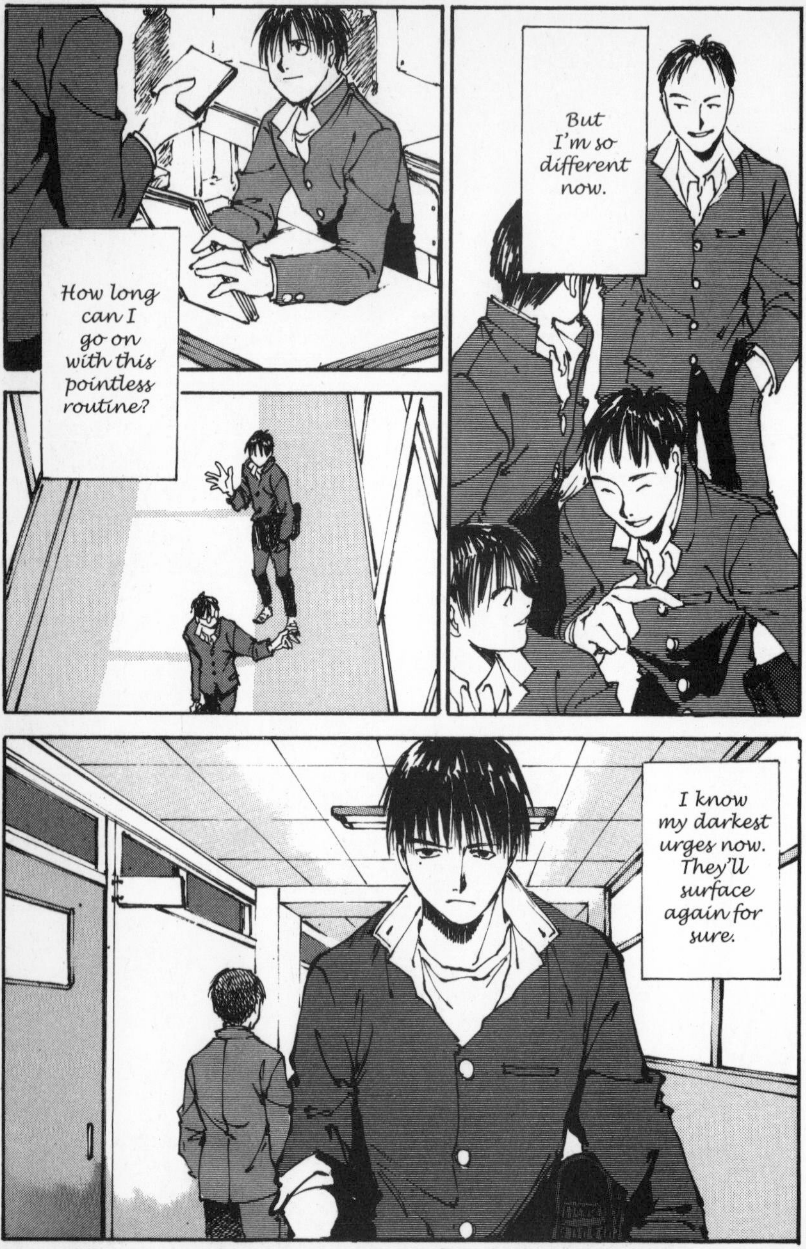
But I'm so different now.
How long can I go on with this pointless routine?
I know my darkest urges now. They'll surface again for sure.

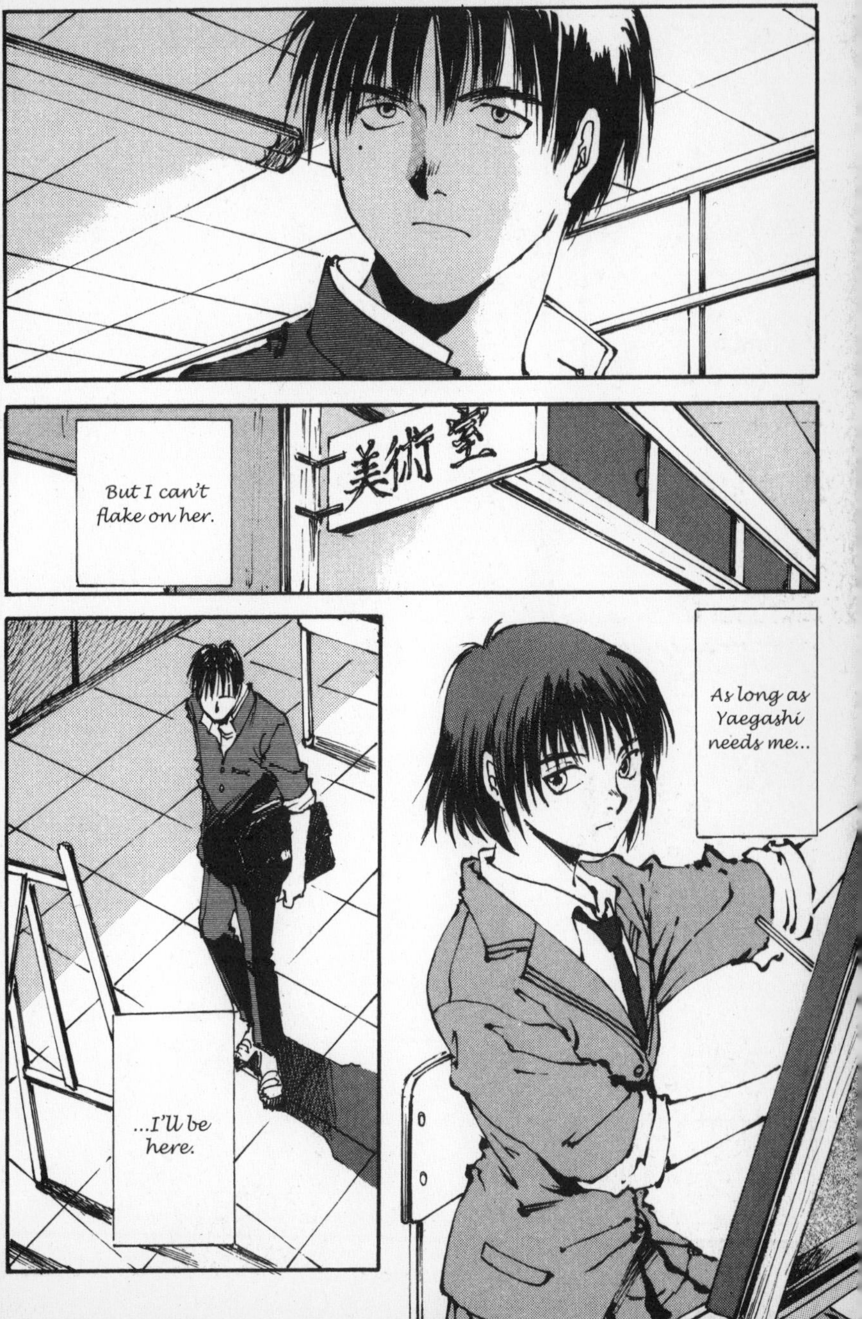
美術室
But I can't flake on her.
As long as Yaegashi needs me...
...I'll be here.

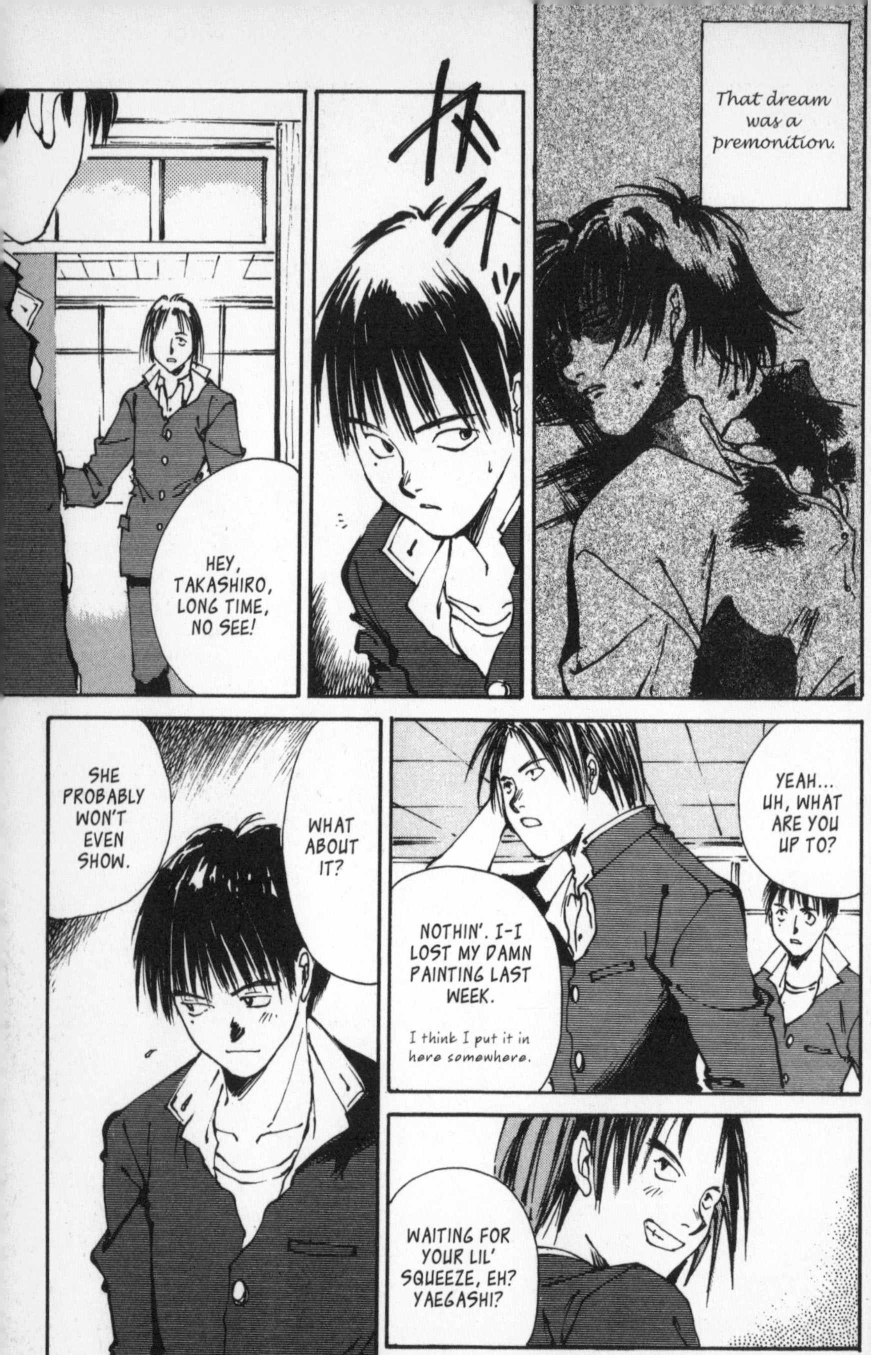
That dream was a premonition.
HEY, TAKASHIRO, LONG TIME, NO SEE!
YEAH... UH, WHAT ARE YOU UP TO?
NOTHIN'. I-I LOST MY DAMN PAINTING LAST WEEK.
I think I put it in here somewhere.
WAITING FOR YOUR LIL' SQUEEZE, EH? YAEGASHI?
WHAT ABOUT IT?
SHE PROBABLY WON'T EVEN SHOW.

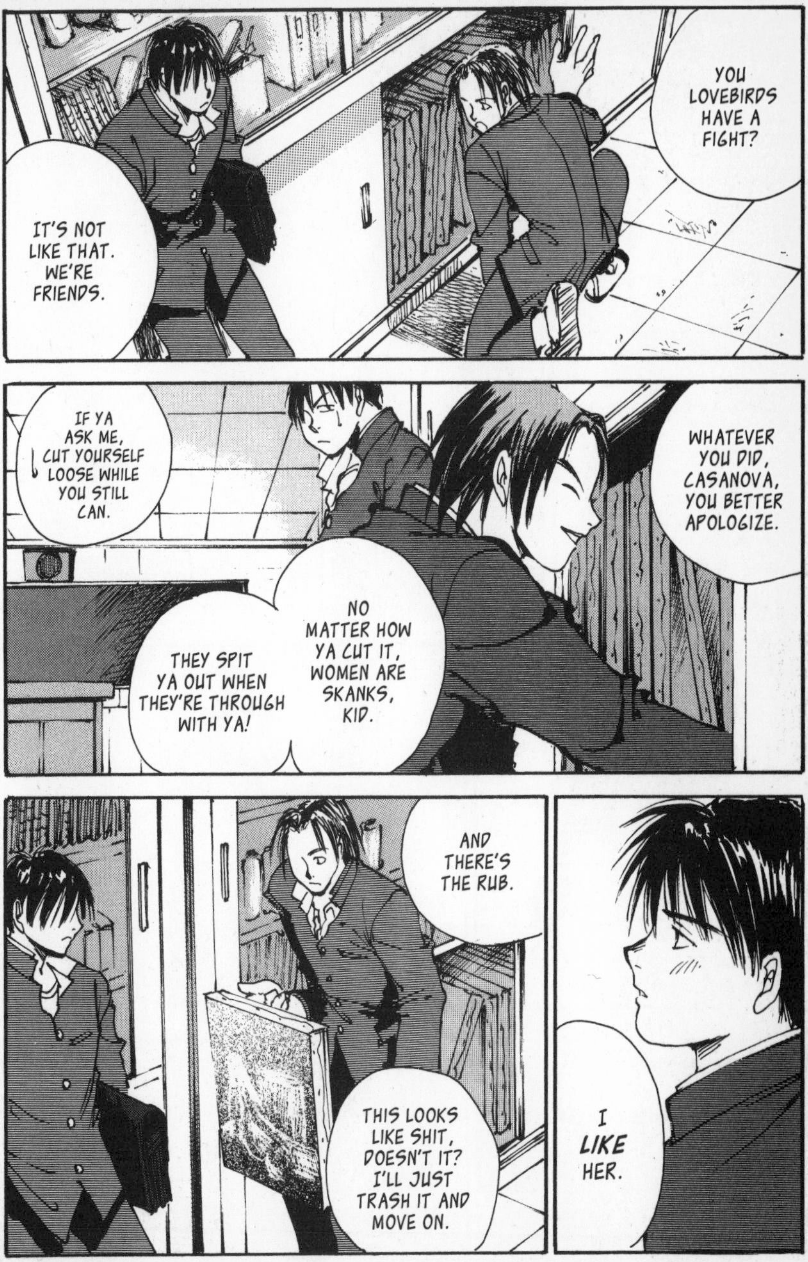
YOU LOVEBIRDS HAVE A FIGHT?
IT'S NOT LIKE THAT. WE'RE FRIENDS.
WHATEVER YOU DID, CASANOVA, YOU BETTER APOLOGIZE.
NO MATTER HOW YA CUT IT, WOMEN ARE SKANKS, KID.
THEY SPIT YA OUT WHEN THEY'RE THROUGH WITH YA!
IF YA ASK ME, CUT YOURSELF LOOSE WHILE YOU STILL CAN.
I ***LIKE*** HER.
AND THERE'S THE RUB.
THIS LOOKS LIKE SHIT, DOESN'T IT? I'LL JUST TRASH IT AND MOVE ON.

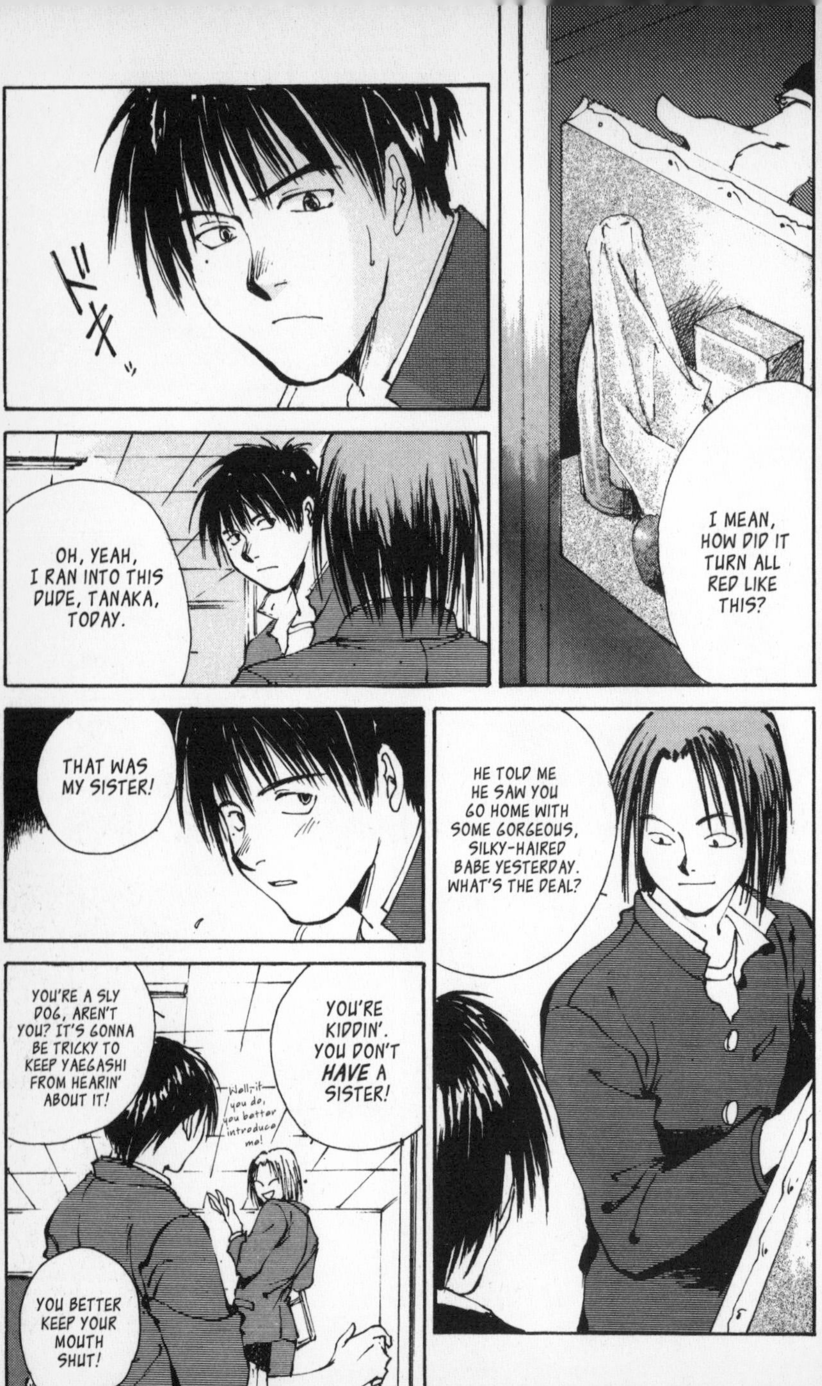
I MEAN, HOW DID IT TURN ALL RED LIKE THIS?
OH, YEAH, I RAN INTO THIS DUDE, TANAKA, TODAY.
HE TOLD ME HE SAW YOU GO HOME WITH SOME GORGEOUS, SILKY-HAIRED BABE YESTERDAY. WHAT'S THE DEAL?
THAT WAS MY SISTER!
YOU'RE KIDDIN'. YOU DON'T HAVE A SISTER!
Well, if you do, you better introduce me!
YOU'RE A SLY DOG, AREN'T YOU? IT'S GONNA BE TRICKY TO KEEP YAEGASHI FROM HEARIN' ABOUT IT!
YOU BETTER KEEP YOUR MOUTH SHUT!

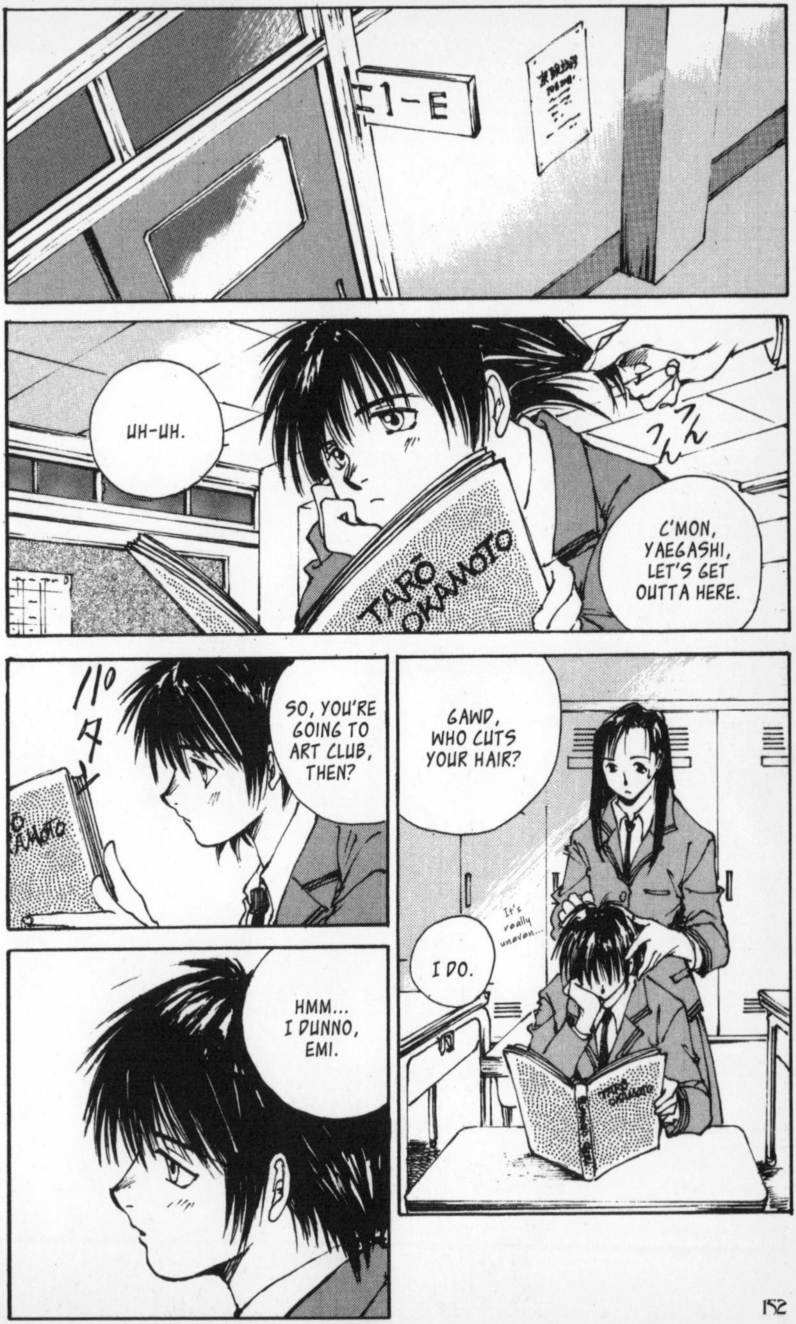
C'MON, YAEGASHI, LET'S GET OUTTA HERE.
UH-UH.
GAWD, WHO CUTS YOUR HAIR?
It's really uneven...
I DO.
SO, YOU'RE GOING TO ART CLUB, THEN?
HMM... I DUNNO, EMI.

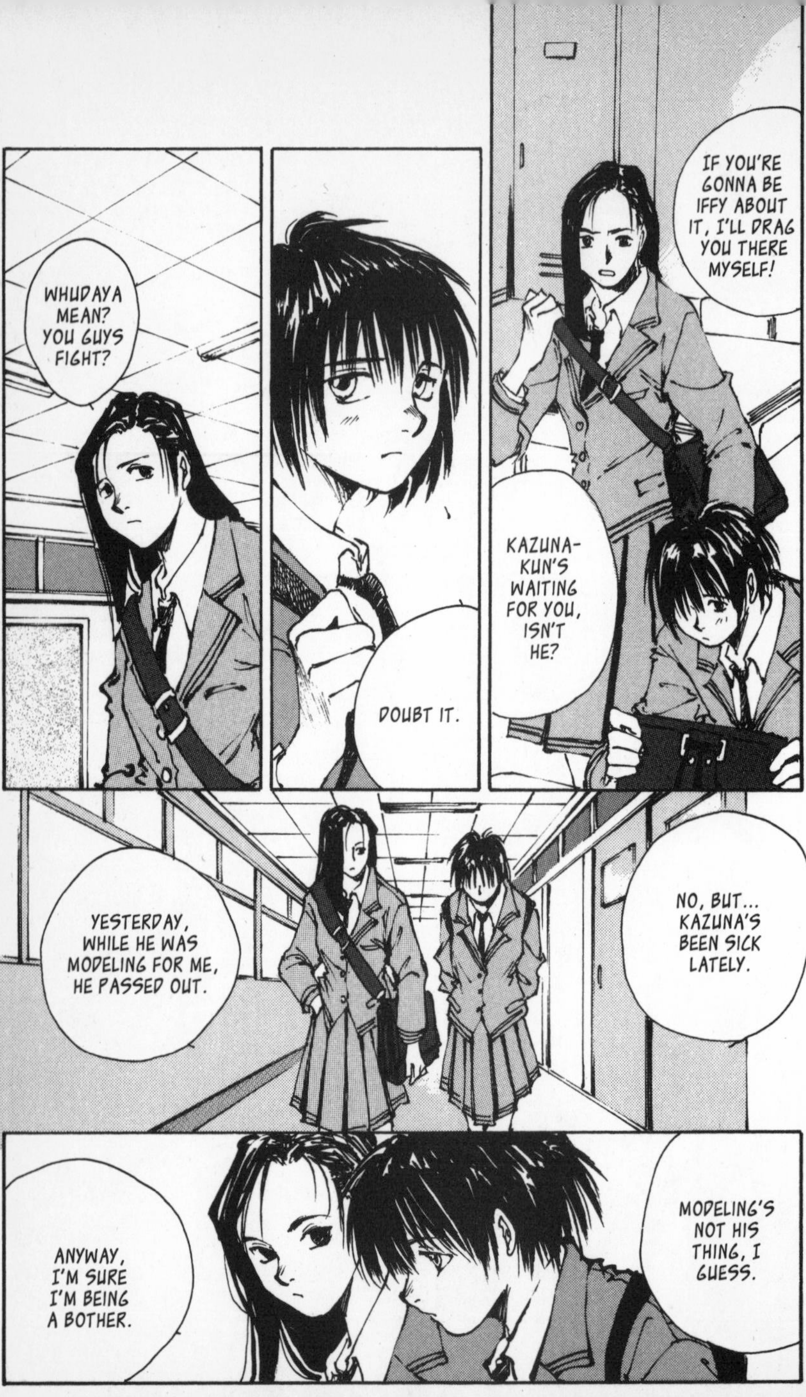
IF YOU'RE GONNA BE IFFY ABOUT IT, I'LL DRAG YOU THERE MYSELF!
KAZUNA-KUN'S WAITING FOR YOU, ISN'T HE?
DOUBT IT.
WHUDAYA MEAN? YOU GUYS FIGHT?
NO, BUT... KAZUNA'S BEEN SICK LATELY.
YESTERDAY, WHILE HE WAS MODELING FOR ME, HE PASSED OUT.
MODELING'S NOT HIS THING, I GUESS.
ANYWAY, I'M SURE I'M BEING A BOTHER.

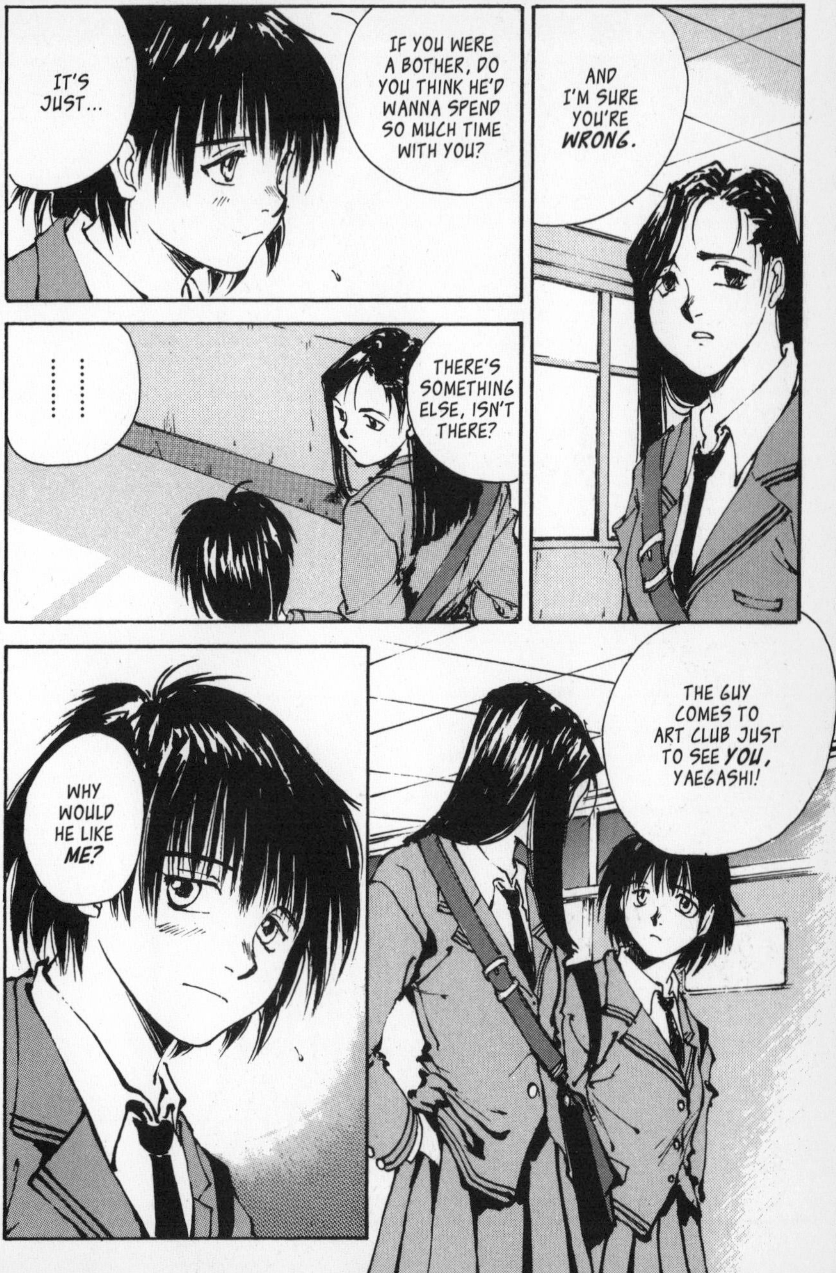
AND I'M SURE YOU'RE **WRONG**.
IF YOU WERE A BOTHER, DO YOU THINK HE'D WANNA SPEND SO MUCH TIME WITH YOU?
IT'S JUST...
THERE'S SOMETHING ELSE, ISN'T THERE?
......
THE GUY COMES TO ART CLUB JUST TO SEE **YOU**, YAEGASHI!
WHY WOULD HE LIKE **ME?**

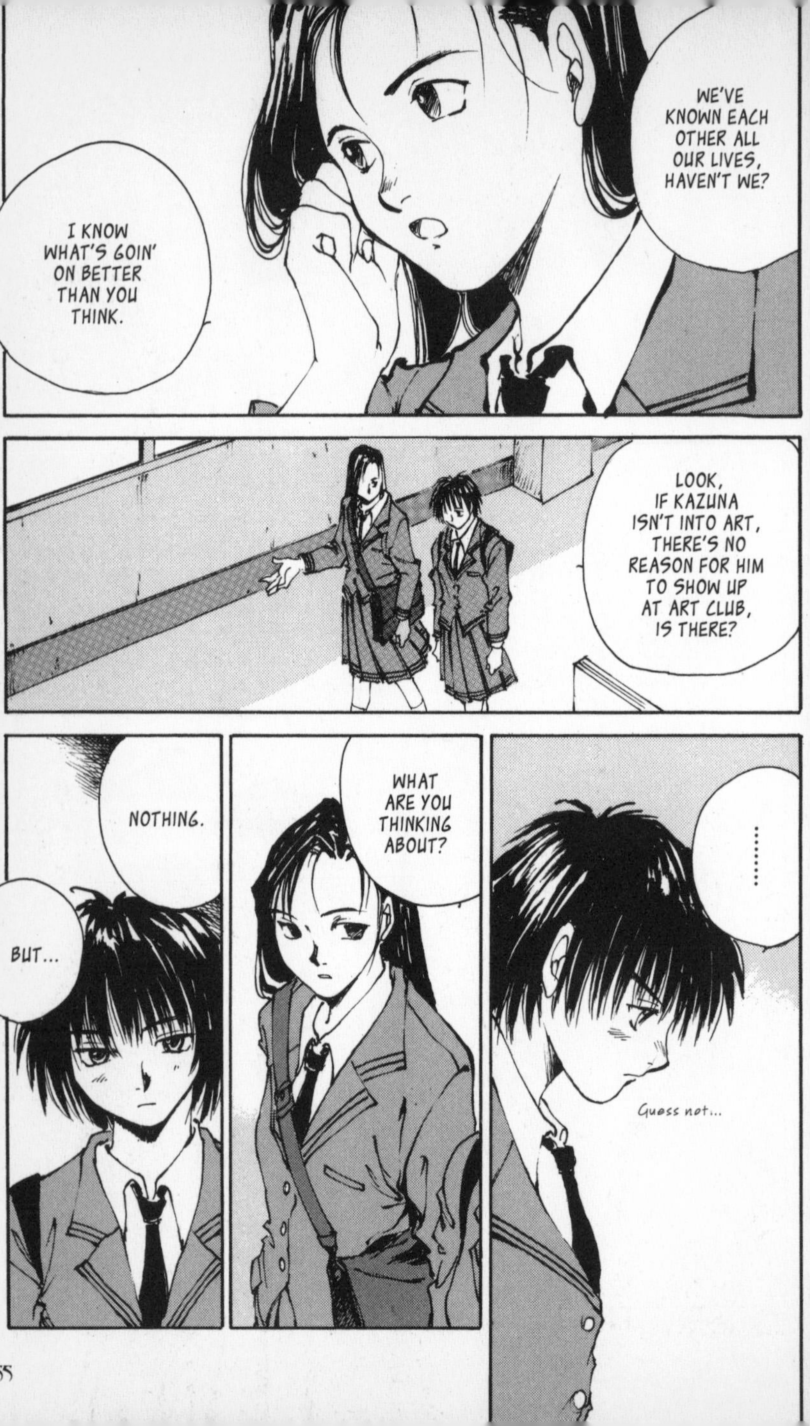
WE'VE KNOWN EACH OTHER ALL OUR LIVES, HAVEN'T WE?
I KNOW WHAT'S GOIN' ON BETTER THAN YOU THINK.
LOOK, IF KAZUNA ISN'T INTO ART, THERE'S NO REASON FOR HIM TO SHOW UP AT ART CLUB, IS THERE?
....
Guess not...
WHAT ARE YOU THINKING ABOUT?
NOTHING.
BUT...

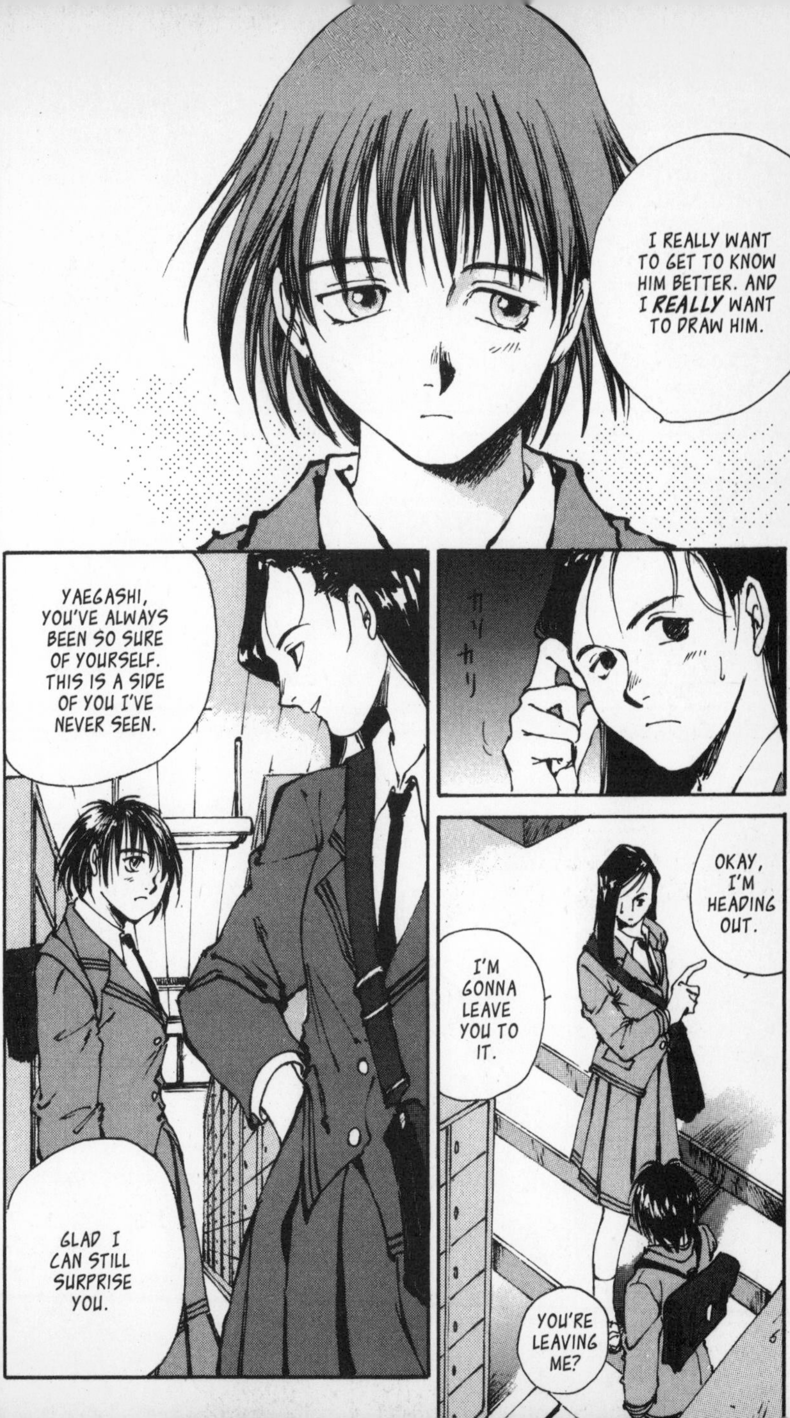
I REALLY WANT TO GET TO KNOW HIM BETTER. AND I *REALLY* WANT TO DRAW HIM.
カリカリ
OKAY, I'M HEADING OUT.
I'M GONNA LEAVE YOU TO IT.
YOU'RE LEAVING ME?
YAEGASHI, YOU'VE ALWAYS BEEN SO SURE OF YOURSELF. THIS IS A SIDE OF YOU I'VE NEVER SEEN.
GLAD I CAN STILL SURPRISE YOU.

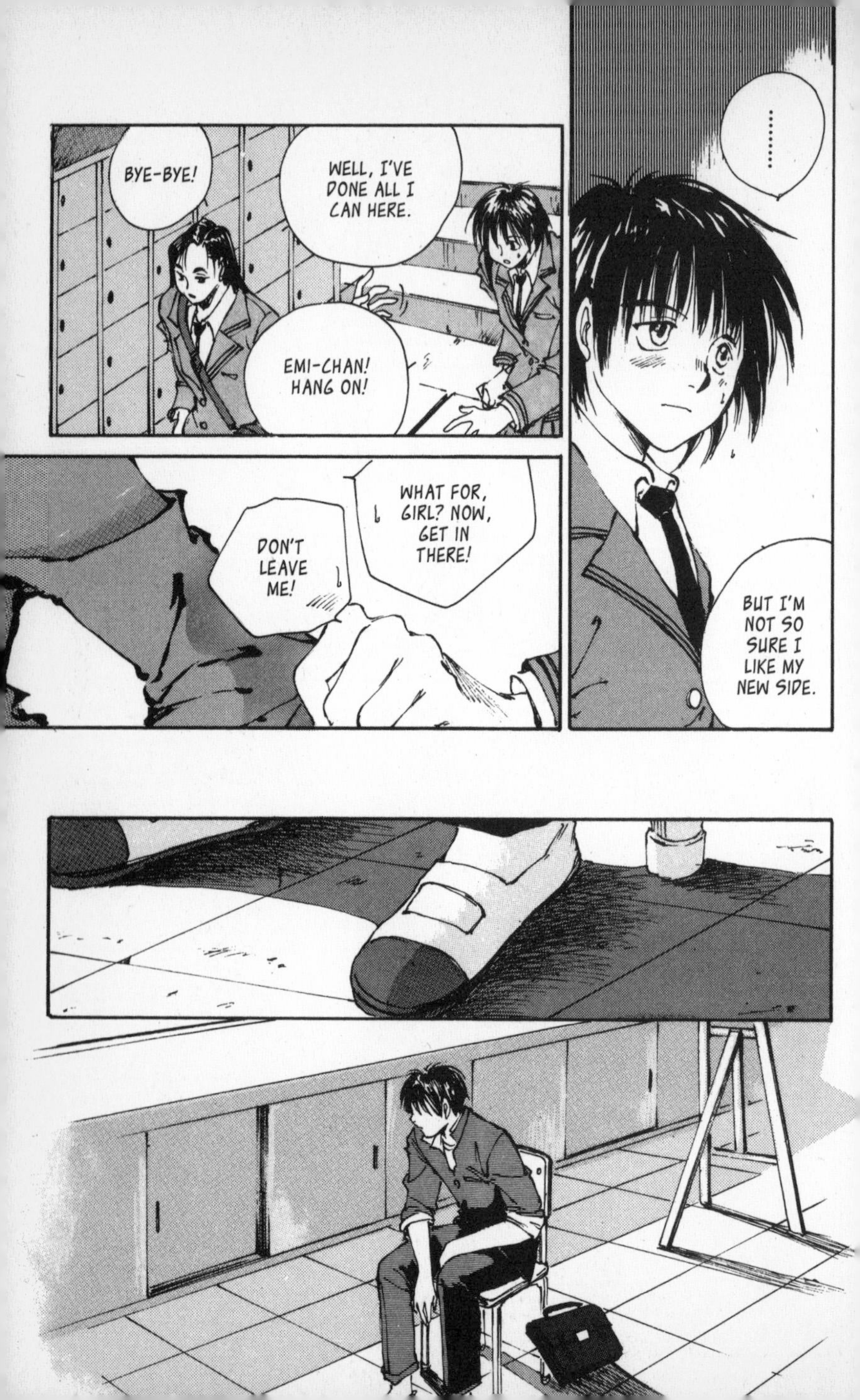
......
BUT I'M NOT SO SURE I LIKE MY NEW SIDE.
WELL, I'VE DONE ALL I CAN HERE.
BYE-BYE!
EMI-CHAN! HANG ON!
DON'T LEAVE ME!
WHAT FOR, GIRL? NOW, GET IN THERE!

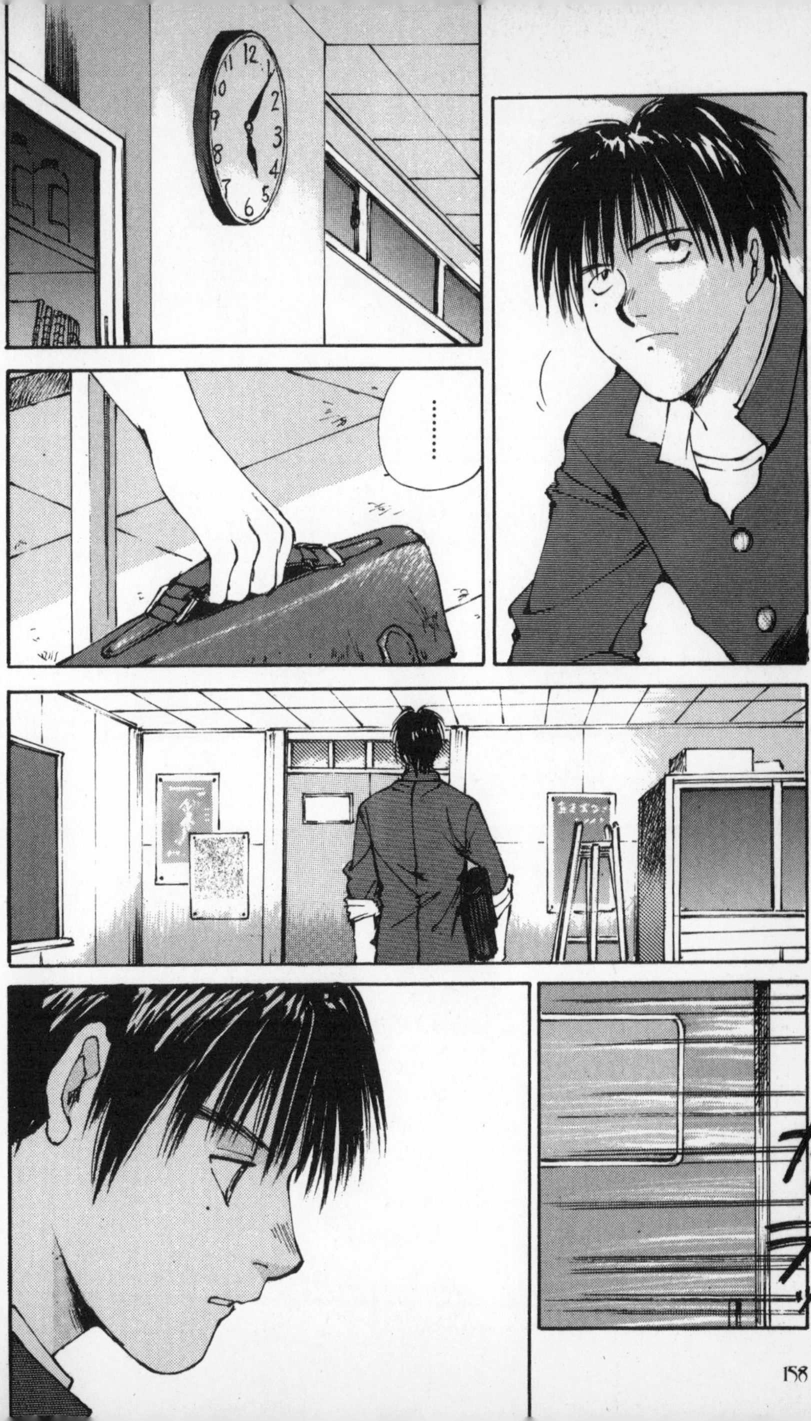
……
ガラッ

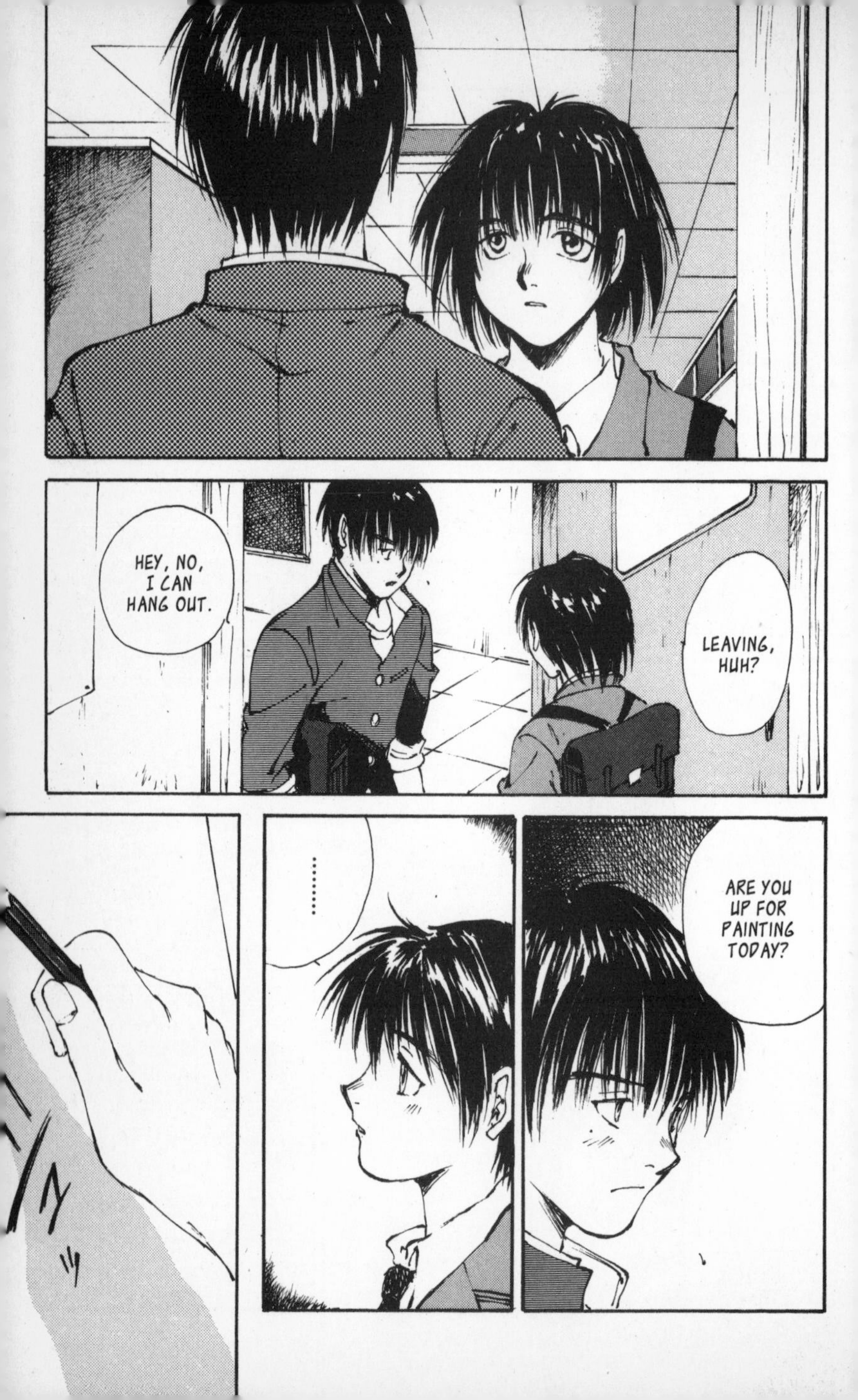
LEAVING, HUH?
HEY, NO, I CAN HANG OUT.
ARE YOU UP FOR PAINTING TODAY?
......

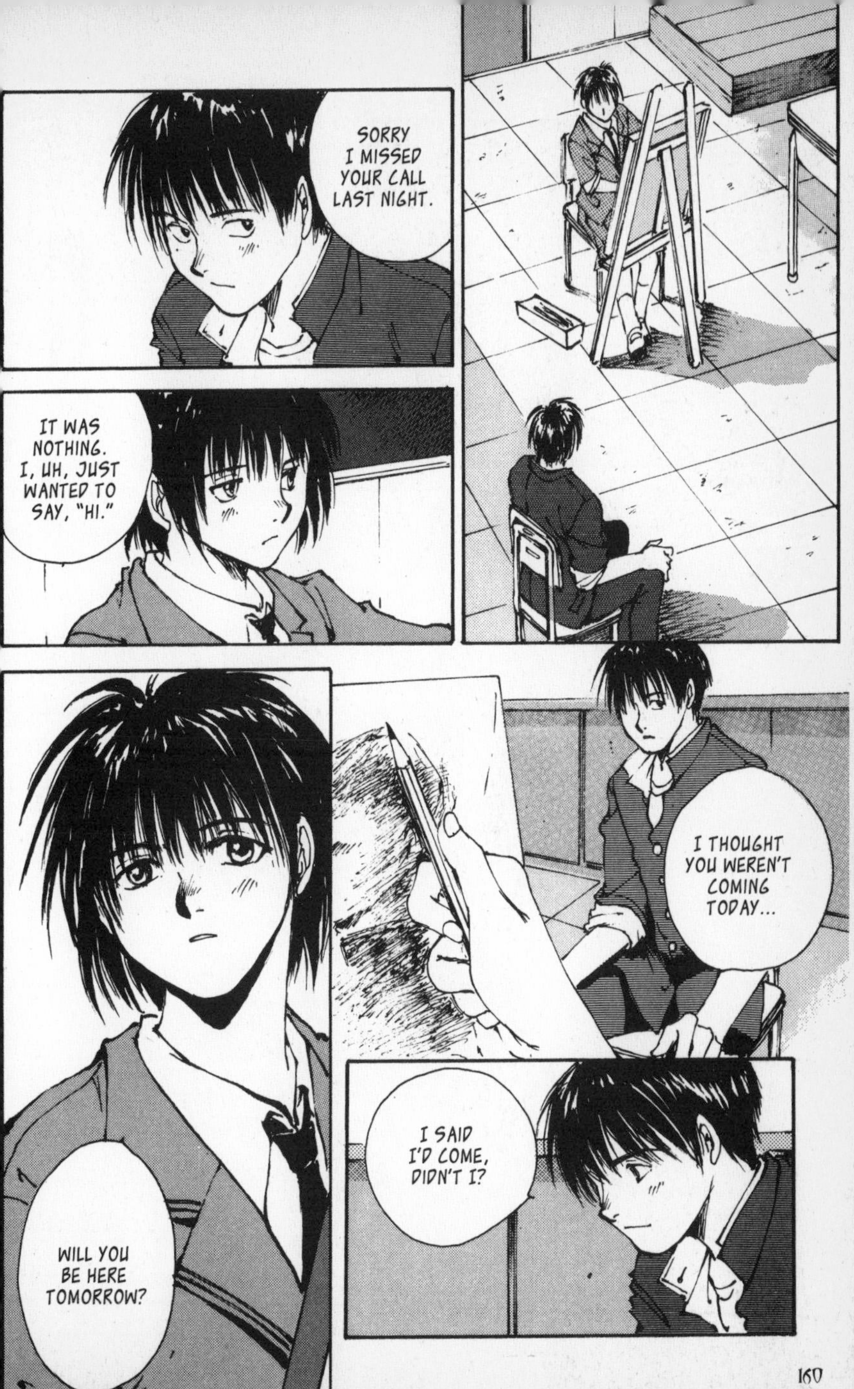
SORRY I MISSED YOUR CALL LAST NIGHT.
IT WAS NOTHING. I, UH, JUST WANTED TO SAY, "HI."
I THOUGHT YOU WEREN'T COMING TODAY...
I SAID I'D COME, DIDN'T I?
WILL YOU BE HERE TOMORROW?

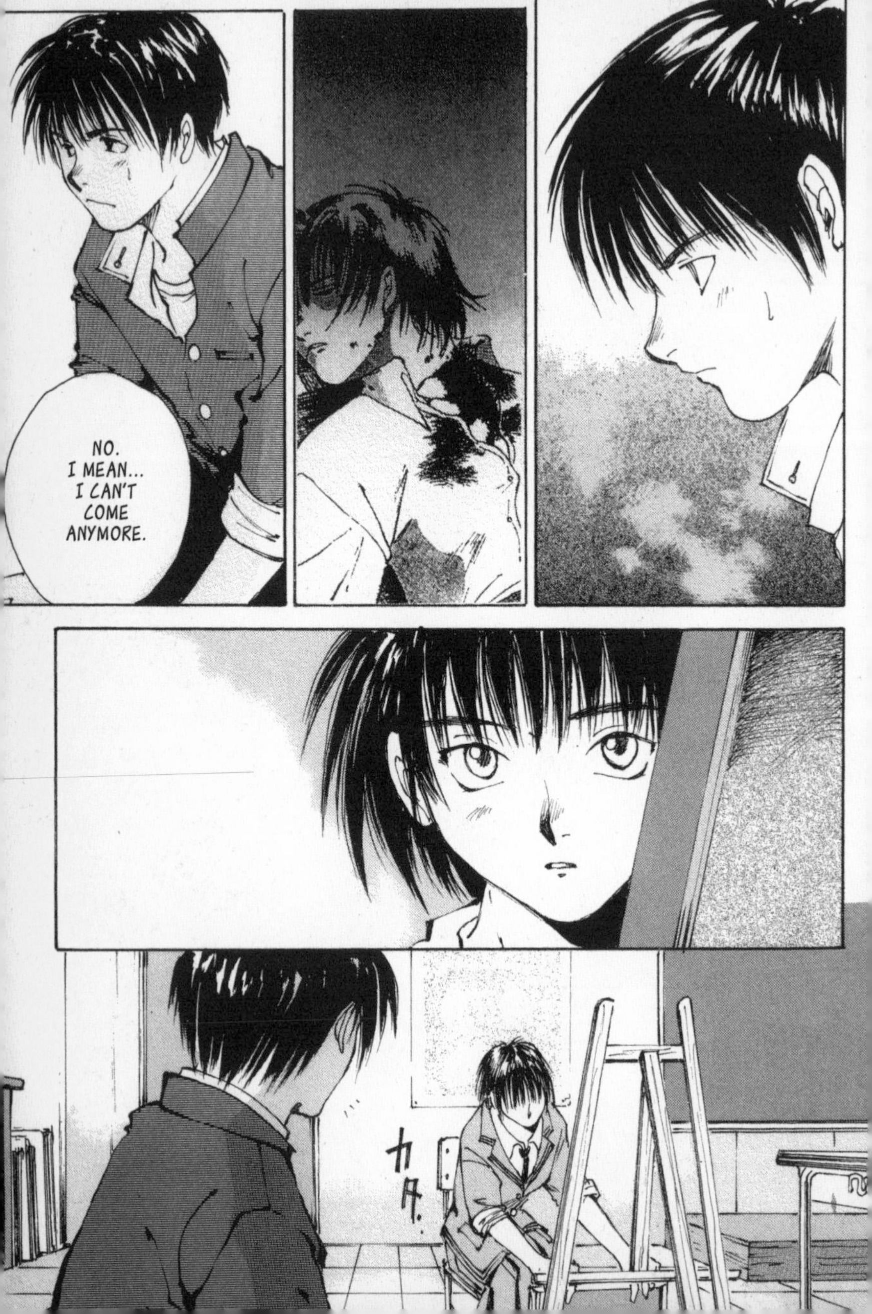
NO. I MEAN... I CAN'T COME ANYMORE.
カタ.

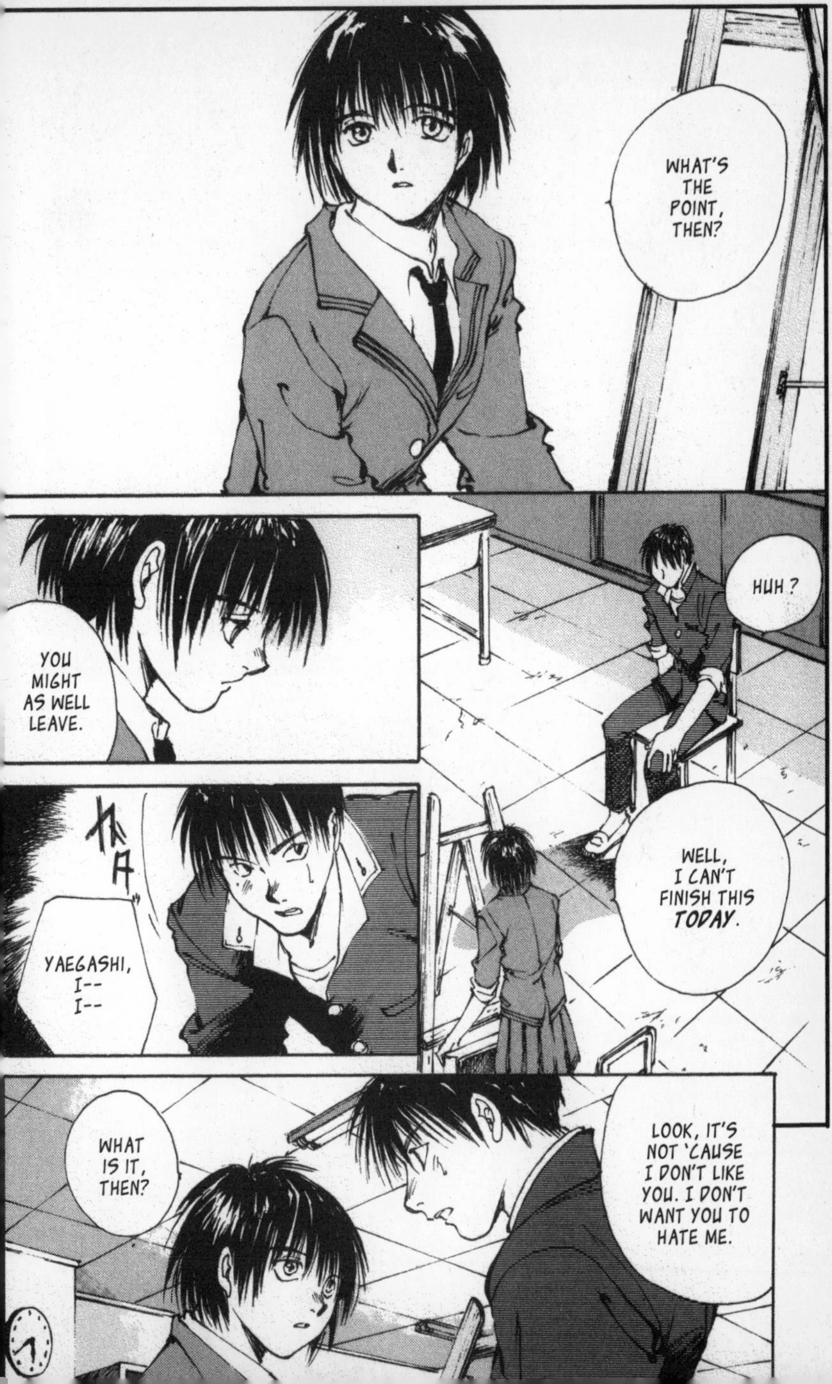
WHAT'S THE POINT, THEN?
HUH?
WELL, I CAN'T FINISH THIS *TODAY*.
YOU MIGHT AS WELL LEAVE.
YAEGASHI, I-- I--
LOOK, IT'S NOT 'CAUSE I DON'T LIKE YOU. I DON'T WANT YOU TO HATE ME.
WHAT IS IT, THEN?

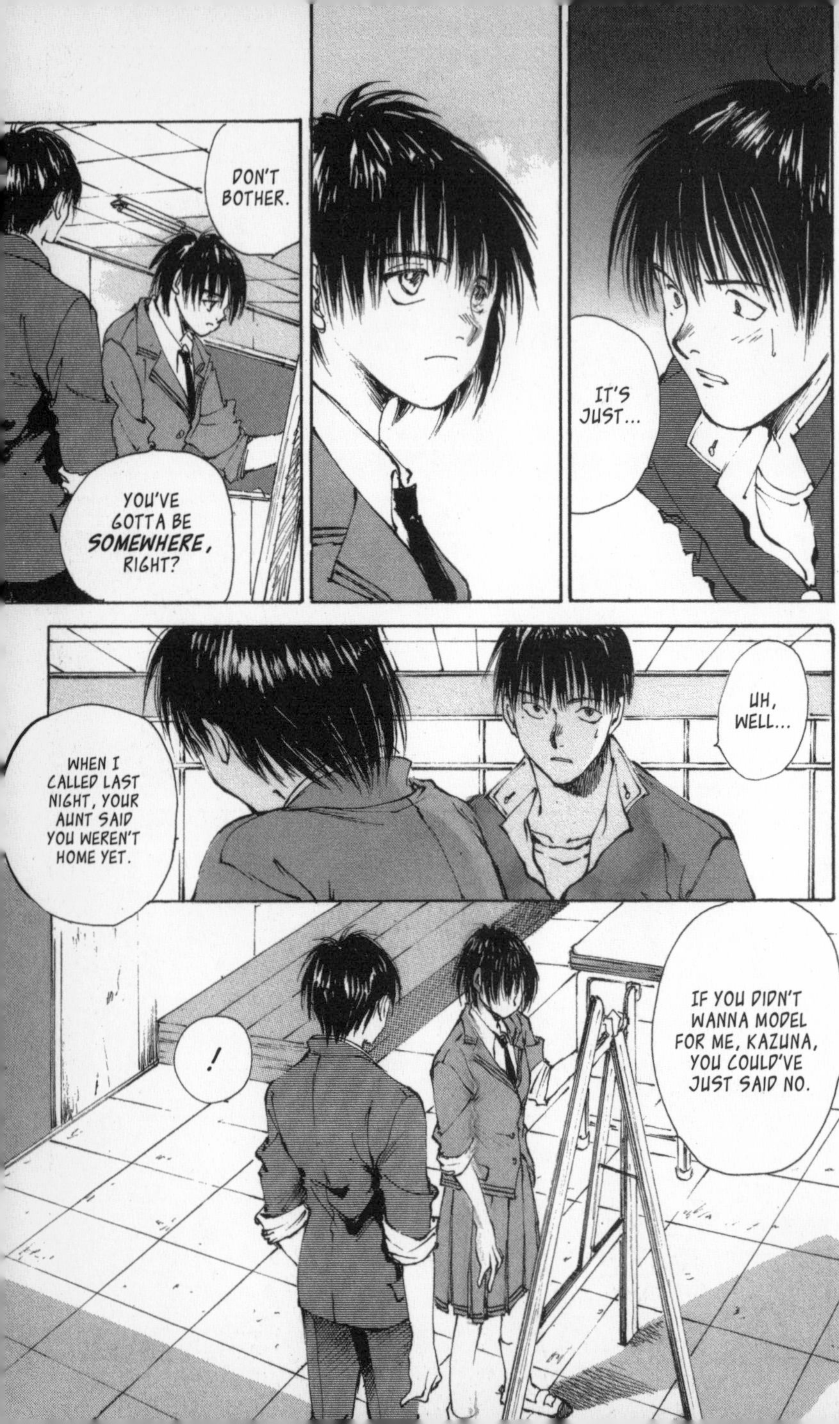
DON'T BOTHER.
YOU'VE GOTTA BE **SOMEWHERE**, RIGHT?
IT'S JUST...
WHEN I CALLED LAST NIGHT, YOUR AUNT SAID YOU WEREN'T HOME YET.
UH, WELL...
!
IF YOU DIDN'T WANNA MODEL FOR ME, KAZUNA, YOU COULD'VE JUST SAID NO.

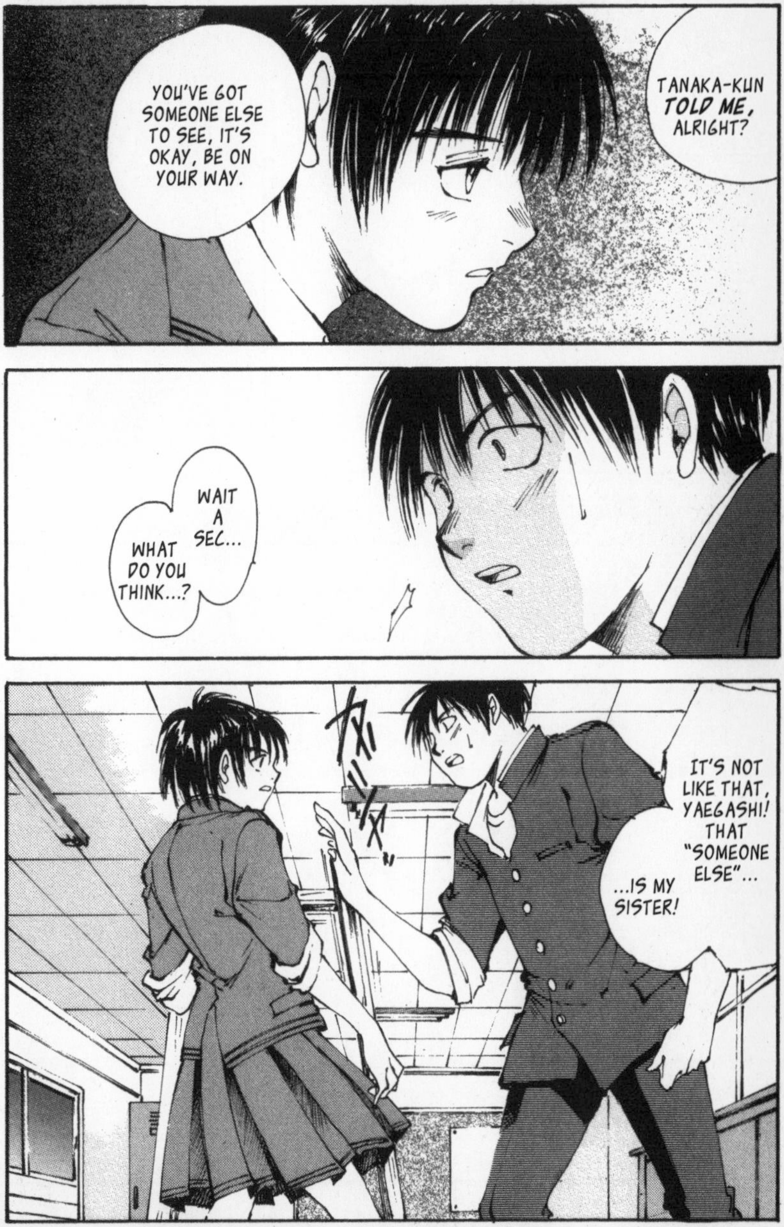
TANAKA-KUN TOLD ME, ALRIGHT?
YOU'VE GOT SOMEONE ELSE TO SEE, IT'S OKAY, BE ON YOUR WAY.
WAIT A SEC...
WHAT DO YOU THINK...?
IT'S NOT LIKE THAT, YAEGASHI! THAT "SOMEONE ELSE"...
...IS MY SISTER!

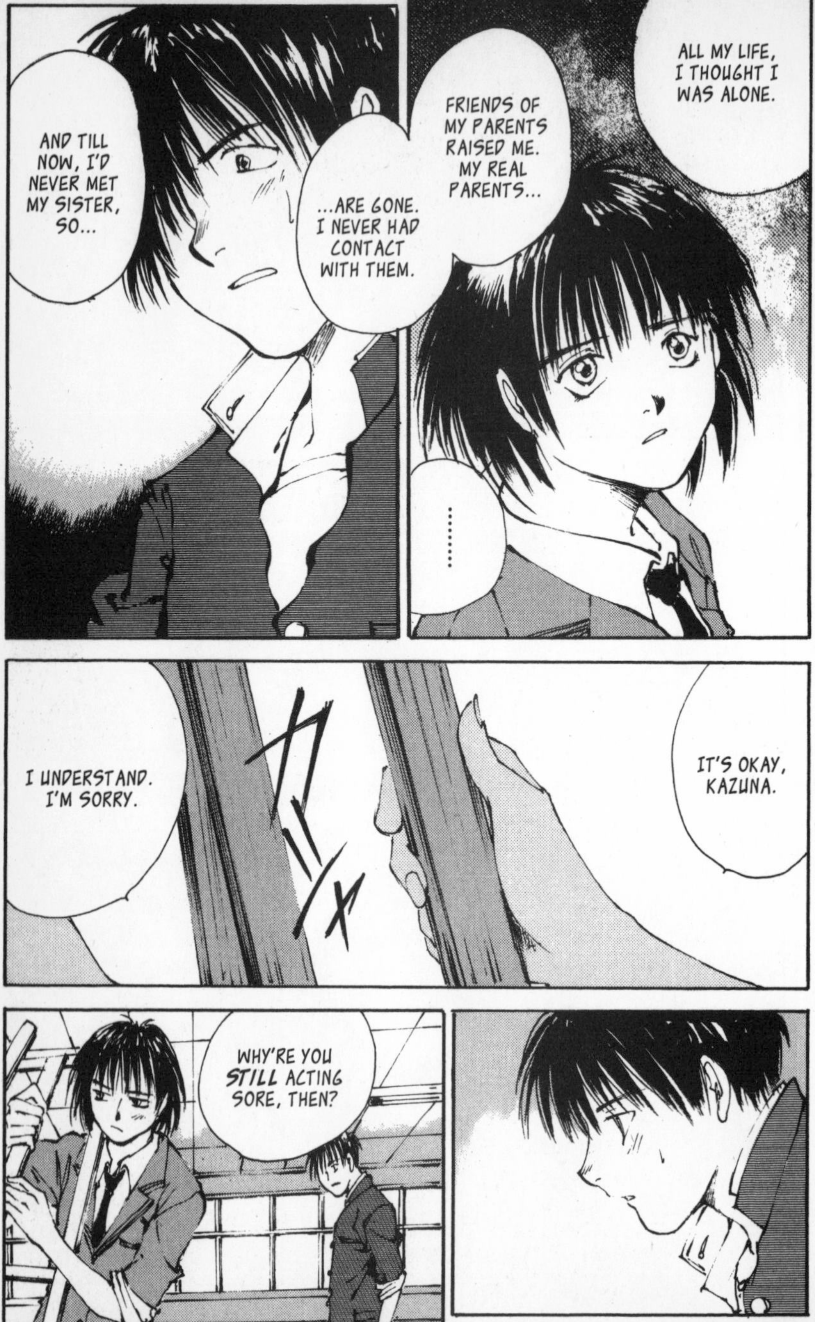
ALL MY LIFE, I THOUGHT I WAS ALONE.
FRIENDS OF MY PARENTS RAISED ME. MY REAL PARENTS...
...ARE GONE. I NEVER HAD CONTACT WITH THEM.
......
AND TILL NOW, I'D NEVER MET MY SISTER, SO...
IT'S OKAY, KAZUNA.
I UNDERSTAND. I'M SORRY.
WHY'RE YOU *STILL* ACTING SORE, THEN?

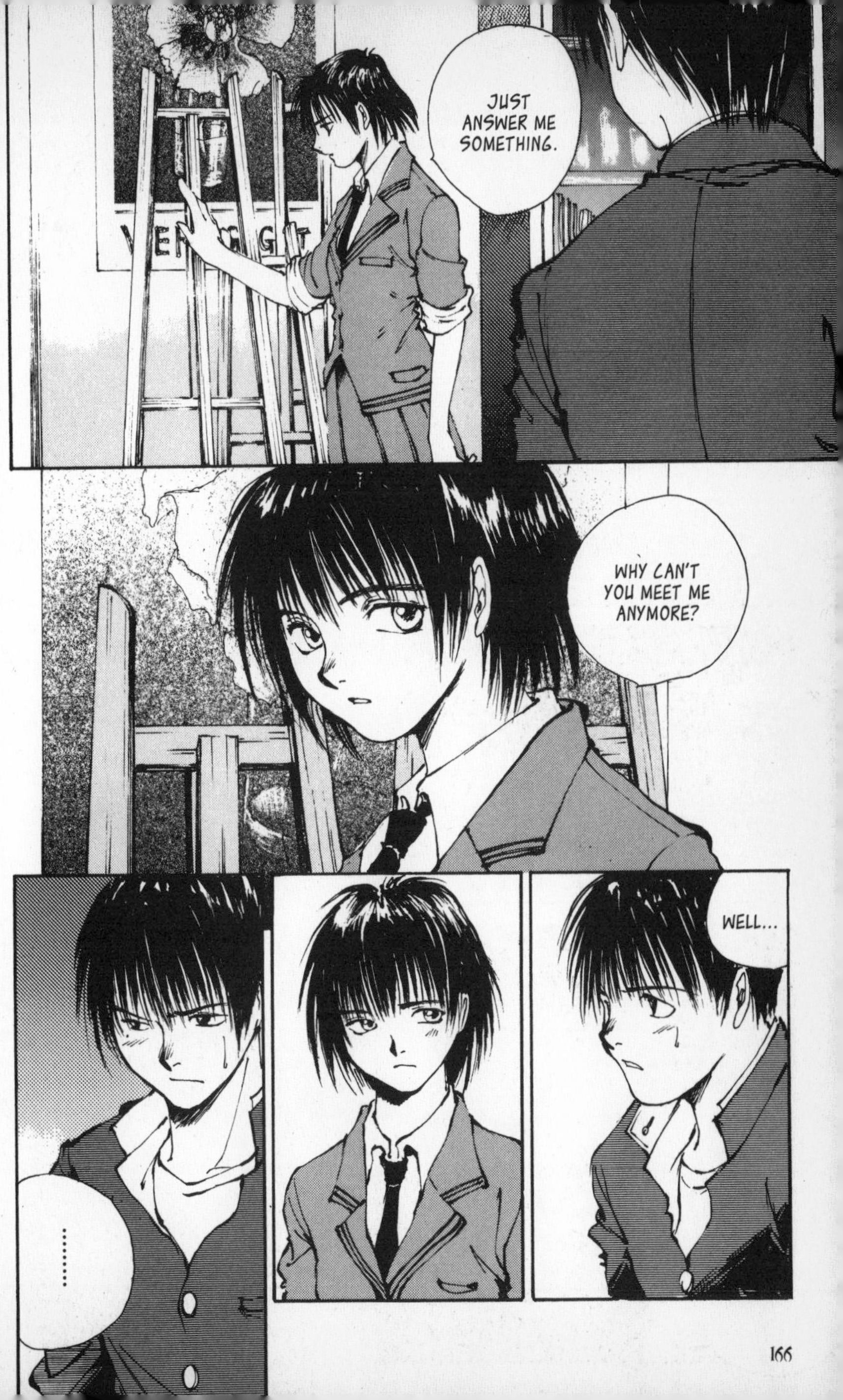
JUST ANSWER ME SOMETHING.
WHY CAN'T YOU MEET ME ANYMORE?
WELL...
....

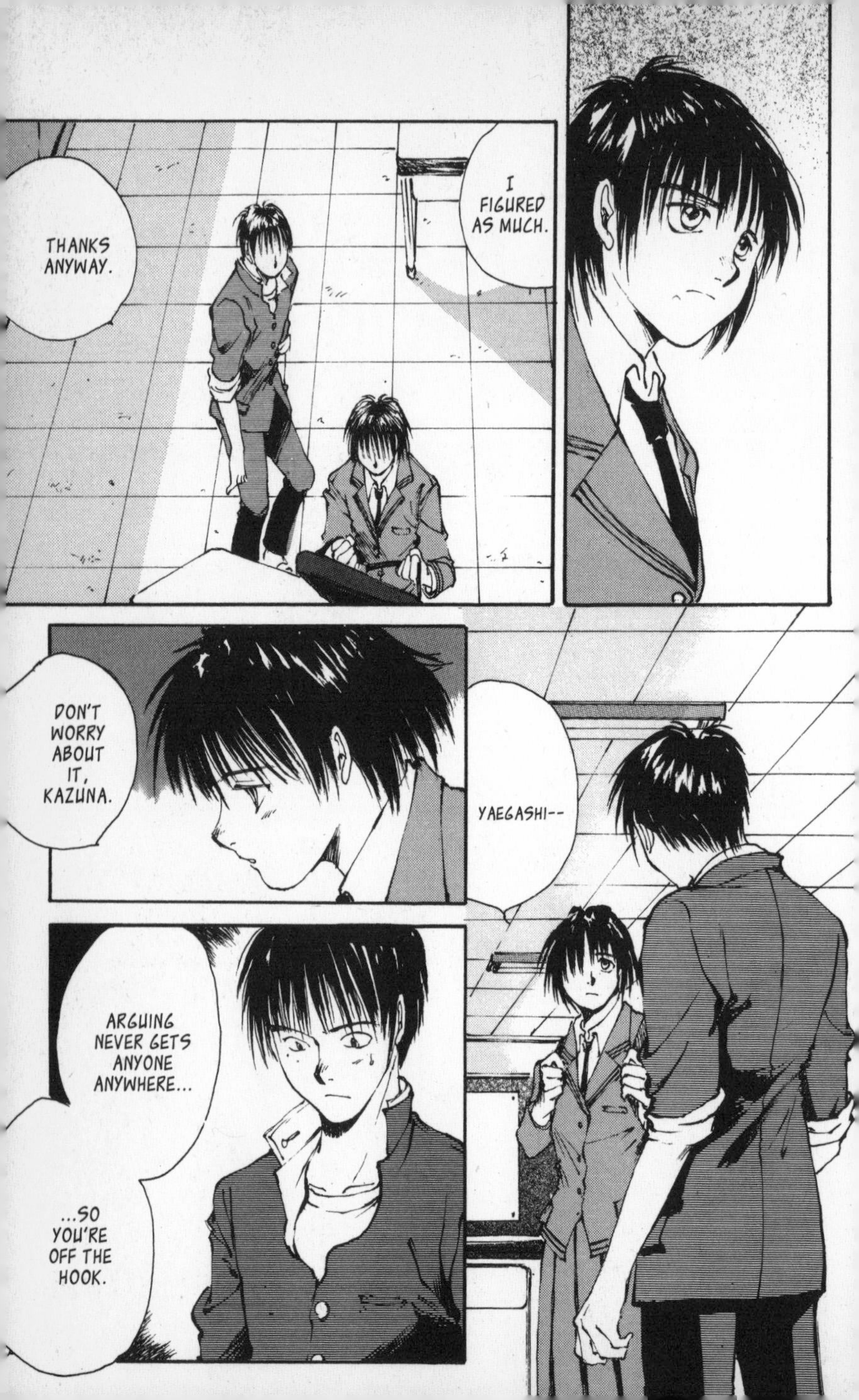
I FIGURED AS MUCH.
THANKS ANYWAY.
YAEGASHI--
DON'T WORRY ABOUT IT, KAZUNA.
ARGUING NEVER GETS ANYONE ANYWHERE...
...SO YOU'RE OFF THE HOOK.

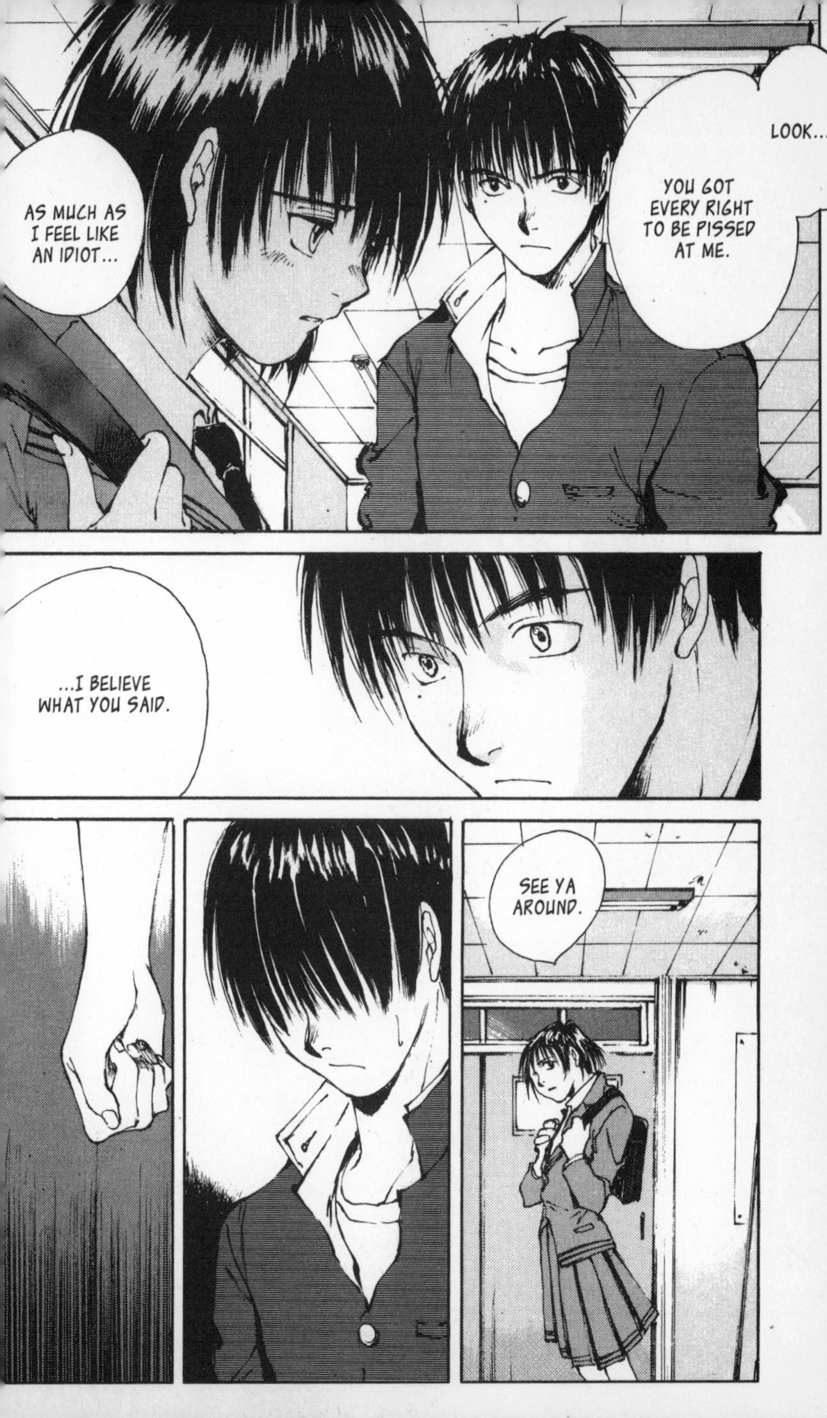
LOOK...
YOU GOT EVERY RIGHT TO BE PISSED AT ME.
AS MUCH AS I FEEL LIKE AN IDIOT...
...I BELIEVE WHAT YOU SAID.
SEE YA AROUND.

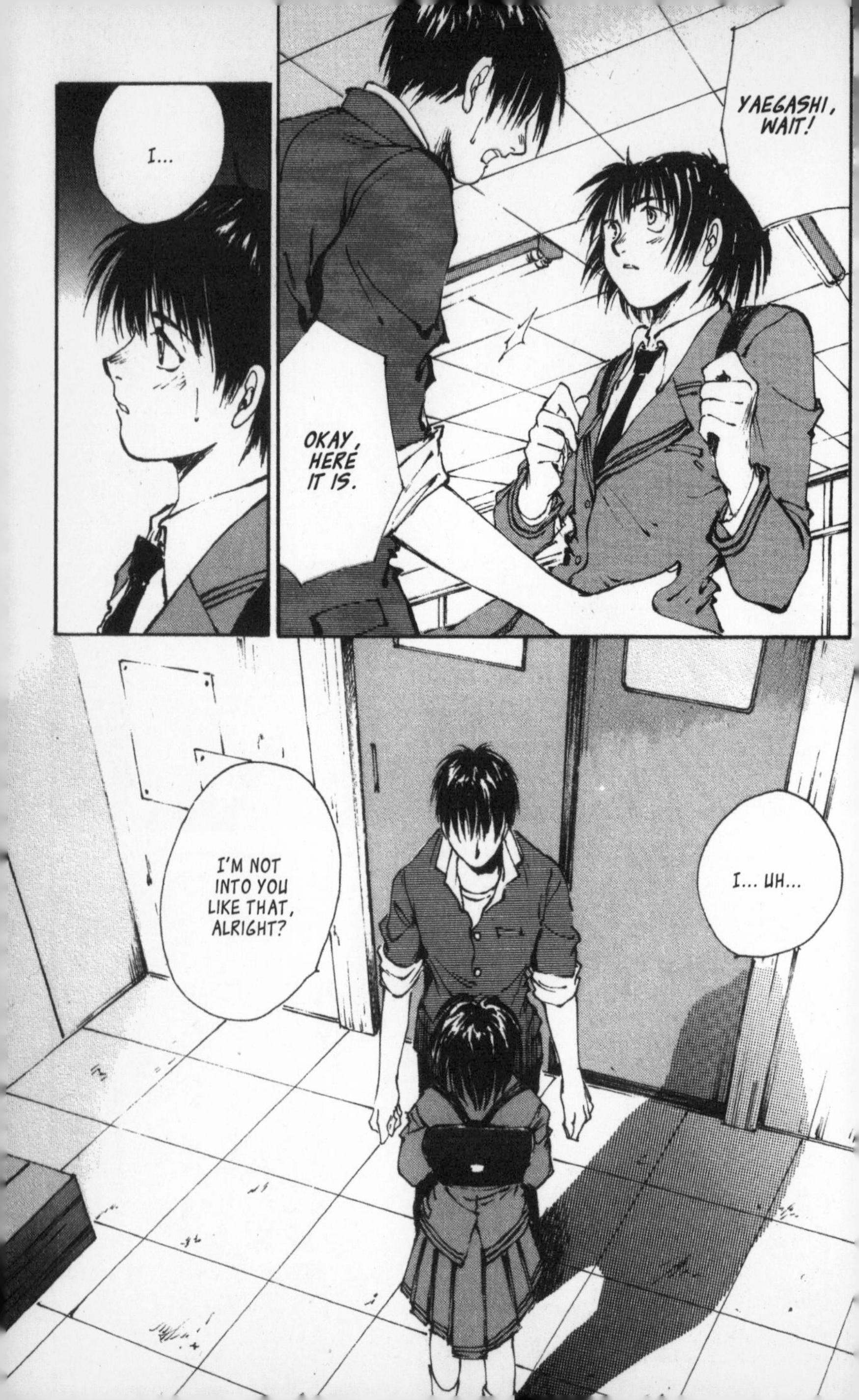
YAEGASHI, WAIT!
OKAY, HERE IT IS.
I...
I... UH...
I'M NOT INTO YOU LIKE THAT, ALRIGHT?

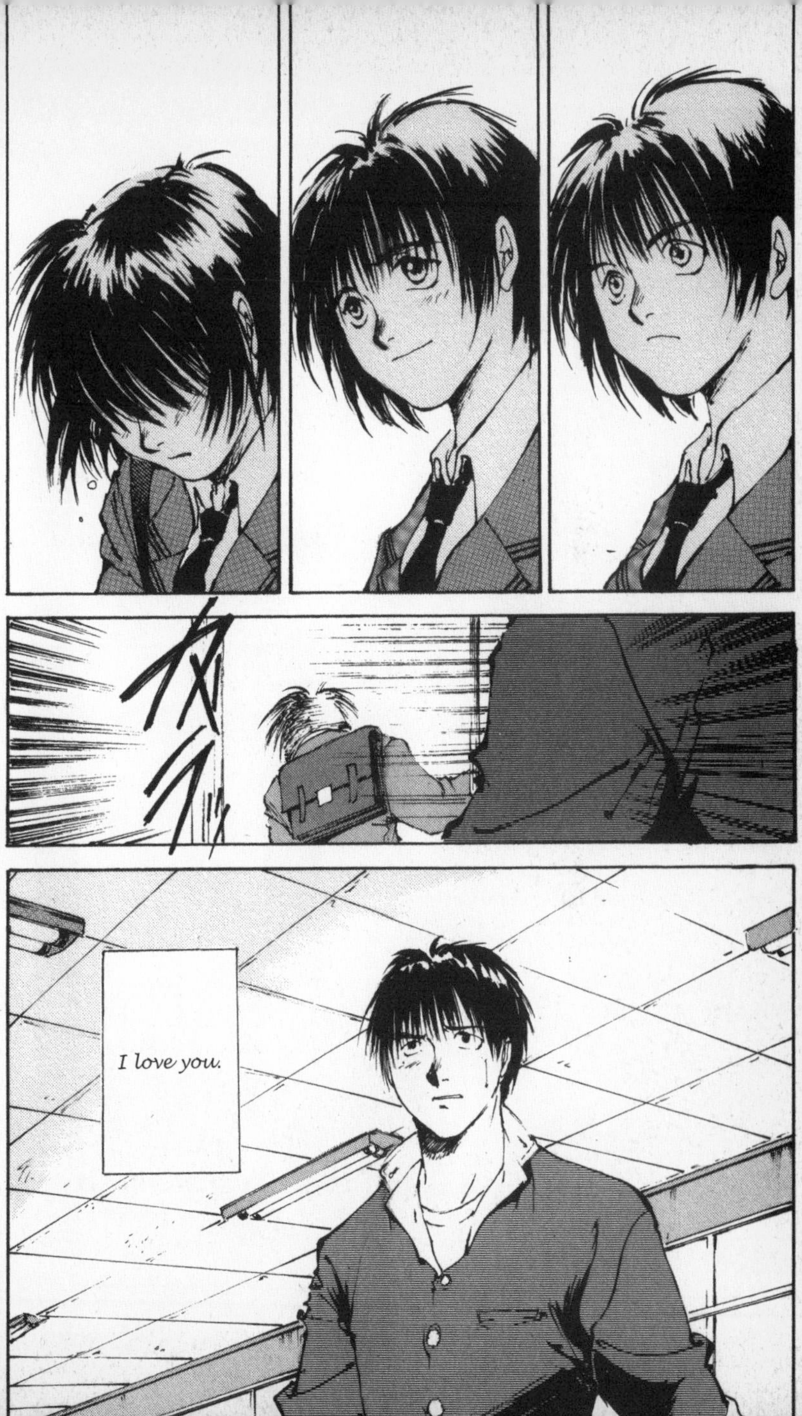
I love you.

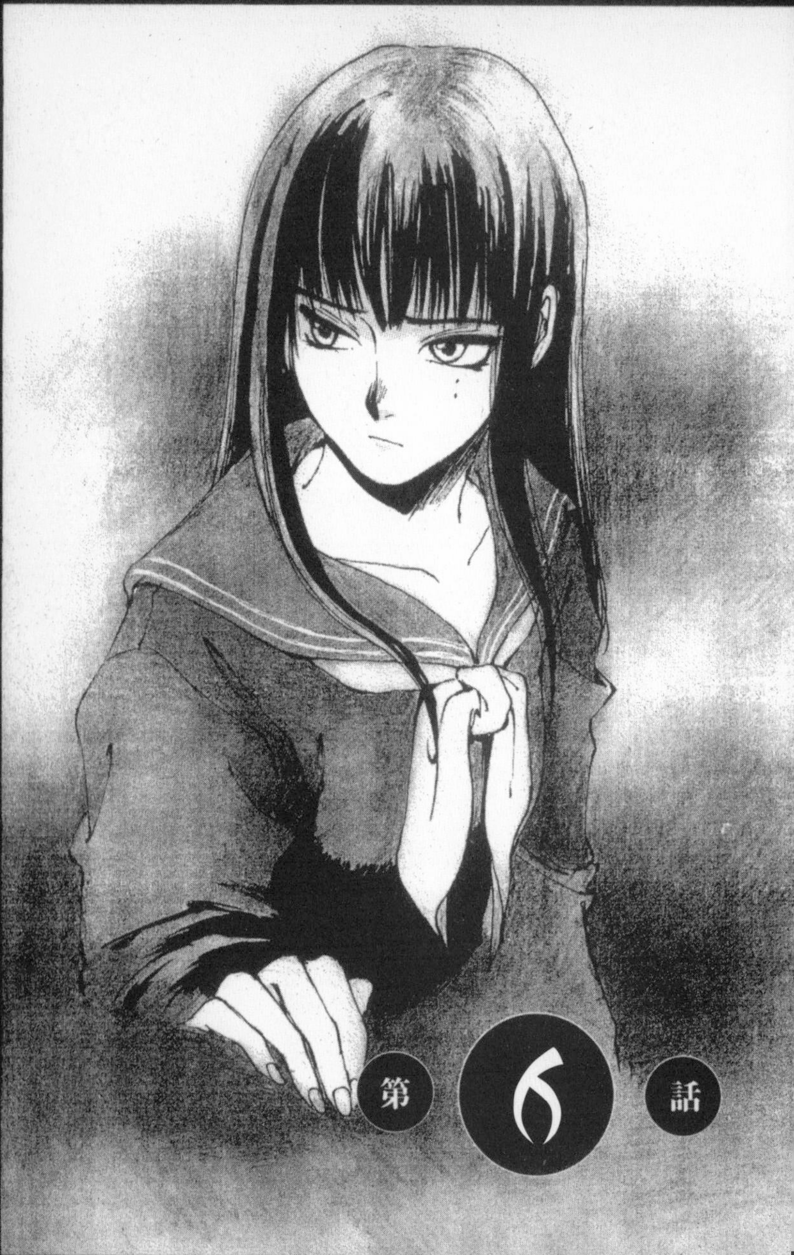
第6話

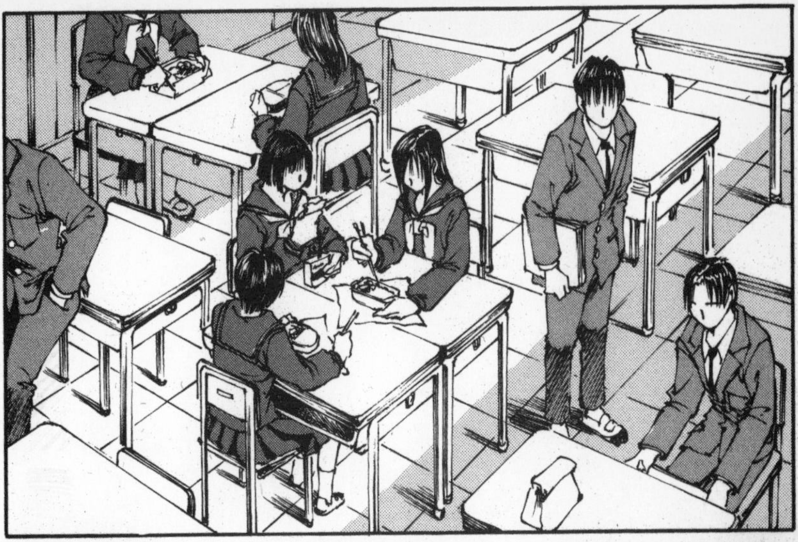
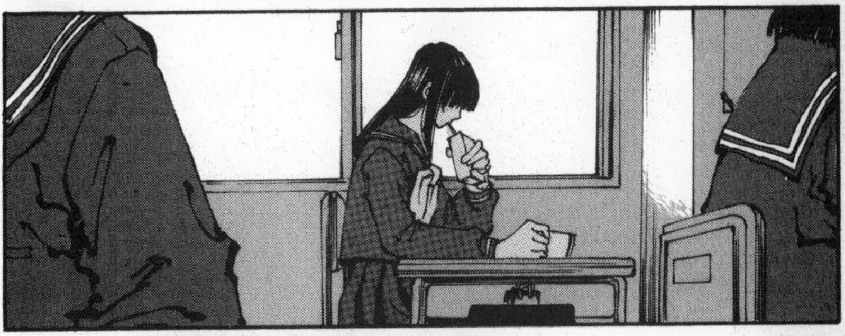
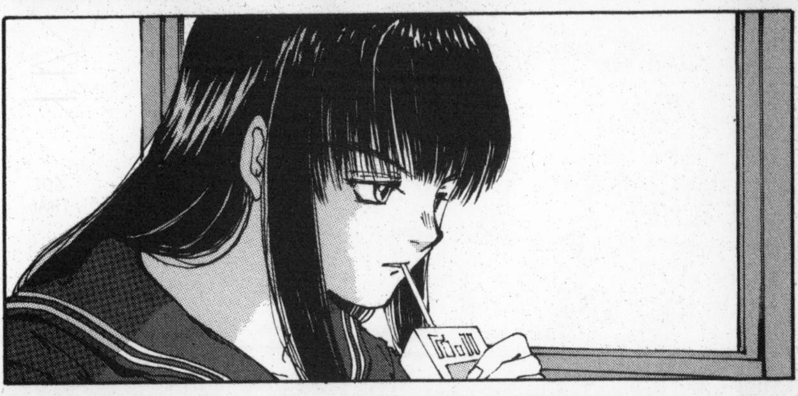

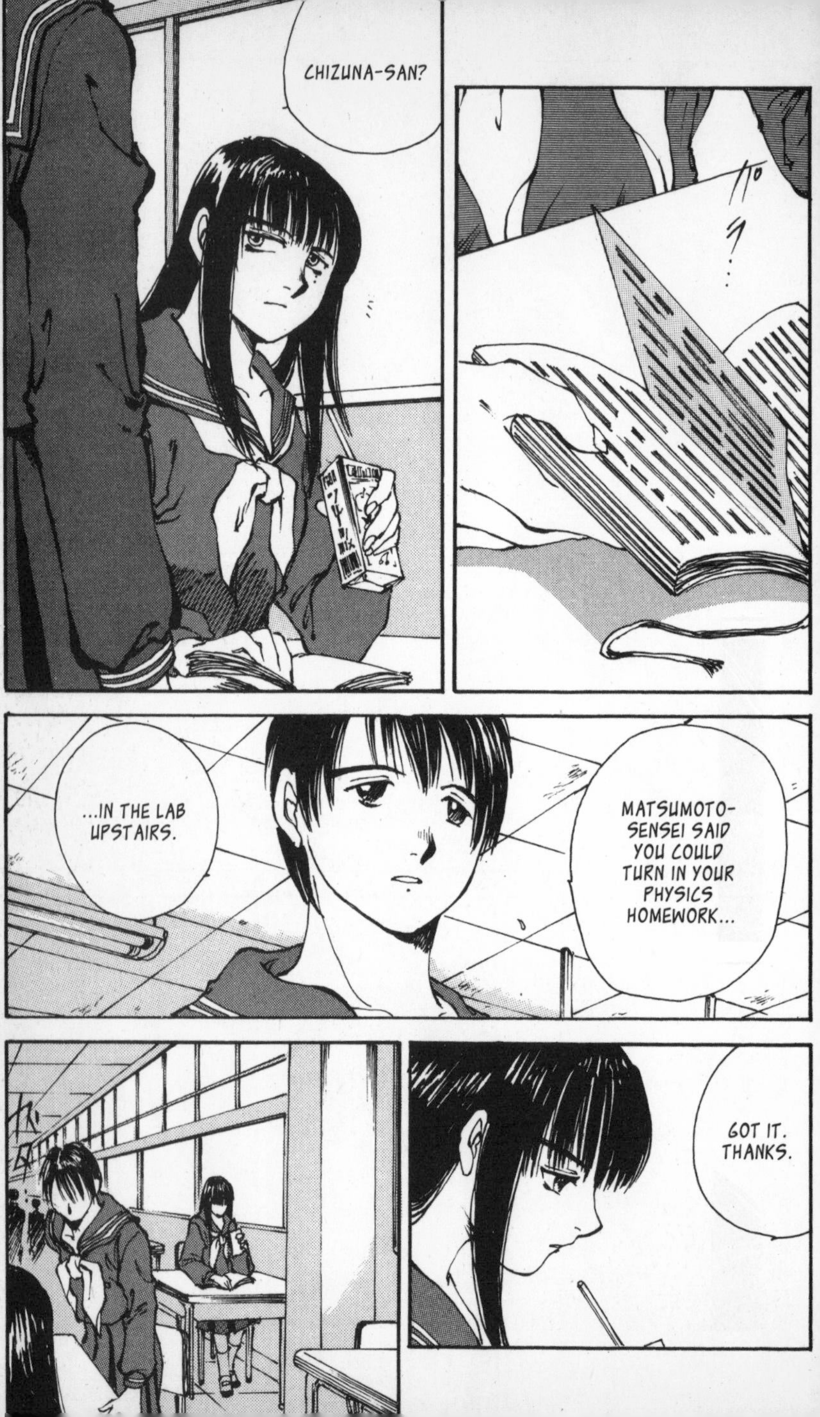
CHIZUNA-SAN?
MATSUMOTO-SENSEI SAID YOU COULD TURN IN YOUR PHYSICS HOMEWORK...
...IN THE LAB UPSTAIRS.
GOT IT. THANKS.

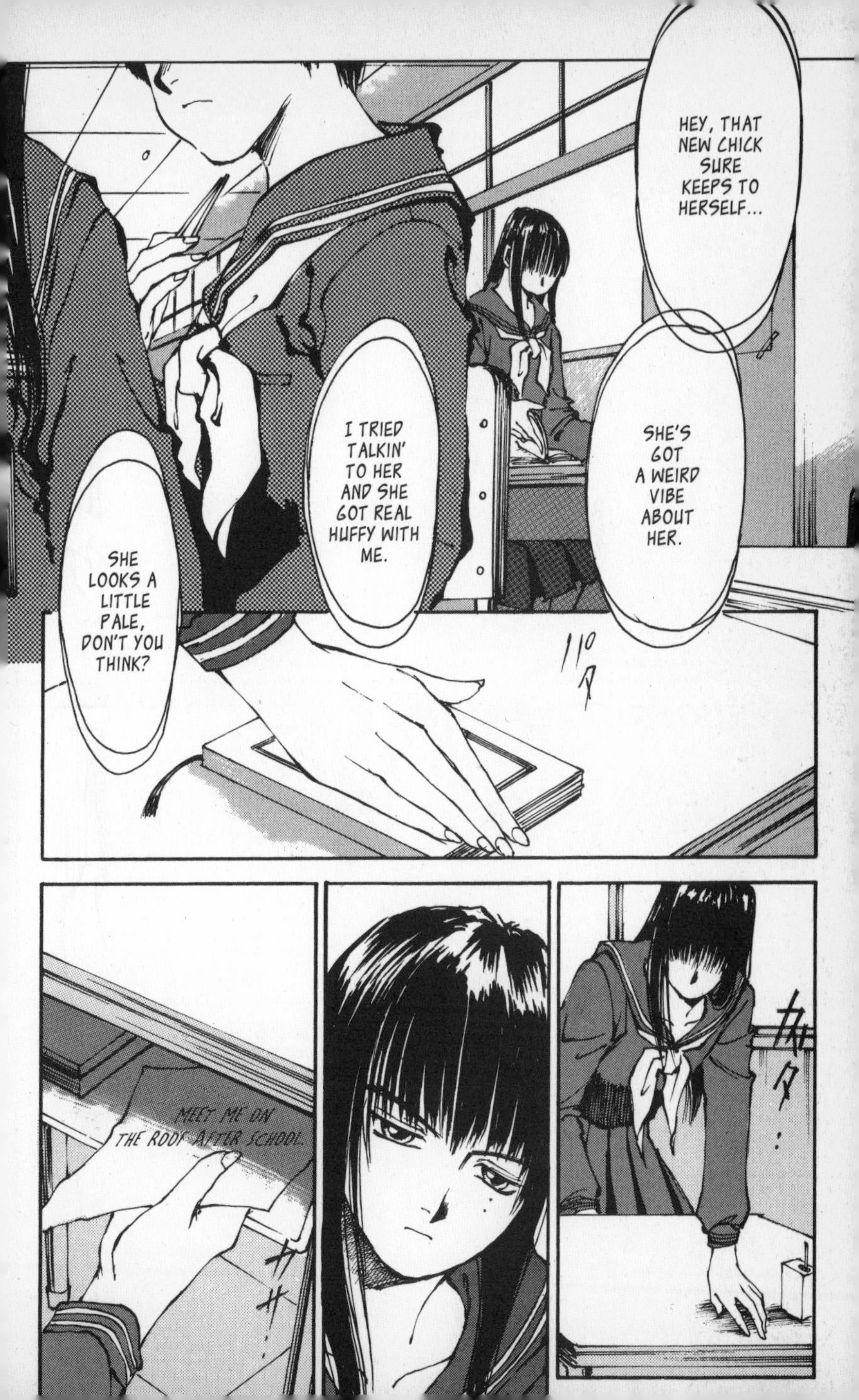
HEY, THAT NEW CHICK SURE KEEPS TO HERSELF...
SHE'S GOT A WEIRD VIBE ABOUT HER.
I TRIED TALKIN' TO HER AND SHE GOT REAL HUFFY WITH ME.
SHE LOOKS A LITTLE PALE, DON'T YOU THINK?
MEET ME ON THE ROOF AFTER SCHOOL.

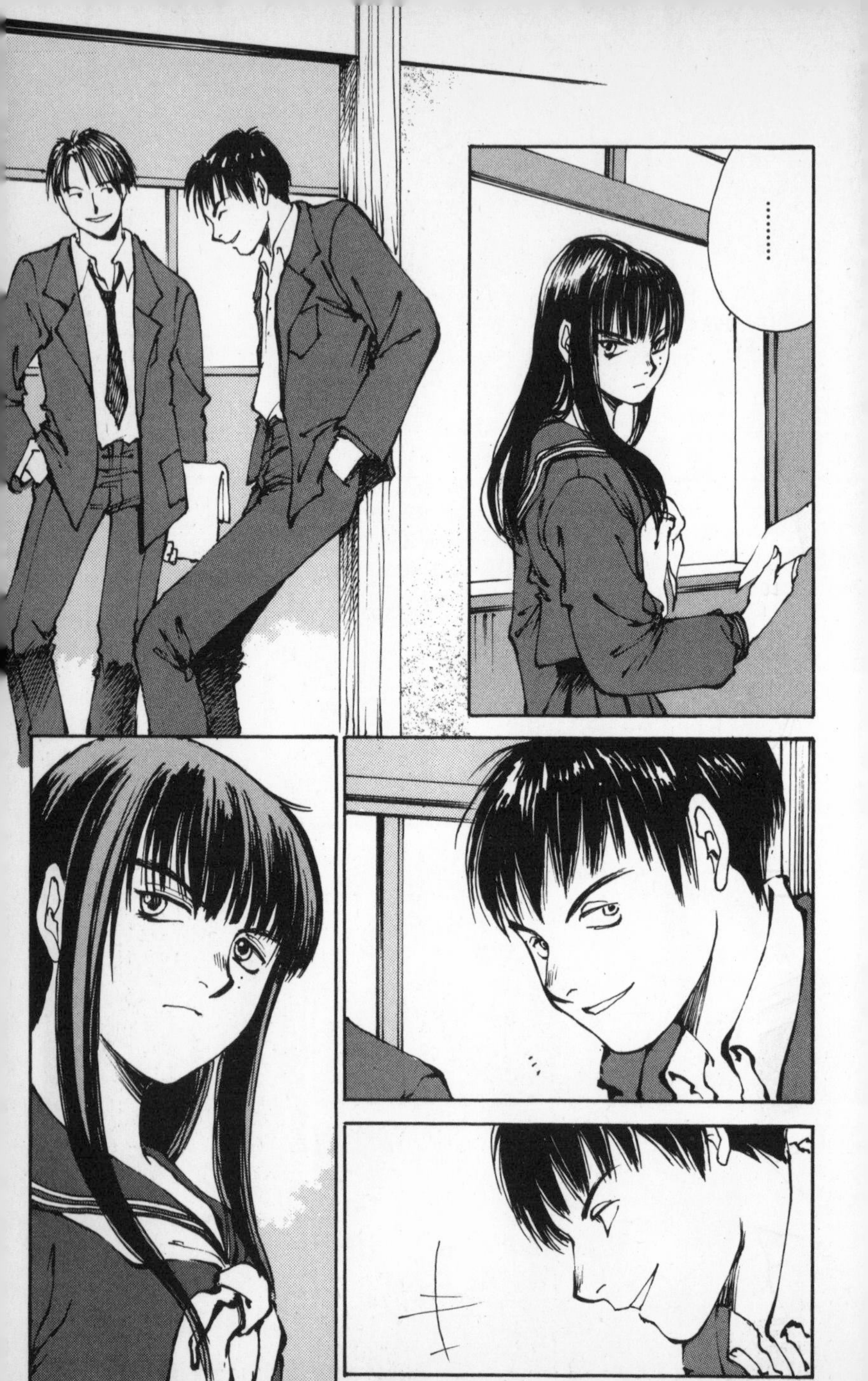
......

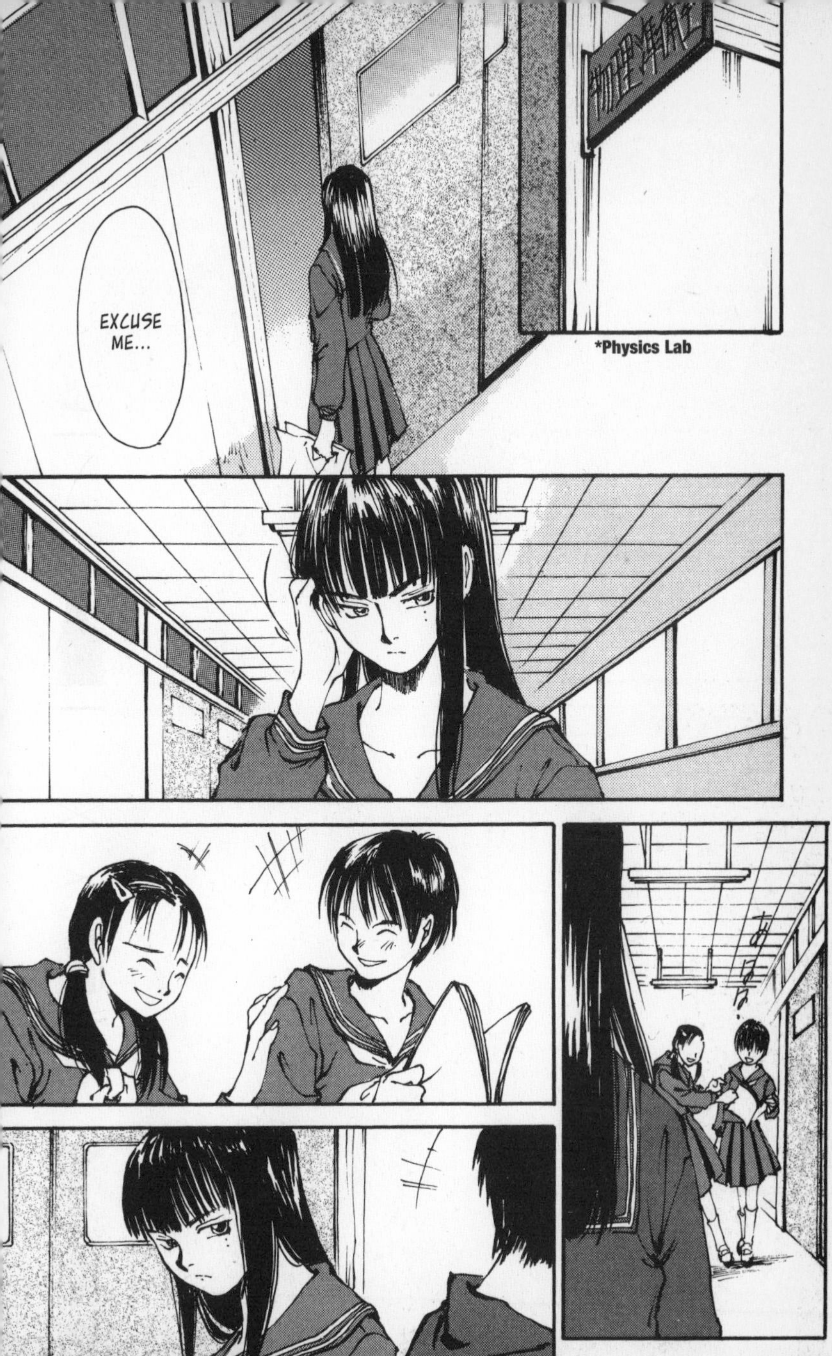
*Physics Lab
EXCUSE ME...
あはは

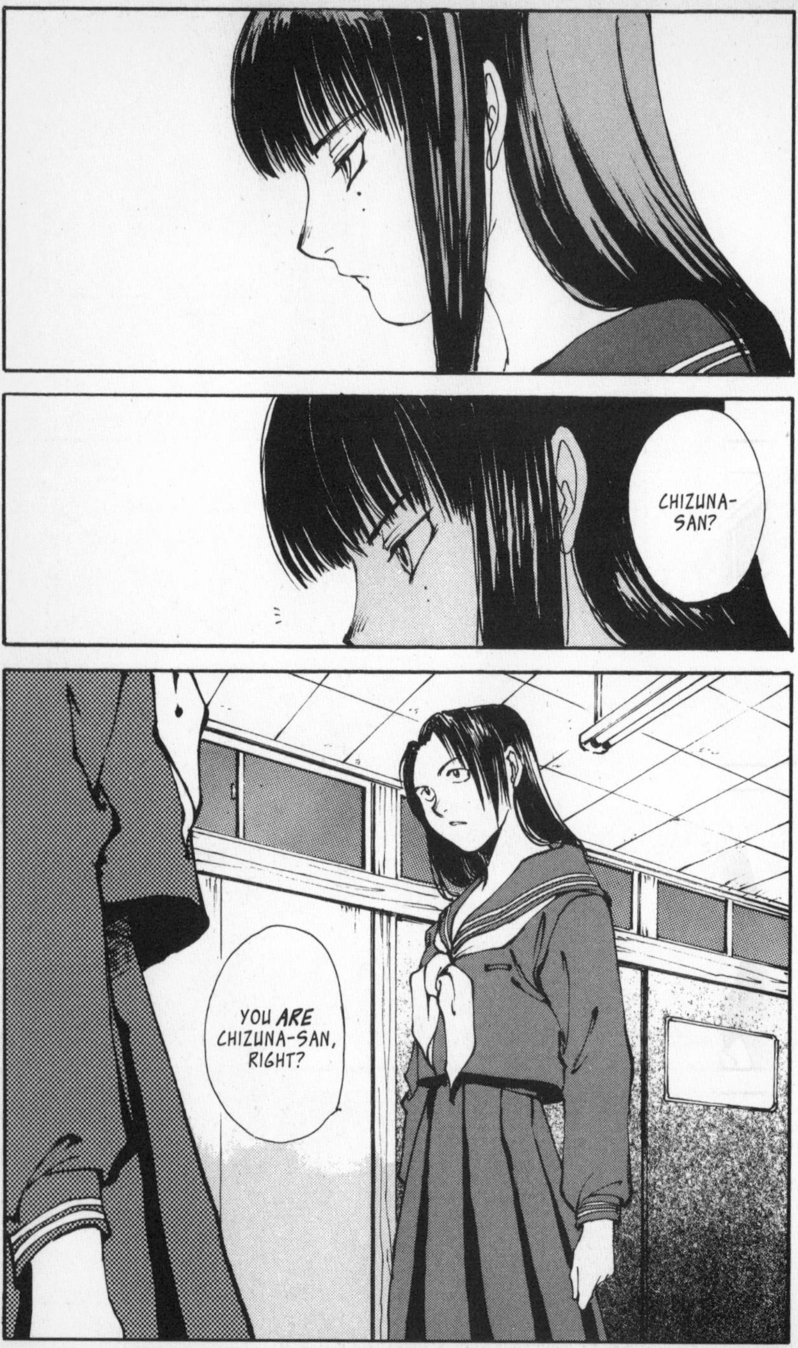
CHIZUNA-SAN?
YOU ARE CHIZUNA-SAN, RIGHT?

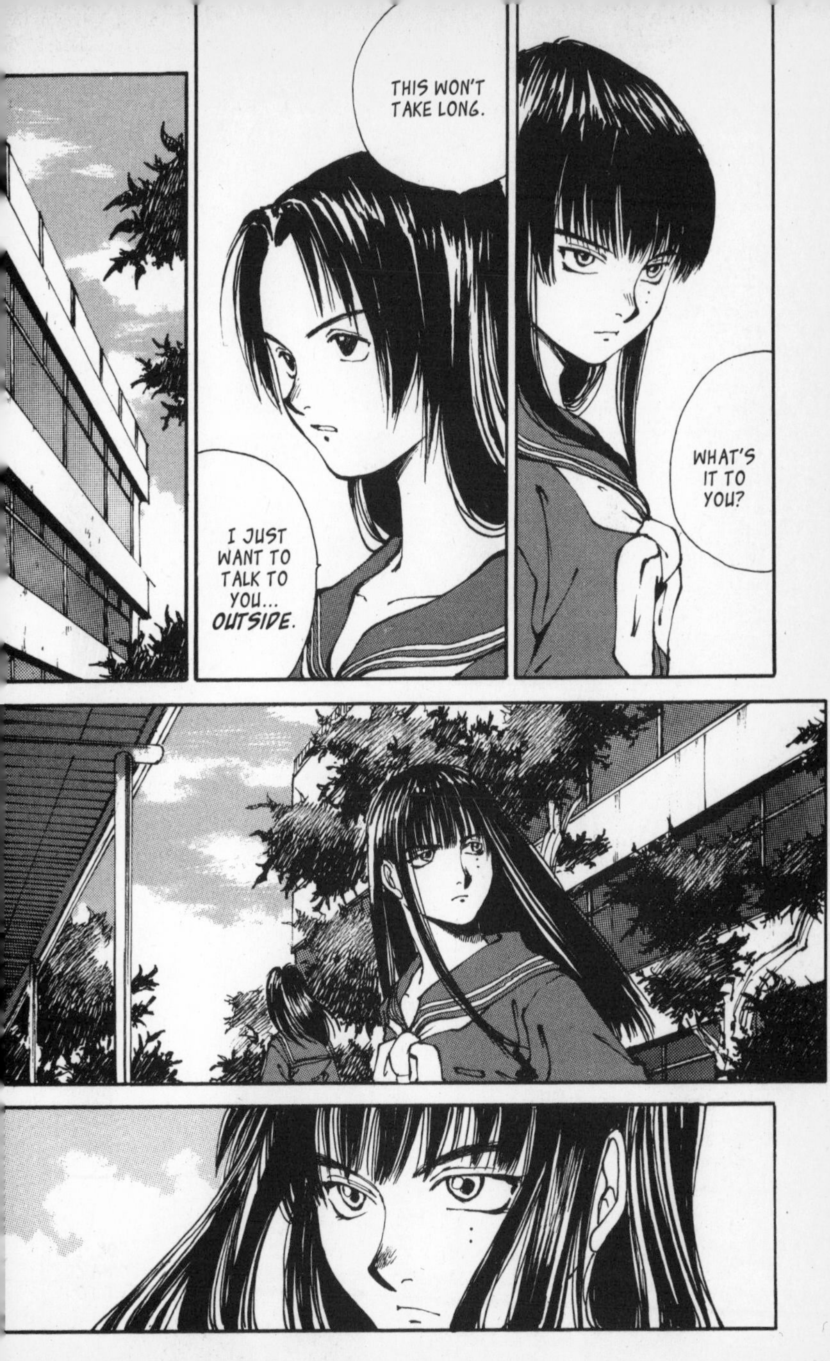
WHAT'S IT TO YOU?
THIS WON'T TAKE LONG.
I JUST WANT TO TALK TO YOU... **OUTSIDE**.

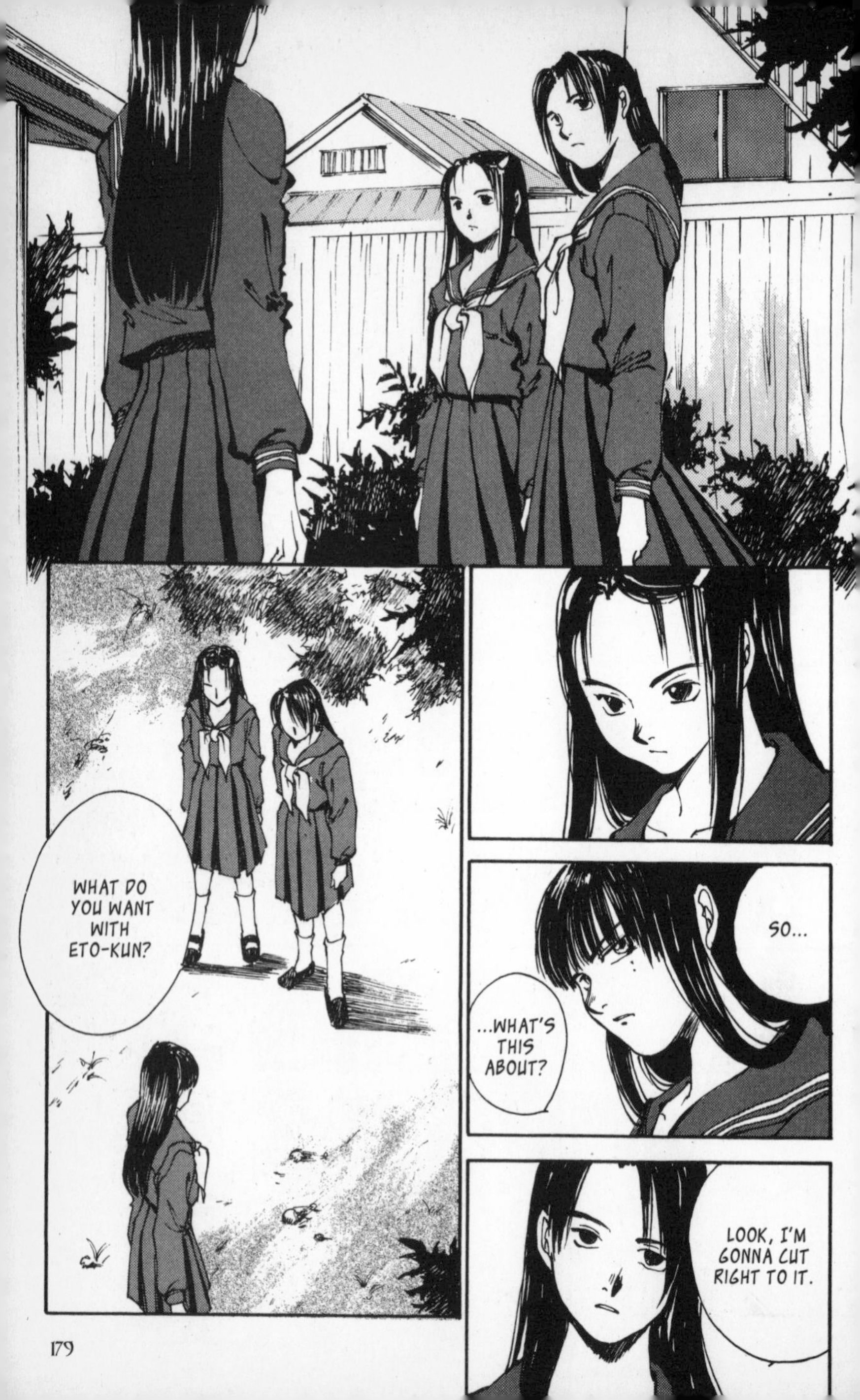
SO...
...WHAT'S THIS ABOUT?
LOOK, I'M GONNA CUT RIGHT TO IT.
WHAT DO YOU WANT WITH ETO-KUN?

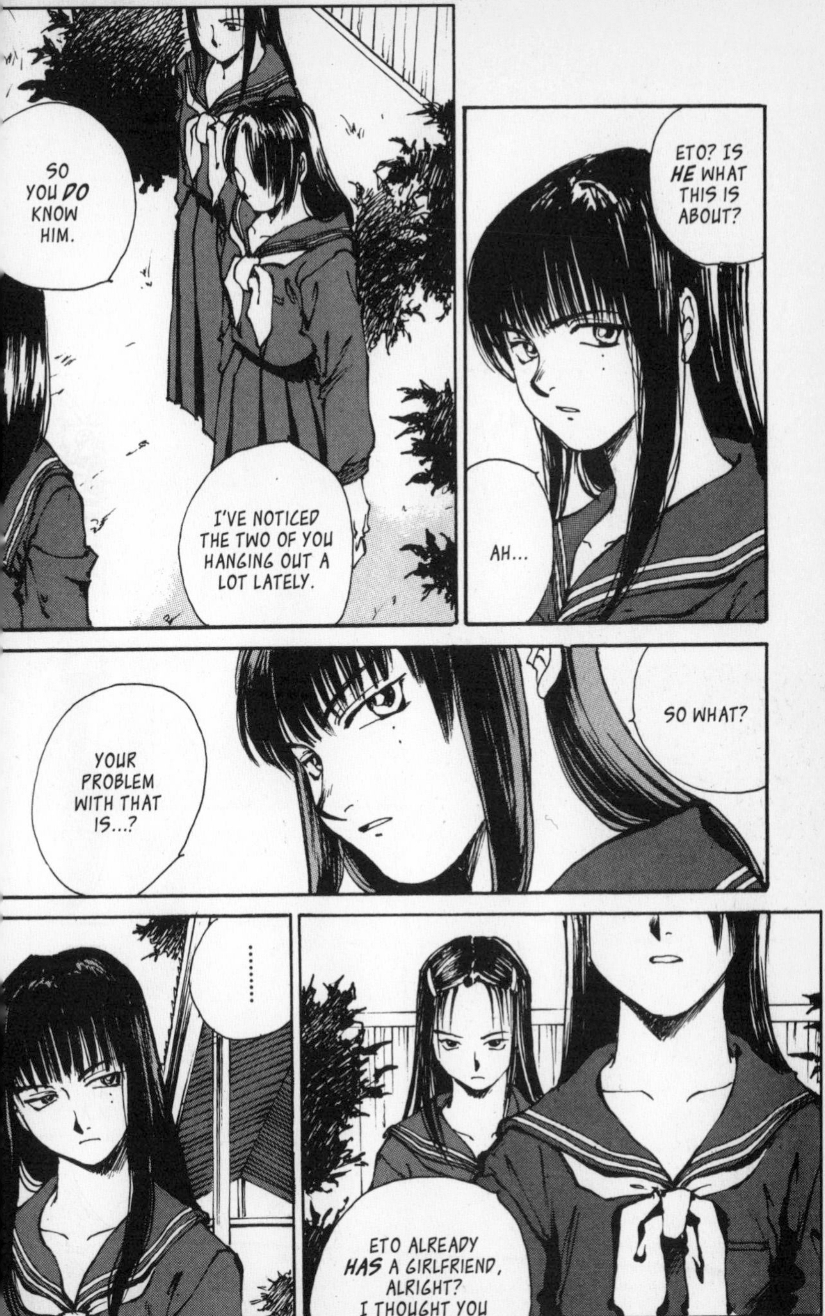
ETO? IS HE WHAT THIS IS ABOUT?
AH...
SO YOU DO KNOW HIM.
I'VE NOTICED THE TWO OF YOU HANGING OUT A LOT LATELY.
SO WHAT?
YOUR PROBLEM WITH THAT IS...?
ETO ALREADY HAS A GIRLFRIEND, ALRIGHT? I THOUGHT YOU SHOULD KNOW.
....

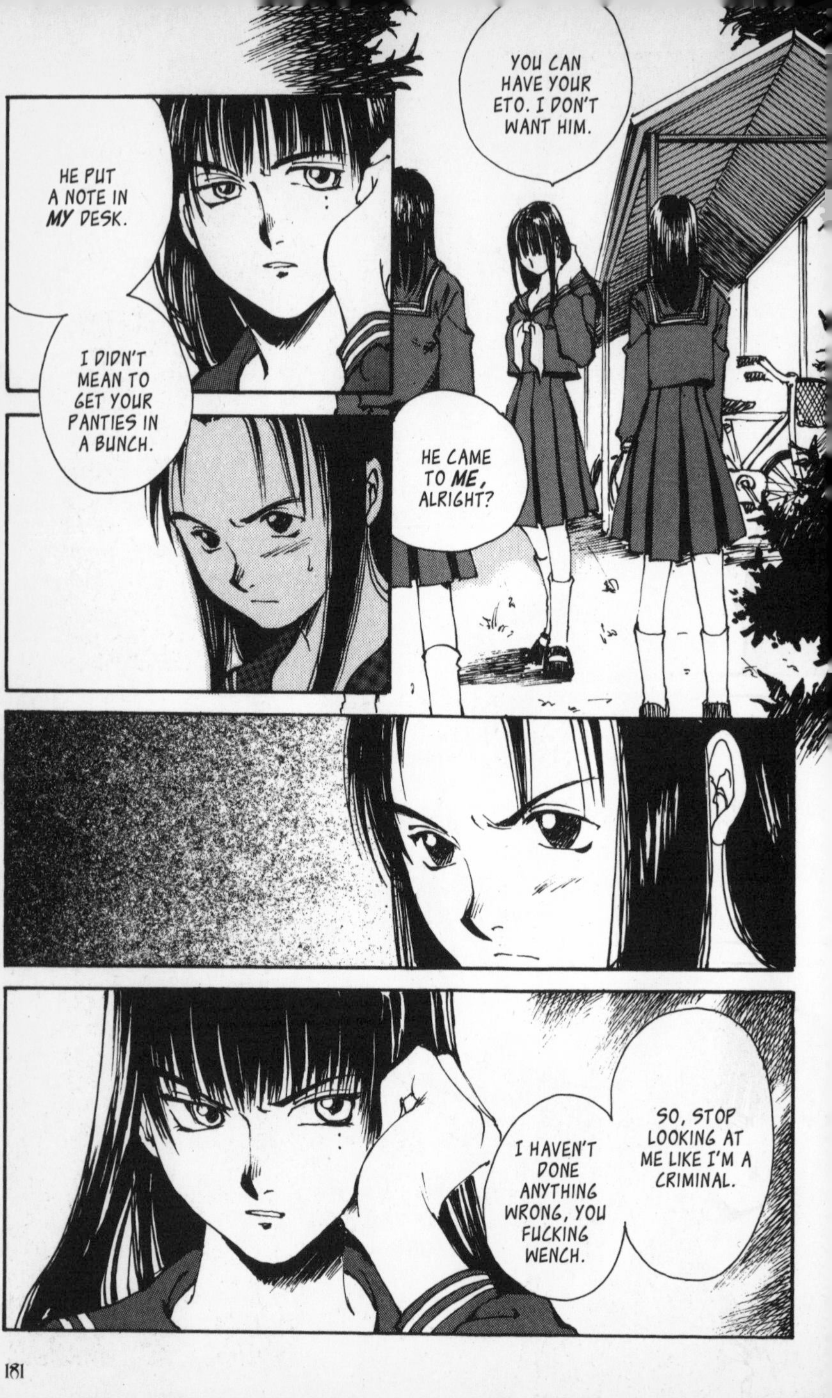
YOU CAN HAVE YOUR ETO. I DON'T WANT HIM.
HE PUT A NOTE IN MY DESK.
HE CAME TO ME, ALRIGHT?
I DIDN'T MEAN TO GET YOUR PANTIES IN A BUNCH.
I HAVEN'T DONE ANYTHING WRONG, YOU FUCKING WENCH.
SO, STOP LOOKING AT ME LIKE I'M A CRIMINAL.

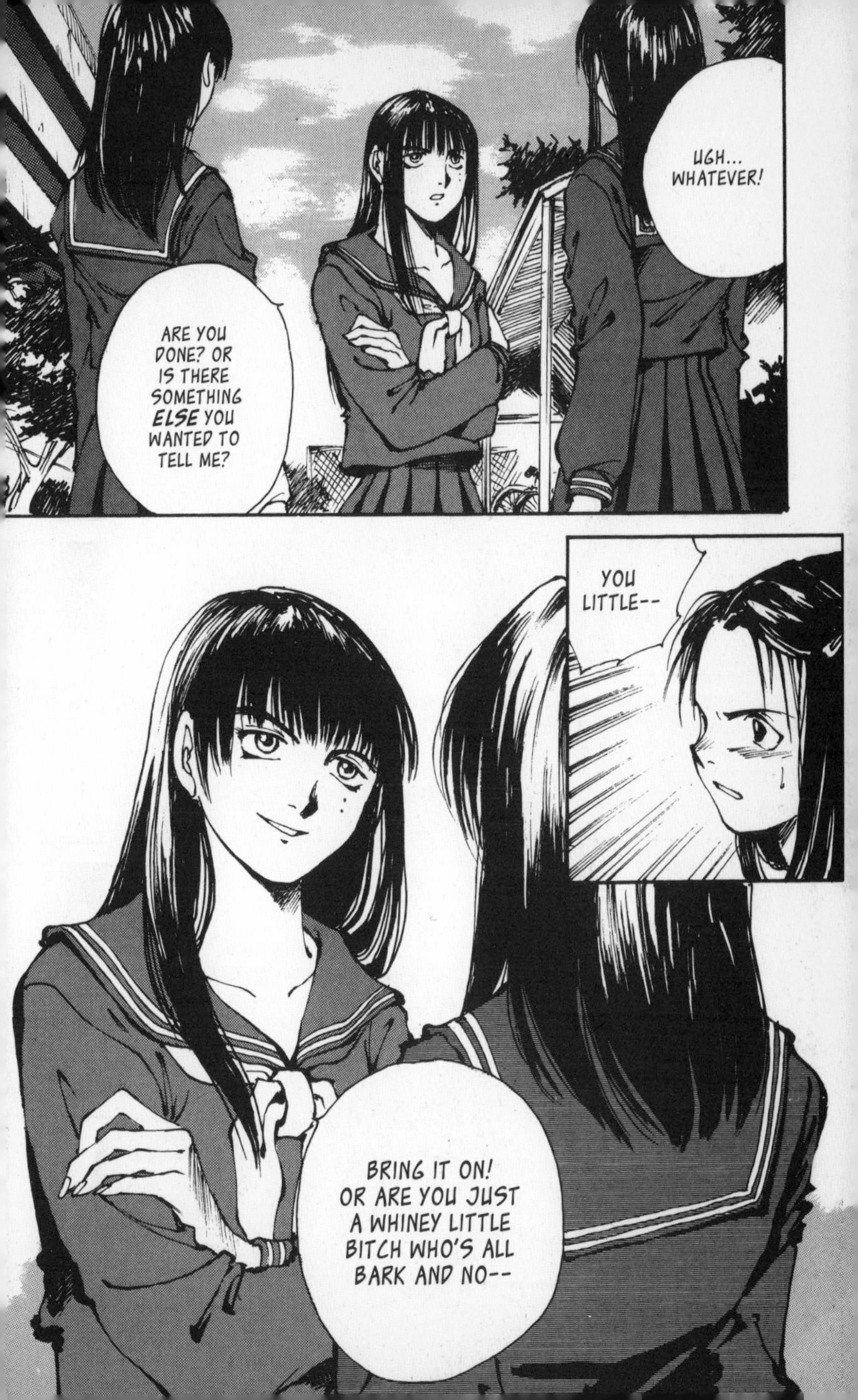
UGH... WHATEVER!
ARE YOU DONE? OR IS THERE SOMETHING ELSE YOU WANTED TO TELL ME?
YOU LITTLE--
BRING IT ON! OR ARE YOU JUST A WHINEY LITTLE BITCH WHO'S ALL BARK AND NO--

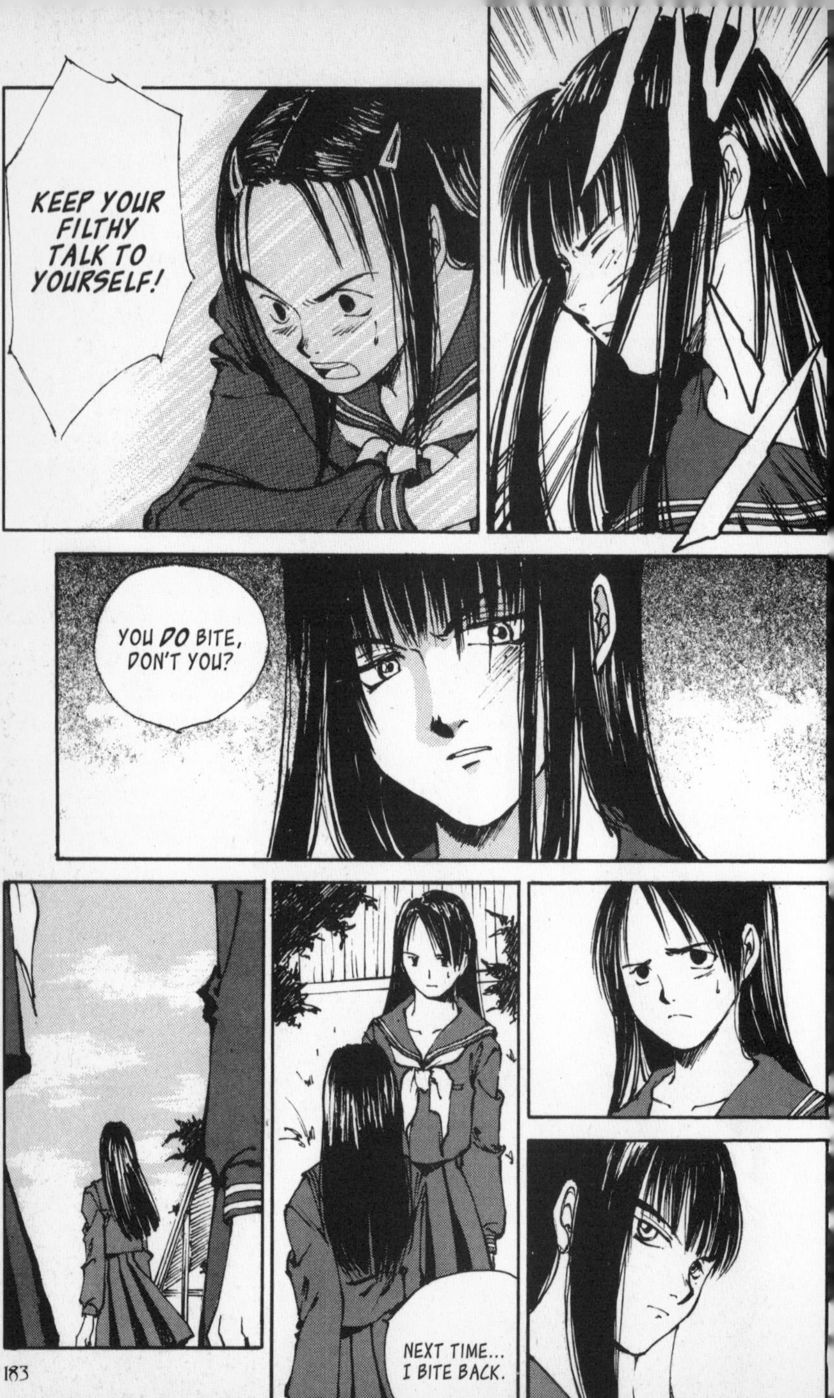
KEEP YOUR FILTHY TALK TO YOURSELF!
YOU *DO* BITE, DON'T YOU?
NEXT TIME... I BITE BACK.

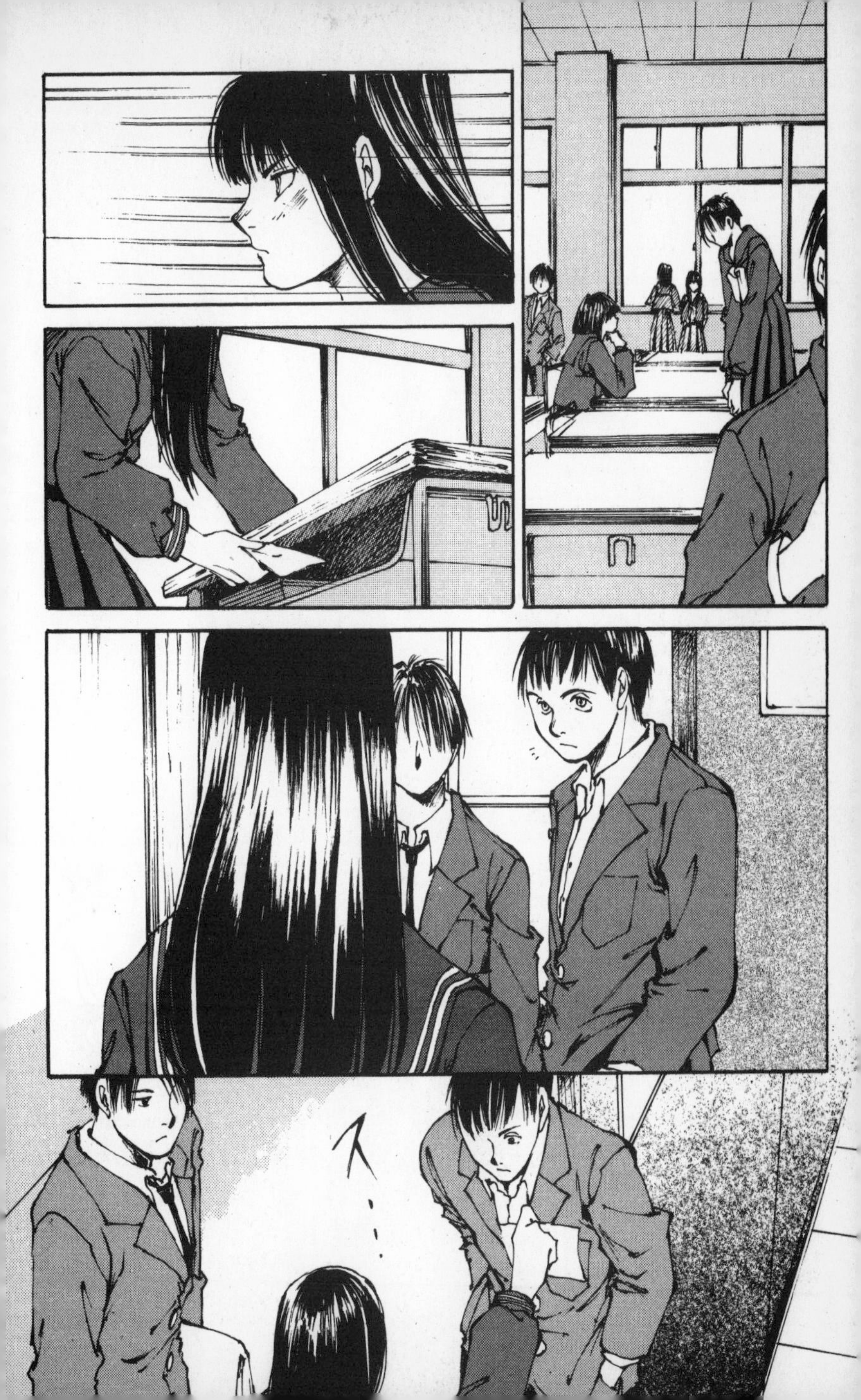
ス

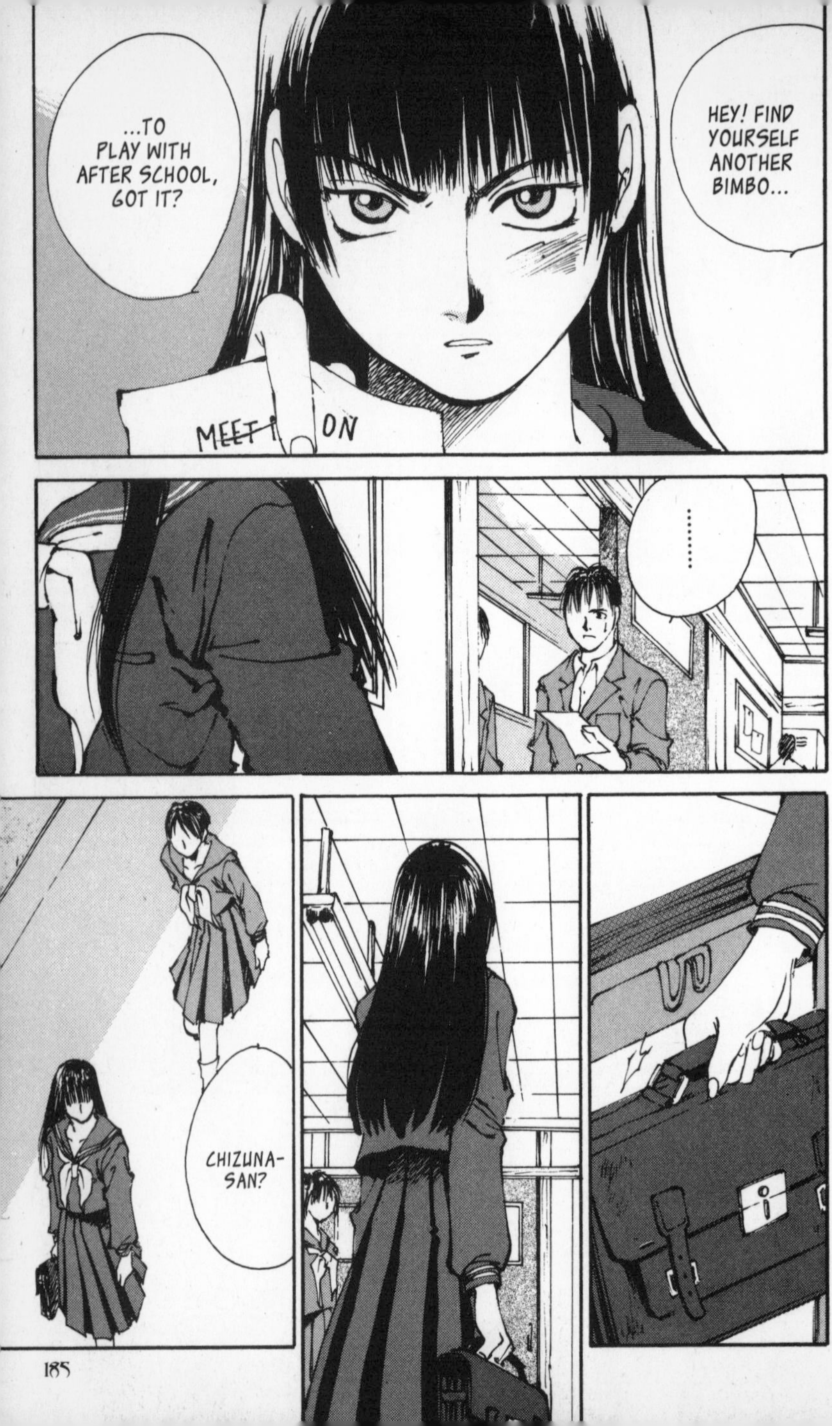
HEY! FIND YOURSELF ANOTHER BIMBO...
...TO PLAY WITH AFTER SCHOOL, GOT IT?
......
CHIZUNA-SAN?

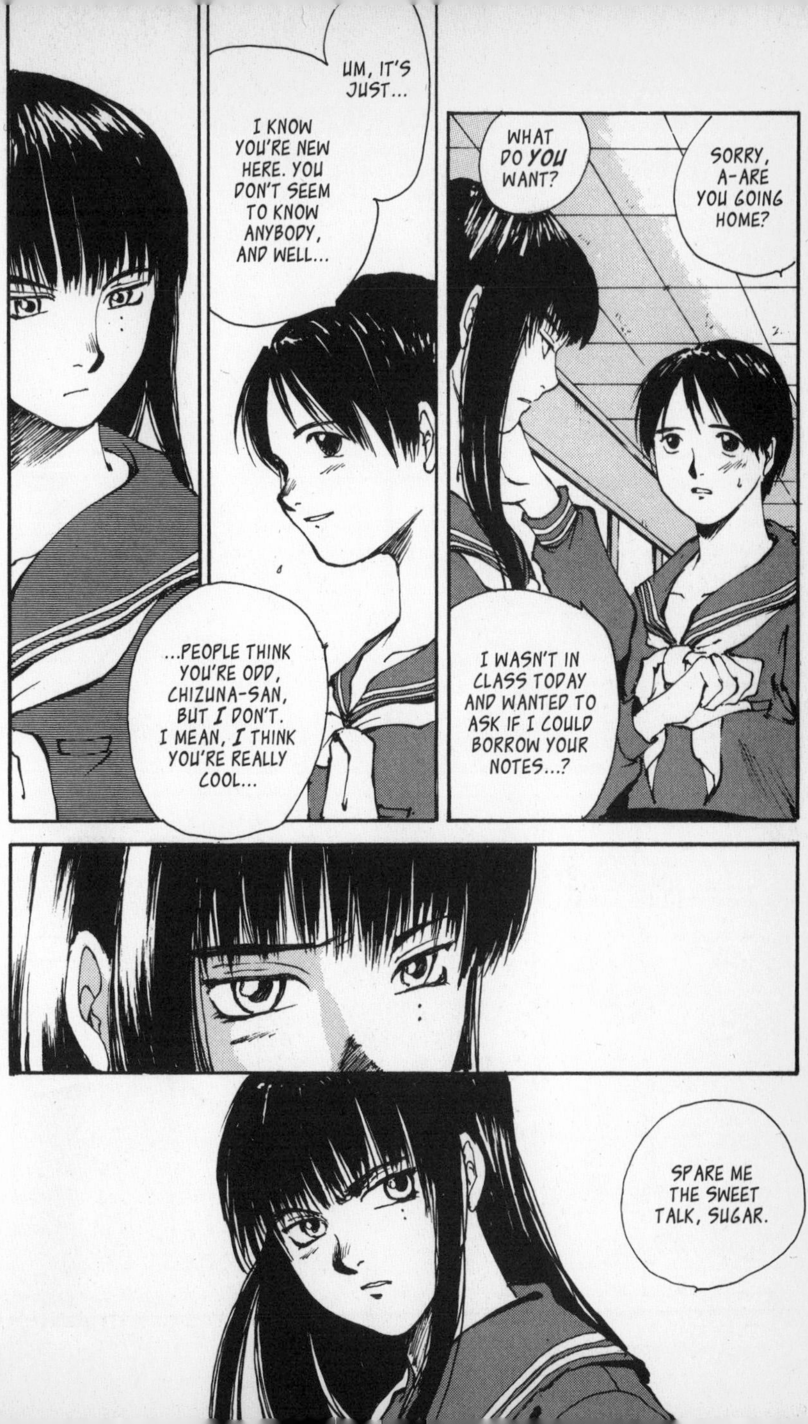
SORRY, A-ARE YOU GOING HOME?
WHAT DO *YOU* WANT?
I WASN'T IN CLASS TODAY AND WANTED TO ASK IF I COULD BORROW YOUR NOTES...?
UM, IT'S JUST...
I KNOW YOU'RE NEW HERE. YOU DON'T SEEM TO KNOW ANYBODY, AND WELL...
...PEOPLE THINK YOU'RE ODD, CHIZUNA-SAN, BUT *I* DON'T. I MEAN, *I* THINK YOU'RE REALLY COOL...
SPARE ME THE SWEET TALK, SUGAR.

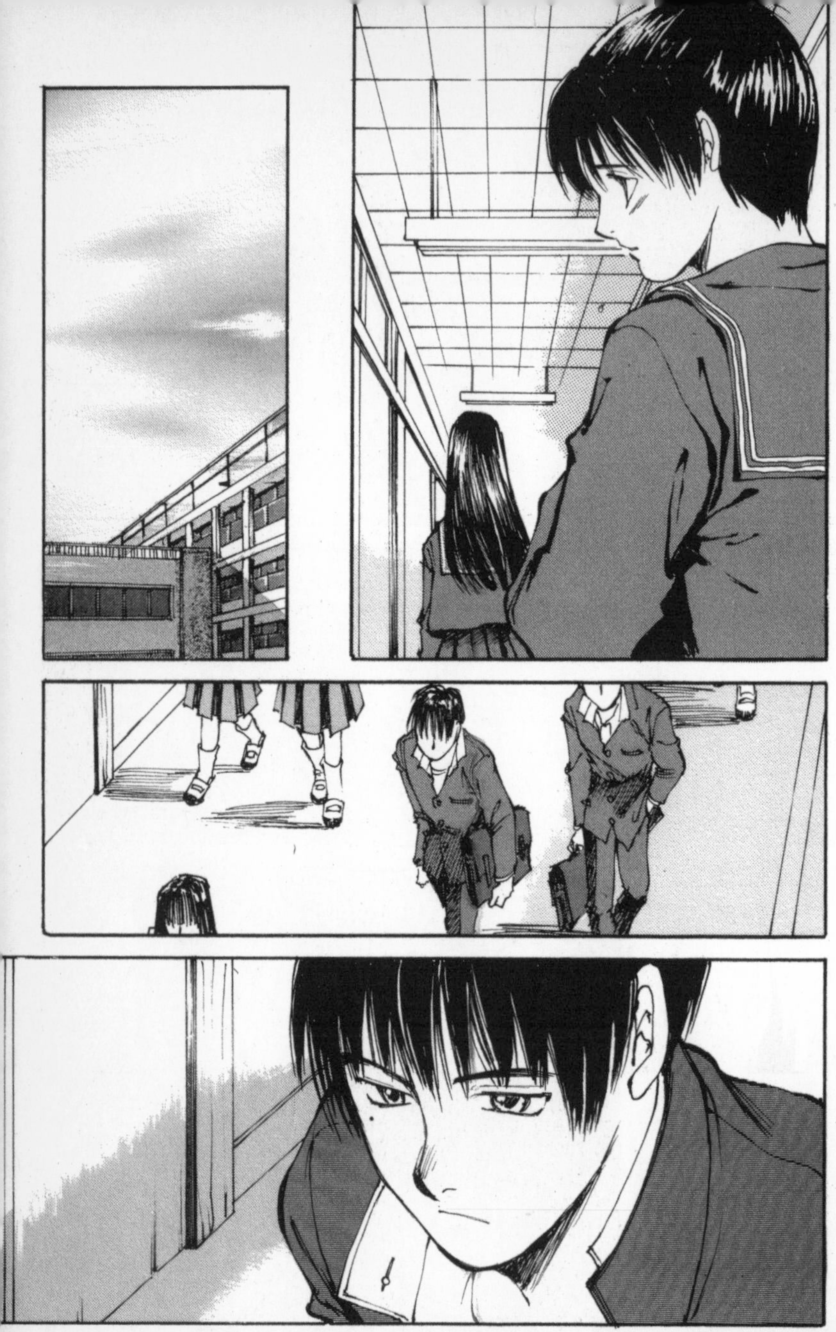

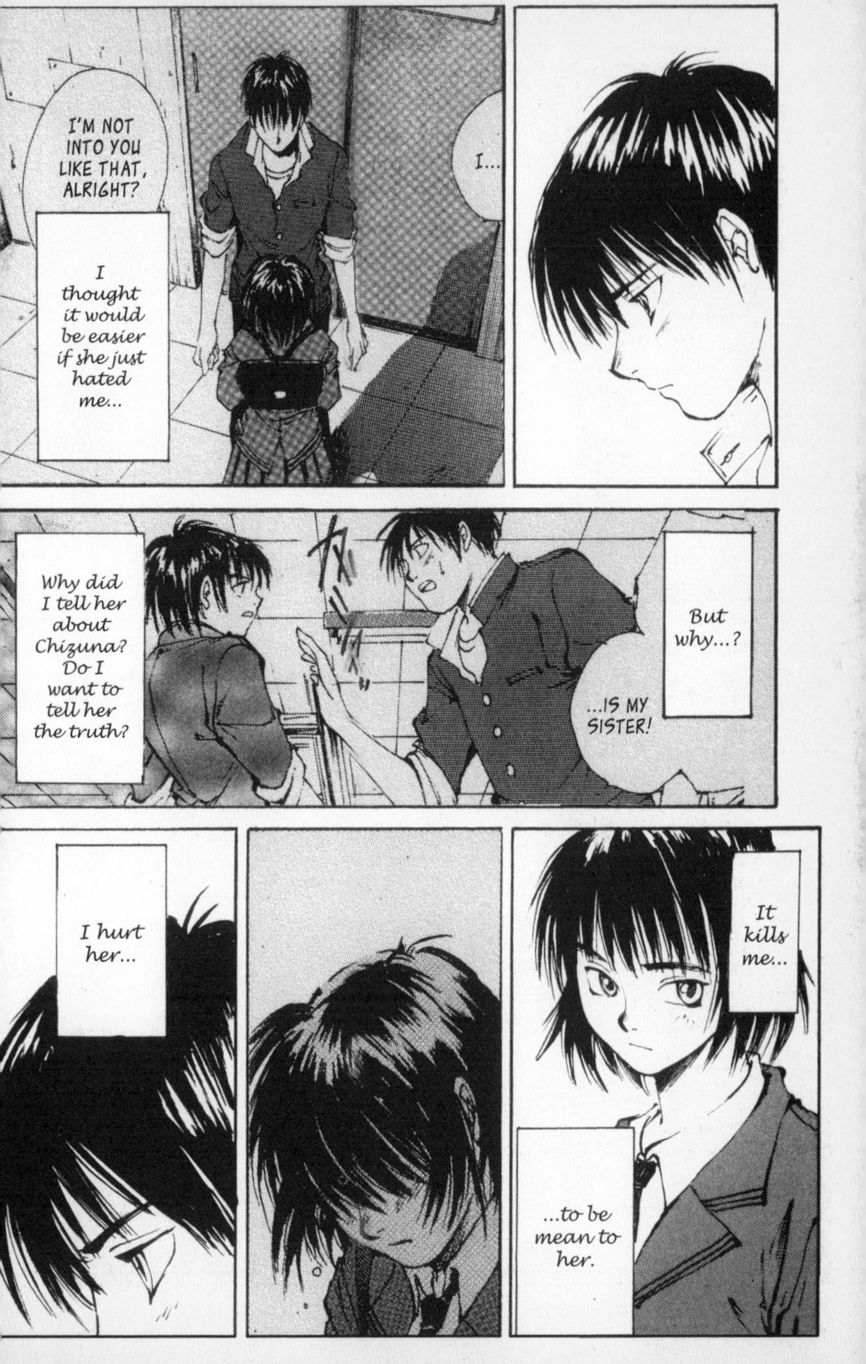
I...
I'M NOT INTO YOU LIKE THAT, ALRIGHT?
I thought it would be easier if she just hated me...
But why...?
...IS MY SISTER!
Why did I tell her about Chizuna? Do I want to tell her the truth?
It kills me...
...to be mean to her.
I hurt her...

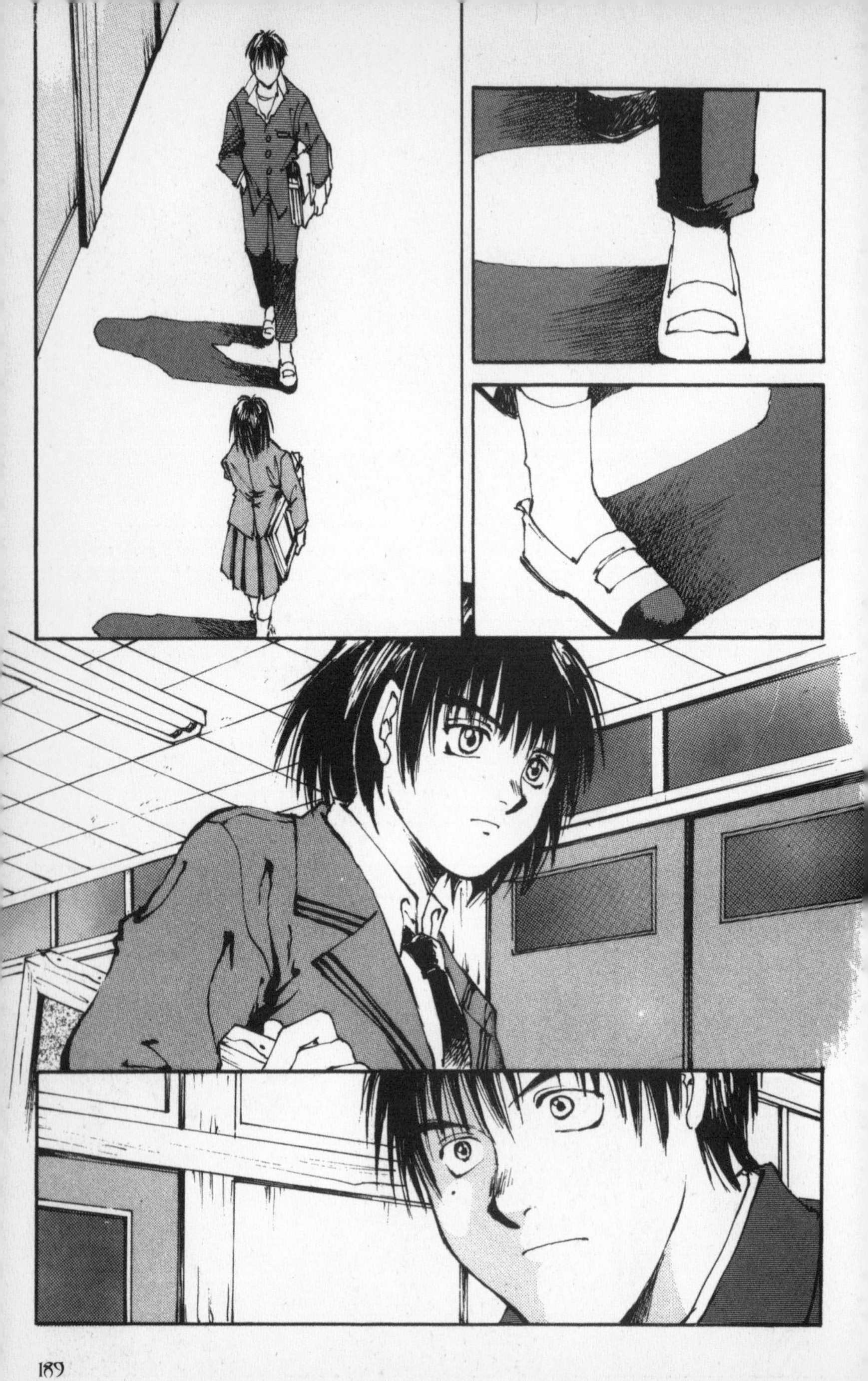

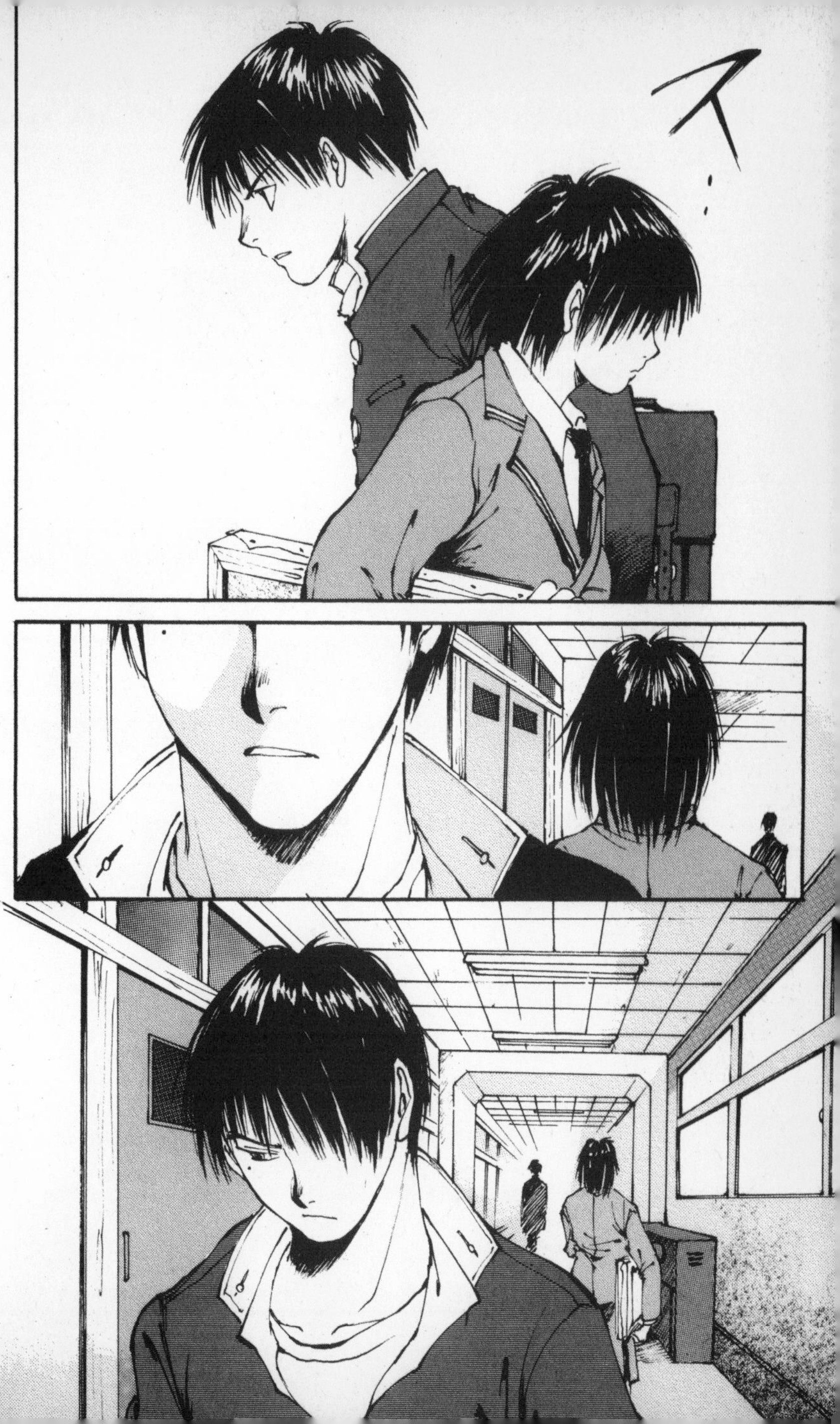
ス…

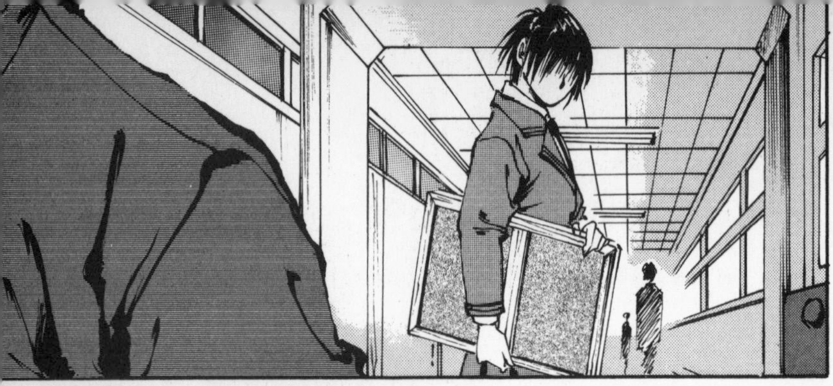
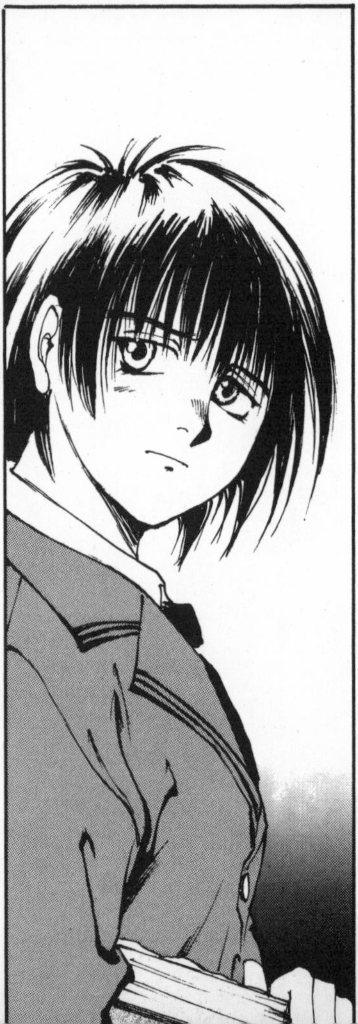
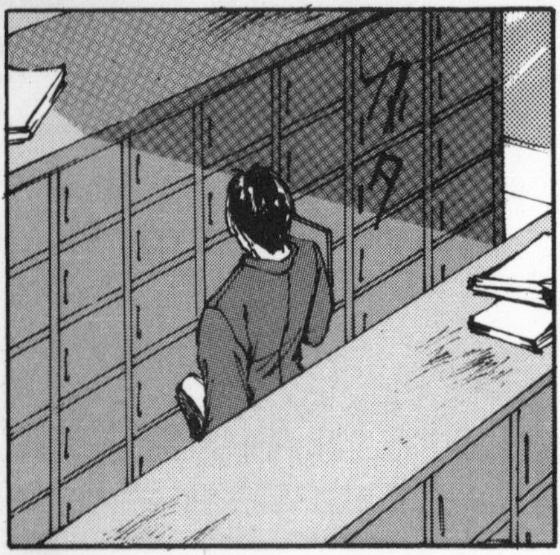
カタ
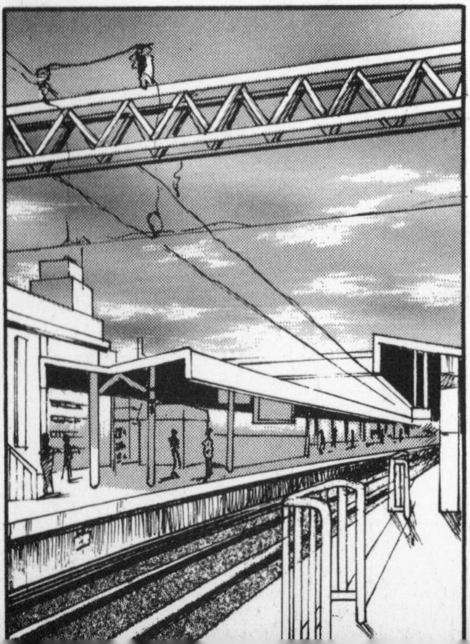

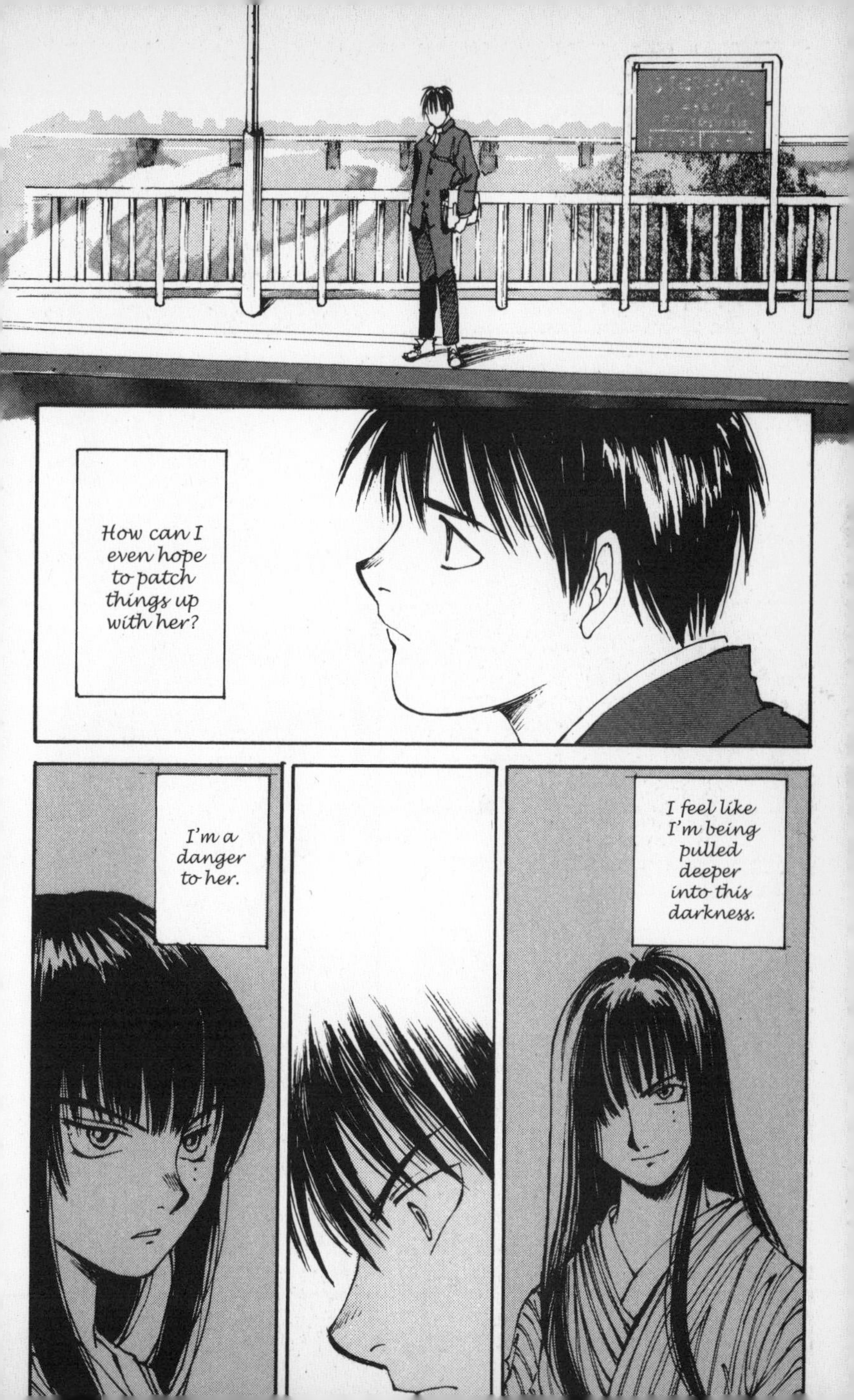
How can I even hope to patch things up with her?
I feel like I'm being pulled deeper into this darkness.
I'm a danger to her.

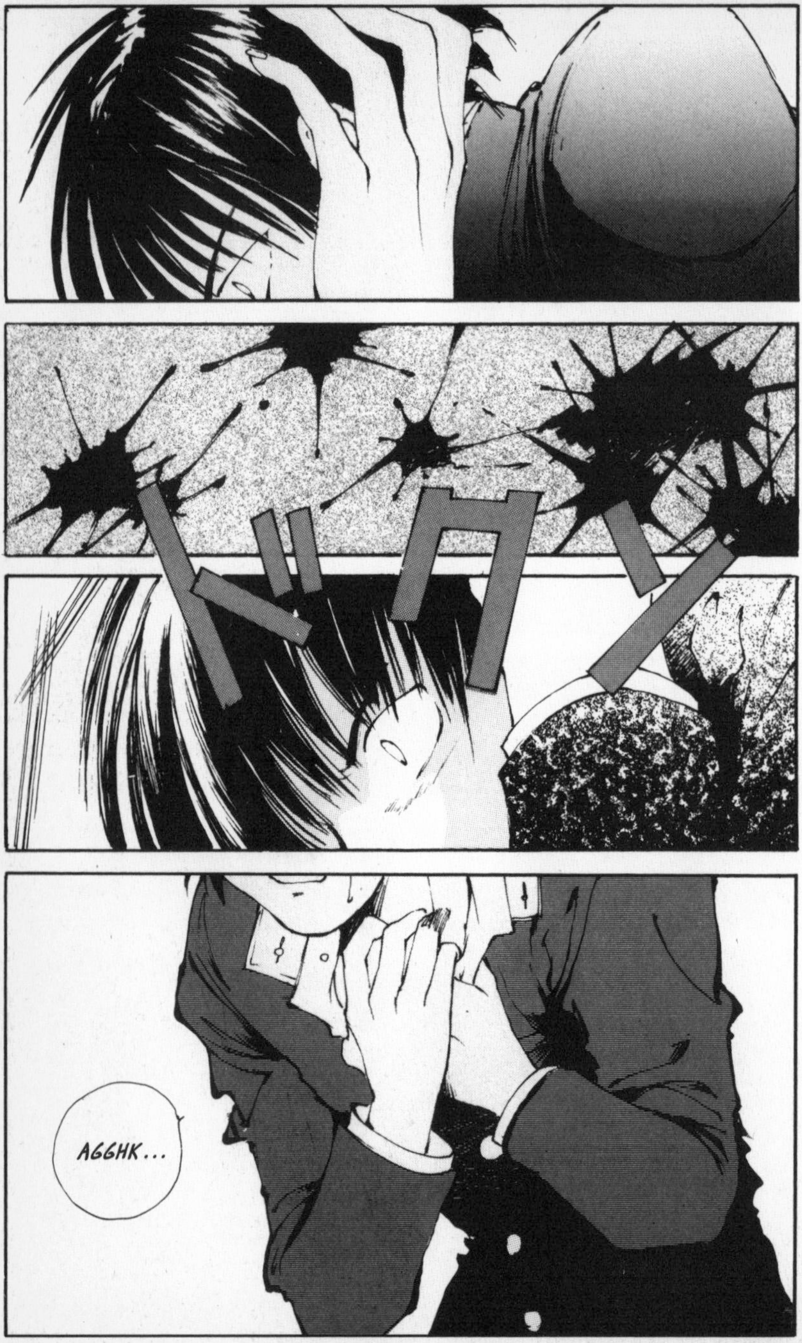
ドクン
AGGHK...

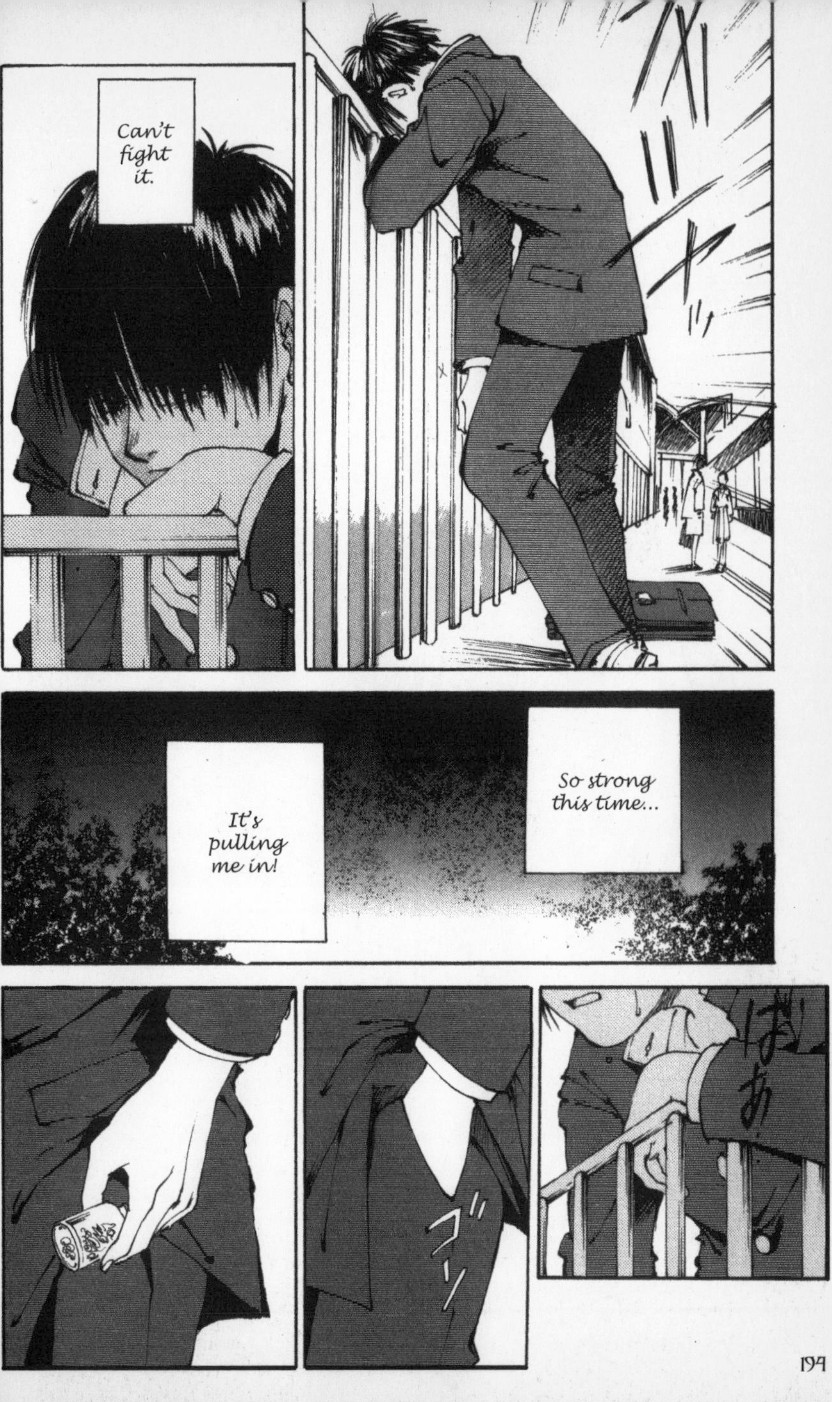
Can't fight it.
So strong this time...
It's pulling me in!

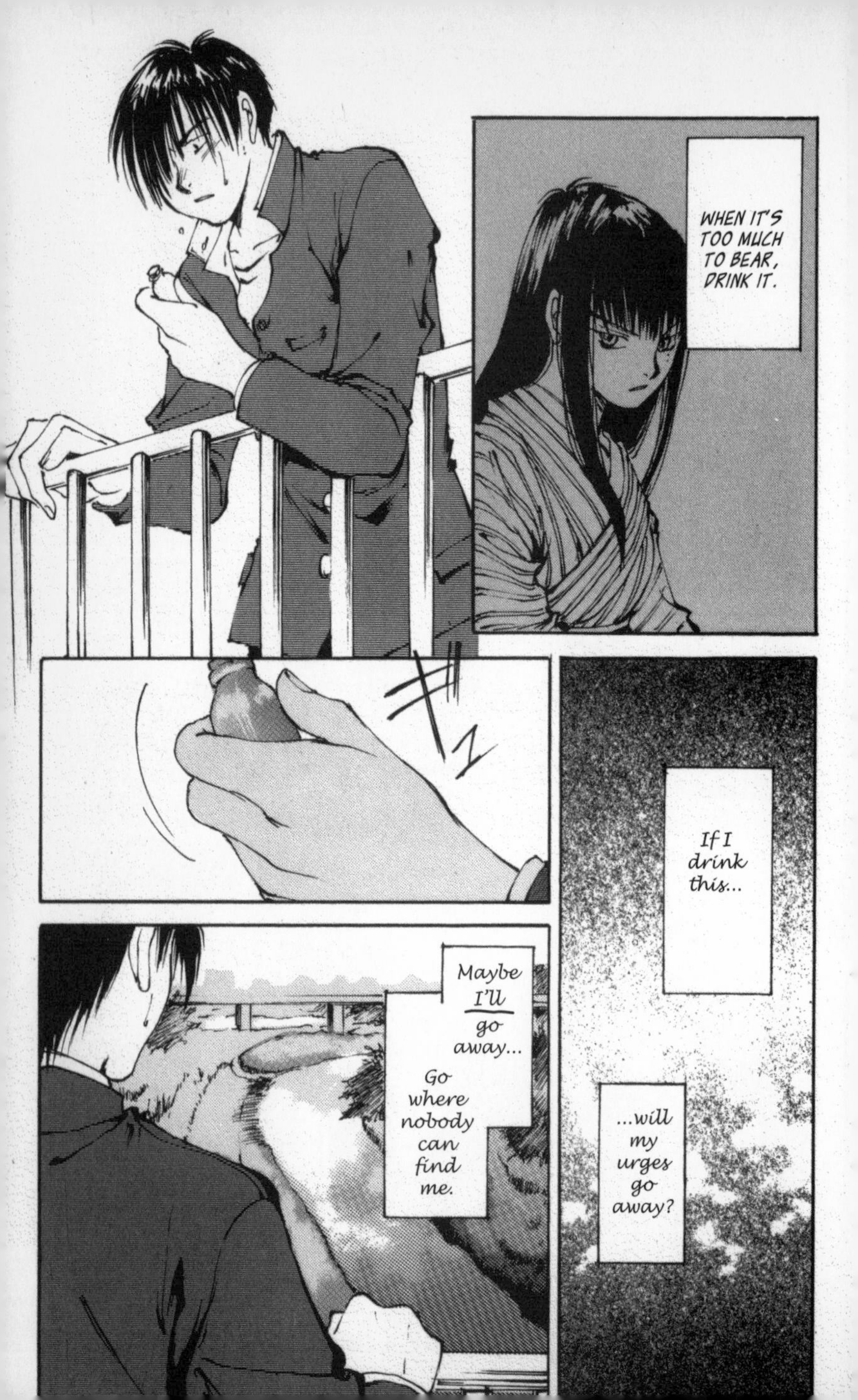
WHEN IT'S TOO MUCH TO BEAR, DRINK IT.
If I drink this...
...will my urges go away?
Maybe I'll go away...
Go where nobody can find me.

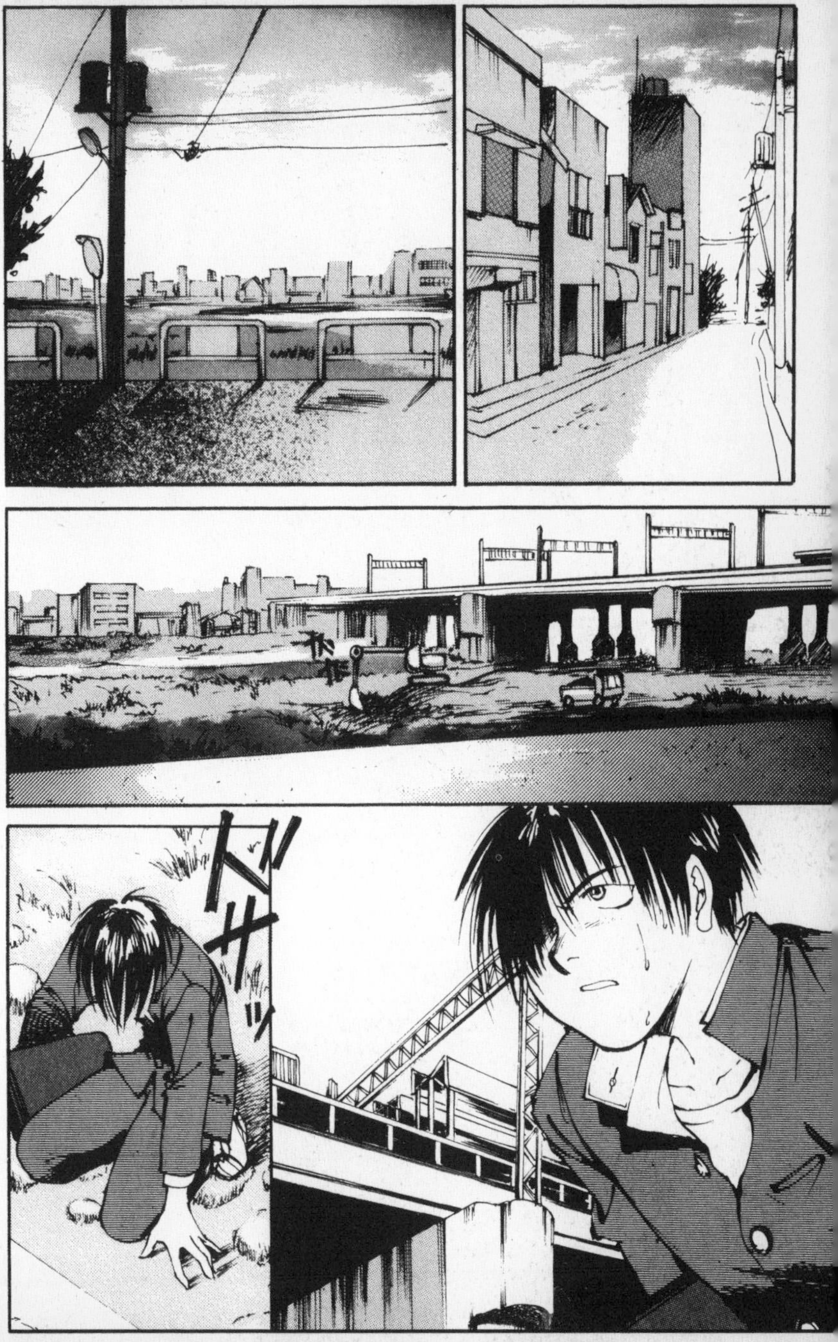
ドサッ

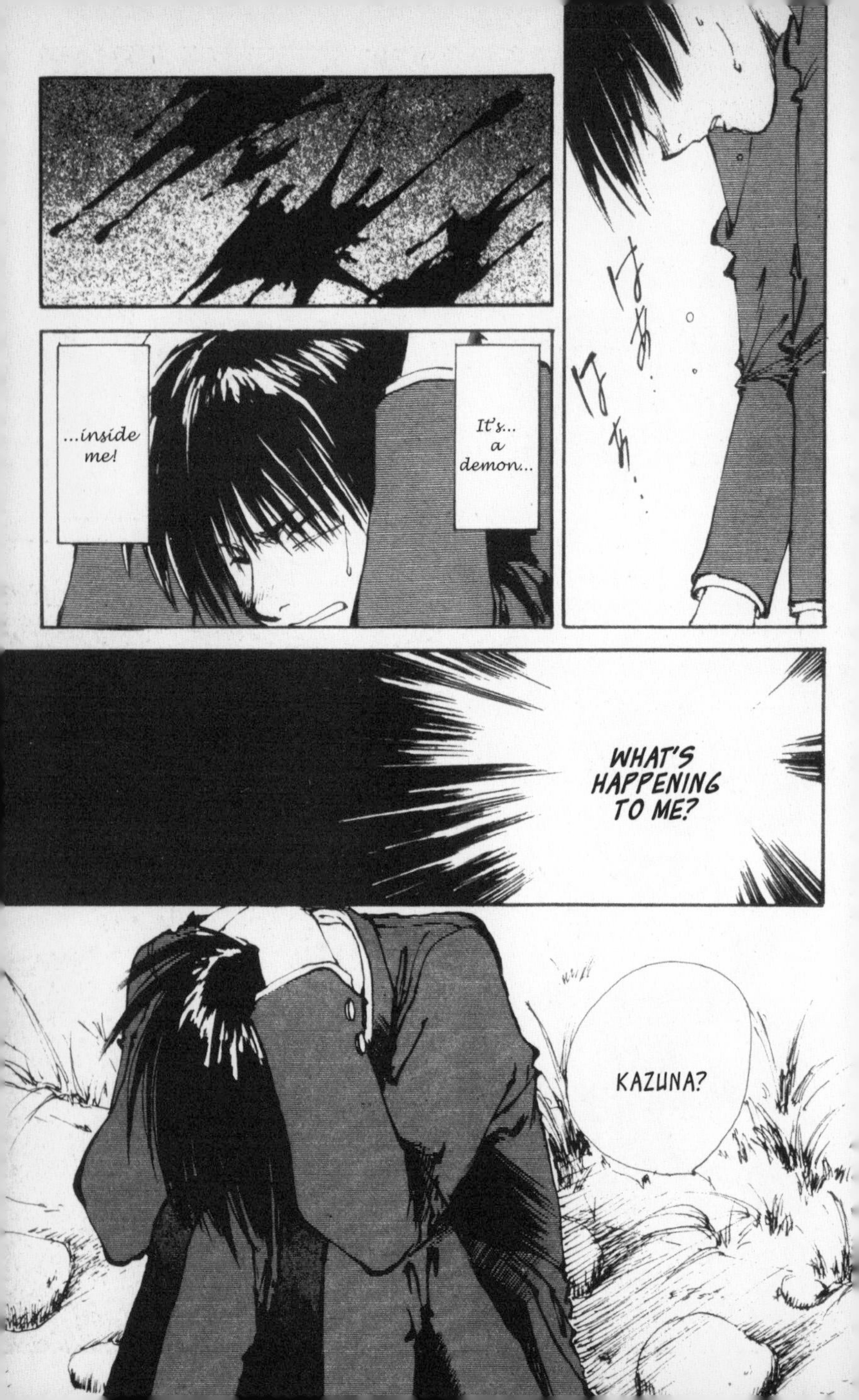
はぁ…
はぁ…
It's... a demon...
...inside me!
WHAT'S HAPPENING TO ME?
KAZUNA?

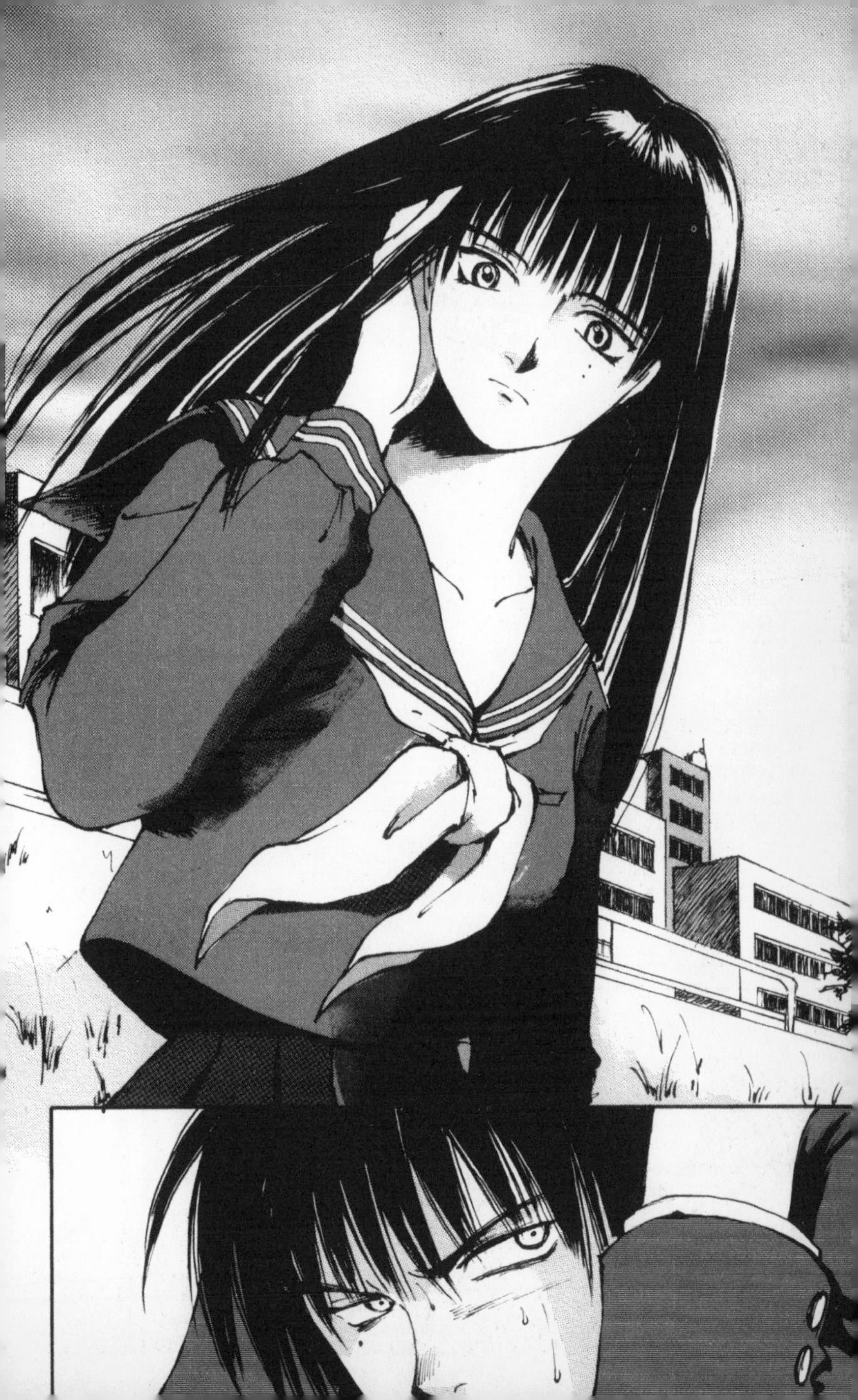

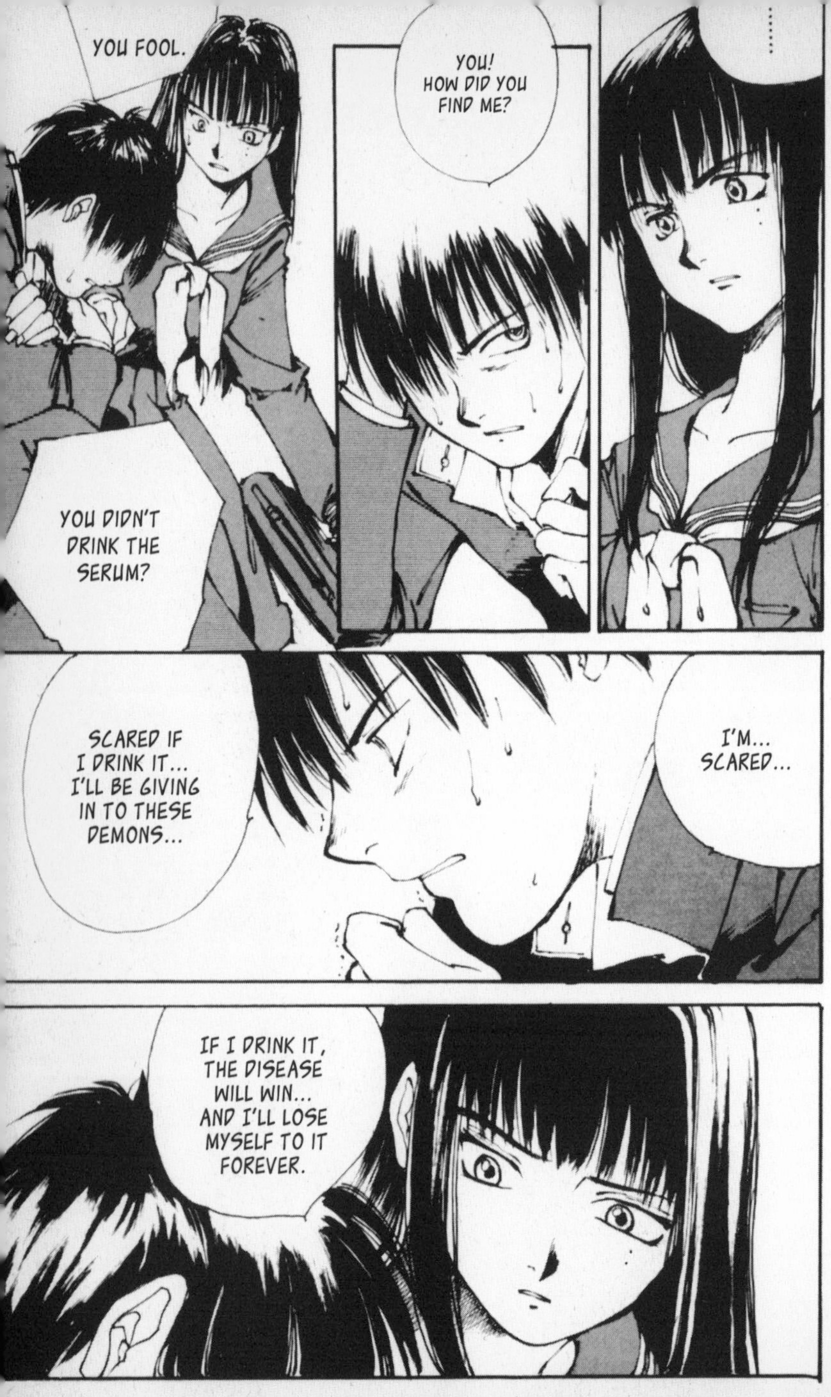
......
YOU! HOW DID YOU FIND ME?
YOU FOOL.
YOU DIDN'T DRINK THE SERUM?
I'M... SCARED...
SCARED IF I DRINK IT... I'LL BE GIVING IN TO THESE DEMONS...
IF I DRINK IT, THE DISEASE WILL WIN... AND I'LL LOSE MYSELF TO IT FOREVER.

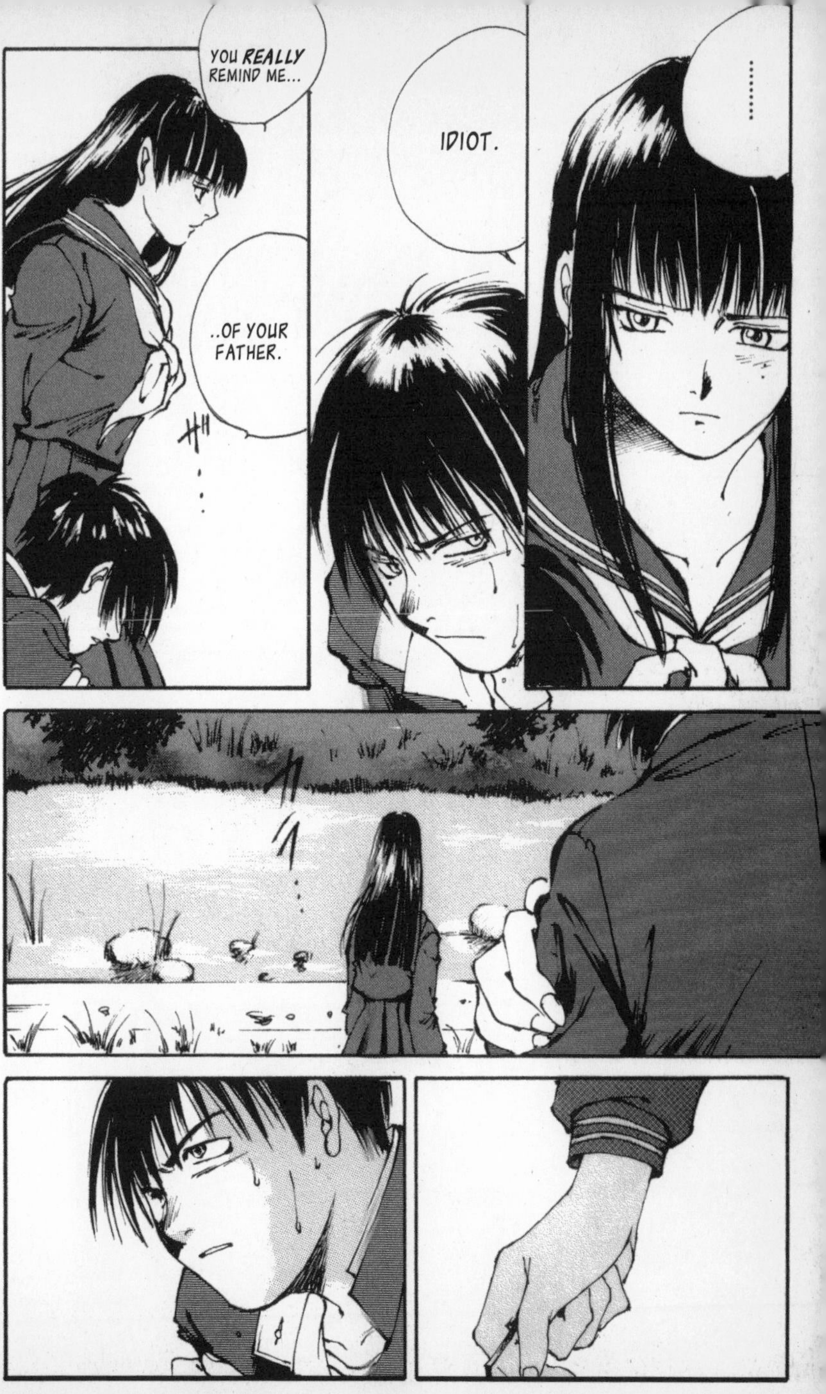
YOU REALLY REMIND ME...
..OF YOUR FATHER.
IDIOT.
....

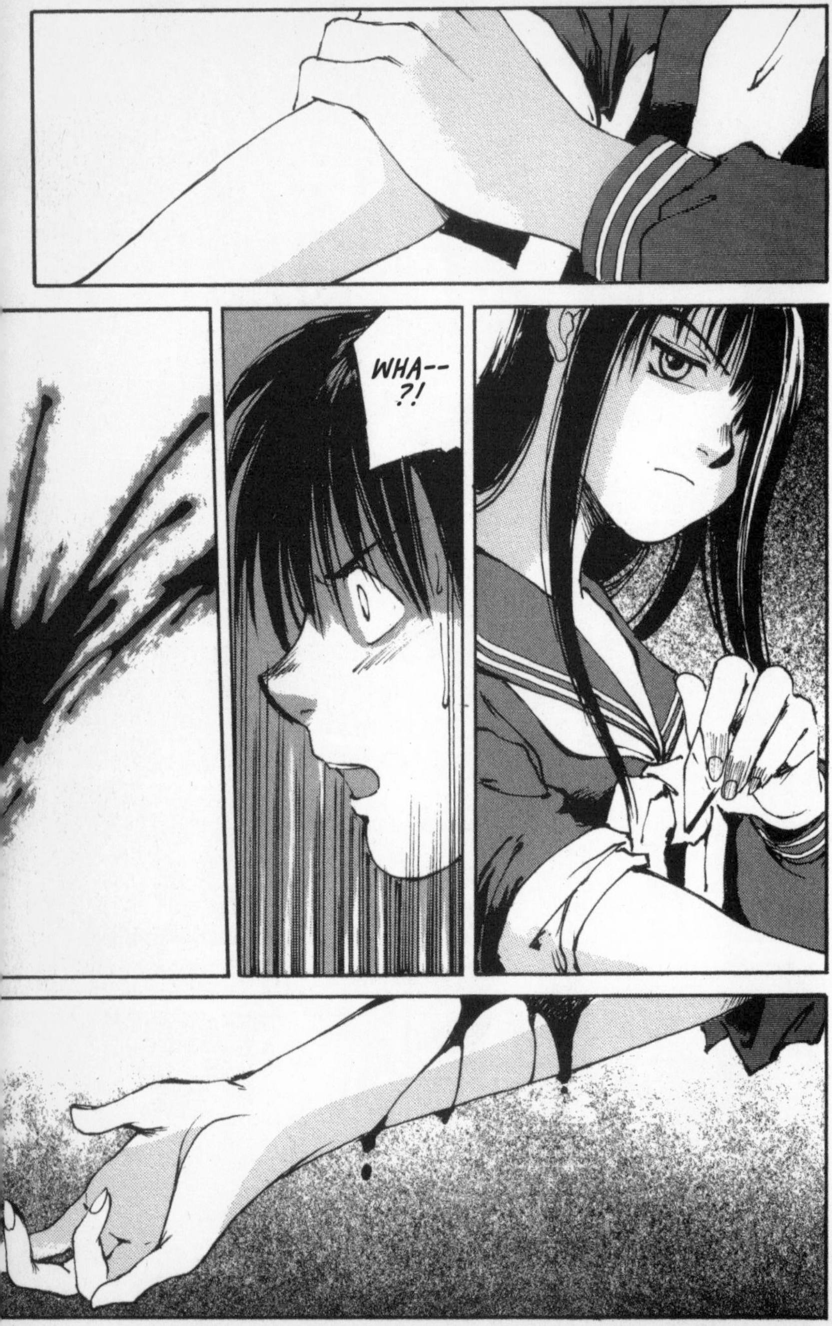
WHA--
?!

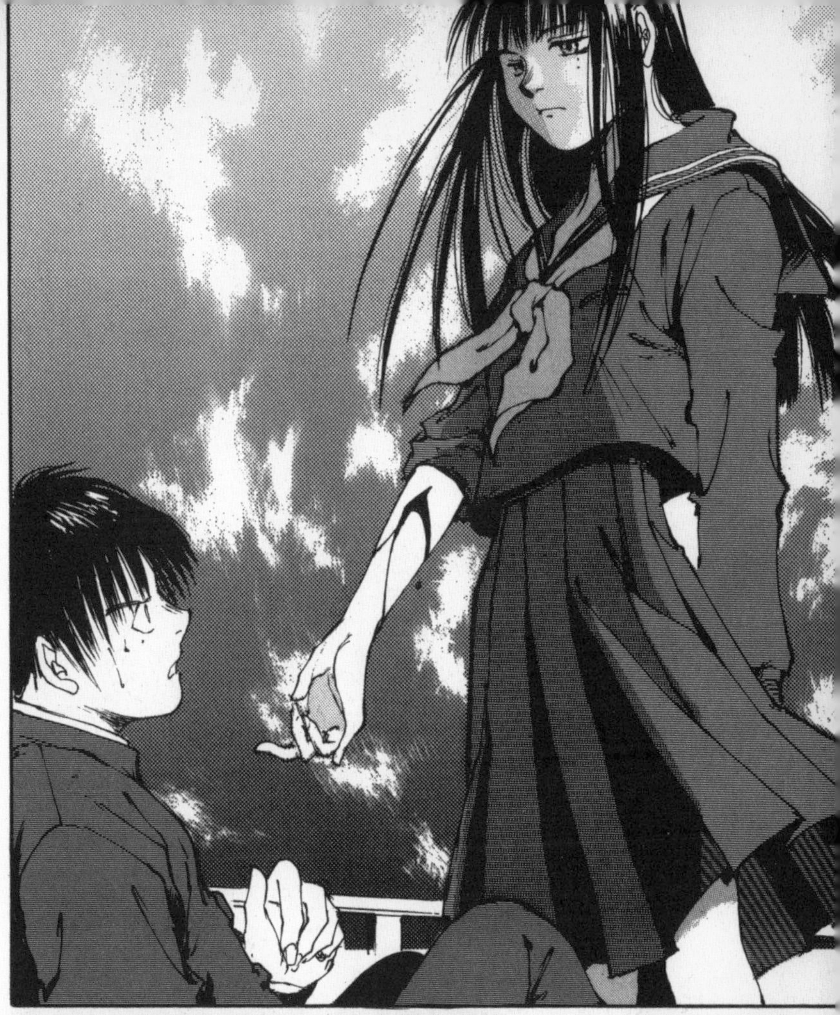
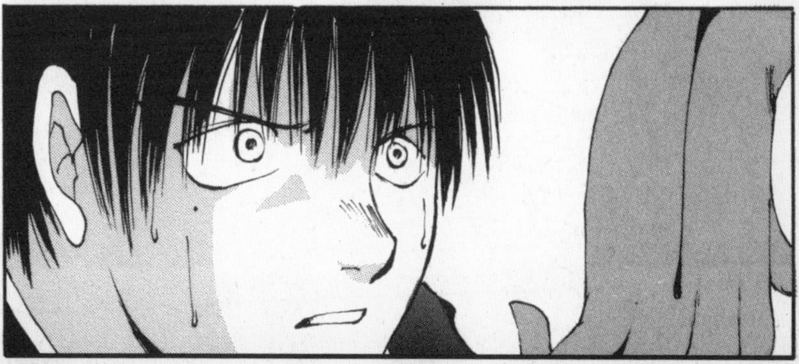

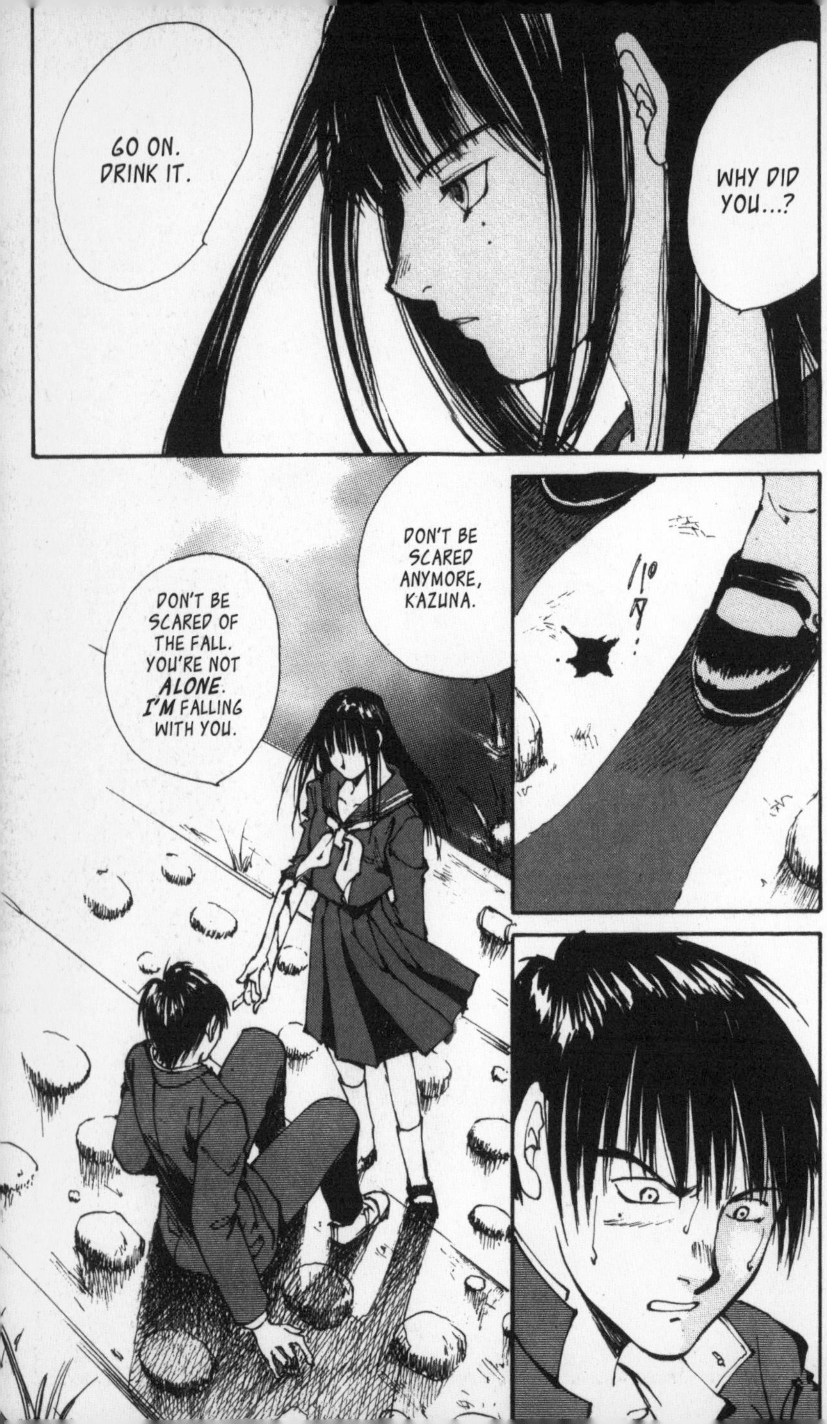
WHY DID YOU...?
GO ON. DRINK IT.
パタ!
DON'T BE SCARED ANYMORE, KAZUNA.
DON'T BE SCARED OF THE FALL. YOU'RE NOT *ALONE*. *I'M* FALLING WITH YOU.

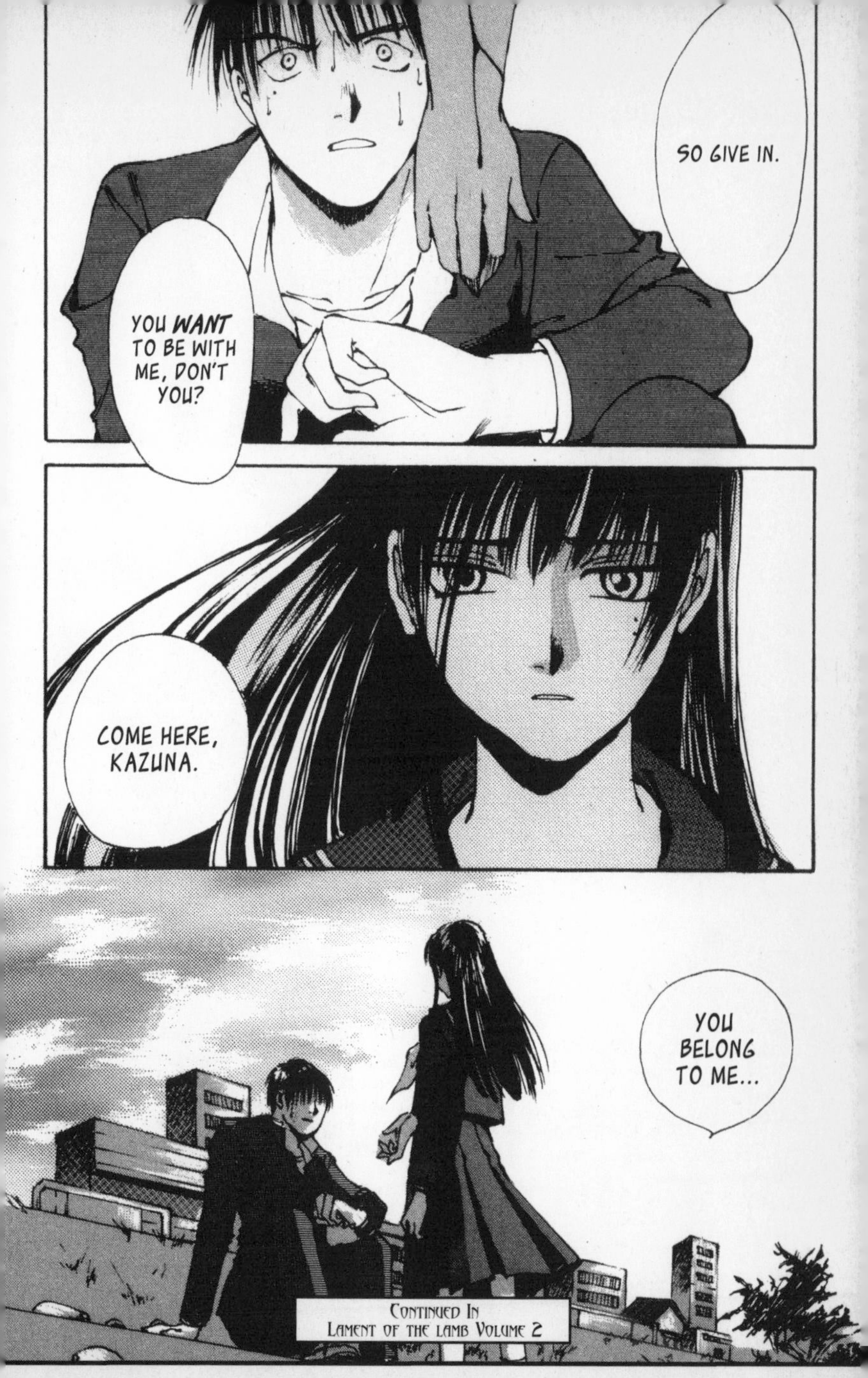
SO GIVE IN.
YOU **WANT** TO BE WITH ME, DON'T YOU?
COME HERE, KAZUNA.
YOU BELONG TO ME...
CONTINUED IN LAMENT OF THE LAMB VOLUME 2

Lament of the Lamb Vol. 2 July 2004

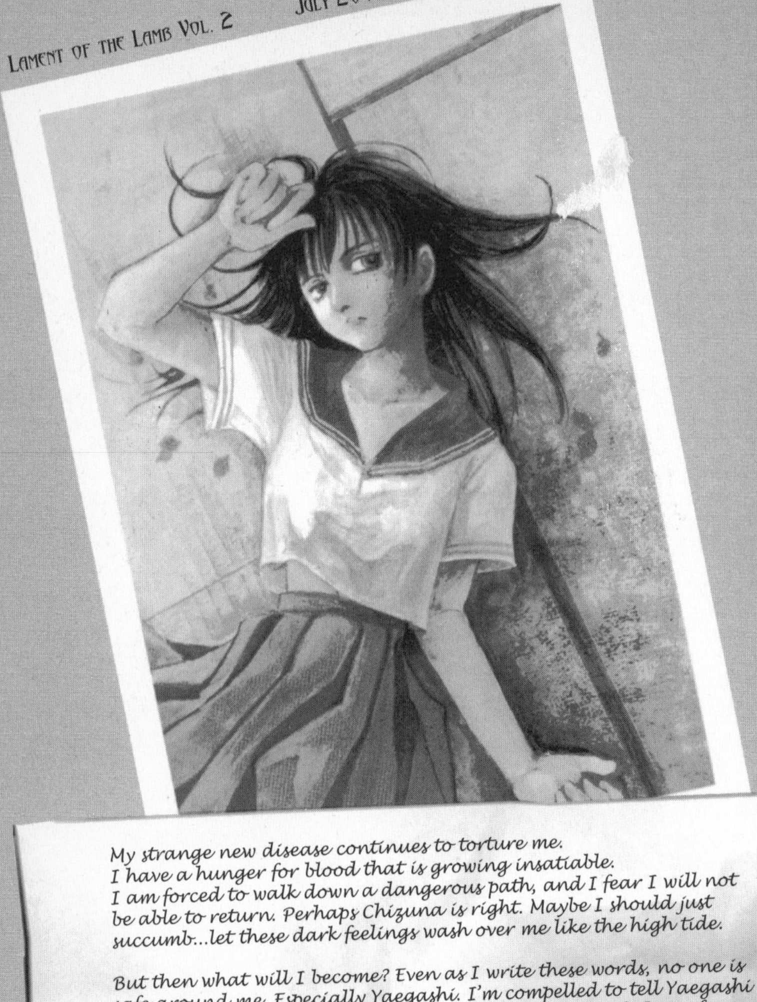

My strange new disease continues to torture me.
I have a hunger for blood that is growing insatiable.
I am forced to walk down a dangerous path, and I fear I will not be able to return. Perhaps Chizuna is right. Maybe I should just succumb...let these dark feelings wash over me like the high tide.

But then what will I become? Even as I write these words, no one is safe around me. Especially Yaegashi. I'm compelled to tell Yaegashi the truth; instead, I push her away. It's hopeless. Our feelings for each other can never be consummated. And as I drift further from the girl I love, it is with a heavy foreboding that I find myself eerily drawn toward a girl who terrifies me--my own sister.

No one but Chizuna knows the pain in my tainted soul. Uncle Shin and Natsuko don't really know me. I'm nothing but a burden to them. I should just move out and leave them be. I must accept that Chizuna is now my only hope for survival. She and I are like lonely binary stars in an empty universe. Unseen forces hold us together, and our fate is frighteningly intertwined.

PLANETES
PRIEST
PRINCESS AI
PSYCHIC ACADEMY
RAGNAROK
RAVE MASTER
REALITY CHECK
REBIRTH
REBOUND
REMOTE
RISING STARS OF MANGA
SABER MARIONETTE J
SAILOR MOON
SAINT TAIL
SAIYUKI
SAMURAI DEEPER KYO
SAMURAI GIRL REAL BOUT HIGH SCHOOL
SCRYED
SEIKAI TRILOGY, THE
SGT. FROG
SHAOLIN SISTERS
SHIRAHIME-SYO: SNOW GODDESS TALES
SHUTTERBOX
SKULL MAN, THE
SMUGGLER
SNOW DROP
SORCERER HUNTERS
STONE
SUIKODEN III
SUKI
THREADS OF TIME
TOKYO BABYLON
TOKYO MEW MEW
TOKYO TRIBES
TRAMPS LIKE US
UNDER THE GLASS MOON
VAMPIRE GAME
VISION OF ESCAFLOWNE, THE
WARRIORS OF TAO
WILD ACT
WISH
WORLD OF HARTZ
X-DAY
ZODIAC P.I.

MANGA NOVELS

CLAMP SCHOOL PARANORMAL INVESTIGATORS
KARMA CLUB
SAILOR MOON
SLAYERS

ART BOOKS

ART OF CARDCAPTOR SAKURA
ART OF MAGIC KNIGHT RAYEARTH, THE
PEACH: MIWA UEDA ILLUSTRATIONS

ANIME GUIDES

COWBOY BEBOP
GUNDAM TECHNICAL MANUALS
SAILOR MOON SCOUT GUIDES

TOKYOPOP KIDS

STRAY SHEEP

CINE-MANGA™

ALADDIN
ASTRO BOY
CARDCAPTORS
CONFESSIONS OF A TEENAGE DRAMA QUEEN
DUEL MASTERS
FAIRLY ODDPARENTS, THE
FAMILY GUY
FINDING NEMO
G.I. JOE SPY TROOPS
JACKIE CHAN ADVENTURES
JIMMY NEUTRON: BOY GENIUS, THE ADVENTURES OF
KIM POSSIBLE
LILO & STITCH
LIZZIE MCGUIRE
LIZZIE MCGUIRE MOVIE, THE
MALCOLM IN THE MIDDLE
POWER RANGERS: NINJA STORM
SHREK 2
SPONGEBOB SQUAREPANTS
SPY KIDS 2
SPY KIDS 3-D: GAME OVER
TEENAGE MUTANT NINJA TURTLES
THAT'S SO RAVEN
TRANSFORMERS: ARMADA
TRANSFORMERS: ENERGON

**For more
information visit
www.TOKYOPOP.com**

03.03.04T

MANGA

.HACK//LEGEND OF THE TWILIGHT
@LARGE
ABENOBASHI: MAGICAL SHOPPING ARCADE
A.I. LOVE YOU
AI YORI AOSHI
ANGELIC LAYER
ARM OF KANNON
BABY BIRTH
BATTLE ROYALE
BATTLE VIXENS
BRAIN POWERED
BRIGADOON
B'TX
CANDIDATE FOR GODDESS, THE
CARDCAPTOR SAKURA
CARDCAPTOR SAKURA - MASTER OF THE CLOW
CHOBITS
CHRONICLES OF THE CURSED SWORD
CLAMP SCHOOL DETECTIVES
CLOVER
COMIC PARTY
CONFIDENTIAL CONFESSIONS
CORRECTOR YUI
COWBOY BEBOP
COWBOY BEBOP: SHOOTING STAR
CRAZY LOVE STORY
CRESCENT MOON
CULDCEPT
CYBORG 009
D•N•ANGEL
DEMON DIARY
DEMON OROORON, THE
DEUS VITAE
DIGIMON
DIGIMON TAMERS
DIGIMON ZERO TWO
DOLL
DRAGON HUNTER
DRAGON KNIGHTS
DRAGON VOICE
DREAM SAGA
DUKLYON: CLAMP SCHOOL DEFENDERS
EERIE QUEERIE!
END, THE
ERICA SAKURAZAWA: COLLECTED WORKS
ET CETERA
ETERNITY
EVIL'S RETURN
FAERIES' LANDING
FAKE
FLCL
FORBIDDEN DANCE
FRUITS BASKET
G GUNDAM
GATEKEEPERS

GETBACKERS
GIRL GOT GAME
GRAVITATION
GTO
GUNDAM BLUE DESTINY
GUNDAM SEED ASTRAY
GUNDAM WING
GUNDAM WING: BATTLEFIELD OF PACIFISTS
GUNDAM WING: ENDLESS WALTZ
GUNDAM WING: THE LAST OUTPOST (G-UNIT)
GUYS' GUIDE TO GIRLS
HANDS OFF!
HAPPY MANIA
HARLEM BEAT
I.N.V.U.
IMMORTAL RAIN
INITIAL D
INSTANT TEEN: JUST ADD NUTS
ISLAND
JING: KING OF BANDITS
JING: KING OF BANDITS - TWILIGHT TALES
JULINE
KARE KANO
KILL ME, KISS ME
KINDAICHI CASE FILES, THE
KING OF HELL
KODOCHA: SANA'S STAGE
LAMENT OF THE LAMB
LEGAL DRUG
LEGEND OF CHUN HYANG, THE
LES BIJOUX
LOVE HINA
LUPIN III
LUPIN III: WORLD'S MOST WANTED
MAGIC KNIGHT RAYEARTH I
MAGIC KNIGHT RAYEARTH II
MAHOROMATIC: AUTOMATIC MAIDEN
MAN OF MANY FACES
MARMALADE BOY
MARS
MARS: HORSE WITH NO NAME
METROID
MINK
MIRACLE GIRLS
MIYUKI-CHAN IN WONDERLAND
MODEL
ONE
ONE I LOVE, THE
PARADISE KISS
PARASYTE
PASSION FRUIT
PEACH GIRL
PEACH GIRL: CHANGE OF HEART
PET SHOP OF HORRORS
PITA-TEN
PLANET LADDER

TOKYOPOP
GTO
GREAT TEACHER ONIZUKA
AS SEEN ON SHOWTIME!
DVD VIDEO
NO BIG EYES
NO MAGICAL POWERS
NO GIANT ROBOTS
GTO
OT OLDER TEEN AGE 16+
©Tohru Fujisawa – KODANSHA – FUJI TV – SME Visual Works – ST. PIERROT.
©2002 TOKYOPOP Inc. All Rights Reserved.
www.TOKYOPOP.com

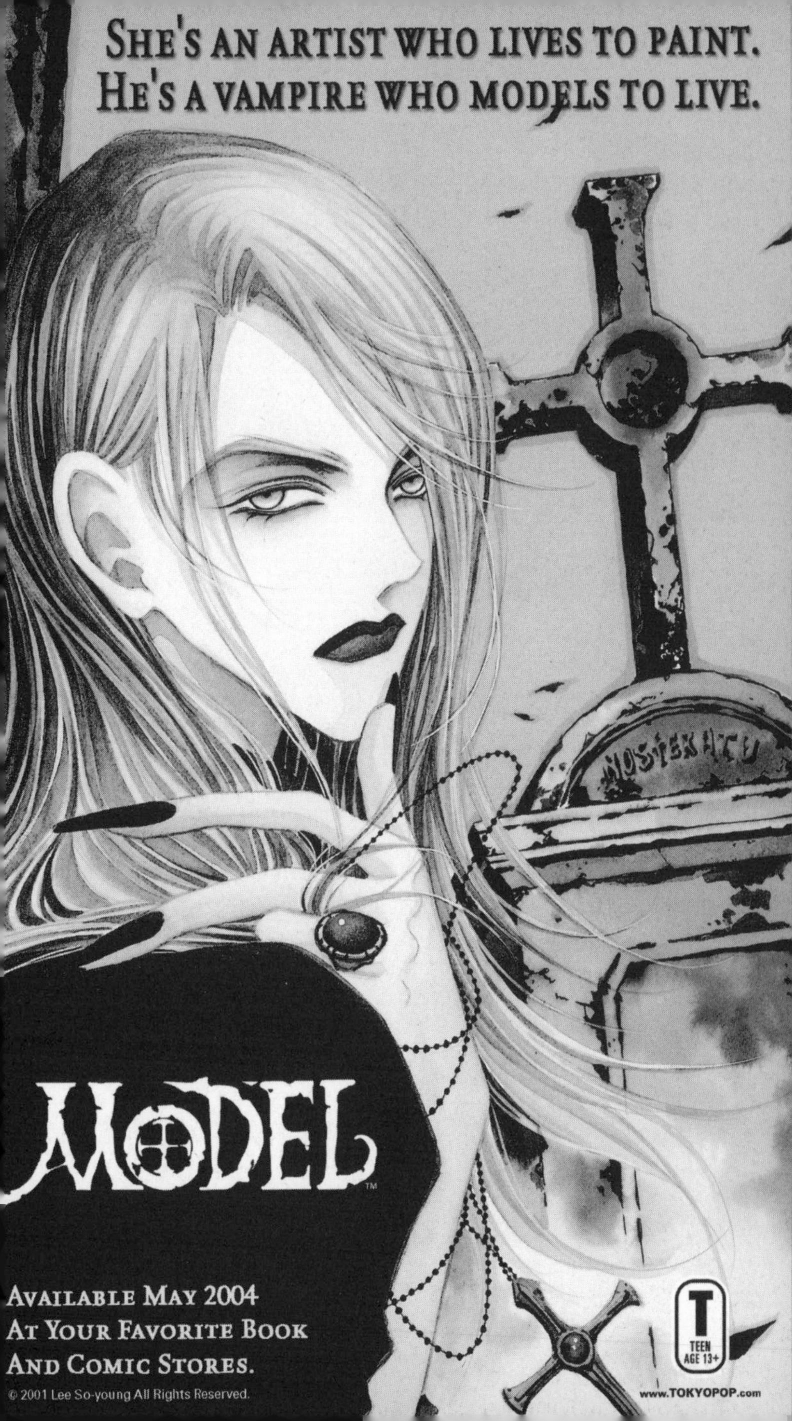

SHE'S AN ARTIST WHO LIVES TO PAINT.
HE'S A VAMPIRE WHO MODELS TO LIVE.
MODEL™
AVAILABLE MAY 2004
AT YOUR FAVORITE BOOK
AND COMIC STORES.
T
TEEN
AGE 13+
© 2001 Lee So-young All Rights Reserved.
www.TOKYOPOP.com

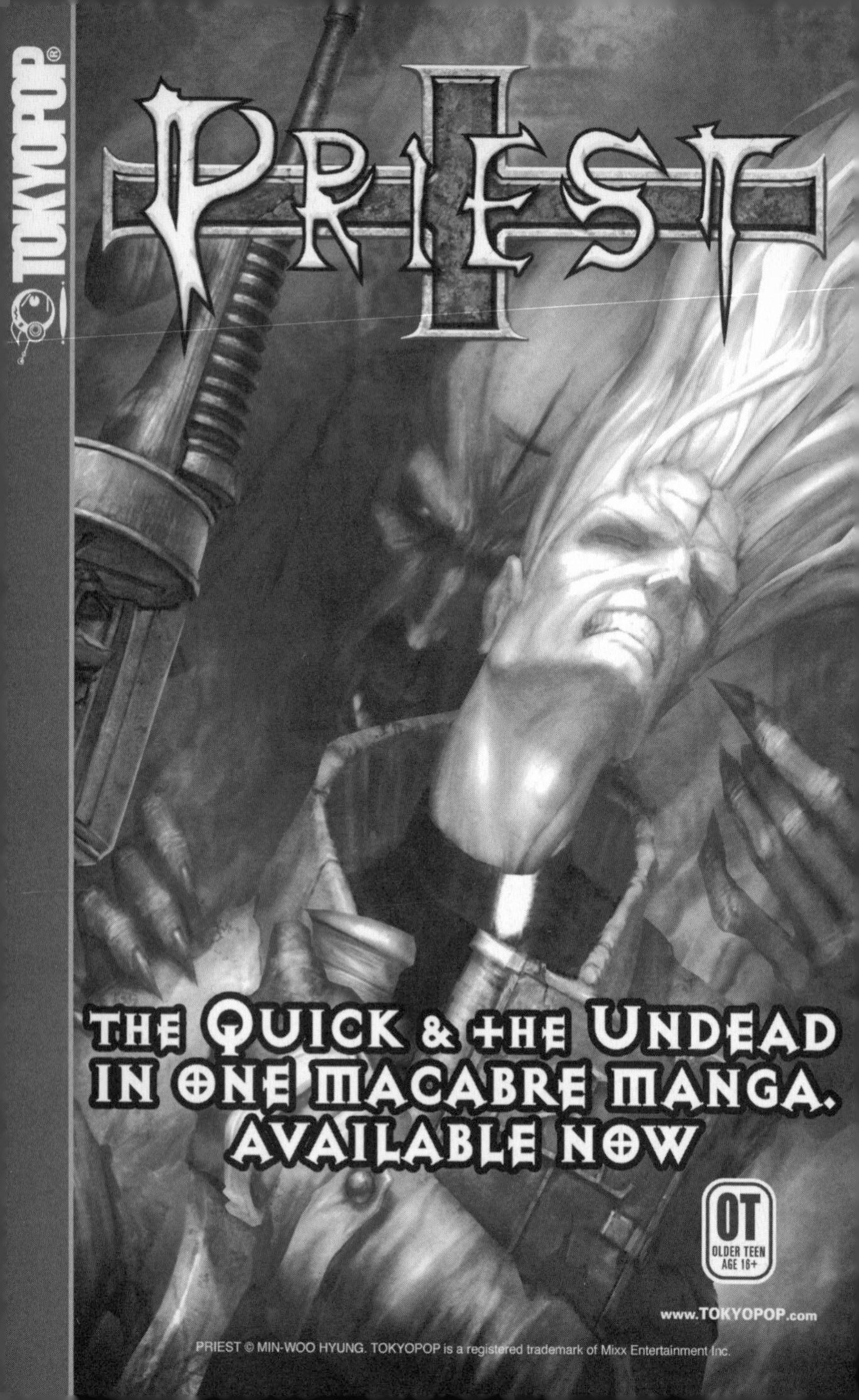
TOKYOPOP
PRIEST
THE QUICK & THE UNDEAD
IN ONE MACABRE MANGA.
AVAILABLE NOW
OT
OLDER TEEN
AGE 16+
www.TOKYOPOP.com
PRIEST © MIN-WOO HYUNG. TOKYOPOP is a registered trademark of Mixx Entertainment Inc.

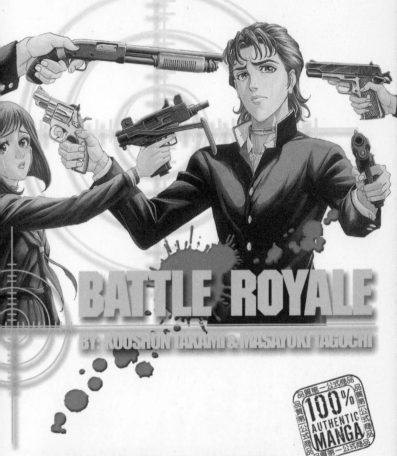

When the curriculum is survival...
it's every student for themselves!

TOKYOPOP®

BATTLE ROYALE
BY: KOUSHUN TAKAMI & MASAYUKI TAGUCHI

100% AUTHENTIC MANGA
品質第一公式商品

AVAILABLE NOW!

MATURE
AGES 18+

www.TOKYOPOP.com

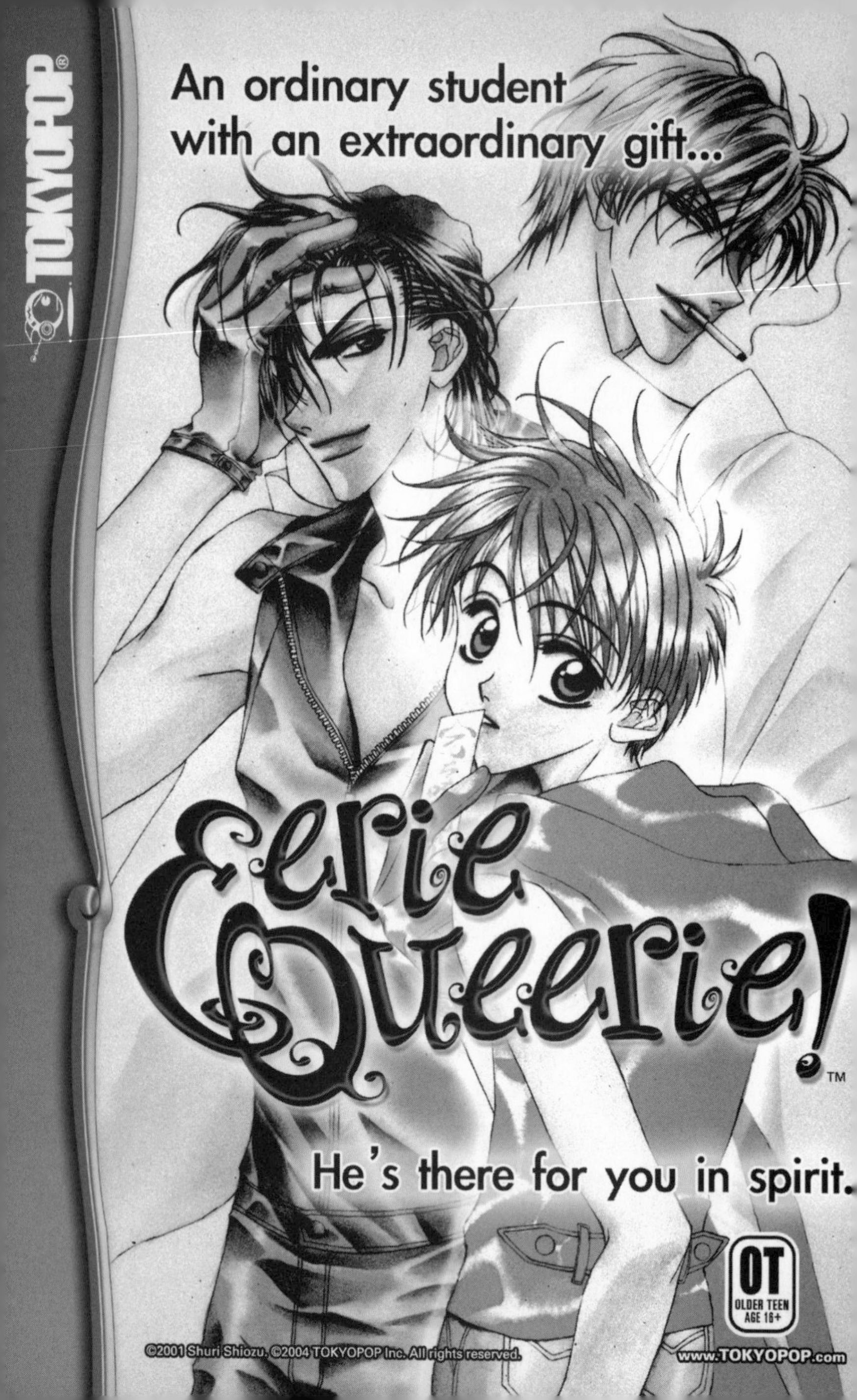
TOKYOPOP
An ordinary student
with an extraordinary gift...
Eerie Queerie!™
He's there for you in spirit.
OT
OLDER TEEN
AGE 16+
©2001 Shuri Shiozu. ©2004 TOKYOPOP Inc. All rights reserved.
www.TOKYOPOP.com

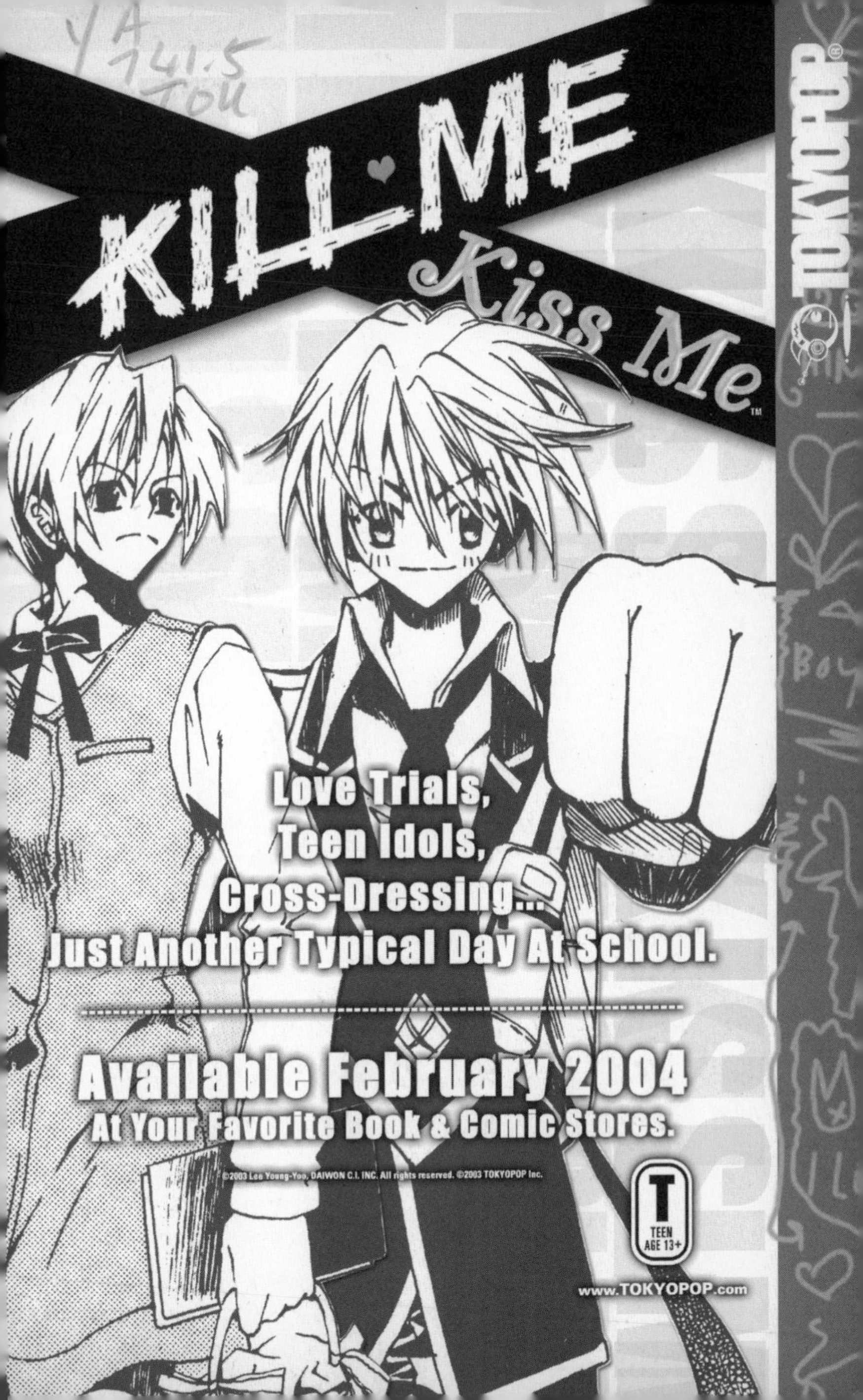
KILL ME
Kiss Me
TOKYOPOP
Love Trials,
Teen Idols,
Cross-Dressing...
Just Another Typical Day At School.
Available February 2004
At Your Favorite Book & Comic Stores.
©2003 Lee Young-Yoo, DAIWON C.I. INC. All rights reserved. ©2003 TOKYOPOP Inc.
T
TEEN
AGE 13+
www.TOKYOPOP.com

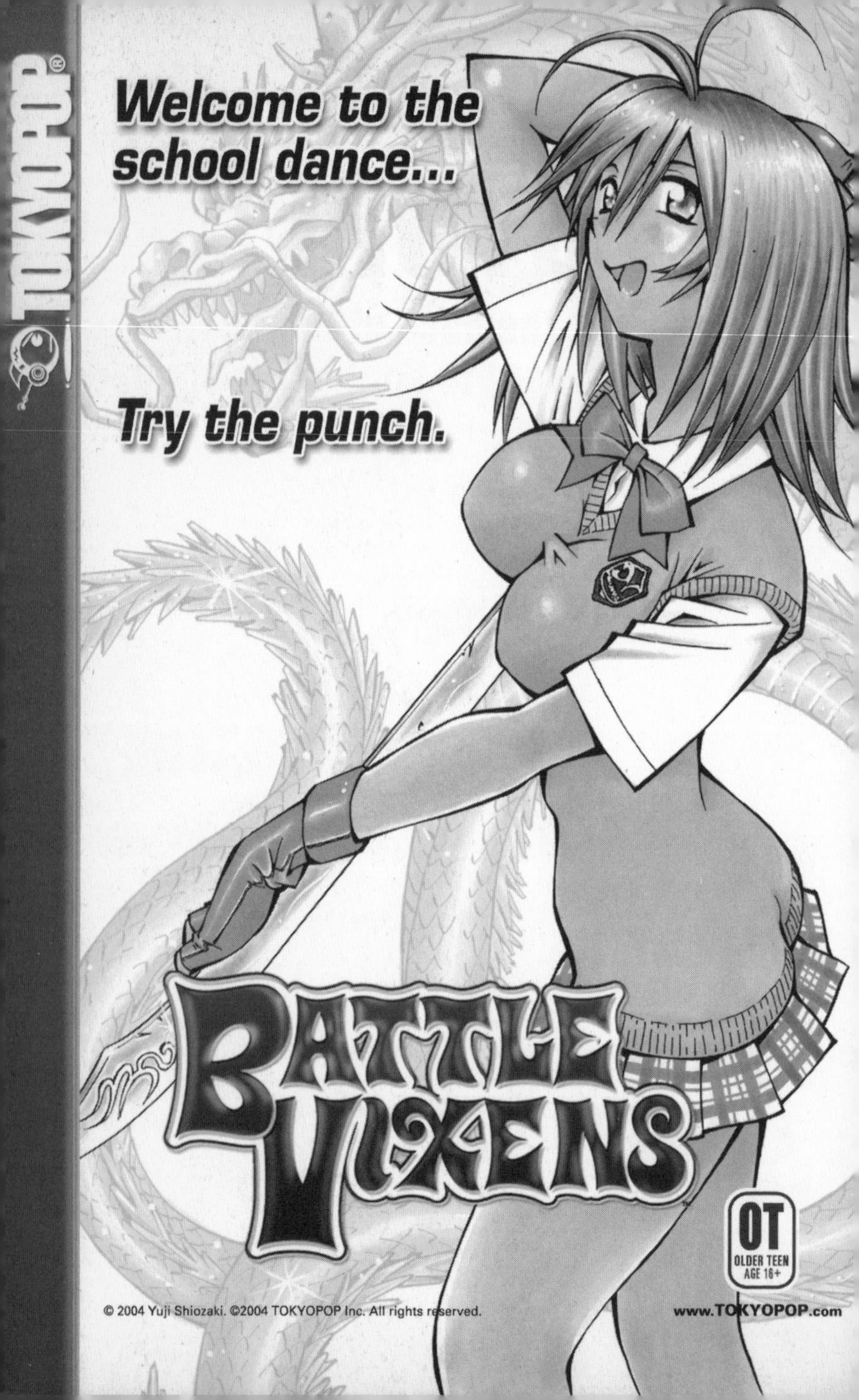
TOKYOPOP
Welcome to the school dance...
Try the punch.
BATTLE VIXENS
OT
OLDER TEEN AGE 16+
© 2004 Yuji Shiozaki. ©2004 TOKYOPOP Inc. All rights reserved.
www.TOKYOPOP.com

This is the back of the book.
You wouldn't want to spoil a great ending!

This book is printed "manga-style," in the authentic Japanese right-to-left format. Since none of the artwork has been flipped or altered, readers get to experience the story just as the creator intended. You've been asking for it, so TOKYOPOP® delivered: authentic, hot-off-the-press, and far more fun!

DIRECTIONS

1
2
3
4
5
6
7
8
9
10

If this is your first time reading manga-style, here's a quick guide to help you understand how it works.

It's easy... just start in the top right panel and follow the numbers. Have fun, and look for more 100% authentic manga from TOKYOPOP®!